PENGUIN BOOKS

HOME
WRECKER

D1342239

ALSO BY
DEANNA CAMERON

What Happened That Night

HOME WRECKER

DEANNA CAMERON

PENGUIN BOOKS

Content Warning: Murder, Uncomfortable Sexual Encounter,
Suggested Drug Use, Underage Drinking

PENGUIN BOOKS

UK | USA | Canada | Ireland | Australia
India | New Zealand | South Africa

Penguin Books is part of the Penguin Random House group of companies
whose addresses can be found at global.penguinrandomhouse.com.

www.penguin.co.uk   www.puffin.co.uk   www.ladybird.co.uk

Published in Great Britain by Penguin Books in association
with Wattpad Books, a division of Wattpad Corp., 2021

001

Text copyright © Deanna Cameron, 2021

Cover design by Laura Mensinga
Cover images © Alexandra Bergam via Stocksy, © Srady via Adobe Stock and
© Vchalup via Adobe Stock
Typesetting by Sarah Salomon

Wattpad, Wattpad Books, and associated logos are trademarks
and/or registered trademarks of Wattpad Corp.
All rights reserved

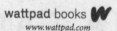
www.wattpad.com

Printed and bound in Great Britain by Clays Ltd, Elcograf S.p.A.

The authorized representative in the EEA is Penguin Random House Ireland,
Morrison Chambers, 32 Nassau Street, Dublin D02 YH68

A CIP catalogue record for this book is available from the British Library

ISBN: 978–0–241–49345–8

All correspondence to:
Penguin Books, Penguin Random House Children's
One Embassy Gardens, 8 Viaduct Gardens
London SW11 7BW

CHAPTER ONE

"*. . . a tornado watch and severe thunderstorm warning have been issued for Greens County and surrounding areas in western New York since this morning and will remain in effect until seven o'clock this evening, so make sure to stay tuned to your favorite radio station, Vibes 104.6, for all the latest weather updates.*"

The voice drifted from the speakers of a rusted blue pickup truck, which idled with the windows down in the high school parking lot a few feet away from me. The engine rumbled loudly as it shook against the tires, almost drowning out the radio. The air was hot, sticky with humidity, and stifling under a sun buried behind clouds, threatening rain. I groaned as another car, a hatchback, drove up behind the truck and was *not* my mother's beat-up, old minivan.

As usual, my mom was late.

I dropped my backpack and sat on the scorching sidewalk, wincing as it burned my thighs, before looking at my phone, again. No response to my onslaught of texts, even though school had let out almost half an hour ago. I knew she was still asleep on the futon, the box fan pointed toward her and the sundress from last night tangled around her legs. Normally, it wouldn't have mattered and I would've walked home. The trailer park was only a mile away, less if I cut through the football field. But today was different. Today, May 31, was the last day of school and we were supposed to go to Plant Nation together to pick out flowers for my garden. It was a promise she'd made me when I'd stormed home last month in the middle of the night after she'd betrayed me, again. I slammed the screen door when we got home, her tennis shoes picking up gravel as she tried to keep up with me, but I locked the door with her still outside.

"I'll make this up to you, baby, I will." Her shrill voice, even through the front door, carried that familiar tremble it did whenever she was desperate. "Really, I will. Look, I'll weed! Right now, I'm going to weed. See, Bronwyn, I'm pulling out this dandelion from your garden." There was a stifled grunt, and then a quiet snap. "I'm going to get a shovel, Bronwyn. I'll find a shovel, and I'll dig that up for you! Right now."

She looked around for a couple minutes, mumbling under her breath until I realized she'd knocked on the door of our neighbor Kingston's trailer in search of a shovel. I nearly fell down the cinderblock stairs in front of our trailer to stop her from waking him up at 2 a.m. She was crying when I let her back into the trailer and promising, in between hiccups, that she would make it up to me as she collapsed onto the futon.

"I'm sorry, baby," she told me, grabbing onto my hands. I didn't let her bring me down beside her but I didn't pull away either. "I'm going to get a job. And with my first paycheck, I'll make it up to you. We'll go to that flower place you love, and we'll buy all the flowers. Vegetable plants, too, and I'll help you plant them even. Baby, I promise."

Her promises never meant much. It wasn't the first time she'd said she was going to find a job—this was usually the first step whenever she tried to reclaim her elusive sobriety—but three weeks ago she actually got an interview. Which wasn't *totally* unusual, but her coming home afterward still sober and with a uniform was. She started working as a cashier at the local Good Greens and, just last week, earned her first paycheck. On the unopened envelope, in thick black letters, she'd written *Bronwyn's Flower Money*. It sat on our kitchen counter, the focal point of our tiny kitchen.

We decided after school let out for summer break was the perfect time to go pick out flowers, mulch, and vegetable plants. I had been researching floral arrangements, deciding which colors complemented each other best, which fertilizers worked well. My mom even seemed to be getting into it, buying a discounted weed killer she saw at work. I mean, the brand had recently been listed during a commercial from a law firm seeking settlements for cancer patients, but *still*, she was finally getting involved in something that wasn't a narcotic, actually doing something *for* me instead of just saying she would.

It almost looked like she was really getting it together this time. She took extra shifts when she could, dumped out all the beer in the fridge—including the ones belonging to her boyfriend, Jude—and even scrubbed the mildew off our shower tiles.

As I said, it *almost* looked like she was getting it together.

Because now I was sitting on the sidewalk outside school, as darkened clouds stretched over the sky. My texts left unanswered. So much for those promises.

"Bronwyn?"

My best friend, Indie, slowly pulled her new-to-her car up in front of me, straining against her seat belt as she looked over the dashboard. "Careful," I warned as she braked. "You might run someone over."

I'd met Indie McKnight a couple years ago when we'd been paired up for a biology project in Mr. Almasi's class freshman year. The mere mention of group work made me feel doomed—since my grade still wasn't where I wanted it to be and I sucked at the partner thing—until I noticed he'd paired me with a girl who color-coded her textbook with pastel highlights and sticky notes. She had deep reddish-umber skin with neat Fulani braids down to her waist, a gold nose ring in one nostril, and she soon became the whole reason I passed biology. She *loved* science. And, already a science tutor, Indie continued helping me even after our project was over. During one of the tutoring sessions, our conversations drifted from scientific terms and theories to our extracurriculars. She was in the robotics club, and I did track. Later that week, at one of my meets, I noticed her in the stands with a poster board for *me*. No one ever had done that for me before.

"Shut up." The car lurched to a halt. "Did your mom ditch?"

The sunlight was almost totally gone now. "It looks like it."

"You want a ride?"

"No thanks. She'll remember eventually, and I don't want to freak her out if I'm gone. It'll turn into a *thing* . . ."

I didn't talk about the stuff going on with my mom, but people usually figured it out on their own. I asked for rides to a lot of places, hung out with my friends and their families after track meets, and packed a medley of random foods for lunch, other-wise known as *whatever's in the fridge*. It was more embarrassing

4

to talk about, though, even if my friends had already figured it out. They had moms who cared, and so did I. It just wasn't always *me* she cared about.

Indie looked at the clouds looming over the parking lot, thunder rumbling quietly in the distance. "There're supposed to be some pretty bad storms today. My dad said there might be hail."

"They always say that and then it's, like, just a short downpour. I'm going to wait for another couple minutes, then I'll cut through the football field."

"You don't want to come over and watch movies? Ride out the tornado watch together?"

"No. Whenever I hear thunder, I have to hide under the bed like a dog and I'd rather do that at my house."

The car nudged forward. "Let me know if you want to hang out or something later. Or if you're still stuck here. I can come back, okay?"

"I'll be fine," I told her, watching as she gingerly drove away from the curb, her tires moving so slowly I could hear the rubber adjusting against the pavement. I couldn't help myself. "*Hey, lady!*" I screeched. "Watch the speed, there are kids around here!"

"I hate you, Bronwyn Larson!"

The cars dwindled to a sparse few in the back lot. When the rain started a few minutes later, I grabbed my backpack and headed for the football field, water beginning to pelt against the bleachers.

Ten minutes later, I reached our trailer park, my hair wet and my sneakers soaked. Thunder crashed overhead as I jogged down the gravel path, the wind in my ears, until I made out the pale orange metal of our trailer. Parked on the grass beside it was my mom's minivan. I was just about to unlock the front door, deliberating between ignoring my mom when I got inside or calling her out when Kingston called out my name. He was under the awning in front of his trailer, water dripping off the edges but dry underneath. I ran over and stood under the cover while he grabbed his lawn chair, folding it and shoving it inside the trailer.

"Hey."

Kingston had moved into the park last summer. After spending the day lounging on the deflating floaties in Indie's pool, I'd come home still in my swimsuit with a pair of cutoffs and noticed movement in the new trailer across from ours. There was a guy, a little older than me, organizing his kitchen. He had shaved blond hair and round glasses without rims. He looked up through the window and saw me standing on my cinderblocks. I waved, and after a beat, he did too.

He was older, a high school graduate with a job at a deli meat factory. Something about him drew me in closer. He was laid-back, casual, *responsible*, something the boys at my high school weren't. Maybe it was the years I'd spent taking care of my irresponsible mother, but being with someone like the guys at my school felt as appealing as wearing wet socks. I liked how Kingston was on his own, and sometimes, it seemed he liked me liking him. We flirted, and it was fun being upfront when I knew it would never really go anywhere. I liked the teasing, the glances, the wondering. The *chase*. Except when it reminded me of my mom, who also preferred the chase. That is, until she'd ended up with me.

"What's up?" Kingston asked.

"Nothing. Thinking about maybe killing my mom or something. Haven't decided yet."

"What she do now?" he laughed.

"It doesn't matter," I mumbled. An ashtray collided with the side of the trailer, making a loud *clank*. Farther into the park, our neighbor's wind chimes clattered violently together and Kingston's awning whipped back and forth. "You should get inside."

"Did you hear there's a tornado warning?" he said.

"You mean a watch, right? A tornado *watch*."

"No. I got an alert, it's an actual warning now."

Dark variegated shades of clouds lingered close like the sky was sinking. Then there was a flash of bright white, without thunder chasing it. Instead, I heard something *snap*, a monstrous groan that shook underneath my shoes. The wind filled up my ears, like a deafening roar. I ran back to our trailer.

"Mom!" I threw open the door. "Mom, come on, we have to go!" The lights were turned off inside, like they had been earlier that morning, and the box fan was still whirring in the corner.

Before I could go any farther, hands grabbed my wrist and pulled me backward out of the trailer.

"Bronwyn! We don't have time. We have to go!"

"I have to get my mom!"

"No, Bronwyn. *Look*!" He gestured at the sky. Debris flew around the air—wood and pieces of metal. And it all orbited around something dark reaching up into the clouds, so close I almost couldn't tell what it was.

A tornado, touching down about a mile away from us.

It churned violently against the ground through the pine trees, dust and rain bordered around it, power flashes igniting at the base. Broken tree limbs, trash cans, even Kingston's lawn chair skidded over the gravel. The wind whistled over a continuous thundering roar that trembled against the ground. Hail hurled against our ankles and our sides, denting the roofs nearby and then shattering.

"*Mom!*" I screamed.

Kingston tugged my elbow, pulling me through the wind-whipped grass between trailers. "Bronwyn, she's not there! If she was, she would've answered you by now, but we can't stay here! That thing's coming this way!"

Kingston dragged me onto the road, rainwater overflowing in the potholes and severed tree branches obstructing the pavement. There was a gas station a few hundred feet from the park, their parking lot flooded as we stumbled inside. The lights were out. A small group of people were crowded into the aisle with the chips and trail mixes.

The clerk, a middle-aged woman named Sandy, with whom I was vaguely familiar, stood behind the counter. "It looks really bad out there," she remarked, eyes wide. "Wait, is that hail? Shoot, my car's out there!"

"It's a tornado," I said, dialing my mom's number and pressing the phone to my ear.

"It was about to hit the trailer park," Kingston added, lifting his shirt to wipe his face.

"A tornado?" Sandy walked closer to the window. "Are you sure?"

A handful of the customers skeptically approached the window as I held my palm up to my other ear, trying to focus on the dial tone instead of their overlapping questions. Then, my mom's voicemail on the other end, telling me she *wasn't* sorry she missed me, she was probably ignoring the call on purpose, but sure, leave a message anyway.

"Probably just a funnel," someone called out. "We don't get tornadoes around here."

"You've got one right now!" I yelled.

I tried to call my mom's number again but instead of the dial tone, an electronic voice informed me my call *could not be completed as dialed*. I was about to ask Sandy if I could use the gas station landline when *something* slammed against one of the walls, a resounding crash that jolted through my chest and seized around my heart. I flinched at the screeching volume and brought my hands to my head. The sign in front of the gas station groaned before collapsing onto one of the cars parked outside. I bumped hard against Kingston's chest as I jerked back from the windows, looking over my shoulder at the girls shrieking in front of the pretzels down the aisle.

"Is there anywhere we can go?!" I shouted, frantically glancing around the inside of the convenience store.

"A bathroom!" a bald man yelled. "The most reinforcement is in bathrooms and stairwells."

"We don't have one," Sandy answered. "They make us walk to the Burger King on our breaks!"

Behind me, someone quietly snorted. "That sounds illegal," a rumbled voice chuckled, sounding either too calm or out of it in a way all too familiar to me, reviving the panic in my chest that my mom was out *there*, on her own. She couldn't even handle normal on her own, let alone a major meteorological event.

"The beer cooler!" Kingston suggested.

The bald man agreed. "Yes, the beer cooler, it's sturdier. People hid in it from a tornado: I saw it on the news once!"

"Isn't that more dangerous?" Sandy called out, searching through her pockets for the keys.

"It has extra enforcements." Kingston nudged me through the other customers crowding in front of the Employees-Only door. "At least, I think it does."

"Do you think my mom was awake? Did you see her at all today—?" I started to ask Kingston, before Sandy unlocked the door and threw it open, the customers rushed in, and I was all but shoved inside. The temperature dipped even though the power was out, and there were stacks of unopened cardboard boxes that made the room feel smaller than it actually was. People trampled over my feet, shoved past my shoulders, and I was pushed against strangers who were sticky with sweat. The building quaked from the force of the wind.

The glass doors to the cooler flapped open, thrashing back and forth as we crouched low to the ground, covering our heads with our arms. The noise was deafening, so horrendously loud I thought the sound would pierce my eardrums. Metal ground together and glass shattered continuously, even when there could be nothing possibly left to destroy. The structure of the gas station groaned, trembling under our feet and against the wind whistling underneath it all, high-pitched and blaring.

However loud it was outside the cooler, it was even louder inside. The girls kept screaming, shrill and piercing. A kid was sobbing. The person who sounded high earlier was more alert now, swearing at each crash we heard from outside. Sandy was shouting, shrieking at every noise. I kept my arms over my head, my nose brushing against the cold concrete wall, my palms over my ears. It was deafening, so chaotic I could barely understand the voices shouting at every impact. But if the tornado was here, maybe it wasn't at the trailer park. Then my mom might see it or get an alert on her phone. She had to know this was happening.

Then, a tree branch burst through one of the cooler's glass doors, leaves and bark grazing my face as shards of glass sprinkled over our heads. Screaming, I dropped onto my back, glass piercing my fingers as I tried to keep my head ducked while scooting away. Leaves and other debris filtered into the beer cooler, torrential rain spraying over everything. A side-view mirror from a car barreled into the cooler before something made a *crunch* sound in the back. I was still screaming, wanting to stop but unable to.

The wind blew the cans and bottles of beer until they tumbled backward out of the shelves, falling between us, beer spraying everywhere, covering my skin in a sticky residue. A can struck Kingston, who was curled low to the ground, his knees close to his face. The tree limb, stripped of its bark, separated us, my view of him obscured through the whipping leaves and the hair stuck to my face.

Then, everything stopped. Sound, the whistling gusts, hail. It all stopped as suddenly as it had started. The loudest noise was water dripping against the concrete.

"Where did it go?" one of the screaming girls asked, her voice hoarse. She was a cheerleader, her normally composed face now splattered with mud. She had shards of glass stuck in her wet hair.

A man warily stood up, his posture hunched as he looked through the shattered windows. "It kept going," he said, blood dripping down his temple. "Tornadoes move about thirty miles per hour."

"It's not dead?" the cheerleader asked.

"A tornado," said the guy who sounded high earlier, "doesn't *die*."

Sandy stood up. "No one's dead in here, right? Is anyone in here dead? There were kids in here, yeah? Are all the kids okay?"

A small, weak voice hiccupped, "I'm not dead."

"One, two . . ." Sandy muttered, counting off with pointed fingers at the cheerleader, clutching onto a girl from the debate team. "I'm missing a third teenager. There were three girls in here—right, the blond one! The one who just came in."

I lifted my hand. "Not dead."

"Where's the boy you came in here with? *Boy!*"

Kingston straightened his back, a sense of relief falling over me. "Boy's not dead either."

When we slowly stumbled out of the cooler a few minutes later, the inside of the convenience store looked as if it had been demolished. Water swished around our shoes and dripped from every surface. The bald man warned us about fallen power lines. The store was still groaning, its hinges and metal struggling to remain upright, concrete slabs under the tiles exposed like raw bone. The corner of the store had been ripped away, collapsed into a pile of rubble, rods of metal sharp and extending. Glass was everywhere, glimmering and crunching under our footsteps as we carefully walked outside. Power flashes sparked from behind the store like small fireworks.

The tornado had ripped the trees from the ground like I would a weed in my garden. Chunks of asphalt had been torn up from the road, and one piece was in the windshield of a car halfway down the street. The motley group of us stood in the parking lot, staring numbly out into a world that used to look familiar but was now dismantled and broken apart.

The girl from the debate team sobbed hysterically, covering her mouth with her hand and clinging onto the arm of the cheerleader. "Look what it did!" she screamed. "Everything is gone! It ripped everything away!"

I stared at her before I turned back to the convenience store, water dripping in through the holes in the roof, tree limbs visible from inside.

Everything really had just been ripped away.

The emergency alert tone blared from the windows of a pickup truck that drove slowly around the debris. Another followed, and then another. Drivers asked if anyone needed a ride to the hospital, people already slumped in the truck beds with their faces bloodied and eyes distant, holding random things like dish towels or T-shirts against their heads. Kingston flagged a black truck down, leading me to it as it slowed in front of a downed tree.

"I have to find my mom," I said. "Her car was in the park. I have to make sure she's still there."

Kingston ignored me as he approached the driver's side of the truck. "Are you heading to the hospital? She was hit in the head during the tornado, and I'm worried her brain might be bleeding inside or something."

"No, I wasn't—" I reached my fingertips to my hairline, feeling shards of jagged glass then something wet, flattening my hair to my temple. When I pulled my fingers back, I could see they were smeared with red. "It's fine. I need to find my mom." I tried to turn around, but Kingston wrapped an arm around my waist again, pulling me back into his chest. I shoved him away, hard. "Kingston, *stop*! I need to go find my mom!"

His forehead was creased, glancing over me worryingly. "You're hurt—*Bronwyn*!"

Taking off, I ran through the ditch next to the shoulder of the road, the longer patches of grass grazing against my legs were bent, snapped, and windblown.

I don't know what I expected, but when I got there, the trailer park had been almost completely flattened to the ground. Pieces of siding and rubble littered the entrance, the wooden stairs to someone's porch were thrown against the sign, which was now collapsed against the ground. The trailers at the front of the park looked as if they had been ripped apart, the centers were missing and the walls pulled off their foundations, leaning sideways against the ground. Each breath I took stung the inside of my nose from the overwhelming scent of the splintered pine trees. The trailer park had been my home for years, and it was *gone*, all of it. And all that had been left behind were pieces I couldn't even recognize.

Someone a few feet away from me screamed, an older woman in a soaked tie-dyed hoodie. She was covering her hands over her mouth, a man standing beside her and swearing as he ran his hands over his head.

"All our stuff is gone!" she cried. "Our house is *gone*! We don't have a house!"

Others came out from under the piles of rubble that used to be their homes. As I moved through the park, the screams continued. People were shouting names that echoed into one another until the garble didn't resemble names anymore. Someone kept shouting for *help, please, help,* but I couldn't see who it was no matter how many times I turned around.

Sirens were soft in the distance. I rounded the corner before our trailer home and my heart clenched sharply when I saw it. The tangerine walls were slanted, leaning in a way they hadn't before. All but one of the lavender shutters had been ripped from the windows and it was barely hanging on by a hinge. My flowers were gone but the bottle of weed killer my mom bought was somehow still there, just leaning against the trailer. The futon was on the grass, upside down without the cushions. Stripped wood was everywhere and a satellite dish that wasn't ours was wedged into the part of the roof that hadn't blown away.

"*Mom?*"

Through the gaping hole where the wall had been torn away, our television was on the floor, facedown, and the blinds were covering the coffee table, bent and dirty. Pine needles were sticking out of the carpet, and crumpled cereal and cracker boxes littered the floor of the living room. "Mom!"

Water was dripping from somewhere inside as I climbed up, hoisting myself into the trailer.

"Mom?!" The floor creaked unsteadily under my weight. I couldn't tell if it was just my imagination, but the ceiling seemed lower than it had when I'd left for school. "Mom, are you in here? Mom!"

Cupboard doors had been blown open, some food still inside but water had soaked through the cardboard boxes, and the refrigerator had fallen forward and was facedown on the floor, exposing the metal backing. The part of the trailer with the bathroom had collapsed on the ground outside, and I peered through the opening in the wall before reaching down, carefully, and lifting the shower curtain. But she wasn't there either.

"Mom?" I treaded to my bedroom, the carpet squishing with water, finding the door was miraculously still attached to its hinges. "Where are you?"

Part of the roof was crumbling in the corner over my bed. The soaked duvet bunched together and caught under my dresser that had fallen onto my bed, clothes spilling out from the drawers. The photos I had tacked to the wall were wet, and when I saw the picture of Indie and me at the beach, with me giving her a piggyback ride while she made a peace sign, sticking out her tongue, my heart twisted.

I pulled out my phone, hoping it would still work, and tapped Indie's name under my contacts. An automated voice told me there was no service in my area. I glanced around my bedroom one last time, and then went back into the living room, but even when I lifted overturned furniture, my mom still wasn't there. When I called out her name, there was never a response.

"Bronwyn?" Kingston's voice suddenly pierced the silence.

Hope soared when I heard him—maybe she was with him, maybe he'd found her while trying to find me. "Yeah?"

He poked his head through the doorway into our mangled living room, "Is she here?"

My hope plummeted. She wasn't with him. "I'm still looking. She could've been knocked out."

"Bronwyn, you need to get out of there. If you haven't found her yet, then she's not here. Come on, we need to go. This place is literally slanted. It's not safe—I'm worried about your head."

I headed back into the kitchen. "This *slanted* place is all I've got. I don't have anywhere else to go. Neither does my mom, so she should be here."

"Unless she went to her boyfriend's?" he offered. "Maybe she went to go hang out with him and rode out the storm there? Doesn't he have an actual house?"

"Then let's go there. I don't have service."

"Bronwyn, your head's bleeding. You probably need stitches or something."

"It's fine. What's not fine is not knowing where my mom is."

"How about we go to the hospital first? You're no good to

anyone if you lose consciousness. Or . . . maybe she's there? We could check there."

"The hospital flagged her years ago for *drug-seeking behavior*. She would never go there."

Kingston sighed, glancing up at the dripping ceiling. "You can't stay here. Look, do you have any paper somewhere? That's . . . not wet? You could write her a note or something."

I knew I couldn't stay—and that I didn't have a reason to since my mom clearly wasn't here—but maybe looking for her wasn't the only thing holding me back.

Maybe it was because I didn't have anywhere else to go.

○

When Kingston and I walked out of the trailer park, a police car was parked on the shoulder. A younger woman in a black uniform with a tight, brown ponytail and glasses, hopped out and passed us on her way to one of the overturned mobile homes. For a split second, as I dodged out of her way, our eyes met, and I glance quickly at her name tag: *Porterfield*.

Her footsteps were splatters in the mud as she ran past us, and she hollered, "Do you need medical attention?"

"No," I answered. "But I can't find my m—"

"There's a shelter being set up at the high school. You should get to a hospital first, though, you're bleeding. And watch out for power lines!" Then she was gone, disappearing as she climbed over the fallen pine trees blocking what used to be my neighbor's driveway.

Kingston nudged me forward and soon we found a brown van inching down the road, avoiding an overturned semitruck halfway in the ditch. The side doors pulled back, revealing a couple of people already inside. The driver, a guy maybe a few years older than Kingston in a pair of scrubs with cartoon dogs on it, let us crawl into the back between the seats. I could barely see through the windows from where I was crouched between the door and Kingston, his ribs grazing against me whenever he breathed.

Once we were dropped off at the hospital, I lost Kingston somewhere in the crowds. I wasn't sure what happened or where he went, but one moment he was following me inside and I was wondering where to go—did I still need to check in, or did I just wait until someone noticed I was bleeding?—when I turned around to ask him and found nothing but a wall of torsos shoving me forward. Eventually, I slumped to the floor in a corner of the waiting room, where people were being stitched up on the coffee tables or against the walls. My hair was sticky from the blood and, hours later, my clothes were still damp. Shivering, I searched every face, but I never found my mom.

I tried calling her again, but there was still no service. I tried to ask the receptionist if I could use her phone to call Jude, who had a landline, but there were so many people clamoring for so many things that she never noticed me. I walked back to my corner, feeling like a little kid lost in the grocery store, and fought to stop my chin from trembling as I let myself wonder about all the reasons I couldn't find her.

"Bronwyn?"

I turned around, believing for a moment it was her before taking in Indie's braids slapping against her windbreaker as she maneuvered around everyone between us. Her arms wrapped around me tightly before she abruptly pulled back. Already, she was crying, and I was too scared to feel embarrassed that it made me cry too. "Are you okay?" she asked, glancing over me, noticing the blood bright against my blond hair. "Your head!"

"I'm okay. But I can't find my mom."

"Bronwyn?" Indie's parents approached us, eyes widening at my damp clothes and the gash above my eyebrow. Mrs. McKnight gently grasped my chin and tilted my head. "Honey, are you hurt?"

"She can't find her mom," Indie told her after I nodded.

Mrs. McKnight reached out for me, wrapped her arms around my shoulders, and nestled my side against her chest. Hearing Indie say it out loud—and feeling her mom embrace me because of it—made whatever thin resolve I had left crack and break into hiccups against her blouse. "It's all going to be all right," she said. "Everything is going to be just fine."

"She's probably out there looking for you," Indie's dad said as he patted me on my back. "With the cell tower down, it's hard to get a hold of people right now."

"That's right. You don't have to worry about being alone. We'll stay with you until you find your mom, okay? TJ's in with the doctor now, getting an X-ray," her mother said, gingerly smoothing back my hair from my ears as she mentioned Indie's brother.

"I should go back to the trailer. I don't know where else she would look for me."

Mrs. McKnight shook her head. "You can't, honey, it's gone. We saw the footage on the news. You can't stay somewhere that's gone."

There was something so final about how she whispered against my hair, rocking from side to side with me in her arms, Indie holding on too. I hadn't really felt it then—the magnitude of the word *gone*—but I would soon.

And I had no idea how hard it would hit me.

CHAPTER TWO

Because I seemed fine—aside from the throbbing gash above my eyebrow—I was overlooked at the hospital for most of the night. The phones at the receptionist's desk kept chirping, sometimes for minutes before anyone answered. Conversations were rushed and abbreviated with keywords as nurses went in and out of rooms. Eventually, well after midnight and several more calls to my mom's phone that never went through, Indie pulled me over to a vending machine, retrieving crumpled dollar bills from her pocket for packaged powdered doughnuts. I was staring down at them, thinking if I ever felt like eating again, these stale dough-nuts would definitely *not* be what I'd choose.

Indie was punching in the numbers for some Keebler cook-ies when the receptionist walked over with the form I'd filled out earlier after Mrs. McKnight instructed me to. "Hi, hon," the receptionist said, her voice soft and tired. "I think you forgot something. We need a parent or guardian's signature right here at the bottom."

"Yeah, I know. It's just I—I don't know where my mom is."

Indie's Keebler cookies dropped to the bottom of the vending machine with a dull thud. "Can't my mom just sign it?" she asked the woman.

"Sorry. The hospital needs the signature and consent of a legal guardian or parent to treat her unless it's an emergency. What about your father?"

I snorted quietly at this. The truth was, *she* probably knew my father, or at least had undoubtedly heard of him. Most people had a figure occasionally gracing their television screens or refreshed Twitter pages with some motivational, encouraging quote edited and tweaked to perfection, all thanks to his publicists and managers. But, despite how accessible he was to anyone with a search engine, he had only ever been far away to me. He lived just a few hours away, but that might as well have been New Zealand or some other distant country as far as I was concerned.

"He's never really been around," I told the receptionist, instead. "Can I try calling my mom? Maybe it'll work on your phone." The receptionist nodded and walked me over to the nurse's station, watching as I pulled up my mom's number under the contacts on my phone. Again, it went unanswered. I dialed two more times, and when it still didn't go through, I tried Jude's number. An automated voice told me that call couldn't be completed as dialed either.

I was dialing his number for the third time when the receptionist sighed. "How about we try giving your father a call? Otherwise, we have to wait for social services and figure out that mess. Does he live nearby?"

"A couple of hours," I said, reluctantly. "He won't come, but his name is . . . David Soliday."

A crease formed between her eyebrows as she paused. "David Soliday? You mean as in—"

"Yep, him. I don't have his number so maybe you could, like, message his constitutional office email or something."

The receptionist stared at me, questioningly, for another moment, but then nodded, before I followed Indie back to where her parents were leaning against the walls, and read the nutritional information for my doughnuts until Mr. McKnight pointed out a couple of empty chairs. I wasn't sure when it happened but, eventually, I fell asleep sitting sideways in the chair.

Then, maybe only minutes later, I was nudged awake by Mrs. McKnight.

"Honey, wake up. You can't sleep with a head injury."

"Sorry," I told her, before noticing the person behind her. Tall and looming, he was dressed in clean and crisp clothing that didn't look as if they'd been soaked in rainwater or whipped through the wind. Then I took in his face and felt mine going pale.

It was my father.

Senator David Soliday.

○

My mother had told me only a few stories about David Soliday, but the ones she did were worn and weathered, like old pages of a book thumbed through countless times before. She'd been a waitress at a little diner on a street corner, with a messy ponytail of dark hair before she started dyeing it, barely twenty-one years old. He came in late one night, alone, and ordered a slice of apple pie. He was her last table, so she had to wait for him to finish before she could leave. Eventually, after my mom approached his booth for the fifth or sixth time, asking if he needed anything else, he caught on.

He asked her if she wanted him to leave, and I assumed my mom's customer service skills needed some refinement because she replied hastily, "Yeah, I do."

But he wasn't offended; instead, he laughed. I suppose she found this charming, because a few minutes later, she grabbed her tips and he grabbed her coat, and they left together. He sat at the same booth every night after that, ordering cups of coffee and apple pie slices until her shift ended. Sometimes they drove around town, listening to music in his car. One night, she brought him back to her apartment, before she lived in a trailer park. They put on a movie, and sometime between that and the end credits, he told her he was married. He said they weren't happy anymore, had two children, made my mother promises that he would end it. A few months later, when my mom told him she was pregnant, he told her he was staying with his wife. My mom must have been scared but she never told me that part.

He never paid child support, even though he came from money and made a lot more at his job as a lawyer. He never called, never asked to see me. I used to wait for birthday cards in the mail, sitting in front of the mailbox for days before and after in case it had gotten lost somewhere. I knew he had other kids, which was more confusing than if he had none at all. Then I would've known he didn't want any, but to know he did and that I just didn't make the cut—it stung more that way.

I met him only once, when I was six years old. It was near the end of summer and close to my birthday. We had a little apartment then, a bunch of narrow houses crammed together into one building. I was sitting at the table in the kitchen while my mom dyed her hair over the sink, the scent filling the room despite the opened window, when I noticed something on the counter beside my mom's purse. She was busy, struggling to rub the dye into her roots, so I got up and walked over, nudging her cracked pleather purse away from a bright pink envelope. Inside was an invitation to a birthday party. For a moment, I thought it might have been for mine until I read the name: *Andi*. Andi's eighth birthday. Andi Soliday.

My half sister.

My flip-flops thwacked against the tiling as I walked over to my mom, holding up the invitation in my hands, waving it around.

"My dad wants me to come to a party!" I exclaimed. Her expression went from vaguely frustrated and disinterested to almost alarmed. She took her gloved hands out of her hair and snatched the invitation from me, getting the dye on the glossy paper. "Mom, you're messing it up!"

She ignored this, reading the front and back, twice, before tossing it on the counter. "You're not going," she said, resuming her dye job.

"But he wants me to." I grabbed the invitation, becoming tearful now. "You could drop me off? I don't have to stay long. You won't have to see him, Mom, I promise."

"Bronwyn, baby . . . those people aren't your family. *I'm* your family. Aren't you happy here with me?" She sounded tired.

"Maybe I could have two families?"

She squirted the bottle of dye again. The chemicals burned my eyes. "You don't need two families, baby. And definitely not with the Solidays. Those are snaky people."

Eventually, after days of endless pleading, her resolve gave in

24

and she agreed to take me to the party, and to the dollar store to pick out a present. I went up and down each aisle twice, even when my mom shouted for me to just pick something. I decided on a surprise bag because I thought the best treasures had to be inside. After all, it was a mystery. She was a mystery, too, at least to me. That Friday night, I picked out my outfit three times and wanted my mom to do my hair special. I even asked if I could wear her lip gloss. Her face was set into a frown as she let out an exasperated grunt. "For goodness's *sake*, Bronwyn."

The Solidays' home was a couple of hours away from ours, and when we finally pulled into their driveway, I was starstruck. It was bigger than any of the houses I had lived in with my mom, with a double front door made of a deep-colored wood, flowers with vibrant petals planted in identical clay pots on either side. The house was white and seemed to go on forever. I was scrambling to unbuckle my seat belt before she'd even turned off the engine.

We went around the house to the backyard. Bright balloons were everywhere, tethered to tree branches or weighted down on table corners, and they had a pool. It was inground, the shape of a large jelly bean, with a diving board and slide. The blue water glistened in the sun. I felt the first twinge of self-consciousness as I stared at the piles of presents on the table—not only were there more than I had ever seen at a birthday party before, but they were pretty, with perfectly tight wrapping and uncrushed bows. My present didn't have a bow but I set it down on the table anyway, smoothing out the piece of wrapping paper where I had written my name in thick, shaky marker, next to the misspelled word *form*. I didn't like the way it looked in comparison to the other tags, but I tried to shake it off, before turning around and realizing there was a bouncy castle.

There was a cotton candy machine under the shade of one of the trees in the corner of their massive backyard. When I went to find my mom to ask if I could have one, she was talking to a couple, her face pinched like she was upset. The man she was speaking to was tall, with broad shoulders; he wore a peach-colored button-down tucked into a pair of khakis, his hair dark and neatly combed. Next to him was a woman with a pair of sunglasses perched on her blond hair, adorned in a sundress with a noticeable bump under the fabric. As I walked up to them, now suddenly hesitant, their attention turned to me.

The man stared at me with familiar, round blue eyes, and after a moment, I realized I had seen those eyes before—every time I'd looked in a mirror. I'd also seen the same lips and thick eyebrows.

"Is this Bronwyn?" the woman asked, already crouching down in front of me, holding out a hand. My mom made a noise in her throat, turned away. "Hi there. It's nice to meet you, I'm Amy. Jason, Andi, and Natalie's mom."

Jason, Andi, and Natalie, I thought. Those must have been the names of my brother and sisters, the ones my mom kept referring to as *his other kids*, never really giving them names.

I shook her hand slowly as the man kneeled down too. "Hey, I'm—"

"David," my mom finished, her tone annoyed. She was still standing, towering over all of us, before she curled her fingers around my shoulders and pulled me back against her legs. I stumbled in my sandals as she started to lead me away. "Come on, honey. Let's go test out that bouncy castle."

I spent the rest of the birthday party with my hand firmly clutched in my mom's, hot and clammy, and she wouldn't let go even when we ate our cotton candy or went into the bouncy castle. We stuck our feet in the pool, my eyes squinting into the sunlight as kids ran around the yard, trying to pick out faces I'd never seen before. My half siblings.

"We could go to my friend Bob's house more often," my mom said, even though I didn't remember anyone named Bob or visiting his house. "He's got a pool. We could swim there."

Something in me deflated. I knew what that meant. We were never coming back to this pool, or this house, or this family. We stayed there, sitting on the edge of the pool until it was time for Andi to open presents. That was when I first saw her, or at least the first time I realized she was my sister. Her hair, blond like mine, was damp against her blue swimsuit. Her skin was more tanned but we had the same blue eyes and lips, maybe nose too. She had her mother's facial structure with pieces of our dad's face in it. She looked like another version of me, one born to a married couple in a nice home with a brother and sister, and a jelly bean–shaped pool in the backyard.

When my mother finally let go of my hand as we stood up, I bolted for the table with the neatly wrapped presents. Beside Andi stood an older boy with blond hair and the same chin and eyebrows, a sunburn stretching down his chest and shoulders, masculine features mixing with a boyish face. Jason. Andi unwrapped two of her presents without really looking up at the friends around her, but I could wait. I was trying to figure out what to say to her when it was my present's turn when I heard a familiar sound that always brought my heart to a screeching halt. That was when Andi and Jason looked up and right past me. To my mother, who was shouting at Amy and my dad.

She was gripping her sandals by the thongs as she yelled at them, red-faced. Everything else went quiet, the laughter and conversation breaking like my heart, and I wanted to cry even though I didn't know what was happening.

She stomped across the lawn, grabbing me by the elbow and yelling as she pulled me toward the side of the house, ". . . you don't know!"

My mother threw me into the passenger seat of the car, slamming the door with a loud bang. She got into the driver's seat a moment later, fumbling with her keys, before letting out a frustrated shriek and threw them at the steering wheel. My breath caught in my throat as she brought her hands to her face, crying loudly. My eyes were watering as I stared at her.

"Mom," I whispered.

She cried for another moment, but eventually her chest sunk into a deep exhale. "Bob has a nice pool," she said, her voice thick. "It's a nice pool. It has a deck that you could do cannonballs off. You'll like it, baby."

"Why were you yelling at my dad?"

"He is *not* your dad," she said. "Or, at least, that's what he thinks, anyway. He says you don't look anything like him and that you're not his."

"But I do! Didn't you tell him he's my dad?"

"He's in politics, baby. He needs to protect his marriage and his real family. He's trying to pretend you're not his kid, so there won't be a scandal stopping him from becoming president or something."

"He's going to be president?"

"No, Bronwyn. But he can't have an extra kid with another woman because that looks bad for him. It means he cheated on his wife." She turned to me, pointing a finger at the house through the windshield. "You see that house, that family? That's his real

28

family. Those are his real kids. He's pretending you're not his because he doesn't want you. You, me, we wreck his perfect little life."

I looked away, curling my knees closer to my chest. "I won't wreck anything," I mumbled weakly. "They invited us, Mom. Why would they do that if he thinks he's not my dad?"

"To look at you, Bronwyn," she snapped, sighing when I flinched. "I'm too stressed out for this right now. He saw you and thinks you look nothing like him. That I slept with someone else and now I'm just trying to get money out of him."

I frowned. "What does that mean?"

She shook her head, before grabbing the keys from the dashboard and aggressively shoving them into the ignition, starting it without putting on her seat belt. "I can't talk about this right now. I'm done. I'm so done with this crap. I don't deserve it."

I blinked as she sped out of the driveway, sinking into the seat because I was what she thought she didn't deserve.

That was the last time I heard from any of the Solidays or saw them, at least in person. But one afternoon when I was thirteen, I was in line at the drugstore with an armful of tampons and discounted laundry detergent while my mom was in the car outside and I noticed him on the glossy cover of one of the magazines. I got out of line to read it, skimming through the quotes on his campaign for senator, then about his family. He talked about his older children, then his younger ones. They had their fourth child a few months after the birthday party, a boy named Danny. I wasn't mentioned.

A couple of years later, I heard Andi Soliday had started a YouTube channel for makeup tutorials after a couple cheerleaders in my geometry class mentioned her product reviews one morning.

I snuck out to the bathroom and pulled out my earbuds to watch one of them, listening as she reviewed the newest high-end makeup products and compared them with cheaper, drugstore alternatives. At first, I watched her videos because I *wanted* to know more about her, that sense of curiosity lingering from when I was six, but within a couple of videos, I noticed just how different we both were. Her hair was always curled in beach waves, gold necklaces shining brightly against her tanned complexion, and she linked items in her description that cost *hundreds* of dollars. In one video, she mentioned a pair of *comfy, casual* sweatpants for *every day, around the house*, and when I clicked on the link, they retailed for nearly three hundred dollars.

That was when I understood how my mom felt about them. Their lives were wrapped up in politics and wealth, reputation and image, and I had been wedged out because I shattered those things. Ignored, forgotten, tossed aside like one of the makeup products Andi said on her channel *just weren't right for her.* And if that was how they'd wanted to live their lives, then fine, so be it.

Eventually, I stopped caring. Stopped watching the YouTube videos, stopped reading the magazines that mentioned him in the grocery lines. Stopped watching his interviews when they came on the television when I was flipping through channels. Stopped wondering what they were like, or why they didn't want to know me.

I ignored them like they ignored me, even if forgetting about them proved to be a little harder for me.

And now, after all these years, he was standing right in front of me.

○

I didn't speak to him at all. The McKnights directed David Soliday toward the receptionist's desk to finish filling out the paperwork so I could get my forehead stitched. After that, I pulled out my phone and pretended to be busy texting while he awkwardly stood around until a nurse called me back, asking if I wanted *my dad* to come with me and I just shook my head in response. My mind was still spinning at the fact he was *here*, barely two hours after I'd told the receptionist about him. After radio silence from him and the rest of his family for the past ten years, he was out there in the waiting room with the McKnights. And what surprised me even further was that he was still there after getting my head stitched, sitting in one of the chairs.

I paused, letting myself take him in for the first time since he'd arrived. His hair was still thick, although it was shorter now, with salt and pepper hair. He wasn't as slender as he used to be, though he still looked fit, and creases around his mouth and his eyes had formed. But seeing him older wasn't a total shock to me; after all, he had been in the news for years.

Then he looked up, his phone screen darkening as he seemed to take me in. Something was shifting in his gaze, and his shoulders rose with a small inhale. But I walked away before I could see anything else—like that piece of him still wondering if I was his—and walked over to the McKnights.

"Can I come home with you?"

Mrs. McKnight smiled softly, then looked over at David Soliday. "Honey, I'm afraid you have to stay with your dad until they find your mom."

I shook my head. "No—"

"It's just until they find your mom—"

"I don't even know him," I murmured to her as he approached

31

us, crossing my arms tightly around my chest. My eyes pleaded with Mrs. McKnight.

She let out a small sigh and turned to him, hitching her purse up her shoulder. "You know, there is just . . . *so* much going on right now. How about you and Bronwyn come over to our house tonight? It's so late and it might make things easier when they find Donna."

I didn't look over or up. Kept my eyes down at my arms wrapped around me.

"That's very generous of you. Thank you," he said, in that *voice*. It was the one from the television whenever he addressed reporters or spoke with other politicians. It was authoritative, practiced, articulate. It was the first time I'd heard it in person since I was six. And then he paused beside me, taking in a breath.

He was about to use it to talk to me. So, I grabbed Indie by the hand and pulled her out of the waiting room, listening to her footsteps stumble for a second as she called out, "Uh, I guess we'll meet you at the car!"

○

There were a few branches down on the McKnights' yard, but the trees on their property still had their leaves and bark for the most part, and according to them on the car ride over—where I was wedged in the backseat between Indie and her little brother— their power was out. The windows in the neighboring homes were dark too—no porch lights turned on as we got out of the car. David's Mercedes pulled up behind us. When we got inside, Mrs. McKnight lit candles around the living room. The smells of various fragrances—ranging from apple cinnamon to tropical coconut—filled the room.

No one said much as Mr. McKnight grabbed flashlights from their coat closet and handed them to us. I was staring down at my phone screen, dimmed to preserve the battery, which was down to just 7 percent, while Mrs. McKnight offered him TJ's bedroom for the night, asking if he needed anything else. He shook his head, his head turned in her direction but his eyes were glancing toward me.

"That's very kind of you," he remarked, and I wondered if he just always sounded like there were fifteen cameras pointed at him. I brought my phone to my ear before he said anything else, deciding to call Jude this time since he *had* to be with her. My mom wasn't someone who could just be on her own. She needed direction, and someone to give it to her. I told her when bills needed to be paid, when her meetings were when she tried to get sober, made most of her meals so she didn't spend her unemployment on takeout. My mom couldn't handle normal life on her own, never mind what was happening now.

But, like every time before, the call never went through.

TJ slept in Indie's room since she had only a twin-sized bed. We slept in the living room together. She grabbed the throw pillows from the couch and tossed them on the floor, beside the sheets and blankets her mother left before she went upstairs.

"Do you want to talk about your dad?" Indie asked.

I was on the floor, careful not to let my stitches touch the pillow. "No."

"Your mom is probably fine," she whispered. It was so dark, too dark to make anything out, but I was still grateful she was facing away from me. "She's probably with Jude. Have you tried calling him?"

"There's no service. Do you think I'll find her tomorrow?" I whispered, my voice weak.

"Yes," she whispered back, quickly and confidently. "She'll probably be knocking on the door before we even wake up. Then you'll be like, *Mom, go away, I'm sleeping!*"

I knew Indie was trying but, somehow, I also knew she was wrong.

○

I woke up early the next morning while Indie was still asleep when the power turned back on, the lights flashing bright in the room and something beeping in the kitchen. I turned the lights back off and shuffled into the kitchen, turning on the TV and plugging my dead phone into the wall to charge it. The local news channel was covering the tornado, and I lowered the volume to a murmur as I sat on a bar stool.

The aerial footage from the helicopter was almost unbelievable—a trail of debris, like the tornado had left breadcrumbs of plywood and siding across Shiloh. There were houses still standing and intact, next to houses that were just piles. Then there was film of the overturned semi we'd passed on the way to the hospital, a reporter standing in front of the wreckage stating the driver was in critical condition.

"There have been fourteen reported fatalities so far," the reporter said, stoically. "The same number of minutes the tornado was on the ground. Experts are saying the ferocity of the tornado, combined with people not heeding weather warnings, are the reasons why the victim count is already so high."

Fourteen. Fourteen people were *dead.*

"Bronwyn?" Indie sat beside me, a blanket wrapped around her shoulders, eyes bleary. "What are you doing up?"

"Fourteen people died."

She turned to the screen, looking slightly more awake now.

"I think my mom has to be one of them," I whispered.

I didn't have to look at her—I knew she was crying in the pause that ensued. It didn't take much for Indie. She cried at movies, really emotional comeback songs from sobering musicians, and basically whenever anyone else did. "Bronwyn! Your mom has to be okay. The odds are so slim. She's probably with Jude."

"The odds are the same for everyone. Fourteen people died. If she isn't one of them, then why hasn't she found me yet?"

"She's looking! Besides, if they did find your mom, someone would come tell you and no one has. That's a good thing."

"Sometimes, to fall asleep, my mom would put on the weather channel after going out," I said, loosely defining meeting her dealer as *going out*, "and they would have these specials about tornadoes. One of the experts said tornado victims are so beaten up, they're unrecognizable."

Indie made a noise between a sob and whimper, but I was almost grateful for it. Indie reminded me of my mom in how emotional she could be, even though they expressed it in different ways, but it always helped me regain my composure in contrast. My eyes would dry, my trembling chin would relax, and I would go back to normal because they needed normal. They needed to be comforted. And it was so much easier to do that than to give in to the feelings I had.

"You're probably right," I grabbed Indie's hand and forced all the confidence I had into my voice. "It takes my mom forever to do anything, right?"

She squeezed my hand, then watched the footage with me for another moment until it went to commercials. "I'm cold. I'm going to go grab a sweatshirt." My phone beeped back to life, but there was no signal. Cellular service was clearly still out.

A few minutes later, footsteps creaked down the carpeted staircase in the other room, and I thought it was Indie coming back downstairs until the footsteps slowed in the kitchen. I didn't turn around, just stared at the commercial about heartburn medication and hoped the footsteps would resume and turn away.

"Good morning," David said, tentatively, before hesitating. "Did you sleep all right?"

I still didn't say anything. Like there was any way I could've slept *all right* after a tornado had demolished my home, whirled pieces of other homes at my face, and brought him into town.

"Last night at the hospital, I left her name with the staff. They're in contact with other hospitals, so they'll let us know if she ended up somewhere else." He paused. "It's possible. The one here in town might have been so crowded, they sent her to a different one."

I leaned my cheek against my knuckles, wishing he would just go away. For the past ten years, that man had had nothing to say to me, and now I had nothing to say to him. He was a stranger to me, a politician out from behind the television screen.

"My house is just a couple hours away. Maybe you'd be more comfortable there," he said. "My wife's actually getting ready to go to our lake house this weekend. But you could rest there, and I could come back to look for your mom for you."

I stood up, leaving the television on, and kept my eyes away from his face as I walked out of the room. "I'm not going on vacation with you."

He started to say something, footsteps resuming on the floorboards for a split second before I went bounding up the stairs.

I locked myself in the bathroom, keeping the light turned off because I didn't want to see the uncleaned scratches across my face, the stitches holding my skin together, blood staining my hair. Because I wanted to slow how fast I was breathing. None of this should've been happening.

I turned the shower on. I couldn't will David Soliday out of the McKnight's kitchen, or the cuts and bruises on my skin to heal, or my mother to find me. I also knew I probably couldn't stop David from taking me back to his home, to his *summer* home, if she didn't surface. But I could wash the blood out of my hair.

After my shower, I snuck out of the house to see if I could find my mom anywhere. And I needed a moment to be on my own without anyone watching me or trying to reassure me my worst fears were just that and not reality.

Besides, it was almost like the tornado didn't belong to them, *any* of them, even the McKnights. There may have been a couple of branches on their lawn, but they'd gone down to their sturdy basement during the storm and had come back upstairs to a house. TJ had sprained his arm falling down the stairs in a panic, but none of them had seen the tornado, felt its harsh winds against their bare faces or the debris hurling against their bodies.

The farther I went out of their neighborhood and closer to town, the more devastated everything looked. Houses were broken in half. Stepped on by the tornado, disintegrating into masses of raw wood under its weight. Firefighters carefully treaded through the rubble heaped onto lawns and had spray painted X's on front doors.

Jude's house was near downtown. Originally a beige-ish yellow, it now looked like most of the paint had been stripped from the house, but otherwise it was still standing. The porch was slanting in a way it hadn't before, slouched in the center, and his car was gone, but I saw enough to know it could've been thrown in the tornado. The window on the second floor was cracked, a piece of cardboard behind the pane.

My mother never told me how she'd met Jude. I found out about him when, one morning almost three years ago, I'd walked into our kitchen to pour myself a bowl of cereal and stumbled upon a man, in his boxers, standing in front of our stove. He was heavier, with a *lot* of chest hair and a thinning dark ponytail over his bare back. He was squinting at a box of pancake mix, a mixing bowl on the counter. Then he glanced over and spotted me there, eyes wide.

"You don't have blueberries, do you?" he asked nonchalantly.

"Mom!"

The man, unbothered by this, set down the box of pancake mix. "It's really not that urgent," he mumbled, pouring an unmeasured amount of milk into the bowl. "Just wondering."

"*Mom!*" I repeated.

Something stirred under the blankets on the futon across the counter. A second later, my mom popped her head out, her hair staticky and eyes bleary as she looked around. "What? What's wrong?"

"You got blueberries?" the man asked.

"We don't buy blueberries. Too expensive." Then she flopped her head back down.

"Do you know him?" I asked.

"Hmm," she mumbled.

He chuckled. "I think *hmm*, translated from the language of the sleepyheads, means *yes, he spent the night* in English. I'm Jude Carney." He grabbed a fork from our disorganized silverware drawer and started to stir the powdered mix into a batter. "Anyway, you like pancakes? I do, but I'm the one making them, so I guess it's all up in the air."

"And we don't have blueberries," I pointed out, slowly, still somewhat baffled.

He pointed the fork at me. "Right. These are doomed." Then he grinned. "It's going to be great."

After that, Jude was always around, sharing the futon with my mom, watching old reruns of comedies or late-night talk shows, their voices quiet and muffled through the thin walls. They were never really that affectionate, at least around me anyway, but they were together, never breaking up or getting into fights. Jude was probably too chill to argue with her. It was refreshing compared to my mom, who got frazzled and emotional over most things.

I was about to walk up the porch steps when a voice from behind me grew louder and closer. "Hey, ma'am? Ma'am?"

Gloved fingers reached around my forearm and stopped me from going any farther. I turned around to see a boy, taller than me but around my age, with thick dark hair and a tanned complexion. I was thrown, hearing someone his age call me *ma'am*.

"Sorry," he said. "I didn't think you'd heard me before."

"I'm not used to answering to *ma'am*. I thought you were talking to somebody else."

"Those stairs aren't safe. We ran out of caution tape earlier, but see how they're sinking in the middle? They're not stable."

"I was going to walk on the edges. My mom might be inside with her boyfriend, and I need to make sure she's not dead. So . . ." I gestured with my thumb to the house.

He shook his head. "We cleared that house earlier this morning. No one's inside."

I noticed the neon yellow *X* painted over the front door, and my shoulders slumped. She wasn't there, but neither was Jude. That had to mean something, like maybe they were out looking for me, and we kept missing each other like some sort of twisted happenstance. Except the cardboard behind the shattered windowpane meant *someone* had been here, and whoever it was, they hadn't come looking for me.

That didn't make sense. My mom would look for me.

The boy was still standing there. I realized he must've been a volunteer from a neighboring town who was helping clean up and search buildings, which explained why I didn't recognize him from school.

I tried to mask the feeling of disappointment sinking into my chest like Jude's porch. "I guess there's no reason to risk my life then."

"You could use my phone if you need to call someone," he offered, pulling out a phone that looked sleek and new. Like his parents bought him a new upgrade every year.

I shook my head. "Cell service has been out since the tornado hit." What I didn't add was that I didn't know my mom's number. I tapped her contact icon whenever I needed to get a hold of her, and that felt too embarrassing to admit. Besides, I had only started to charge my phone at Indie's and it was already dead again, so I couldn't even look it up.

"I'm sorry," he told me.

I shrugged, inching farther away from him because he actually *sounded* sorry, like he wanted to say more than that and I didn't want to hear it. "It's fine, whatever. Thanks."

"Ethan," he added, then held out his hand. After a beat, he pulled off his glove before extending his hand again.

I hesitated but then shook his hand. His fingers tightened around the back of mine in a firm handshake, which was just another example of how he was *clearly* not from around here. Handshakes here were rare and flimsy when they did happen, loose like your hand might accidentally slip out, and they never came from teenage boys.

"Bronwyn," I said, pulling my hand back and shoving it into my pocket.

He smiled, nodding. "Nice to meet you, Bronwyn. See you around."

I watched as he took a step back from me and then turned around, slipping his leather glove on again before walking across the street where other volunteers in similar colored shirts were loading up the bed of a mud-splattered black truck with logs of sawed wood as a chainsaw revved in the distance. I shook my head, mumbling, "Not likely."

o

David agreed to spend another night at the McKnights', hoping to hear something about my mom but the next day, when we hadn't, he decided it was time to head back to his house a couple hours away. He kept trying to reassuringly tell me the authorities knew how to get in touch with him, and at least his phone would be working where he lived. I refused to go until I saw the trailer again, check one more time to see if she was there. I wasn't sure what I thought I'd find, what I could've salvaged or repaired, but in the unforgiving afternoon daylight, it was obvious there wasn't much left. David was behind me, surveying what used to be my neighborhood, my world, but I could tell it was nothing but dingy and wretched to him.

It had been almost *two* days, and my mom was still missing.

I didn't know how I was supposed to just leave, and it was pulling my nerves apart. My mother was gone. Except she wasn't because she had to be somewhere, but I couldn't look. I couldn't help. I couldn't find her. I was just supposed to leave with a stranger on vacation with his *real* family. I couldn't even find anything to bring with me, grasping at shards of my old flowerpots or brushing my fingers against the ruined pillows. The tornado had torn everything from me and tossed it in places I couldn't reach or find.

The gravel crunched under David's footsteps as he approached me. "I talked with the sheriff earlier this morning. They'll contact us the moment they find your mom. And they will."

I didn't acknowledge him, or his clumsy attempt at reassurance, because I wasn't totally afraid of them finding my mother. I was becoming more afraid they would. I knew what it meant when it took *days* to find someone. If my mom were okay, she would've found me by now.

"Have you found anything you want to keep? I could—" I glanced at him, for the first time that day, and he went quiet. "How about I go talk to your neighbors? Let them know how to get a hold of us in case she comes back here?"

I closed my eyes, breathing in the scent of the sap exposed from the pine trees, felt the wind ruffling my hair. Took in my home for what might be the last time. Then, while he was speaking to Mrs. Reynolds, an older woman still in her nightgown because it was the only clothing she had now, I slipped around to the back of the house. The walls were dilapidated, like the tornado pulled them apart by the seams, but it was just enough space for me to stick my hand through and grasp the picture of me and Indie at the beach. It was stiff, the corner bent, but it was the one thing not completely ruined or reeking of mildew. My mom had taken that picture, raving about how we looked just like Cher and Dionne from *Clueless*, but prettier, much prettier. Then, I was embarrassed, worried she'd offended Indie but later, we watched the VHS tape my mom still had and ordered pizza. It was the first time I'd brought a friend over to meet my mom and for a second, I wasn't ashamed of her or our trailer. I stuffed the picture into my pocket and then stepped away, wishing I could cling to everything that used to embarrass me or make me feel ashamed.

But I couldn't. It was all gone.

CHAPTER THREE

The drive to David's house felt longer than it had when I'd been an excited little kid in the backseat, asking my mom if *that was his house, was it that one, how about that house* until she told me to be quiet. This time the radio was on, tuned to a news station for about five miles before he asked me if I wanted to change it to something else. When I didn't say anything, he switched it to a station with bubbly pop songs I never listened to. I was used to classic rock and Dolly Parton, the kind of music my mom listened to on hot summer afternoons. But he didn't know that about me—he didn't know anything about me. He was probably filling in the blanks about me with stuff that was true for his real daughters, who probably loved pop music.

He tried to be polite in the way a senator would be—asking how school was going, what my favorite subject was, what my college plans were, which stung deeper than I thought because I couldn't afford it now—but each question enforced just how much of a stranger I was to him. He talked to me like my barber or a teacher at school. When I didn't answer him, he tried a new tactic.

"Do you want to stop somewhere, maybe get something to eat?" he offered. "We haven't eaten since breakfast. Is there somewhere you want to go?"

"No," I mumbled indifferently. "And you don't have to do *this*"—I made a broad gesture with my hand—"because I'm just going right back home when they find my mom."

He hesitated. "Bronwyn, you do—"

I reached out for the volume knob and twisted it until a Taylor Swift song drowned out his voice.

○

It was nearing nine at night when the homes we passed felt familiar before I spotted the one I recognized. The garage door was open and light spilled onto the pavement, revealing a sleek Suburban with the trunk open. Two people were leaning inside it, the interior light shadowing their faces.

Amy. I hadn't seen her in years, but I could make her out. She had a shorter haircut and was dressed in capris and Birkenstocks, rooting around the trunk. When she heard us pull in, she looked up, squinting in the headlights, and then waved.

"Do you remember Amy, my wife?" David asked.

This is temporary, I reminded myself as I grabbed the door handle without answering him, forcing myself to set one foot onto the smooth asphalt. *You're going to find Mom and we'll go live with Jude or something. None of this will stick.*

This is temporary.

When we stepped inside, I could see the suitcases lined up on the tiled kitchen floor beside the refrigerator. We hadn't gone into the house the last time we were here. And it was *huge*.

A door opened while I was in the expansive kitchen, looking at a *television screen* on one of the doors of the fridge, and Amy walked into the kitchen with canvas bags looped around her wrists, smiling, taking me in. Then she brought me into a tight embrace as soon as she set the bags down on the floor. It was weird, and almost unsettling, how enthusiastic a stranger could be to see me.

"You've grown up so much," she said, taking a step back. "You've become such a beautiful young woman, Bronwyn."

"Thanks," I mumbled, frowning somewhat at how warm she suddenly was to me, after a decade of ignoring my existence and my paternity, as clear as the thick eyebrows and the eyes staring bemused at her. But she was the wife of a politician, used to performing in front of cameras and adapting to whatever role she needed to take on.

"I wasn't sure what size you were." She searched through a couple of the bags, grabbing a set of black silk pajamas from inside. "So, I got a couple of different ones for you to try on. Until we can go shopping and you can pick out what you want for clothes other than the ones you're wearing."

I took them only because I didn't want to sleep in Indie's jeans. "These are my friend's. I'll need to get them back to her," I mumbled.

"Yes, of course," Amy said. "Change into these, and I'll wash them. We can drop them off next time we visit Shiloh."

"Sure," I said, "but I'm not going to be *visiting*. I'm going back when they find my mom. But, um, do you have chargers for my phone? I lost mine, obviously, and I used my friend's earlier, but my battery died again."

46

"No, not for an Android," she said with a soft, apologetic sigh as she glanced at the phone in my hand, the screen cracked and dark. Then reached for the purse still over her shoulder, patting the leather once before nodding. "But I'll go out and grab you one. There's a Best Buy just down the street. And your dad has been on the phone with the police—as soon as he hears anything, you'll be the first to know."

The aggravation I felt at hearing her refer to David as my dad was blanketed by a new current of dread washing over me as I realized even with first responders searching specifically for *her*—no one had been able to find her. This was happening. My mom was missing.

She might really be gone, and I'd never see her again. I would've walked out that morning before school, mildly frustrated she was still asleep while casually glancing at her then leaving. That was it. We hadn't even spoken to each other. I wasn't even sure what I'd said to her the night before, the last time we'd talked.

"Thanks for these," I murmured, feeling like I was about to cry and taking an abrupt turn for a hallway, even though I didn't know where it would lead. "I'll just go . . . change."

"Bronwyn—?"

"Don't worry. I'll find a couch or something to sleep on."

The walls, like the ones in the kitchen, were painted a light shade of gray, with tall white baseboards stretching from the hardwood floor. The doors in the hallway were closed, and it didn't feel right to open them to find a bathroom, so when I spotted an open door leading into a laundry room, I decided it would work. I ducked inside, closing the door and leaning my forehead against it, eyes closed, forcing my mind onto something else other than my mom.

Then someone cleared their throat.

My eyes flew open wide and I spun around, clutching the pajamas to my chest. There, standing in front of the dryer, was a girl around my age in a white and blue school uniform, white knee socks sliding down her shins. Her hair, a similar shade of blond as mine but with added highlights, was pulled into a messy bun. Her expression was obstructed by a sheet mask over her face, but even then, I knew who she had to be. *Andi.*

Her eyes, visible through the eye holes, narrowed as she took me in, then the silk pajamas I was holding. Even though I'd showered at Indie's house after the tornado, I still felt dirty in comparison.

"There's a bathroom across the hall," she finally said, before turning back to the dryer, pulling out a pair of drawstring shorts from inside. "Second door on the left."

I had nothing but resentment for David and incredulousness for Amy, but I wasn't sure how I felt about Andi. I was never really able to define or label how I felt about her, at least not after her eighth birthday party. It wasn't like any of this was her choice, but she was still a stranger to me, not really a sister. Plus, she was eighteen. If she wanted to reach out, she probably could've.

She, like the rest of the Solidays, clearly hadn't wanted to.

Andi glanced up again. Even through the thin material of her sheet mask, I could tell she was shooting me a look. "Do you need me to show you where it is?" she asked flatly.

Slowly, I shook my head, finding my voice. "No. I'll . . . no."

Andi went back to the dryer, pulling out the top of a bikini, and I hesitated before slipping out of the room, going back into the hallway until I found the bathroom.

Eventually, I found a couch in one of the most spacious living rooms I had ever seen in real life. The floor plan was almost open concept, except the only concept was the living room and then, more living room. There were three white couches in total, not including armchairs, with cushioned ottomans in the center. There was a flat-screen television mounted to the wall, the screen practically a mirror tracking my reflection as I tentatively sat down, careful not to disturb the delicately arranged throw pillows. I leaned carefully against the cushions, staring at the ceiling until my eyelids reluctantly grew heavy.

○

The next morning I woke to my ankle bumping against something warm and soft. I tried to nudge it away, thinking it was one of their throw pillows, but it didn't budge. There was a beige dog curled up at the end of the couch, resting its chin on its front paws.

"That's Miles."

Across the living room on one of the other couches was a younger girl still in her pajamas, curled up against the armrest, her dark hair tangled from sleeping, her eyes bright and awake.

"Miles?" I croaked out.

"Dad named him that. He thinks it's funny to say *I walk Miles every day*," she said, her smile revealing bright pink rubber bands in her braces. "He got it from one of his friends, Brian. The worst dad joke, ever."

"Are you Natalie?"

"Yeah." Her smile widened. "We picked out clothes for you to wear today. We bought them yesterday when Dad was picking you up."

She got up, hurrying over to a bag slumped against the archway leading into the hallway. "You didn't have to do that," I said hesitantly. "I could've just put my friend's back on."

"You need something to wear at the lake," she told me, pulling out a crop top and a pair of high-waisted shorts. "It's going to be hot today, but it'll feel a little cooler at the lake. Do you want a cardigan to go with it?"

"I don't really wear crop tops."

"Okay," she said, grabbing a basic T-shirt from inside. "Do you like this? If you don't, we can return this stuff when we go shopping later."

"That one's nice," I said, noticing the excited glint coming into her bright brown eyes.

"Thanks. I kind of like fashion stuff, but Andi's better at it. She's got a YouTube channel, you know, where she does all makeup tutorials, but, sometimes, she does ones about outfits too."

"Yeah, I heard." There was a pause, then almost reluctantly, I asked her, "What are *you* better at?"

"I'm on the swim team at school. And when we go skiing, I can go faster than Andi. This winter, when we go again, I can teach you how to ski if you want."

"Maybe," I told her, even though there was no way I would be going *skiing* with them in the winter.

"Cool. We need to get dressed. We have to leave soon."

"You're right about that one," I mumbled under my breath.

It wasn't until the Solidays were loading their suitcases in the back of the Suburban that I met the youngest sibling, Danny. His hair was blond like mine, natural and not highlighted like Andi's, still sort of wet with comb tracks. He ran around to the trunk and chucked his backpack inside, ignoring David standing in front of it with a concentrated look on his face, staring at the luggage.

"Danny," he said with a sigh, grabbing the backpack. "You can't just toss your stuff in here. It needs to be *arranged*, carefully."

Natalie was already in the car. "To optimize space!" she called out, like it was the punchline to a joke she'd heard all her life. It probably was, considering how Amy laughed. It, along with everything else around here, was just another thing I didn't understand.

Then, there was a loud *thunk* from the front porch. Andi finally emerged from inside. A ring light wobbled under her tight grasp as she trudged slowly to the car.

"And that," David concluded, "is why we need to optimize space, everybody."

Without a sheet mask on, I could see her face more clearly. Her complexion looked smooth and even, devoid of acne or scarring. Her hair was curled in her signature beachy waves, and I could smell the coconut perfume as she reached the car.

Natalie must have noticed me eyeing the light because she said, "It's for her YouTube channel."

Amy held out a granola bar to me, one that prided itself on having only three ingredients. "She has almost a million subscribers!" she mentioned. "Maybe she could do your makeup sometime!"

"Maybe," I said.

After another few minutes of struggling to fit the ring light in the trunk, during which I climbed into the backseat beside Natalie when she started patting the seat next to her, Andi eventually slid into one of the middle seats beside Danny. She was on her phone, and never looked over her shoulder at me. I stared out the window at the rosebushes against the side of the house.

David let Miles in the backseat. He approached Andi, tail wagging and panting with his lips curled, as if into a smile. She didn't look up from her phone, but she scratched his head.

"Okay," Amy said as David got into the car. "Jason and Kimberly said they're already about halfway to the house, so they'll just meet us there."

"Kimberly is Jason's fiancée," Natalie informed me. "They're getting married in July."

"Ah."

"When we go shopping, we should look for a dress you can wear."

"Wait, you want me to come? To their *wedding*?"

Amy gave me a funny look over her seat for a second. "Of course, we do."

David flipped on the turn signal. "Well, hang on. Let's not pressure anyone here. It's not really our decision to make."

It wasn't like I wanted to be a part of their family, but there was still a piece of me, deep and buried, that felt the familiar throb of knowing it wasn't entirely one-sided. They weren't all reaching out, waiting for me to accept their hand. Instead, more of them were like me, waiting for things to go back to our separate normals.

o

Despite the fact it was only a forty-five-minute drive to their lake house—which, turned out, was located about halfway between their house and Shiloh—David stopped at a gas station halfway there. Partly because Danny was clamoring for a bathroom, despite us only leaving twenty minutes ago, and partly because this particular gas station had the best price per gallon.

Something told me David's insistence on saving money wasn't so much a necessity—like it was for my mom—but a point of pride.

Danny bolted out of the car as Andi unbuckled her seat belt. "I want something to eat," she said.

"Do you want something to eat, Bronwyn?" Amy asked, glancing over.

"Okay," I mumbled, even though I didn't, but my phone was charged again and I didn't want Amy or Natalie listening in when I tried to call my mom for at least the twentieth time that morning, just in case someone finally answered with a totally reasonable explanation of why she hadn't before.

Amy held out a twenty-dollar bill, and I paused halfway out of the car. "Did you want me to get you something?" I asked, confused.

"No, I thought you wanted something?"

"Oh, yeah. But you don't have to . . ." My mom or Jude never handed me money that easily, not unless they wanted me to run into the store for them. It felt foreign to even say *you don't have to give me money,* so I let my sentence trail off, shaking my head. Money wasn't talked about where I lived, not unless you were making jokes about how you didn't have any.

"You shouldn't have to buy your own food," she said, holding out the twenty. "Go get something to eat, some snacks for the weekend maybe. Oh, and don't forget to use our loyalty card. Dad's got it but they'll let you just use a phone number."

"Sure, thanks," I said quietly, slipping the bill into my pocket and pushing the door forward, not bothering to mention I had no idea what their phone number was.

When I went inside, I tried not to remember what had happened the last time I'd been in a gas station, glancing at the ice cream freezers and the beer coolers with a weird pang squeezing in my chest. *It's fine, it's just a gas station*, I told myself, venturing farther inside, cautiously, like I expected it all to just collapse like the one on the road to our trailer park back home.

Danny was near the bathrooms, looking impatient, while Andi examined bags of white cheddar popcorn. She was already holding a bottle of water, with swatches of shimmery pigments on the inside of her forearm.

I breathed out.

It's not raining, it's not windy, there's no tornado. It's just a gas station. There's no reason to be this freaked out right now. Get it together.

I found a corner of the store, grabbing a random bag of barbeque chips so I wasn't totally lying to Amy about getting something to eat, and pulled out my phone. I dialed my mom's number again, and like every one of the other hundred times I'd tried calling it, it went straight to voicemail.

One of the doors to the beer cooler slammed shut, and I flinched. But it was just an older guy in a baseball hat, grabbing a beer, and I focused on exhaling.

I tried Jude, expecting to hear the automated forwarding when on the last dial tone, I heard a click. Then a muffled, groggy, "Hello?"

"Jude?"

"Bronwyn?" he asked, his voice rumbling against the receiver. "That you, kid? Hey, where you been?"

Danny's flip-flops thwacked loudly against the floor as the bathroom door finally opened. "Jude! I . . . can't believe you answered. I'm . . . on my way to Shelridge," I said.

"Shelridge?" His voice was louder now. "What are you doing up there?"

"I'm not staying long," I said. Andi was already at the cash register, so I didn't have a lot of time. "Look, is my mom with you?"

"No, your mom's not here," he said. "I swung by your trailer looking for you guys, but no one was there. Your neighbor told me you were okay but didn't know where you were staying. I thought he meant both of you."

Kingston.

"I haven't seen her since I left for school the morning of the tornado. I can't get a hold of her. I don't know where she is," I said.

"I haven't seen her," Jude said. "Maybe you should call a couple of hospitals. If she's out of it, they might not know who she is."

Amy said David had already let the first responders and hospitals know to look out for her, which so far had come up with nothing. "Maybe," I said. "I should probably go. Thanks for . . . answering."

"Wait, why are you up at—?"

I hung up before Jude could finish asking me why I was halfway to a lake town. She wasn't at the trailer or the hospital, or with Jude. That was the last flicker of hope I had left, extinguished just like that. She had disappeared, just like the tornado, withering into the atmosphere, nowhere to be found, and leaving everything behind in places it didn't belong.

The Solidays' Suburban was still beside the gas pump, David clutching the nozzle as the numbers on the screen behind him crawled, and I decided that before I paid for the barbeque chips I *really* didn't want now, I'd call someone else.

"Bronwyn?" Kingston answered. "Hey, where are you? I lost you at the hospital."

"I'm on my way to Shelridge," I explained, "it's a long story, but I need to know if you've seen my mom? Like, has she come around looking for me?"

"No," he responded. "But I've been crashing with my parents. I haven't been around the park much."

"I think something happened to my mom, Kingston." I turned my back to Danny, who stared at the beef jerky selection near the registers. "No one can find her, she's not with Jude. The police are looking for her, she's not in any of the hospitals."

"Wait, where are you? Are you staying with Jude?"

"I wish," I muttered, then paused. "I'm with the . . . Solidays. Like David Soliday."

"The *senator*?"

I looked over at Danny, still in front of the Slim Jims. "Yes."

"Why is a senator getting involved?"

"Because he's . . . I'm—there's some paternity thing happening, but it's not—it's temporary."

Springs creaked in the background. "Are you saying David Soliday is your dad?"

"Only if you ask my DNA. Look, I gotta go. Let me know if you hear from my mom, okay? And don't tell anyone about the Soliday thing. It's weird, and I don't want to deal with that when I get back."

"You're coming back?"

"Yes, I'm coming back. Kingston, please—"

"I know, and I won't. Go have a good time with the *Solidays*," he said, feigning what I was pretty sure was supposed to be a posh British accent, and I rolled my eyes.

"They live in Fairview. They don't have different accents."

"Whatever. Don't get spoiled or anything. Then you'll be intolerable."

"You'd put up with me anyway."

"Probably."

I laughed—for the first time in days—just for a second before Danny ran up to me. "Did Mom give you money?" he asked, holding three packages of Slim Jims and a can of Coke.

I was thrown for a moment, hearing him address Amy as *Mom* to me. "Yeah, she gave me a twenty."

"What?" Kingston asked.

"I'm talking to Danny," I explained.

"*Danny*?" he repeated.

Danny held up the packages of Slim Jims, careful not to drop his Coke, and raised his eyebrows. "Can you buy me these? Mom just gets trail mix, but the kind with, like, dried fruit instead of M&M's."

"Can you have that stuff?"

"I'm not allergic," he said, "she's just a health junkie."

"Who's Danny?" Kingston asked, confused.

Danny, apparently hearing this, leaned in closer to me and shouted, "I'm her brother!"

"Danny! Kingston, I have to go. I'll talk to you later." I hung up quickly, before Danny had a chance to yell anything else into my phone. "You can't just shout things into my phone like that."

"Who were you talking to?"

"No one. Just go get in line," I grumbled.

"You only say no one when you're talking to someone if you *like* them. Was that your *boyfriend*?"

He dumped his food onto the counter as I dropped my bag of barbeque chips, unfolding the twenty-dollar bill and handing it to the cashier. "Just because you're nine doesn't mean you have to act like it. Liking someone doesn't have to be embarrassing."

He opened the package of Slim Jims after the cashier handed me the rest of Amy's change and we walked away from the counter. "Why did you say you were going back?"

"Because I am. When they find my mom, I'll live with her like I did before."

My fingers tightened around the limp dollar bills in my hand, the sinking feeling in my chest sharply returning.

"Are you scared they won't find your mom?"

The sinking feeling gave away into a cavity, a black hole sucking down rib bones and muscles and the air, a dizzying haze entering my mind with it.

"No," I lied, to him and me. "They'll find her."

o

The lake water sparkled between the pine trees through the window before the car slowed into the driveway of a sprawling home of dark wood, gray stones, and expansive windows. While smaller than their other home, it was still bigger than most back in Shiloh. Kayaks were on the ground near the water, life jackets tossed aside on two wooden Adirondack chairs on the porch. There was a dock in the backyard, leading out to the lake, a hammock beside it lazily swinging back and forth, bare feet smoothing over the grass. Another car was parked in the driveway, a black coupe with the windows rolled down. I hesitated in the backseat as everyone else crawled out of the car. Everything was so . . . *much*.

Natalie tapped her knuckles against the window. "Bronwyn? Come on, you have to meet Jason!"

Right, Jason, I thought. *There are* more *of them.*

Arrangements of azaleas were bright and in full bloom, edged in front of the porch, reminding me of the paycheck on the counter my mom had saved to buy flowers. Then a girl raced past me as the hammock in the backyard spun, now empty. To my surprise, for the first time since I arrived, Andi was beaming as she was enveloped in the arms of the girl, stumbling backward but laughing.

I glanced over at Natalie, mouthing, *Kimberly?*

"Taylor-Elise. Andi's best friend," she explained, before hollering over her shoulder. "Hey, *Andi*! Get your stuff! I'm not carrying this light."

"We are going to do so many videos this summer! Look at your hair! It's so cute!" Andi exclaimed.

For the entire car ride, Andi had been nothing but disinterested and vaguely aggravated. Seeing her so excited, even enthusiastic, was jarring. I assumed it was her personality but this, whatever it was, was even more confusing.

"Hi, Taylor-Elise," Amy said. "How are you? Were you waiting here for us?"

She nodded. "Yeah, this place is boring without you guys."

David lifted Andi's light from the trunk and nodded over to the front porch. "Tell your brother he's been doing a good job keeping up with the lawn. He should make a business out of it." Then he laughed, another joke I didn't get.

Natalie groaned. "Dad."

"Taylor-Elise," Amy said, "This is Bronwyn. She's—"

"She knows who she is, Mom," Andi interrupted, her previously enthused tone waning and returning to the one I was more used to.

But for Taylor-Elise to know about me, Andi must have talked about me at some point, but what would she have said? *She came to my birthday party one time and her crazy mother ruined it by screaming at my parents before cake and ice cream?* I never even told Indie about that, just that Senator David Soliday was my father. But, apparently, Andi had talked about me.

Taylor-Elise hesitated. "Hey," she said, then added, "Bronwyn."

I waved at her awkwardly. She was shorter than Andi, her teeth were bright white against her olive-toned complexion, with freckles dotting her nose beneath round, wire-rimmed glasses. Her hair was thick and dark, trimmed into a blunt shoulder-length bob.

"I'm going to go look around," I said to no one in particular, turning toward the backyard. It was just so *awkward*, like I was an exchange student no one asked for, but worse.

I focused on the glittering dark patches in the water as I ambled into the backyard, breathing in the scent of the water against the rocks. Jet Skis were cutting through the surface, their motors loud and rumbling. Pine trees were on the other side of the lake, another couple of docks lazily bumping against the current.

I heard someone behind me and turned, assuming it was either Amy or Natalie. But there stood a boy who had grown into a man since I'd seen him ten years ago, his blond hair darkened and his features broader. His eyes were wide and a deep shade of blue, his lips parted as he took me in like I was a memory he wasn't quite sure he had.

"Bronwyn?" he asked, almost uncertainly. But not like because he doubted it was me.

I nodded. "You're Jason, right?"

"I didn't think you'd come," he said, instead of answering.

"Sorry to disappoint," I mumbled, before walking around him toward the house. "I should go find out where I'm sleeping."

I heard him take in a breath behind me like he was about to say more. But a second later, there was nothing but the lake brushing against the shore as I went inside alone.

CHAPTER FOUR

Where I was sleeping, it turned out, was the floor. More specifically, the floor in the bedroom Andi and Natalie shared, with their twin-sized beds pressed up against opposite walls. The floor was at least carpeted—and unstained—and Amy brought me a sleeping bag while apologetically informing me about a bunk bed they planned to order.

"You don't have to do that," I said. "It's not worth it for a couple of nights."

"It would still be good to have," Amy said with some hesitation, "in case you ever wanted to visit."

I nodded, not because I was agreeing with her but because I didn't want to get into it. That might mean she would try to *prepare* me for what would happen if they couldn't find my mom, or if they did. I didn't need to be prepared for something like that—it was all I thought about.

I spent the rest of the day in the bedroom, on my sleeping bag, constantly calling my mom's number, then going through the apps on my phone over and over again, texting Indie about the lake house and how everything—and everyone—seemed so weird here. Natalie asked if I wanted to go kayaking, but I told her I was sore from the tornado, which wasn't entirely untrue. Hours later, I could hear laughter coming from the kitchen down the hall, the patio doors opening and closing as they lit the grill.

It wasn't until later that night someone knocked on the door, and I looked over to see it was David.

He stared at the sleeping bag I was sitting on, then swallowed. "Are you comfortable enough?" he asked, his voice softer and quieter than I expected it to be.

"I've slept in worse places," I said, hoping it struck a nerve. It was painfully obvious he had money, enough to splurge on expensive cars and kayaks and lake houses, but apparently not enough for child support.

Something came over his face for a moment before he sat on the corner of Natalie's bed. His eyes looked far away. "I, um—" he cleared his throat. "The Shiloh Police Department called."

The screen on my phone went black. My heart sank somewhere deep inside me, bottomed out, stopped there.

"They found your mom," he said. He wouldn't meet my gaze, the veins in his neck were pronounced, and there was nothing even resembling relief anywhere on his face. And he would've been if they'd found her okay. "She was a few miles from your trailer—"

"Stop," I whispered. There was no way this was real.

"She was in the creek," he said, softly. "They think the tornado—that the wind carried her there from your trailer."

Everything in me emptied and poured out over the floor. "It's not her."

"Bronwyn—"

"No, on the news they said people could be unrecognizable after a tornado," I insisted, hearing the frantic certainty in my voice as I spoke. "The debris, the—it all damages their faces and they can't make identifications. That could be someone else."

He shook his head. "It's her, Bronwyn. They checked the dental records."

"They're busy—"

"Bronwyn—"

"No, they're busy! They could've gotten the dental records mixed up. And Mom hasn't even been to the dentist in years. Maybe her teeth changed!"

"It doesn't work that way, Bronwyn."

"That's not my mom," I snapped. "I would know if my mom was dead."

"Your mother did die, Bronwyn. She passed away in the tornado."

I hoisted myself up with my trembling hands. "You are the *last* person who should ever talk about my mother."

Everything in me rattled as I stormed down the hallway, fingernails digging into my palms. I didn't know if it was because of how easily he could give up on my mom, *again*, or because he'd just confirmed what I already knew, even if I didn't want to think it. I wanted to cling to the anger—the burning I felt in my lungs when I breathed, the surge of rage it gave my blood instead of the heart-stopping fear of something too big to fit into my mind.

I reached the kitchen a second later, where the rest of the Solidays stood around the island. Amy stared blankly at the sink. "Bronwyn," she said, bringing everyone's distant gazes back to me, the same pity I saw in David's eyes in theirs. "I am so, so sorry, sweetheart."

"Just stop," I whispered, the words shaking as I spoke them. "First, that's not . . . my mom. Stop acting like you know anything about my mom, *or* me. You don't."

"I know you just met us, and there's so much happening right now," Amy said. "But do you want to sit and talk about it?"

"What?" I laughed, the sound breaking like fragmented pieces against my teeth. "Talk about it? What are you going to do next, give me a list of *resources* that might help me? Like, are you even for real?"

"Bronwyn—"

"*I understand that this must be hard for you,*" I finished for her. The anger I clung to was waning, giving in to something else I didn't want any of them to witness. I stomped toward the back door. "Leave me alone," I whispered.

Which shouldn't have been hard for them. After all, it was the only thing they'd ever done my whole life.

○

Somehow, without my noticing, Miles had snuck out into the backyard with me.

His tags jingled behind me, his steps shifting the dock where I dangled my legs into the black water. A wet nose brushed against my arm, the skin above his eyes wrinkling like concerned eyebrows again, and after a soft snort, he slumped his body against mine.

I had been out there for a few minutes, maybe longer, I didn't know. Words were jumbled in my brain, half sentences started and abandoned as my mind jumped from one thought to the next, wondering how any of this could be real. An emptiness closed in on me, accompanied by the realization that it might last forever. My mother was gone.

My face crumpled again as I thought of it, her, tears sliding out from the corners of my eyes. My heart sped up with every thought entering my mind—that I'd seen her for the last time without realizing it and hadn't even talked to her. That she'd died while we were still kind of fighting over that night, how I'd never really forgiven her for it.

She woke me up late one night in April during a spring snowfall that had sent cold drafts through the sides of the windows. Suddenly the overhead light was turned on, everything bathed in bright yellow as I squinted, my winter coat shoved so close to my face the zipper hit one of my teeth. She was on something again. Probably her personal favorite, oxycodone.

"Mom," I groaned, pushing the coat away. "I don't need a coat. It's not that cold."

She sniffled. "Baby, honey, I need your help."

"Why?" I mumbled, closing my eyes again. Last time she *needed my help*, she forgot how to use the defrost setting on the microwave. We had nothing to defrost; it just suddenly worried her in the middle of the night that she couldn't remember how to do it.

"I need money," she whimpered, not actually crying but like she wanted to, her voice raspier than normal. "I owe someone money and I don't have anything to give him. We need to go get some."

I hoisted myself up and she draped the coat over my legs, smoothing it delicately. "Who?"

She shook her head, tugging the zipper up and down.

"Mom."

"Just someone I know, okay?" she finally said, and I nodded, because of course. It was her dealer, whoever gave her the pills she was on right then. I had never met him before, didn't know his name because she pretended he didn't exist. He was always just *someone she knew*.

"How much do you need?"

She leaned against my knees, pressing her face into my parka. "I shouldn't even be asking you. I'm supposed to take care of you."

I pulled my knees away. "Mom, what do you need? Like a hundred bucks or something?"

My mom laughed. It was the first time she seemed almost like herself. The sober version. "I need a couple thousand," she said, her face crumpling but her eyes still dry. "Baby, I know—I know."

"I didn't say anything."

"But I know what you're thinking! You're disappointed, but it's going to be okay, baby. I'll pay you back, I promise, promise. Okay, here, pinkie swear?" she said, holding out her finger. When I just stared at her, her eyes finally glistened. "Bronwyn—"

Pushing back the blankets, I grabbed my coat by the hood. "Whatever, let's just go."

I was quiet the whole ride to the drugstore, listening to the staticky music from the classic rock station on the radio, focusing on Tears for Fears and Journey instead of the fact a couple thousand was *all* the money I had in my college savings account. I had earned some from babysitting and working last summer at the community pool with Indie, skimming the water and refilling the soda machines. I had been saving ever since I was eleven and realized what college could be for me: an escape. I could live in a dorm room in another state, leave everything behind, never stumble upon my mom passed out somewhere or worry she'd taken too many pills. Instead, I could worry about normal things, like finals and unforgiving professors. It was something I dreamed about whenever my mom got too much.

And because of my mom, that dream was gone.

We had to drive to a couple of ATMs because there were limits on how much you could take out. Each time we stopped, my mom did that breathy cry and started apologizing before I got out of the car. I knew better than to let her come with me and see my PIN number.

But I was doing it, and I couldn't even understand why other than she needed me to. She needed money, like she always needed someone to pay her bills, cook her meals, tell her I loved her when she was ruining me. The more I thought about it, the angrier I felt. I had to do everything for her. There wasn't one normal mom thing about her. She hadn't packed me a lunch in years, never took me out to the movies or the mall, never helped me with my homework. The one time I asked, she got so frustrated she started crying and I had to comfort her. And if that didn't sum up our relationship, then I didn't know what did.

When I finished draining my savings account, silently handing her the final stack of twenty-dollar bills while I sulked, she finally stopped crying. "Baby, I'm so sorry. But I love you so much. You're everything to me," she said, reaching out to touch my hair but I jerked back.

"Don't you see that's the problem? I'm *everything* to you. I do everything for you. You can't do one simple thing on your own. Not even paying off your dealer," I snapped.

I angled myself to stare out the streaky passenger window,

but judging from the watery sniffling sounds, she'd started crying again. "I know, honey. I do, I really do. And I'm sorry. I'm going to do better, I promise. Okay? This time I swear it."

I couldn't look at her, hating how if I did, she would notice how blotchy my cheeks were. None of what she said meant *anything* to me. I'd heard it all before. The money she took was a real promise. One of college, away from here, from her.

Except, that promise did mean something. It was the first one she'd kept in a long time. She stopped using, her eyes were clear, and she could have normal conversations without being overly affectionate. She got a job; she came to meets at my school again. She saved her first paycheck for me. And even though she apologized a thousand times for taking my savings, I never apologized for snapping at her. For hating her, something she probably knew even if I'd never told her.

She died knowing exactly how disappointed I was in her, in her flakiness and her addiction. But she did so many things right too. She'd stayed. She'd tried. She'd cared about me. I never had many people in my world, but my mom was the only one who was always there, right from the beginning.

It felt like it sometimes, but I was never really on my own. I had her, a mom would who come into my bedroom with her clunky laptop to watch movies or curl the hair at the back of my head for me. She cheered at my middle school graduation even after the principal had asked parents to remain quiet during the ceremony, taking so many blurry photos she never deleted from her phone. When I started my compost, she saved her scraps too. I normally had to pick out the produce stickers, but I liked the feeling of knowing something that mattered to me also mattered to her.

When I leaned against Miles's fur, I felt a vibration in his throat that became a low growl. I jerked away from him, thinking he was growling at me, but he was staring out at the water, alert. He barked, jumped up with his ears turned back. Eventually I spotted a blue kayak out in the lake. It was too dark to see who was inside—not that I'd recognize them anyway—but after a few seconds, it was clear it was coming closer, nearing the dock I was sitting on.

I brought my feet out of the water, purposefully not looking over at the kayak as it approached. I patted my thigh to get Miles's attention, but his attention was on the water.

"Miles," I said. "Come."

The dog's tail wagged, thwacking against my knees. In the moonlight, I could make out the outline of broad shoulders as the kayak paddled closer. Inside was a boy, and considering he was about to use the Solidays' dock, I imagined it was someone they knew—if not *another* of them, like a cousin or something—and I did not want to make another set of introductions right then.

"Miles, come," I commanded again, but it felt foreign in my mouth, like a suggestion instead of an actual order. Miles completely ignored me. "Miles, come on."

"You're fine!"

The boy in the kayak lifted a hand in a wave to me. If I didn't want to leave so badly, I would've laughed at this, at someone saying that I was *fine*.

"You don't have to leave," he called out, the tip of his kayak bumping against the dock, the glow from the motion sensor lights spilling over his face. His hair was dark, dampened in a way that caused slight curls; his eyes bright, warm, and green like the faultlessly manicured lawn behind me. There was something vaguely familiar about him, but I shook the thought away. "You don't have to go," he repeated, angling his kayak closer to the shore. "I don't need the dock."

I took in a breath, which turned into an unwitting sniffle. "I was just leaving," I mumbled, swatting a bug from my ear. "Miles, come *now*."

He grasped onto the side and withdrew one of his legs from inside, sinking his boat shoe into the water and standing up. For a moment, relief unclenched my chest as Miles darted down the dock only for him to run into the water, to the boy. "Hey, Miles."

Of course he knew the dog. Which meant he knew the Solidays, which meant he already knew which one of these things was not like the other. And maybe that was supposed to be my life now, the Larson surrounded by Solidays, a piece that somehow had gotten thrown into the wrong puzzle box.

"Miles." I kept blinking, trying to ward off another onset of tears in front of a total stranger. "Miles, come on. Let's *go*."

The boy paused. "Are you all right?"

I fought the urge to shake my head, not because I wanted to answer him honestly but because no one around here could take a hint. "Fine," I retorted. "Can you stop petting him, though? I'm trying to get him to listen to me."

"Sorry," He lifted his hand. "Do I know you from somewhere?"

"Nope."

"You look familiar."

Yeah, probably like Andi Soliday if she'd been raised in a trailer home with a different nose. "Pretty sure I don't."

"No, not at the Solidays' house—" He paused, and dread came over me like when Taylor-Elise first heard my name, a recognition dawning her face. Maybe Andi had told this guy too. He clearly knew the Solidays well enough to use their dock and pet their dog, so why not well enough to know their dirty laundry too?

But then he said something else, something I wasn't expecting. "You're that girl who wanted to use the broken stairs."

"What?"

"Bronwyn, right? That's your name?" He looked over to the lake house behind me, the dim lighting stretching out from the patio casting shadows over his face. I knew he had to be that teenage volunteer from in front of Jude's house, but I couldn't remember his name. "What are you doing up here?"

I let out a soft breath. "I don't know," I whispered, an honest part of myself cracking open and leaking out without my permission. But then I grasped Miles by the harness, leading him away from the boy whose name I couldn't remember.

When I reached the patio, I heard a voice softly call out, "Goodnight . . . then."

The lake house was quiet when I crept down the hallway, although I thought I might have heard a door closing but didn't see anyone as I approached Andi and Natalie's room, someone softly snoring inside. I hesitated, grateful it sounded like they were asleep, then braced myself for a night of lying on the floor in a sleeping bag.

The light from the hallway spilled into the bedroom as I nudged the door open, using my foot to feel around for the sleeping bag but all I felt was the carpet. Someone had taken it off the floor. I sighed, about to head to the living room for another couch to sleep on, when I noticed blond and brunette hair tangled together on the bed in front of me. I opened the door farther to let in more light to reveal Andi and Natalie sleeping in the same bed.

The sleeping bag was arranged on the other bed, over Andi's duvet, replacing her pillow with the one given to me. The sleeping bag was even unzipped, the flap pulled back so all I had to do was crawl inside and fall asleep.

But still I hesitated. I knew this had to be Amy. She'd probably told Andi to sleep with Natalie so the new kid didn't have to sleep on the floor after finding out her mother was dead. It was polite and kind, but I didn't need that from them. It couldn't have been how they felt. I was tearing their lives apart, too, tarnishing their good reputation, and now it would be permanent. And all they could do was be polite about it.

I went to grab the sleeping bag from the bed, thinking they could give me all the handouts they wanted but that didn't mean I had to accept them like the defenseless orphan they were making me out to be, when I heard a voice mumbling from across the room.

"Get in the bed, Bronwyn."

"What?" I whispered back to Andi.

"Get in the bed," she repeated instead of answering, her voice not quite a whisper. "I'm not in the same bed as Natalie just so you can go back to the floor. *Take* the bed."

"It's your bed. You can have it. I'm fine with the floor."

Even in the low lighting, her glare was evident. "Take the bed," she warned me, "or else."

"I'd do it if I were you," Natalie whispered, although her eyes were still closed. "She was on the lacrosse team at school."

"Wait, really?"

"Go to bed," she responded gruffly. "That one, over there."

"Do it. The pain isn't worth it. Trust me." Then, a pause. "It still hurts when I sneeze," Natalie said.

"Shut up," Andi told her, but her tone was lighter now. They were teasing each other, like actual sisters.

"All I did was use a spritz of perfume. Then *wham!* Suddenly, all I could smell was," Natalie said, laughter starting to break apart her words, "was *blood!*"

I sank into the bed as they both laughed, Andi telling her she was being dramatic and Natalie continuing with said dramatics, a heaviness starting to anchor me down. I leaned into the sleeping bag, letting the sound of their voices mixed together drown out my sigh.

If someone asked me where home was, I wouldn't have an address to give them.

My mom was dead.

I closed my eyes, breathing in and out. *Not here, not here, not here.*

"We're sorry about your mom, Bronwyn," Natalie said a moment later, before I even realized they had stopped laughing.

I kept my eyes closed.

"Go to sleep," Andi whispered, and I almost thought she could've been saying this to me.

CHAPTER FIVE

It didn't feel like I'd slept at all until I was stirred awake by a loud sound outside. Metal clanking together, the deepened rumble of a loud engine, doors opening and closing. Natalie and Andi were still asleep. Then, I remembered everything that had happened the night before. Why I was in Andi's bed instead of the floor, why I was in the Solidays' lake house instead of my double-wide, why I could never go back: my mom was dead.

The familiar black hole reappeared in my chest, dragging down everything until all I had was this sense of fear, so palpable it vibrated through my bloodstream and whirled my thoughts together into breathless unspoken words. She was just gone. But it didn't feel real, either, like there was still this part of me that expected everything to undo itself, somehow. There was no way this was happening.

There was another clunk from outside. My mom was dead. Completely dead. Cold dead. I blamed TV dramas for making death feel like a plot point instead of a real thing. It just *seemed* like that character had died, but then an episode later they were alive and everything was fine. But that's not what happens. In real life, death isn't reversible.

I needed to get out of the room, out of my head, because now I was blaming television networks for my denial.

The scent of brewed coffee drifted out into the hallway as I ambled into the kitchen, a carafe on the island beside a plate of blueberry waffles, which apparently weren't too expensive for them. No one had noticed me yet as Amy poured the batter into the waffle iron and David stood at the counter with a cutting board, his back turned. Jason was standing at the open front door, staring out at what I assumed was the source of the metal clanking. And a woman with shiny black hair, adorned in a yoga outfit, was shifting things around inside the refrigerator. Kimberly, I presumed.

Amy looked up, lowering the lid of the waffle iron. "Bronwyn," she said, and then everyone paused. She looked like she was about to say more, then hesitated. "Do you . . . want some waffles?"

"No, not really."

"You should eat something. You barely ate yesterday."

I glanced over to the front door where Jason was standing. "What's going on?"

David looked over his shoulder, resuming his careful slicing of what I could see were strawberries. "It's the bunk bed we ordered for your room," he explained. "We had it delivered today."

"Fast," I remarked, keeping the *and expensive* part to myself.

"Hi." I turned, realizing Kimberly was now beside me, a bottle of orange juice in one hand and her other extended out to me. Her engagement ring glinted like the lake water outside. "I'm Kimberly Seoung. Jason's fiancée."

I shook her hand, nodding.

"I'm so sorry about your mom, Bronwyn. I was praying they would find her okay," she said.

"I'm sure you were," I mumbled.

"Bronwyn, I could make toast if you wanted," Amy said to me. "We have a lot of decisions to make today."

"Decisions?"

Amy fiddled with the waffle iron. "Planning. For your mom's funeral."

A *funeral*, for my mom. She couldn't just be dead, there had to be this event to remind everyone of it too. "I don't want to."

"I know it's hard to think about, but you should have a chance to say good-bye. So should her friends, people she loved."

I thought about Jude, then wondered if he even knew they'd found her. Dead. "I don't want to have a funeral right now. The tornado just happened. There probably isn't even a place to *have* a funeral," I said, not adding that a funeral made this all too . . . *real*. This couldn't be some freakish nightmare for me to wake up from if there was a funeral.

"How about we just meet with a director?" Amy suggested. "Get an idea of what needs to be considered—"

"Why are you acting like you have a say in this? She's *my* mom. None of you even knew her." I glanced over at David. He might have met her, impregnated her, then dumped her, but he never really *knew* her. And, besides, it bothered me that suddenly now they cared. *Now* they cared about my mom, not when she was a single mom raising David's mistake. Child support, simple acknowledgment, no. But, sure, yeah, they would *love* to put her in the ground.

"Having a funeral for your mom could be a way you show

your appreciation for everything she did for you," Kimberly inter-jected tentatively. "She was a single mom who raised you into an obviously strong, opinionated woman. That life deserves to be celebrated."

My resolve weakened. "It can't be, like, this *thing*, okay? Not what you would want at your funeral, but what *she* would've wanted."

"Absolutely. You can choose everything she would've wanted. We'll just sit back and write the checks," Amy said.

"Right," I murmured just as one of the deliverymen approached the front door, holding a tablet, somewhat red-faced.

"Okay," he said, his gaze falling on me for a second, "so where do you want this thing?"

○

I called Jude later that evening, sneaking out onto the patio while the Solidays were still inside, eating dinner. I'd spent most of the afternoon wondering how I was going to do this, what I was going to say to him. I couldn't even tell Indie or Kingston and just texted them instead. It would make Indie cry, and I didn't want to hear that because I was too afraid of what it would make me do. Kingston was different though. Truthfully, I was angry with him. If he hadn't rushed me to the gas station, then I would've gotten to my mom. I was angry with myself about that too. I could've fought harder, but I didn't. When he texted back, I deleted the notification without reading it.

But I had to tell Jude. I wasn't sure if he'd already heard it from someone else, but if he didn't, I knew it had to come from me. So, when he answered, I blurted, "They found my mom," before he could even say hello. "They found her in a creek a few miles away from the park. She was dead."

I heard nothing on the line for a moment. Then, a soft shuddering exhale. "I figured as much," he said, "when you mentioned you didn't know where she was."

Stop, stop, stop, I thought to myself as that familiar feeling started to overtake me again, tightening my throat and prickling my eyes. "Yeah, so," I said. "I'm planning the funeral, in case you wanted to have any say in that?"

"That's all right, kid," he replied, his voice also thick. "I don't know anything about that kind of stuff, what'd look nice, things like that. I don't want to get in your way or anything."

Please get in my way.

Please don't let me be the only person doing this who loved Mom.

"Yeah, no problem," I said instead. "It's next week, on Friday, if you want to come."

"Yeah, yeah. Of course, I'll be there." There was a sniff on the other end, something clunking around in the background before he said, "So, you holding up okay?"

No, I wanted to say, but didn't. It felt harder, like pulling out pieces of a Jenga board game. Touch the wrong one and everything comes crumbling to the floor. "Yeah, I guess."

"I should probably let you go. Don't want to hold you up."

"I'll see you next week."

The lake splashed over the pebbles near the dock, the wood creaking against the soft undulation. I left the lake behind and turned to the garden beds lining the back of the house.

Wandering around the backyard, I went searching for a hose. It might not have been my garden, but I hadn't realized until then how much I missed pulling out weeds or plucking the dead flower blossoms from stems still bright green in color. Maybe I missed having something to take care of, and I wasn't sure if that meant I missed my garden or if I missed my mom.

The hose was around the side of the house, coiled around a plastic reel. The nozzle was more elaborate than the one I had at home, which stuck if I squeezed it too tightly. I had just turned the water on, unraveling the hose and feeling the weight of the nozzle in my hand when I heard someone behind me.

"Hello?"

I whirled around, my hand involuntarily squeezing, sending a jet stream over the grass and toward the boy from last night, splattering water all over his collar. I uncurled my fingers around the clamp, lowering the nozzle.

Water trickled from his eyelashes as he used the hem of his sleeve to wipe his face. "Good evening to you too."

"What are you doing here?"

"Mr. Soliday hired me to take care of their plants. I was coming to water them when you"—he gestured to himself, his shirt soaked—"sprayed me."

"I didn't do it on purpose. You snuck up on me."

He shrugged. "I was getting hot anyway."

I paused, not sure what to make of him. "I can water them," I said, even though I wasn't sure that was true. It wasn't like I'd asked permission or anything. "Sorry for spraying you."

He watched me for a couple of seconds trying to unravel the hose. "You can just pick up the reel and take it with you, you know? Just, like, lift it."

"I'm old-fashioned," I retorted, but the real reason was I'd never used a reel before—the hose I had at home was around twelve feet long and was shoved against the foundation of our trailer instead of being put *away*.

"Are you a friend of Andi's? Is that why you're staying here?"

"No," I snorted. "Are *you*? That why you're always over here?"

"I'm their *neighbor*," he replied, pointing through the shroud of pine trees between properties, to where enormous windows glinted in the warm colors of the setting sunlight. Unlike the Solidays' stone lake house, theirs was constructed of stained wood. Windows basically made up the walls, the light reflected obscuring me from seeing inside. "We're the Denvers."

"Okay," I said.

"My sister's here all the time. Taylor-Elise?"

"*She's* your sister?" I blurted out. "You're their neighbor and she's your sister?"

"Yeah. They've been best friends ever since her family bought the lake house and moved in next to ours."

"Do you live here, year-round?"

"Well, I—no. It's a summer home," he answered, turning to look at it over his shoulder. "People don't really live year-round in Shelridge. Not in this neighborhood, anyway."

He talked like it was so normal, like of course no one lived here for longer than the summer, but there was also a hesitation in his voice. Like he realized how it sounded to have a summer home now that he was talking about it out loud. He wasn't just privileged—he was ignorant of it. I felt a twinge of annoyance thinking about it, how money could mean nothing to people like him, like the Solidays. It was something they never had to worry or care about. It was always just there, no matter what, and the whole time their noses would be turned up at everyone else. People who barely had one home, never mind seasonal ones.

"That's nice," I told him. "Do you also own a winter cabin?"

He hesitated again, beginning to look sheepish. "It's not so much—"

"Sorry, right, I mean, do your parents own one? I'm assuming your parents are the ones who earned the money to buy multiple homes. *They're* rich?"

"They're lawyers," he answered.

"So, it doesn't matter what you do then. You don't have to worry about college or not finding a job after college. Because you have parents who'll pay your bills. But I bet your parents also have *connections*, so you'll be employed your whole life until you retire at a reasonable age. It's like you have nothing to worry about, ever. Someone's always there to take care of you."

His brow was furrowed, confused. "My parents don't—"

I shook my head, feigning an innocent look as I watered the rosebushes. "It's not a bad thing," I explained to him. "It just means you're better off than most people. A lot of people, actually, who have to go out and earn their living."

Or a teenage girl, struggling to hide her mom's unemployment checks from her so it went to bills instead of drugs, handing in applications at stores that wouldn't hire her until she was eighteen, buying pasta and rice with food stamps because those were cheapest.

"For someone I barely know, it sounds like you know everything about me," he remarked. The friendliness was starting to slip away from his tone and his eyes were giving in to something almost *annoyed*. Which was more refreshing and familiar to me than unwavering politeness.

"Am I wrong? Your parents are lawyers who can afford multiple homes, right? That's what you said. They probably made sure you had the best education, maybe sent you to a private school?" I smirked when he looked away. "That's a yes. And I'm guessing the reason you waste time watering the Solidays' garden is that he's one of those *connections*, right? A senator's approval could get you into a lot of places."

"Is that why *you're* here?"

I couldn't stop now if I tried, "I'm just saying it's a tactical move to be so involved with a senator's rosebushes. Take good care of them, and who knows? He could send a handwritten letter of recommendation to his alma mater."

"Because well-off means that you have to have ulterior motives for everything. You can't just be nice if you're affluent."

"The fact that you said *affluent* and *well-off*," I laughed, "shows even *you* know what it means to be called rich and you're tiptoeing around the word because of it." I pulled a weed, shaking off the dirt and looking over my shoulder as if to say *missed one*.

It wasn't that I disliked him personally. I couldn't even remember his name, but there was a part of me that liked saying what I thought out loud after feeling stifled ever since I'd arrived here. I didn't know how to be unwaveringly polite like the Solidays were. But I knew back and forth, how to be combative. This was what I was comfortable with, and it was like slipping back into your bed after a long, hard day.

"I'm not *tiptoeing*," he countered slowly. "Those are just word choices."

"Right. Sorry. You're from a private school. Must have taught you all the big, fancy words while we just got the basics."

"Well, you're here at the same *summer home* as me so I don't think—"

"You know *I'm* not from here."

He paused, eyeing me for a moment. "You look a lot like Andi," he remarked, and my grip around the nozzle weakened slightly. "You might not *be* from around here, but you *look* like you belong here."

My gaze narrowed, one part of me fearful he might have pieced together who I was, another part crushed because it wasn't like I had my old life to go back to. But to be told that I *looked* like I was from around here, like I grew up with summer homes or expensive clothes—that rattled me. I had only what the Solidays had handed me, stripping me of who I used to be to fit into this perfect little world where this boy thought I belonged.

"I don't think those were just *word choices*," I said icily. "You're trying to distance yourself from it, from how easy you have everything. That's why you volunteered after the tornado, right? Because you have all these beautiful houses and hundreds of people didn't, and you felt guilty. So, you threw on your rattiest Gucci shirt and spray painted a couple of houses, then called yourself a good person for it."

"Did they find your mom, Bronwyn?"

I whirled around, the cold water from the hose dripping over my socks as I gaped at him. His expression softened, not aggravated or uncertain anymore, just sympathetic. *Sorry.*

"When we met, you said you were looking for your mom and you seemed upset last night, so I thought—"

"*You* thought she was dead," I clarified. "And you were right, she is. They found her in a creek."

"I'm so—"

"I know what you're doing," I interrupted. "You don't think I could just not like you. There must be something else on my mind, something like a dead mom that makes me want to pick a fight, right? Then you'll tell me how sorry you are, and you can walk away feeling like a good person. Just like you did when you volunteered after the tornado. You use people's worst-case scenarios to feel better about yourself for being nothing more than a rich lawyer's kid, living the best life *you* didn't earn and will never have to prove."

Finally, after what felt like forever, he said, "You're over-watering the violets," and turned to walk away.

"I don't need your help . . . *Adam*," I retorted

"Ethan," he called from his property now. "Guess you don't know everything about me after all."

CHAPTER SIX

A couple days later, I was in the bedroom on the top bunk when Andi and Taylor-Elise walked in. They had been out shopping, paper bags from outlet stores dangling from their wrists like bracelets. Natalie was out paddleboarding with her friends, which left me in the room alone—until that moment, anyway. Andi dumped her bags on her bed and signed into her parents' Netflix account, preparing to binge-watch episodes of *Gossip Girl*, ignoring me on the top bunk.

Andi had resumed ignoring my existence after forcing me to sleep in her bed the other night. She never really spoke to me, just went about her summer like I wasn't part of it. She had a job at a local drive-in theater and spent most of her nights there, creaking open the door around three in the morning and quietly slipping into bed. It was almost familiar, like when my mom let the rickety screen door slam shut behind her while I was dozing off in my room. Close, but not quite the same.

Taylor-Elise, however, wasn't as used to ignoring me, glancing up at me as Andi asked if she wanted to restart the episode or pick up where they'd left off. Within a few minutes, they were on her bed, talking about what snacks were in the house, and I decided to leave without saying anything. If they were going to pretend like I wasn't there, then I might as well not be.

Besides, I'd never seen *Gossip Girl* so even if they restarted the episode, I was still going to be behind.

After wandering around outside for a few minutes, I couldn't figure out what to do with myself, and it just kept bringing up thoughts I was trying to keep buried, so I came back into the house. As I walked into the kitchen I could hear popcorn popping in the microwave. Taylor-Elise walked in from the other doorway, laughing at something Andi shouted from the bedroom. She saw me as she reached for the microwave handle like she had done this a thousand times before, her eyes widening before she quickly looked away. There were swatches on the inside of her arm like the ones I normally saw on Andi's arms, probably doing something for her YouTube channel.

Taylor-Elise grabbed a bowl from the cupboard. The resemblance between her and Ethan was more noticeable now I knew she was his sister. I wondered if he'd told her about what I'd said to him a couple of days ago. Maybe that was the reason she wouldn't look at me.

"Oh," she said as she tore open the bag and poured the popcorn into the bowl, black-tinged kernels steaming at the top. "I can't believe I burned *popcorn.*"

I glanced up, not sure if she was talking to me.

"I make popcorn at work," she explained, like I'd asked her. "At the Starbright Drive-In down the road. I make popcorn every *day.* I should know how not to burn popcorn."

"You can still eat it."

"I hate microwave popcorn. At work, there's this big popcorn machine and it spits the popcorn out from a metal tin when they're done."

"Don't leave it in as long next time."

"I *hate* microwave popcorn," she reiterated then paused, like she realized who she was talking to, and a crease formed between her eyebrows.

"*Tay! You're missing the best part!*" Andi called out from down the hall.

Taylor-Elise looked over her shoulder, grabbing the bowl of burnt popcorn. "I should—" She awkwardly gestured to the hallway with the bowl.

"Yeah, you're missing the best part."

I took my phone out of my pocket to text Indie—deciding I would launch straight into how *rich* the Solidays were instead of acknowledging anything about my mom—when Amy walked in the kitchen.

"You didn't want to watch TV with the girls?" she asked.

"Never seen the show."

She sat down on a bar stool. "Do you need help with writing your mom's eulogy? I wrote one when my mother passed away. If you wanted, I could help you with it?"

"It's going fine," I lied, because I had no idea what I was supposed to say. My mother was so complicated, and my feelings for her were the same. She was there for me, but there were so many times it didn't feel that way. She loved me, but she needed her pills more. She took care of me, but I still felt like I was on my own. How was I supposed to capture everything about her into one speech and make strangers understand that despite her smoker's voice and unfocused eyes, she was still beautiful? Or was I supposed to just ignore that side of her? Even that felt wrong, like I was rewriting her history. Plus, it's not like I'd ever been to a funeral before, or even heard a eulogy. The Solidays were well practiced when it came to wording obituaries or discussing plans with the funeral director. David and Amy had gone back to Shiloh with me the day before and we'd met with the funeral director, and Amy ended up taking over completely. I didn't know what I was doing, so I just let her. It bothered me even more, like after years of handling everything on my own just fine, suddenly I was thrust into a world where I couldn't understand the most basic things.

"Okay, well, if you change your mind . . ." I looked out through the kitchen window, at the black lake waters tousling the dock. "There is something else we should talk about, Bronwyn. You already know your father is a public figure, right? It seems as if the media *knows* about what's been going on. There are rumors, and we feel like it's time to address them. In a press conference."

"You want to do a press conference? And say what, exactly? The senator has a bastard love child living with his real family now?"

She paused. "Is that how *you* feel?"

"It's not like you wanted me here before you had to take me in."

"Honey, we—"

"It's whatever, I don't care," I interrupted. "You'll do this press conference with David and what? The media will back off?"

"We planned to do the segment here as a family. The local morning news crew will take care of everything. We also thought it would be a good idea if you met with your—with *David's* press secretary to go through some techniques to help you deal with the press."

"Wait." I hoped I was hearing this wrong. "You want *me* to be there? And answer questions; I can't do that!"

"If you don't want to answer any questions, that's fine! David and I will be doing most of the talking."

"What are you going to say?"

"We'll explain you're David's daughter from a separate relationship and since your mother has passed away, you'll be living with us. But the techniques will be helpful for more than just the press conference. Even after this, there will probably still be speculations, questions about you, for you. It's good to know how to respond to them."

"Strangers are going to be gossiping about me," I clarified.

"In plain terms, yes. But we'll help you deal with it."

"Can't you just lie and say it's all made-up or something?"

"If we tried to hide you like dirty laundry, it would look like we're ashamed of you," she said, and smiled softly. "And we're not, Bronwyn. Truly. And, it's best not to hide things from the media. It just looks worse in the end. We're only waiting this long to give your mother a peaceful funeral."

There was a crease formed in between my eyebrows as I stared at her, confused because before I was their dirty laundry, hidden and kept away from everyone, including the media, but it unraveled when she mentioned the funeral. Right. Because my mom was dead. And now I have to live in a world of press conferences and media techniques and *politics*.

I was going to be living the life of a *rich kid* now.

CHAPTER SEVEN

Amy and David were driving me to the funeral, but I didn't expect *all* the Solidays to be in the kitchen when I came downstairs. Even Taylor-Elise was there, although not dressed in formal black attire like everyone else, pinning back strands of Natalie's hair into a braid crown with the bobby pins between her teeth.

Amy was going over the sleeves of David's blazer with a lint roller, dog hairs from Miles sticking to the paper. "Hey, Bronwyn," she said, taking me in and frowning. "Is that what you're wearing today?"

I looked down at the outfit I had assembled from the clothing Amy had given me, a pair of *distressed* jeans that probably cost more than my phone and a basic dark T-shirt. When I went through the bags, I had found only one dress. It was olive green and the fabric was soft; too nice for my mother's funeral. Like, I felt like I'd be rubbing it in how I was so much better off without her. I had a lake house and a dog and a wardrobe of beautiful, expensive clothing, all because she was dead.

"All of my clothes were destroyed in a tornado so . . ."

"Do you think she could wear one of your dresses, honey?" she asked Andi.

I quickly shook my head. "She doesn't—"

Andi, holding a dark blue smoothie in a mason jar with a steel straw, looked me over. "I don't think they'll fit her right. They'd look too long on her."

"This is fine—"

"I could change?" Kimberly piped up. "We're about the same size, and I've got another dress. It's not black but it's not too loud for a funeral."

"That's okay," I insisted.

Amy sighed. "I should've prepared better. Bought something appropriate for you to wear. I don't know what I was thinking."

She was rolling the lint roller over David's elbow so aggressively, he nearly spilled his coffee. "She's still dressed nicely," he remarked. "I think you look very nice, Bronwyn."

I stared at him, unamused with his placating tone. Then, after a second, he looked away.

"I . . . I have a dress. Bronwyn can borrow it," Taylor-Elise said. I almost forgot she was there. "It's black, appropriate for a funeral. And washed."

"Really—" I started.

Amy beamed at her. "Oh, Taylor-Elise, that would be perfect. Thank you."

"I'm done with your hair, Natalie. Bronwyn, we can head over and get ready at my house." Then, she turned to Andi. "You want to come?"

She spoke around her straw in her mouth. "Nope."

That's what I wanted to say.

◦

The inside of the Denvers' home smelled like lemons. Taylor-Elise led me through their living room, and houseplants were *everywhere*. Varying shades of green in a house that otherwise looked minimalistic. The furniture was white, the walls were white, the cupboards in the kitchen were white. It almost made the Solidays' houses look lived-in.

Taylor-Elise's bedroom wasn't much different, also painted white with a white duvet perfectly made and fluffed. As she went over to her closet, I found myself surprised she even owned a black dress.

"Was that how you wanted to do your hair?"

"What's wrong with my hair?"

"It's flat against your head and kind of wavy in the back. Like you slept in it wet."

"That's what happened," I said defensively.

"It's fine if you're just hanging around but you're going to a funeral. You want to look your best."

"My mom didn't care about me looking my best even when she wasn't too dead to notice," I snorted softly.

"I'm sorry," she said. "I'm not trying to make you feel worse. I've just—well, my family has always taken funerals really seriously. You honor the deceased by looking your best. Making some kind of effort. And maybe that makes up for all the times you didn't give them your best when they were alive." She made a face, moving aside a sweatshirt. "But you're probably right. They're all too dead for that."

I paused, glancing down at my jeans and T-shirt, at my best for my mom. "What would you do with my hair?"

"Probably a Dutch braid. It's simple, so it doesn't take long and it looks nice. Not too much, which is also a funeral *don't*. You have to look respectful, but not too great, you know? You're still in mourning and too much looks like too much."

"Do you just go to funerals on the weekends for fun or something?"

Taylor-Elise laughed. "No, my parents are older. They kept putting off having kids to focus on their careers until they were almost in their forties, had to do IVF, which is how they got me and my brother, and we're seventeen now—"

"You're twins?"

She nodded. "Anyway, all of our grandparents have died, one of my mom's sisters. A few old friends, I guess. And our parents always make us go. It looks better that way."

"People around here sure do care a lot about the way things look," I remarked quietly.

"It's what happens when your parents have high-profile jobs," she said with a shrug, clearly more used to it than I was. "They're prominent members of the community. My behavior reflects well on them."

"Doesn't that take away something from you, though? Like you're not your own person, you're just someone's daughter?"

Taylor-Elise considered this for a moment. "I don't think so. I don't think not caring about certain things would make me who I am. And I am someone's daughter. I'm not ashamed of my parents and I don't want them to be ashamed of me. I don't think that's a bad thing."

"Your parents should accept you for who you are."

"And they do but, like, that's not an excuse for being inconsiderate or ignoring something important to them." She pulled out her phone. "What time is the funeral?"

"Two."

"I don't like this one," she declared, shoving the dress back inside her closet. "Like, it looks nice but it's not *you*. I want something that looks *you*, or *you* adjacent. Something familiar. *Ethan*!"

My eyes widened, alarmed. "Why are you calling him?"

"I don't want you to be late. He'll braid your hair while I pick out a dress for you. *Ethan*!"

I shook my head. "That dress looks fine—"

"*What*?" a muffled voice called from down the hall.

"Come here!"

A pause. "*Why*?"

"I don't need my hair braided—"

Exasperation flickered across her face, poking her head out the door frame. "I need your help with something, now *come on*!"

There was a groan in response, which appeared to satisfy Taylor-Elise as she turned back to her closet. Meanwhile, I was frantically trying to come up with a way to get out of Ethan Denvers *braiding my hair* when a door opened and footsteps shuffled down the hall.

His hair was tousled and uncombed, but still perfected in some way—like maybe he had combed it and just didn't want it to *look* like he had—and he was wearing a black T-shirt with a Champion logo on the chest. A crinkle formed between his eyebrows when he noticed me standing awkwardly at the foot of Taylor-Elise's bed.

"Why are you here?" he asked.

"I need you to braid her hair," Taylor-Elise answered for me.

"Braid her *hair*?"

"She needs her hair styled and braids are fast," Taylor-Elise ordered. "We're in a hurry. You remember how to do them, right?" She looked over at me, elaborating, "Before I knew how to braid my own hair, Ethan did it for me. He's pretty good."

"Okay," I said. "But that's—he doesn't . . . have to. It's fine."

"In that case . . ." he replied, turning to leave.

"No, Ethan, come on." Taylor-Elise's expression softened. "Her mom died and she's going to her funeral. All her stuff got wrecked in that tornado so I'm trying to find her a nice dress and her hair needs to look better than *that*. So, go do a Dutch braid."

"You know what? It's fine," I blurted out, hating how choked and tight my voice sounded, but I needed to leave, now, because I really couldn't listen to them talk about my mom like that—her death was starting to feel too real. "Don't worry about it."

I attempted to go around Ethan in the door frame, tearful eyes pointed at the floor when a hand reached out for my wrist. "Bronwyn," Taylor-Elise whispered, pulling me to her bed and nudging my shoulders until I sat down. "Just sit, okay?"

Ethan sighed before abruptly heading out of the room.

I wiped my knuckles over my cheeks, pressing them into my eyes until colors burst across my eyelids. There it was, it happened. I was crying in the Denvers' house.

Taylor-Elise went back to the closet, the sound of hangers screeching against the rod resuming as I kept my knuckles against my eyes for a moment longer. Then footsteps neared and I felt heat close to my arms.

"I'm going to touch your hair now," Ethan said, before his fingers brushed against my back as he lifted my hair. "Don't freak out."

The teeth of a comb gently grazed against my scalp as I took my clenched fists away from my eyes. "You don't have to braid my hair."

His voice was low to keep Taylor-Elise from overhearing. "Have to prove I'm not just a rich kid somehow."

I slumped until my shoulder brushed against his stomach and then I straightened up so fast that the partial braid in his hand tugged against my head. He hesitated, then resumed braiding my hair. "I shouldn't have said that," I said.

"Did you mean it?"

His fingers grazed my earlobe as he gathered more of my hair, the movements gentle and soft. "I was wrong. I was angry, and not at you but it just kind of . . . came out at you. Sorry."

"But you meant it."

"Maybe."

Ethan separated the sections of my hair and wove them together. We sat there in silence until he was done and had wrapped a small elastic around the ends. "Then I guess it doesn't matter how you said it."

"Okay, this dress will work," Taylor-Elise announced, walking over to the bed. The black material was draped over her arm as she took in my braid, frowning. "Ethan, that's a *French* braid."

He shrugged. "It looks fine. She'll look like a million bucks."

His eyes met mine for a fleeting second, a knowing glint reflected in them. I stifled a groan because he knew. He knew exactly why I was staying with the Solidays now.

Guess you don't know everything about me after all, he had told me.

"She'll probably be *rich* with compliments on that French braid," he continued.

Taylor-Elise narrowed her eyes. "Why are you talking like that?"

"Bronwyn knows." He shoved his hands into his pockets and walked out of the room.

"You know what, exactly?" Taylor-Elise asked.

"It's nothing," I said.

"Try this on."

She handed the dress to me, and I changed in her en suite bathroom. It was sleeveless, with a higher neckline than I was used to, but she insisted it looked good. It was formfitting, making me somehow feel both older and too young at the same time. She reached behind my ears, loosening a few strands to frame my face, and ran a chilled jade roller under my eyes to decrease the splotchy puffiness there.

"Why are you doing *all* of this?" I asked. "You don't even like me."

"I don't *dislike* you or anything," she explained, taking the roller away from my face and placing it back into a small refrigerator where she kept her skincare products. "But Andi—she's . . . my best friend. And having you around is hard for her. She's popular, but she doesn't have anyone she can talk to. I'm just trying to be there for her."

"I'm not trying to make things hard for her. I don't want to be here either."

"She knows that. It's just hard for everyone, I guess." She glanced down at her phone and then showed me the time. "You'd better go if you don't want to be late, which is another funeral *don't*. Also, you'll need mints. Old people tend to hug and then speak to you while they're still kind of hugging you, like super up close. It's weird, but whatever. And you look great. You know, if you cared about that today."

"I didn't," I said as I looked into her full-length mirror. "But the jade roller worked."

"Yeah, they're great. Andi gets them in PR packages all the time. Ask her for one."

"No, thanks." Then I paused. "But thanks for . . . this. You didn't have to."

She shrugged. "I'm a sucker for a makeup montage."

CHAPTER EIGHT

The inside of the church was sweltering because it didn't have air conditioning. I hadn't even been into the sanctuary yet; instead, I was standing around the entrance, where the windows and doors were propped open. We were the only ones there so far, except for the minister and a couple of deaconesses from the church who were arranging the flowers around the casket and folding the programs. The others were inside the sanctuary, fanning themselves with the programs, except for Amy and David. They excused themselves after tires splashed through the mud puddles outside and I assumed they'd left to go speak with the funeral director.

I was concentrating on my phone, not looking toward the casket, when I got a text from Indie. Just pulled in. I stepped outside to wait, noticing David and Amy having a hushed conversation at the side of the church. Except it wasn't either of them I heard speaking.

". . . acting suspiciously, inserting himself into conversations, talking more about her death than Donna herself. He might pay special attention to your daughter, or the rest of your family."

I peered around the corner to where the Solidays were standing with a man who wasn't the funeral director. He had a comb-over of thinning brown hair and an unbuttoned blazer, a belt too tight around his waist. The woman beside him also had brown hair, her glasses speckled with raindrops. They were both dressed in black funeral attire. It took me a moment to realize she was the police officer I'd seen right after the tornado, running into the trailer park.

But I didn't *know* her, and it wasn't like my mother was *that* social. Mom spent most of her life confined to our trailer, asleep on the futon or watching television after dry-swallowing pills. I couldn't think of a reason the officer would be here at my mom's funeral, standing next to a man I didn't recognize at all, speaking with the Solidays about someone acting suspiciously.

"If you think he'll be here then is it even safe to have the funeral? If it could involve our kids . . ." There was a concerned crease between Amy's eyebrows as she spoke, glancing almost nervously to David beside her.

I frowned, using the wheelchair ramp as a shortcut to get down to the parking lot. "Why wouldn't the funeral be safe?" I asked. "Who do you think will be here?"

Amy and David paused when they noticed me approaching them. "No one, sweetheart," Amy said quickly. "We're talking about the weather. They're expecting more thunderstorms this afternoon."

I shot her a look. "The weather's not a *person*."

Then I felt myself being propelled forward as arms from behind enveloped me. The man and woman nodded politely to the Solidays and then headed inside the church.

". . . I haven't seen you in forever!" Indie was saying as I hugged her back, still staring skeptically at Amy and David as he placed a hand on her back and started to lead her toward the church as well.

"It's nice to see you again, Indie," David said without pausing in his steps.

"You too," Indie said. "Sorry! I shouldn't be all happy right now. And I'm not happy. I've just missed you."

"It's fine." I shrugged. "You know I don't know how to handle somber anyway." I looked over to the parking lot, seeing her family's red minivan. "Where's your baby? I was kind of hoping it could be our getaway car."

"Being repaired." Indie pouted. "A microwave went through the windshield."

"That sucks."

"It's fine. It's just my car—it's not . . ." Her face started to crumble, her nose scrunching as she sniffled. "*Sorry*."

I held out my hand. "You'll get through this. Your windshield will come out stronger for it."

○

If I looked over my shoulder and tilted my head enough to the right, I could see Kingston a couple of rows back. The cuts across his cheekbones were starting to heal, the bruises fading. He caught my eye for a moment, but I turned away and stared down at Indie's hand clutched in mine. I didn't realize it, but I hadn't let go of it when I walked up to the front pews, near the closed casket.

The Solidays were sitting up front, too, crammed hip to hip when Indie plopped down beside me. Jude came a few minutes later, wedged tightly between Kimberly and Danny. He offered to sit somewhere else, but I adamantly refused. He deserved the front pew more than any of them did. I was actually annoyed they had the nerve to take the front when it should have been reserved for those who had cared about her. Who *knew* her.

I looked at the casket in front of me, white and expensive, with my mom inside. She was right there. If I wanted, I could get up and walk over to her, lift the lid, and see her. But I didn't want to because she'd been thrown by a tornado, left in a creek for days, dead. She wouldn't look like my mom. I tried not to think of what she looked like now. Because then I thought of how much I wanted to see her again, to reach out and feel her touch one more time. I couldn't even remember the last time I'd hugged her, like *me* initiating it instead of tolerating it when she hugged me. I wanted to breathe her in, the cigarettes and the three-in-one shampoo, conditioner, and body wash. Her.

She was right there, and I was right here, but there was nothing I could do. I couldn't plead, cry, or scream to make her snap out of it. She was *gone*. Somehow thinking about it like that felt worse than thinking she was dead.

The reverend approached the pulpit, a somber expression on his sweating face. "Afternoon, everyone," he said, and I wondered if he purposefully left out the *good* because there was no way spending an afternoon at a funeral could be a good anything. "Thank you for joining us in the celebration of the life of Donna Annabeth Larson. A life ended so young and tragically will always be a sorrowful occasion for us here on earth but we remember the promises God has given us. Of eternal life in paradise."

The Solidays nodded, like this was something they knew and

believed in. But I wasn't sure if my mom did. She'd never talked about dying, about paradise.

"Now, join us in singing the hymn, 'Nearer my God to Thee.' The words are provided on the third page of your programs. Please, let's stand."

The first notes of the hymn drifted through the air. Everyone else stood, but I couldn't move. I wasn't even sure if she liked this hymn, my mind blanking when the reverend asked me which songs we should sing during the funeral. Eventually, I told him the hymn they played in *Titanic*. She liked *Titanic*.

Now she was dead, like everyone else who'd been on the real *Titanic*. I wondered if she was in paradise with them, asking if it was anything like the movie. Maybe they asked her if dying during a tornado was anything like *Twister*. Maybe Bill Paxton could ask her about that.

Bill Paxton was in both movies.

I tried to think of more Bill Paxton movies instead of my mom, in paradise or a few feet away from me. Either way, dead and far away in every way that mattered. But I couldn't think of any more Bill Paxton movies.

Natalie sat down on the other side of me. "You look like you're going to be sick," she whispered, then grabbed her program, fanning my face.

"You know if Bill Paxton was in the first *Predator* or just the second? Or was he even in the second one?" I asked.

She frowned. "Are you doing that thing when you want to say one thing, but your brain changes the words? Like when you're having a stroke?"

Indie sat down, too, still clutching my hand. "What's going on?"

"I think she's having a stroke," Natalie whispered.

"No, I'm not. But I need to think of another Bill Paxton movie," I blurted out, a little too loudly as the hymn concluded and my voice echoed throughout the quieted sanctuary. The reverend smiled and looked away. I slumped in the pew.

"Please be seated. And now we'll hear from Donna's daughter, Bronwyn Larson."

Right, the eulogy.

I stood up, and Indie released her grip. My palm felt sweaty, but I didn't want to wipe it against Taylor-Elise's dress. Indie whispered, "Don't talk about Bill Paxton!"

Jason, on the other side of her, murmured, "Wait, why is she talking about Bill Paxton?"

"I thought Bill Paxton was dead," Kimberly added.

"Was he that guy in *Titanic* looking for the necklace?" Indie asked.

I sighed, purposefully avoiding the casket as I approached the pulpit. I already knew *that* Bill Paxton movie.

There were handwritten notes scattered across the shelf inside of the pulpit, and a Bible turned to a page stained with highlights. The program with my mother's picture printed on the front was used as a makeshift bookmark.

I'd given up on trying to write her eulogy a couple of nights ago, deciding to wing it in honor of my mother, who had winged most of her life. I took in all of the faces staring at me expectantly and realized as the rain started to pound against the roof that there was a reason I hated it whenever my mother *winged* it.

Then I noticed near the back of the sanctuary an arm lifting in the air, grasping something. Kingston was holding up his phone and on the screen was the movie poster for *Apollo 13*.

Bill Paxton, Kingston mouthed.

I smiled, just a little. That was a new one.

"My mom winged everything," I said, and he nodded because he was one of the few people here who really knew her. "She never planned anything. That's how she ended up with me. So, I haven't planned this speech. I'm just going to word-vomit here and hope it sounds all right to everyone."

There was an echo of quiet laughter throughout the room. Kingston lifted his phone again, the movie poster for *A Simple Plan* on the screen.

"I loved my mom. But I didn't always like her. She flaked, like a lot. She made a lot of bad choices. That sounds terrible to say now because she's gone, but that's how it was. A couple of times I wished I could've been on my own. Because then, I wouldn't have to deal with it.

"And I think it's the stupidest thing in the world that you only want to deal with that crap when you don't have to anymore," I said, my voice tight. "And now I just want my mom. I keep thinking the one thing that would make this easier would be my mom."

I hesitated, like I was waiting for someone—for her—to say something back. But everyone in the sanctuary was like her, dead silent. Kingston looked around and held up his phone again, this time with a photo of Bill Paxton in *Aliens*.

"I'm sucking at doing a eulogy," I laughed, running the heel of my hand under my eyes. "I'm supposed to talk about how amazing my mom was, and she was. I guess I can only think of all the ways I miss her instead of the other stuff. But she had a lot of it, a lot of good stuff. So, um, thanks."

I stepped down from the pulpit, taking my seat in the front pew before the reverend even stood up.

Natalie stared at me quizzically. "I know you're grieving and don't take this the wrong way," she whispered, "but Dad's media manager has got a *lot* of work to do on you."

○

After the funeral, there was a dinner in the church's basement with various baked pasta dishes and a salad bar. I was sitting at one of the tables, poking at the ziti on my plate and watching as the female officer got up from her table for the third time. I was eavesdropping on a conversation Andi was having with a couple of girls from my school—they said a lot of *yeah, of course, cool* as Andi told them about her upcoming million-subscriber milestone—when I noticed the woman walk toward the bathrooms.

I grabbed my empty glass and told Indie I needed a refill. She nodded and went back to talking about wedding plans with Jason and Kimberly—apparently conversing about Bill Paxton had struck up some sort of a bond between the three—and I slipped away, placing my glass down on the beverage table as I passed it. And followed the woman into the bathroom.

It wasn't my proudest moment, lingering inside the restroom as I waited for her to come out of one of the stalls. Then my elbow accidentally triggered the motion-sensor hand dryer and I grimaced at the deafeningly loud sound. She stepped out a moment later, glancing at me as she walked to the sink.

"You're a cop, right? I saw you after the tornado, dressed like one."

She lathered her hands together. "I'm a police officer."

"Did you know my mom?"

The woman ran her hands under the water for what seemed

like at least a minute, which meant she was trying to think of something better than the truth. "Not directly, no."

"Why was Amy wondering about the funeral being safe? And if you don't know my mom *directly*, then why are you here? Why are you watching everyone?"

"Maybe you should talk to Amy and David about this."

I stepped in front of the hand dryer as she moved to approach it, hands dripping water against the tiles, and hot air blew against my back. "She's *my* mom. If something's going on, you should be talking to me, not Amy and David—"

The bathroom door opened, and Amy stepped into the room, concern etched into wrinkles on her forehead. "Bronwyn," she said. "People want to say good-bye before they leave. You should come to see them off."

"Why is a cop my mom didn't know at her funeral? Is this about that thing the guy said earlier, about suspicious behavior? Are you thinking someone's, like, targeting me because they found out I'm a senator's daughter?"

"No, that's not what's happening," Amy said. "Bronwyn, this is Officer Clara Porterfield and the man you saw her with was Detective Ben Marsh. They are . . . investigating your mother's death."

"Why?"

"Sweetheart, the police think your mother might not have been killed in the tornado. They think—it seems as if your mother was already dead when the tornado touched down."

"Like," I said, my mouth suddenly dry, "she OD'd?"

"No," she answered softly, shaking her head. "They think she was murdered."

That didn't make sense to me, like she was saying the words

out of order or maybe having a stroke like Natalie thought I was earlier.

"Maybe we should go somewhere to talk—"

"Why do you think she was murdered?" I interrupted, turning to Officer Porterfield. "She died in the tornado. Are you sure you're not just wrong?"

"Her injuries aren't consistent with the other tornado victims. At least not in the sense that she was alive when they were inflicted. They happened after she died."

"But you could be wrong about that. It could just look like that but not actually *be* that."

"Bronwyn," Officer Porterfield said, in the same way everyone said my name now, like it was a sympathetic yet cautious warning, a leading front for bad news. "The preliminary autopsy results suggest your mother was . . . the injuries she sustained before her death are typical with deaths caused by strangulation."

"Sweetheart," Amy said, her fingertips brushing against my elbow as I stepped away from them, reaching for the bathroom door handle. The thought was so foreign in my head, to know something was true but not believe it, dizzying and nauseating. Like the merry-go-round when it spins too fast and no one reaches out to stop it to let you catch your breath. After numbly stumbling out of the bathroom, I found myself leaving the church basement. Then the parking lot. Then the street, ignoring the texts vibrating my phone. Before I knew it, I was ambling down familiar streets until the scent of pine sap greeted me home.

It was only about a twenty-minute walk from the church to the trailer park. Or, at least, where it used to be. A soft rain was falling, just enough to make our already sodden town damp once again. Even a week later, some of my neighbors were still here, among the rubble, searching through debris, whatever the tornado had left of their homes. It seemed strange to me that all of us could have nothing and yet so much left to deal with. David had already hired someone to sift through what was left of my home sometime next week, save anything of value, toss the rest in a dumpster.

Home. Where the furniture always smelled a little like cigarettes, the cupboards had mostly junk food, and my mom watched soap operas. Now it smelled like wet earth, the food in the cupboards was ruined, and my mom was gone. Not just gone, murdered. *Strangled.* I heard once it takes minutes to be strangled. Minutes of struggling to breathe, of panic, thinking there must be something you could do to save yourself, but you can't, and you didn't because you were dead.

I heaved the few bites of baked ziti I'd eaten earlier into the grass. My nose was burning when I opened my eyes, wet and hot, something shifting out of the corner of my eye. Kingston stood across the gravel, purposefully *not* looking at what I'd just vomited onto the ground.

"I'd offer you a towel, but I don't know where one is right now," he said, glancing toward the shambles of his own home. "I'm sorry about your mom. I texted you that when you told me. But I never heard back from you."

I pulled out the tin of mints Taylor-Elise gave me earlier, the sound of them rattling inside filling the silence as I tossed a couple in my mouth, now grateful for her suggestion. "I was mad at you."

Oh, he mouthed. "Why?"

"I thought my mom had died because you'd stopped me from helping her," I admitted, brushing the wet clumps of leaves from our cinderblock steps and tentatively sitting. "Sorry."

"It wasn't like I wanted to leave your mom behind. I got scared, man. I thought we needed to leave, like, right then."

"You were probably right. If I'd gone inside, we'd be dead. I mean, she was."

"What do you mean she was?" Kingston asked, confused. "What are you talking about?"

"There were detectives at her funeral. They said it looked like she . . . like someone had strangled her before the tornado."

"Wait—" he said, sounding even more confused. "That she was *what?*"

Then something jolted sharply in my chest when I realized that when she was murdered, I was at school, but he would've been across the path from her. "Did you see anything that day, before the tornado?"

He shook his head, his eyes wide. "No. I mean, I can't think of anything weird," he said after a moment as he then—almost, sort of hesitantly—sat down on the cinderblock beside me. "Jude was over there, though, in the morning."

"Jude wouldn't do something like that," I said. "I've never even seen him get mad, like, normal mad, let alone strangle-your-girlfriend-mad."

"Are you sure they're right? Can't you get all sorts of banged up in a tornado?"

"The police seem pretty convinced."

"Do they have an idea of who did it?"

"I don't know." I shrugged, "I ran out of there. Honestly, it didn't even occur to me to ask, which sounds kind of dumb now that I think about it."

"That's . . . I can't—I mean, are you okay? Aside from the throwing-up part?"

I took in his gaze as it lingered on me, watched as it softened. I chose to focus on this instead of his question, instead of all the thoughts screaming for my attention. My mom was murdered, next week a morning news crew would film the press conference about me and the Solidays, and I wasn't even sure what came after that. But Kingston was here, side by side with me, and I wanted it to stay that way, clench my fingers around it, hold on, never release.

He was sitting so close to me, and I memorized all the bursts of color in his brown eyes. He was familiar, one thing I still had that hadn't been stolen away from me. Suddenly, hints weren't enough. I leaned in, and after a second, he did too.

"You didn't answer me," he murmured.

"I'm not thinking about it. I don't want to."

He shifted a little closer to me. Rain was still spitting against our necks, thunder rumbling somewhere in the distance. It seemed wherever we went, we brought a storm. I could smell the toothpaste and cigarettes on his breath when tires crunched against gravel. I ignored the sound until a voice yelled, "Bronwyn!"

Kingston and I jerked away from each other as the headlights of a Suburban beamed over us. Behind the wheel was Andi.

"Who's that?" Kingston asked.

I sighed, the windshield wipers going back and forth, obscuring her expression as she rolled up the window. "Andi," I said. "One of David's kids."

"So, you have to go then?"

"I don't want to." A second later, the horn blared. "I'm coming back next year, though. When I turn eighteen."

"You can still visit, right?"

"Do you want me to?" I teased, leaning in closer again.

"*Bronwyn!*" Andi hollered again.

"Thanks for coming to the funeral," I said, even though it felt like the smallest of things I could thank him for. "See you around, Kingston."

As I yanked open the passenger door, Andi was scrolling through Instagram on her phone, double tapping the screen to like the posts she barely took in. The car idled in the park as Kingston ambled back to the crumbled ruins of his trailer. Then she dropped her phone in the cupholder.

"Did you really sneak out of your mom's funeral to go make out with *that* guy?"

"No," I retorted sharply, my irritation flaring because of how judgmental she sounded. "I went home. And he was there. He's my neighbor."

"Why?" she asked, signaling to leave the trailer park. "Nothing's here anymore."

"You don't get it, okay? *That's my home.* I'm not like you, I don't have multiple *furnished* houses and all this money to replace everything. *Nothing* is all I have."

"Except, you do have all those things. If you wanted anything replaced, my parents would buy it for you in a heartbeat. You just have to tell them. They're practically begging you to already."

"It's not about actual stuff. And I don't want your parents to replace everything, because they can't. My home, my—" I looked away, out through the rain speckled window. "It's just not replace-able and I don't want your parents throwing their money at it like it is."

The sound of the windshield wipers filled the inside of the car. "That's not what they're trying to do," she said. "They're just try-ing to give you the best there is. And there—"

I interrupted her by snorting. "Yeah, now, after sixteen years."

"What are you talking about?" There was a pinched look to her expression, lines forming between her eyebrows as she glanced at me.

"You guys waited until my mom was murdered to finally—"

"Wait, what? Are you talking about, like, murdered by the tornado?"

"Really? *Murdered by the tornado*?" I repeated, deadpanned.

"Well, that's what it sounded like, because she died in a tornado. Some people take nature personally."

"She didn't die in the tornado. Someone strangled her first."

"What are you talking about?"

"Your mom told me she was murdered. I found your parents talking to a couple of, I don't know, undercover cops or something at the funeral and she said someone strangled her before the tornado."

"Do they know who did it?"

"Probably not, because why would they need undercover cops for a case that's already been solved?" I asked, which earned me a withering glare in response.

"I'm just—" She shook her head without finishing her sentence, clenching her jaw. "Forget it, whatever."

"Yeah, whatever," I muttered, realizing after a moment I was clenching my jaw too.

○

I wasn't sure what I expected from Amy and David when Andi drove us back to the church. Inside, Amy was speaking with one of the women who'd arranged the flowers and David shook hands with someone from the catering company, complimenting the grilled chicken recipe. When Amy saw me, her lips caught mid-smile, hesitating. But then she went back to her conversation after shooting me a quick nod.

That wasn't what I expected.

It wasn't until we drove back to the lake house that either of them acknowledged I'd left in the middle of dinner when a low-toned Amy said after all got out of the car, "Kids, go inside, please. Bronwyn?"

"Yeah?"

"Why would you just take off like that? We were worried about you," Amy said. She and David looked so *parental*. "You knew the police thought the person responsible for your mother's death might have been there. What if he'd followed you?"

"Were you ever going to tell me about what happened to my mom?"

"We were going to tell you after the funeral," David placated. "We thought with everything else going on, it would be best to give you a little time to process things. And we only found out ourselves a few days ago."

"And the police were okay with that? They didn't want to talk to me or anything?"

"I might have . . . convinced the lead detective to put that on hold. Just until you found out. Plus, we were confident that if you knew something, you would've mentioned it by now."

I scoffed, glancing away because I didn't want them to see how much this bothered me. Her death, her *murder*, them using their connections, maybe even their money, to keep it from me. "Aren't the first days, like, the most important?"

"Bronwyn, we were doing what—"

"Since you're such buddies with the police department, can you at least pull some *more* strings so I can talk to them? Tomorrow?"

David nodded slowly. Almost like he felt guilty. Almost. "Yes, I think we can arrange that."

I didn't say another word. I just walked around them into the house.

CHAPTER NINE

Air conditioning blasted over me as I sat in an interrogation room at the Shiloh Police Department the next afternoon. The only furniture was a table against the wall with four chairs, two on either side. A camera was mounted in the corners, pointed at the table where I was sitting with David. Detective Marsh was across from me. Officer Porterfield was in the other chair, wearing a patrol uniform, which I thought was strange. But I was also expecting a one-way mirror so maybe I didn't know as much about police procedure as I thought.

"Afternoon, Bronwyn, Senator Soliday," he greeted. "Bronwyn, I don't think we were properly introduced yesterday. I'm Detective Ben Marsh. I'm going to be investigating your mother's homicide."

I tried not to flinch at the word *homicide* being spoken so closely to *mother*. "Okay."

"I'm very sorry for your loss," he continued, glancing over to David, like he was saying this to him, too, which made the muscles in my jaw clench. I didn't even want him there. But he and

Amy had insisted either their lawyer or David had to be there. "Today, we're going to go over a few questions about your mom. That sound good with you?"

"Yeah."

"When was the last time you saw her?"

"She was asleep on the couch when I left for school that morning, but the last time I'd talked to her was the night before."

It was almost unfair how normal everything was that night, as if there should've been something I felt or vaguely understood. Like the meteorologists warning us on the evening news about the severe thunderstorms for the next afternoon. It left the biggest piece out—*severe thunderstorms are expected in the southern Greens County region for most of the afternoon, with the potential for a couple of isolated tornados up near the Shiloh area and the certainty of Donna Larson's murder*—and because of that, the last time I spoke to her was normal. I cooked spaghetti for dinner while she was outside smoking, the scent of her cigarette drifting in through the open windows. When it was done, I leaned over the sink to the window, seeing her on the cinderblocks, her lit cigarette bright like an orange firefly.

"Spaghetti's done if you want any."

She came in a few minutes later, brushing the dirt off her sundress and plopping beside me on the futon, with a paper plate of spaghetti smothered in butter and tomato sauce. Her breath still smelled like smoke when she asked me, "Are you excited for the last day of school tomorrow?"

I shrugged. "I don't know. I mean, it's not like anything happens."

"Except when you get out," she said, nudging me with her elbow until I smiled back. "We're going to get every kind of flower you want, baby. And vegetables too. We'll become a greenhouse."

"I don't think your check has *that* much in it."

We spent most of the evening talking about what kind of flowers I wanted to plant, which ones she thought would look nice with our tangerine exterior, which vegetable plants neither one of us wanted to grow—green beans, decidedly. She asked me if I had any tests tomorrow, then threw out our plates while I packaged the leftovers in the fridge. After that, I went to go take a shower. When I got out, she was asleep on the futon with the television still on. I turned it off and went to bed, and that was it. The last time I ever talked to my mom.

And all we'd talked about was flowers and school. And green beans, the worst vegetable.

I didn't tell her I loved her, and I didn't hear it from her either. Other than her nudging me with her elbow, we didn't touch each other or hug. It was boring and normal, which shouldn't have been how it ended for us. There should've been some feeling, pulling us back, reminding us of something we didn't yet know.

"And you were at school, all day?" Detective Marsh asked, bringing me back. "You didn't skip class at all, or leave during lunch period?"

"No. I got home late because she didn't come to pick me up. I had to walk home."

"When was she supposed to pick you up?"

"Around two thirty, maybe closer to three. She wasn't all that punctual."

"What time did you get back home?"

"I'm not sure?" I said sheepishly. "It was about an hour after school let out, so . . . three thirty? It was just as the storm was getting really bad."

"And you didn't see her inside the house when you got back?"

"I never actually went inside. The tornado touched down before I could, and I had to run to a gas station."

"Okay. Can you think of anyone who might want to hurt your mom? Someone who had a grudge against her, maybe?"

"No. My mom didn't *do* much. She basically slept all day, hung out with me and her boyfriend."

"And who's her boyfriend?"

"Jude Carney," I answered, watching him write his name down on a pad of paper. "He and my mom had been together since I was fourteen, so almost three years, I guess?"

Detective Marsh nodded. "Did he and your mom have any problems? Fights?"

"No, not really. Like, couples have disagreements on stuff, but they never really *fought* or anything. Jude's supermellow, he kind of lets everything roll off his back, you know?"

He was still nodding, and I wasn't sure what that meant. "And was there a lot, rolling off his back? I mean, I didn't know your mom personally—"

"Right."

"—but from what I've heard about her, she could be a little high-strung. Emotional. Was she ever like that with Jude, even if he was mellow about stuff?"

It felt like answering that honestly was a slight against my mom. It seemed wrong to count her flaws against her, like this happening could all be pinned on her hair-trigger emotions. "Sometimes, but he never did anything. And she'd apologize for it. She was normally only like that if she was on something."

Out of the corner of my eye, I noticed David turn sharply to me. Detective Marsh, however, seemed undeterred by this but it wasn't like it was a secret. She had even been arrested a few times, so it was probably still somewhere on her record.

"How would you describe her addiction? Was she a heavy user?"

"Yeah," I admitted. "She had been, anyway. Mainly oxycodone, but a lot of times, the pills were in Ziploc bags and she wouldn't tell me what they were. But she was clean before she died. For real this time, she had a job and had stopped using."

"Did she have anyone in her life who might have been upset by this? Her getting her life together?"

"I don't know. She never talked about it with me. I think she liked to pretend I didn't know about it so she could feel like a better mom."

"Did you wish she was a better mom, Bronwyn?"

"I think that's a little—" David interjected.

"No," I lied, interrupting. Then my voice softened as I told him something true. "I loved my mom, and I didn't want anyone else. I still don't."

o

"Are you sure you know your way around the neighborhood well enough?"

Miles's claws clicked against the tiles in the kitchen as Amy held out his retractable leash. He seemed to recognize it, ears perked and eyes intently watching as he sat at her feet, front paws tapping the ground. When Amy hesitated, he scooted closer to her and whined.

It had been a couple of hours since David and I had returned, after spending the drive feeling drained and dissatisfied. The questions had been endless, including ones I didn't even know the answers to, and I went from thinking I knew my mom better than anyone to realizing I didn't know much about her at all. I didn't know the names of any of her ex-boyfriends except for David, nor where she got her pills from. I didn't even know why she used or remembered when it started.

And I couldn't even talk to anyone about it because Detective Marsh informed us they intended to keep the investigation private, which basically meant hiding it from the media. According to him, David's political status would turn the murder investigation into a scandal, tearing into our lives for the sake of public intrigue and entertainment while hounding the police. It was a mess, Detective Marsh had put it, best to avoid.

After arriving back at the lake house, Amy was with Miles in the kitchen and I felt like I needed to do *something*. Ever since we'd gotten back, I just wandered around. I couldn't even garden because I was still trying to avoid Ethan in case he decided to use the dock or tend the garden.

I had always wanted a dog, though, and now I kind of had one. Or, at least, I lived with one. Which was how I ended up asking Amy if I could take him out for a walk.

"I used to walk everywhere," I told her. "I can figure it out."

"Do you have your phone with you?"

I rolled my eyes, pulling it out of my pocket. "Yes, *Mom*," I groaned before I realized what I'd said. My skin flushed as I looked away before it occurred to me that made me seem embarrassed, like I wanted to call her mom, which I *didn't*. I reached out and took the leash from her, fumbling with the clasp.

"Bronwyn," Amy said. The metal kept slipping out from under my thumb as I tried to open the clasp because I didn't want to hear her say I could call her mom if I wanted. "I know what you meant. You don't have to—"

I finally managed to keep my thumbnail against the clasp to attach it to his harness, when Miles suddenly opened his mouth and reached out for my hand. I jerked back, dropping the handle onto the floor with a *crack*, which caused Miles to jump, too, claws scampering against the floor.

"Hey, hey," Amy said, bending down to grab the handle. "He wasn't going to bite, sweetie. He does this—"

"Um, yeah, he was," I retorted, trying to ignore that for some weird reason, it stung. It meant even the *dog* knew I was the last person in the world, or at least in this household, who should be taking him on a walk.

She pulled the leash from inside the handle, then clicked down the lock and attached the clasp to his harness. Miles was more hesitant now, but he still opened his mouth and reached out again, grabbing the loose leash next to her hand. "He likes to hold the leash in his mouth," she explained, holding the handle out to me. "You still want to take him for a walk?"

"Yeah," I said, even more embarrassed now for overreacting. I led him out of the kitchen, leash still in his mouth as he happily trotted out in front of me.

"Have a good walk," she called out. "Call if you get turned around!"

○

I walked for about twenty minutes with Miles before noticing a beach with an adjoining parking lot. The water drifted back and forth against the sand, smoother than the mud and rocks around the dock in the Solidays' backyard. Beach chairs were planted near the water, towels stretched out with grains of sand in the folds.

The sand made my footsteps heavier as I ambled onto the beach, Miles eagerly running in front of me. Everything was *peaceful* here, I thought, looking at the water. Families were enjoying the weekend like whatever had happened the previous week didn't matter. I tried to do that, too, to just let everything melt away and into the water, polluting it with all the feelings I didn't want anymore.

Suddenly, Miles dragged me from the shore, an abrupt tug coming from the leash as the dog broke into a run. "Miles, stop."

There, on one of the beach towels, was Andi in a black bikini with oversized sunglasses shading her eyes. Taylor-Elise was beside her, speaking to another girl on the sand, her natural hair pulled tightly into space buns and her teeth bright against her russet-brown complexion. There was one more girl with them, with a red pixie cut shaved close to her head in the back but floppy bangs over her forehead. She was tall, probably standing at almost six feet. But Miles wasn't running toward them; instead, he was darting for a shirtless Ethan Denvers.

He was farther from the girls, gripping a football because, *of course*, he was the kind of guy who tossed a football around at the beach. I almost laughed as Miles slowed because Ethan had *abs*. Not incredibly defined ones, but there was some definite rippling down his surprisingly sun-kissed chest. Teenagers back home *definitely* didn't look like him. No one could afford the time or money it took. Ethan tossed the football to a guy down the beach before spotting me with Miles out of the corner of his eye and pausing.

"Hey," he finally said, his tone not *entirely* unfriendly. "What are you doing here?"

"Oh, well, I'm here for the Abercrombie commercial. Isn't this where it is?"

It was slight, so subtle I wasn't even sure it was there, but it almost looked like his expression relaxed. "No, no. You're thinking of the one at the park. This one is for Gucci."

"Ah," I remarked drily, realizing with some surprise his joke was a callback to the Gucci remark I'd made last week. "Well, I should go. But I'll let you know if I see anyone in desperate need of a washboard, okay?"

There was an amused glint in his eye as he caught the football and tossed it back. "Are you really leaving because you saw us here?"

"Yeah, this beach isn't big enough for the both of us," I said flatly. "No. Get over yourself."

"Sorry. Force of habit for us rich kids."

I groaned. "Are you seriously going to keep bringing that—?"

Before I could finish, I was interrupted by the football colliding with my face. Pain radiated across the bridge of my nose, throbbing in my teeth as tears sprang to my eyes. Down the beach, I heard a guy yelling, "Holy sh—I'm sorry!"

I dropped the dog leash and brought my hands to my nose, afraid to look at them in case they were covered in blood. I was doubled over, angled away from Ethan, but he reached out and tentatively touched my arm.

"Hey, are you okay? Bronwyn?"

Footsteps jogged through the sand as I closed my eyes. I didn't want to overreact, like I had with the leash and Miles, because it was just a football. Ethan had probably been hit in the face with footballs all his life. But it *hurt*. "Wait, that's Bronwyn? I hit *Bronwyn*?"

"You know who I am?" I asked, my voice muffled through my hands.

The guy didn't respond before someone else piped up, "You did *what* to Bronwyn?"

I looked over Ethan as he crouched down, too, trying to look past my hands, to where Taylor-Elise was lifting her sunglasses. Andi was still lying on her towel, but she had hoisted herself on her elbows, staring at us too. So were the other girls with them.

"I hit her in the face," the guy yelled, grimacing. "I didn't, like, break your nose, did I?"

I shook my head, even though I didn't know. "I'm fine."

"Bronwyn," Ethan said, touching the inside of my wrist. "Can I look at it?"

"I'm fine," I repeated, pulling one of my hands away to grab the leash sinking into the sand beside my sneakers, ignoring the blood on my fingers. "Next time, for bystanders' sake, will you just . . . keep your eye on the ball?"

"Sorry," he said, frowning as his gaze drifted down to my nose. "Do you need some ice? There's probably some in the cooler."

"And lemonade," the other guy offered.

"I'm fine."

I tugged on Miles's leash, pulling him out of the shallow water and watching—with some satisfaction—as he shook out his wet fur beside Ethan. He barely reacted, though, because he was still *looking* at me. I wasn't fragile—a lifetime of living with a single, addicted mother had taught me that—and being treated like I was made of glass infuriated me.

"You sure you don't want anything? We could give you a ride back, at least."

"Yeah," the other guy echoed. "I kind of hit you hard. But I didn't mean to. I was aiming for a nut shot on Ethan because he wasn't paying attention."

"I'm good. But if you still want to go for that nut shot, don't let me stop you."

I walked away from them and out to the parking lot, scraping the sand from my shoes and looking over my shoulder to where they were all sitting on the beach towels. The guy mimicked tossing a football, then threw back his head dramatically like he was pretending to be me. He gestured to Ethan, sipping from a water bottle as he shook his head, suppressing a laugh.

I knew they were talking about me, how awkward I was. What strangers thought of me—what *rich kids* who had it easy their whole lives thought of me—didn't matter. And that was what I told myself the whole walk back.

CHAPTER TEN

"Was this afternoon the last fitting for the dress?"

Even though Amy was speaking to Kimberly across the dining table, she was glancing out of the corner of her eye at me, more specifically the bruise forming over the bridge of my nose. She hadn't mentioned it since calling me for dinner, only hesitating when she saw me, maybe because she was instructing Danny how to properly set the table. I slipped into the kitchen while she was still focused on the knife placement.

Not surprisingly, David hadn't said anything, either, but he didn't keep looking over at me like Amy did. He was focused on slicing his grilled chicken breast.

"Yep. The alterations are finished and it's finally ready for next month."

"Good. It's about time you're officially a member of the family." I tried to keep my facial muscles smooth as I stabbed my fork through the disgusting buttered green beans.

"So, Bronwyn," Amy said. "What happened to your nose? It looks like you're getting a bruise there."

"Ryan Pembroke hit her in the face with a football," Andi explained before I could.

Now David looked up. "Ryan Pembroke? Why would he hit you in the face with a football?"

"I didn't know you even *knew* Ryan Pembroke," Amy added.

"She *doesn't*," Andi said. "She was at the beach and Ryan hit her in the face by accident."

"Did you break your nose?" David asked.

"No. It's just sore."

Although there was some concern in Amy's eyes, she looked almost hopeful for a second. "You went to the beach with Andi and her friends?"

"I found the beach when I was walking Miles."

David chuckled around the mouthful of food he was chewing, and Natalie groaned. "Dad, the joke's *not* funny."

"Did you all hang out after . . . Ryan hit you in the face?" Amy asked tentatively.

"No-o-o," I said slowly, like it was obvious, because it *was*.

She thought I was lonely. But what Amy didn't get was that I *did* have friends. I wasn't as popular as Andi, but I didn't live in a hole. My friends were back home. And the thought that they assumed I was friendless because I didn't hang out with rich Shelridge kids gave the chicken a bad aftertaste in my mouth. Because that wasn't the truth, but it wasn't like I could call Indie either and go to Scoops for ice cream or hang out at the pool like last summer. I *had* a life. It was all mine. And now, it wasn't, and I was stuck here pretending to like green beans and feeling pitied because I didn't hang out with Andi's friends.

On Sunday morning, it was still dark outside when the early morning talk show crew positioned the cameras in the living room. The
scent of coffee brewing filled the first floor of the house, boxes of
doughnuts and sliced fruit were on the island as I shuffled into the
kitchen. My eyes were squinted shut, my cheeks were swollen and
creased from the bedsheets, and if my reflection in the windows
were any indication, I was nowhere near camera ready.

I'd spent over three hours the night before with Deshaun Warren,
David's PR manager, after he arrived at the lake house after dinner
in a car that made the Solidays' Suburban look modest, a phone
clamped to his ear as he shook our hands with quiet smiles and nods.
As he coached me on what to say, I was instructed to be vague about
my circumstances before coming here, focus more on embracing my
new life. Deshaun also told me to deflect questions about David's
affair and his role in my life. *David's going to interject his involvement
was limited because of his political status. Your parents wanted to keep
you out of the media and kept you under wraps because of it.*

I knew that wasn't the truth, but his political reputation had to
be protected. It was what he'd wanted sixteen years ago and what
he needed now. His career came first.

I sat at the island, rubbing the powdered sugar from my
doughnut off my fingers, watching as crew members walked in
and out of the house, untangling microphones and arranging the
lights. It was like this was normal, boring even, to everyone else
as they got ready. But I couldn't tear my eyes away.

I'm awake on Sunday before noon

Indie texted, including a series of sleeping emojis.

I can't believe you're going to be on TV! We
already have it on, but it's just the weather.

I don't want to do it.

Indie's text bubbles appeared, then disappeared, reappearing
a second later.

It's just one segment, Bronwyn. It won't even be
ten minutes.

This is supposed to my LIFE now.
Not just ten mins.

For one year, then you can move back home.
MOVE IN WITH ME!

But now people know. The MEDIA knows.
They'll never leave me alone.

Come on. One senator isn't that important. After
a couple of months, everyone will forget about
you.

Promise???

Complimenting you is weird. It's like I'm
insulting you, but you're flattered. You might
be a supervillain.

Well, duh. I'm the daughter of an unfaithful
lying politician and a murdered druggie.
Comic books WISH they had that kind of
tragic backstory for their big bads.

If you ever need a bumbling henchwoman, you
know where to find one.

I smiled down at the screen, thinking of a response when
another text came through.

WAIT
Why did you say your mom was MURDERED??

My eyes widened.

BRONWYN???

Before I could think of something to text back, a man in a partially zipped hoodie stepped into the kitchen, holding a small corded microphone. "Hey, we just need to get you miked up now."

> Are you still there?? Pls call me when the interview is over, Bronwyn! I'm so confused right now.

I nodded slowly, and turned over my phone. "Right."

○

"Going live in five, four, three, two . . ." Instead of completing his countdown, one of the crew members held up his index finger. We were strategically arranged on the couch. David and Amy were seated in the center, with me beside David, of course. Andi, Jason, and Kimberly were on bar stools behind the couch, while Danny and Natalie sat next to Amy. Sitting across from us was Kelly Bright, a television reporter with a straightened blunt bob and powdered complexion. Her smiling teeth were so perfect they didn't seem real.

"Thank you, Jack and Sandra," she said, and I fought the urge to glance around the room, even though I knew Jack and Sandra were anchors back at the station. "If you're just tuning in, I'm here with Senator David Soliday and his family. It's so nice to meet with you, Senator Soliday, Mrs. Soliday. Thank you for having us."

David grinned like his eyes weren't blinded by the glare of the lights around the room. "It's our pleasure, Ms. Bright. Thank you for coming."

"Of course. Now, I understand there have been some rumors surrounding your family for the past couple weeks and you wanted to take a moment to address them with us."

"Yes. I would like to introduce the public to my daughter, Bronwyn Larson. Until recently, she was living with her mother, who unfortunately passed during the Shiloh tornado."

"It's great to meet you, Bronwyn. And I'm so sorry about your mother," Kelly said.

It took me a second before I realized I was supposed to respond. "Thanks."

"What has been your reaction to all this? This must feel very sudden for you."

"Yeah," I said, very aware this was being broadcast live while my mind blanked on all the techniques Deshaun tried to teach me. Then, to sound less inept, I added, "It was."

"And you grew up knowing Senator Soliday was your father," she commented, and I nodded. "And yet, there was this conscious decision to keep you out of the public eye. Why was that?"

"It was an agreement her mother and I had come to when she was born," David answered. "We thought it was best for her to grow up without so much public scrutiny."

"And there would be a lot of it considering she was born outside of your marriage. Tell me, how exactly did that happen?"

"It's something I've felt guilty about for years. But I could never regret what happened, because if I did, I would regret my daughter. Which I don't. Absolutely not."

"How did you come to meet her mother?"

"I met Donna—her mother—when Amy and I decided to separate early in our marriage. Donna and I were involved, romantically, for a short time. But I still loved my wife and I had an obligation to my children, so Donna and I ended our relationship."

I focused on the camera lens like a crew member had told

me to earlier, but I wanted to look at David. He talked about a separation I'd never heard of before. How he and my mother met, what it was like before—before she was pregnant, before he left her—all that was exactly like the fairy tale my mom had told me all my life. And never once had she mentioned a separation.

Kelly nodded, almost somberly. "You say you had an obligation to your children. How long was it before you knew you had one more obligation to think about?"

He already knew, I thought. That was the part of the fairy tale where my mom's voice got a little louder, a little angrier. It was minutes after telling him she was pregnant that he told her he was staying with his wife.

"We found out not long after Donna and I ended our relationship," he replied.

I hated how he made everything sound. Like their affair was something they *both* decided to end, or that he found out about me after they broke up. It was just another embellishment to protect his reputation from crumbling.

"And, Amy, how did you feel learning not only that David had been seeing another woman but that she was pregnant?"

Something came over her eyes, a momentary flicker in her otherwise poised expression. "It was hard, of course. And unexpected. But it didn't take long to fall in love with her. I wouldn't have our family any other way."

She reached out and grasped one of my hands, limp on my lap. Everything in me wanted to recoil because she was lying too. No one had fallen in love with me—not then, not now. David was embarrassed to look at the souvenir from his adulterous affair, Amy was polite because years of being a politician's wife had brainwashed that into an automatic response. Jason barely acknowledged me, Andi outright hated me, and Natalie liked me only because I was nicer than Andi. Danny acted like he thought I was a long-lost cousin or something. Miles was the only one who seemed to tolerate me for me.

"How amazing," Kelly concluded. "Thank you all so much for having us and we look forward to hearing more from you and your loving family soon."

"Thank you, Kelly."

"Back to you, Jack and Sandra."

"And . . . *cut*! All right, thanks, everybody. Good job," a crew member echoed from behind the camera as movement suddenly resumed after moments of constrained silence. I stood up and headed for the hallway, frustrated and exhausted by this—by all the things that wouldn't stop happening.

"Uh, wait, you still got our mic on . . ." someone called out awkwardly from behind me, and I reluctantly turned back into the living room.

After a couple of months, everyone will forget about you, Indie told me.

I just hoped she was right.

CHAPTER ELEVEN

The day after the segment aired, I was on the back patio, my legs pulled close to me, scrolling through the unanswered text messages Indie had sent me since. She told me I looked *freaking cute* in the black shirt I was wearing and totally at ease, which I knew was a lie. Then she asked me to call her. When I didn't answer, she sent twelve more messages throughout the morning and afternoon before they stopped. Her last text was without exclamation points or question marks, short and final in a way I hadn't expected.

Talk to me, Bronwyn.

I deleted the notification from my phone. My silence should've made it clear I didn't want to talk to anyone, even her. If I called her and told her the rest of the truth, she would cry and tell me how sorry she was, ask me what I needed. Hearing those things from her, from someone who really cared, would unlock something in me I wanted to bury deep and far away.

Instead of responding, I called a different number.

"This is Detective Marsh," he picked up.

"Hi, Detective. This is Bronwyn Larson. You're investigating my mom's murder? Donna Larson?"

"Hey, hello, Bronwyn. What can I do you for?"

"I wanted to ask if you had any new information on my mom's case? Any suspects or anything?"

The clanking of keyboard keys echoed on the other end for a moment before he answered. "We have a few leads that we're working on," he said. "It's still early in the investigation, but we're doing everything we can to solve it."

He was using one of the techniques Deshaun had told me about earlier: deflect the question and answer a different one that's easier. "What leads do you have?"

"I'm afraid I can't discuss an open investigation like that, Bronwyn."

Which meant he had nothing. He had nothing because she was a drug addict murdered right before a tornado, dispersing whatever evidence there might have been miles away. Soon he would tell me the investigation was shelved due to lack of evidence and she would become another unsolved murder everyone forgot.

"Detective Marsh," I said, listening as the clanking paused. "She was my *mom*. I get there's a lot going on right now, but . . . she was my mom. She was a person who didn't deserve this."

"Her case is important to us, Bronwyn, and we'll get this guy. I can promise you that."

I knew this was supposed to reassure me, but I felt empty hearing it. "Yeah. Okay."

"All right," he said, and if he could tell I wasn't persuaded, he ignored it. "I gotta get back to it. But I'll be in touch if we find anything."

I hung up, frowning, as a notification for a text appeared. I thought it was Indie, but instead it was Kingston.

> Had my uncle tape you on the news yesterday
> and just watched it. You did good.

I was dying. I hated it.

> You didn't look it.

I hesitated, sent my reply before I could change my mind.

And how did I look?

A flame emoji appeared, followed by a drooling one.

I smiled, shaking my head.

Gross. Control your spit.

"Hey. Bronwyn?"

I glanced over my shoulder, where Amy was standing in the door frame. She was holding a coffee mug and her face was bare, eyelashes and lips pale against her complexion as she smiled, sitting in the chair beside me.

"It looks like a beautiful day to be out on the lake," she remarked.

I stared down at my phone, watching as it lit up with another text from Kingston.

> I thought you looked cute. Very cute.

"Bronwyn," Amy said, "I'm worried about you. You spend so much time alone. There's so much going on for you right now—"

"Those things don't just go away even if you do have a social life."

"I know, but getting out of the house and . . . meeting new

people, finding things to do. Maybe it could help you cope with losing your mom and moving away from your old friends. And they can come to visit too."

"I'm fine."

"I've spoken with a good friend of ours," she said, and my stomach dropped. "He owns the Starbright Drive-In theater a couple of miles away. Andi and Taylor-Elise work there. Anyway, I've asked him if there was a position available for you."

I shook my head. "Wait—"

"He said yes. And he wants you to start tomorrow night. You'll work four nights a week, from seven to after two in the morning. It's only for the summer, obviously, but I think it'll be good for you. You could get to know more of the kids around here, and feel a sense of accomplishment."

"You want *me* to get a sense of accomplishment? Like I'm the one sucking on silver spoons and sitting on trust funds."

Amy measured her words carefully, "Bronwyn, sweetheart, *you* have a trust fund."

"Wait, what?" If finding me a job at a drive-in movie theater with Andi and her best friend surprised me, then this *stunned* me. "Why do I have a trust fund?"

Amy laughed. "We set one up for all our kids. Before any of you were even born."

"That's not what my mom said."

She was midsip of her coffee, and the mug lingered at her lips for a moment after she swallowed. "We must have forgotten to mention it to her then. But we did set one up."

"Okay, but still. I don't want to go work with Andi and her friends. That would be . . . weird. And, like, isn't Andi a famous YouTuber? Why does she even have a job?"

"She's worked there for years, before her YouTube channel. Now, she works there to hang out with her friends."

I shook my head, incredulous how some people had to work minimum wage jobs just to break even while others acted like it was some sort of hobby. "So, you think I'm going to get depressed and instead of sending me to a shrink, you send me out into the workforce? That makes people even *more* depressed."

"Oh, you're going to therapy. But I didn't think it would be beneficial for you to start seeing a therapist here in Shelridge and then find a new one when we move back in August. You'll start seeing Dr. Sandbel in the fall after school. You'll like her, I really think you will."

I paused, hoping I was hearing this wrong. All of it. "School. You mean as in…?"

"As in the one Natalie and Danny attend? Yes, that one. Andi graduated last month."

"Don't I get a say, or David? He's my actual biological parent. Why are you making all the decisions?"

"You get a say, just not the *final* say. And your father agrees with everything. He thought you would be more receptive if I told you."

"He was wrong then."

"Hopefully you'll feel differently in the future." She stood up and headed for the doors, then paused, giving the arrangement of potted flowers a quick look. "You're letting these die."

"What?"

"Our gardener—well, I guess you know him, Ethan Denvers? He lives next door. He quit last week. Told us you liked to garden, and you should do it instead."

I looked at the wilting floral arrangement, the petals drooping. "Why would he quit? That doesn't make any sense."

"Maybe you already have a new friend," she said, and headed inside, leaving me there to look over at the glass house next door. A moment later, I got up and went around the side of the house for the hose.

○

The sign at the entrance of the Starbright Drive-In was massive, with twisted neon lightbulbs forming the name with yellow stars and crescent moons around the corners of the *S* and the *N*. There were five screens in total, hedges separating them to prevent screen jumping, and a concession stand in the center, which was where Andi parked. She was quiet after coming into the bedroom about a half hour earlier, telling me as she ripped her uniform from its hanger, "We're leaving in ten minutes."

I wasn't sure when Amy had told her about my new job, but Andi's reaction was obvious, especially now, as she got out of the car and walked into the concession stand without glancing back to see if I was following her or still in the passenger seat. And it wasn't like I wanted her to wait for me, to tell me where I was supposed to go or who I was supposed to talk to, but I was totally out of my depth here, and I hadn't even left the car yet.

The doors were propped open with wooden wedges, the scent of buttered popcorn drifting out to greet me as I walked inside the concession stand. Andi was in a booth near the windows, a view of the first screen behind the pane, with Taylor-Elise and one of the girls from the beach. I approached the counter where a woman with dull blond hair and a pen between her teeth stood.

She glanced at my shirt—which wasn't the uniform one—

and then, with a confused look, asked me, "Are you here for the restaurant?"

"No, I'm Bronwyn Larson. The new hire?"

The woman stared at me for another second, her pale eyebrows furrowing together when realization dawned on her. "Right!" she exclaimed. "Bronwyn. Right, Bronwyn. David's new girl, yeah?"

I wasn't sure how to respond to this, so I just nodded.

"Sheila Rogerson. I'm Hank's wife."

I shook her hand, assuming Hank was the owner. "Amy said I'm going to be working outside. Like, showing cars where to park?"

"You got that right," she said, heading outside, and it took me a moment to realize I was supposed to follow her. "I'll get you a uniform and a vest in a minute. You're going to be up front at the beginning of each movie, directing traffic and checking trunks. Then, you'll start walking around and making sure things are good. No smoking, no filming, no taking up extra parking spots. There's a hoverboard you can ride, but you'll probably have to fight Ethan for it."

I stopped, hoping maybe Ethan was just a popular name around here. "Who?"

"Ethan. You know, Ethan Denvers. He's going to be the one training you."

"Wait, he works here?" I asked, wondering if this was some sort of prank. It had to be. There was no way this could be happening otherwise.

But then a glint of bright orange zoomed past me and there he was, riding on the hoverboard Sheila had mentioned and wearing a reflective vest. "Looks like it," he said, his voice sounding weird, garbled. "And she's right, I'm not sharing the hoverboard."

I realized he was speaking with an Australian accent, or at least *trying* to anyway. Sheila called out, "There you are! Got a recruit for you!"

I hadn't even clocked in yet, and I already knew I was going to hate this job.

Two hours later, Ethan was still speaking with the fake Australian accent. He called everyone around him *mate*, his accent shifting into a Boston one when he explained larger cars park in the back. It wasn't until he started talking like that to drivers pulling up to us that I spoke for the first time aside from mumbled *okay*s and *got it*s.

"Are you really going to keep talking like that?" I asked as the driver of the sedan popped his trunk, revealing an unfolded mess of blankets and collapsed lawn chairs inside.

"I am, *mate*," he said. "Ryan bet me I couldn't keep up a British accent for a whole shift. If I win, he has to use Andi's Instagram to post a video of himself singing a Taylor Swift song and tag his ex. So, yeah, I am."

"You're doing a *British* accent?"

He laughed, carving out a single dimple in one of his cheeks. "No. I literally called you *mate* two seconds ago."

"If you lose, what do you have to do?"

"I'm not going to lose."

"But you must have wagered something."

He shook his head. "Nope, not happening."

He was embarrassed about whatever it was. Which made me want him to give up the fake accent even more. "Is it something humiliating? Or painful? Or maybe both? Wait. Are you getting a Brazilian?"

He made a face. "*No.*"

"You're getting a Brazilian, aren't you?"

"No," he reaffirmed. "I saw you on the news the other morning."

"I know what you're doing. You're trying to distract me, so I won't figure out you have to give up the abs or something."

"Still no," he told me. "It looked like you hated it."

It wasn't like I wanted to be good at press conferences, but after reading Indie and Kingston's texts, I thought I at least held my own. "If you shave your head, I'm not sure you'll keep the teen heartthrob status."

"You know, you talk about my body every time you feel uncomfortable about something."

"Maybe it's your body making me feel uncomfortable."

"You looked pretty uncomfortable on TV, and I wasn't even around," he pointed out. "I was almost expecting you to just randomly yell about me right there on camera, it's becoming such a habit."

I tilted my head, hearing how he phrased this. "You mean, yell about your abs, right? You can't even admit you have them, because that would make you attractive, right? It's like when you said *affluent* all over again. *You're* the one who's uncomfortable, except it's not about being on TV, it's about being who *you* are."

Something unfamiliar came over him as tires crunched against the pavement. It wasn't annoyance like I'd seen before. It was softer than that as he turned to the driver. "Hey there. Which screen you headed for?" he asked, the fake Australian accent suddenly gone.

He directed them toward screen three, and I said, "You lost."

Realization replaced the look on his face, his shoulders slumping slightly. "Crap."

"What'd you bet?"

"Still no."

As another car approached, I mouthed, *Brazilian*.

Once we'd directed all the cars to movie screens and assigned parking spaces for the first screen nearest to us, Ethan told me it was time to wander the property. He still hadn't admitted what bet he'd lost to Ryan. Other than my occasional guesses—he didn't have to perform a Taylor Swift song himself, dye his hair, or get any other part of him waxed—we barely spoke. Fragments of movies drifted out rolled-down windows, the pounding explosions or muffled dialogue, but it wasn't until we passed a convertible with their volume dangerously high that a woman screaming startled me.

I jumped, looking at the screen. The woman on the screen slipped over a banister and down a flight of stairs, breaking the relative quiet of the summer night. Then, a man stood at the top, watching her before ominously following her down the stairs.

"You good?"

Instinctively, I nodded, still watching the screen. It was an older movie, but I didn't know the name of it. "Why are they showing such an old movie?"

"Because it's a classic," Ethan said, like it was obvious. "Wait, have you never seen *Halloween* before?"

I shrugged. "Why are they showing *Halloween* in June?"

"It's Horror Movie Tuesday. On the fifth screen, they do theme nights. Fridays are animated movies. Mondays for superhero films. You get the idea."

The woman was crying and screaming on the screen, and for a second it reminded me of my mom. I hoped she hadn't cried or screamed when it happened, but I knew that wasn't realistic. I pushed the thought away, almost grateful for the distraction when Ethan spoke again.

"You sure you're all right? You know, as far as horror films go, *Halloween* is pretty tame. The original is, anyway. The kills get more creative, and ridiculous, as the series continues."

"The kills?"

"Yeah. There are kills, usually ranging from dull to innovative, with the Final Girl normally getting the last kill. Or it looks like the last kill, but then the slasher mysteriously lives and hints at a sequel."

"You know, it's kind of creepy how happy you sound talking about murder."

"It's not real murder," he pointed out. "I don't condone actual violence, but the horror genre has produced some of the greatest cinematic masterpieces. The amount of foreshadowing, tension. Especially when you get into Jordan Peele films, but that's another Tuesday."

"Oh my gosh," someone hollered, once again startling me, but Ethan spun around as if he expected this. "Do *not* get him started on *Get Out*. He'll literally text you articles on why it's awesome."

Ethan shone his flashlight on Ryan Pembroke's face, the boy from the beach. "Because it is," he said, matter of fact.

Ryan shielded his eyes. "Dude, watch it," he scolded, before grinning triumphantly as Ethan turned the flashlight off. "You're not doing the accent. You lost!"

"Yeah, yeah, I know."

"You know what this means—"

"I know," he interrupted, his voice low and firm, but Ryan ignored this.

"—*send it*!"

Even though the darkness shrouded most of his face from me, I could still make out the glare he was giving Ryan. "Send what?"

"Ethan has to—"

"Get a Brazilian," he interjected quickly, turning to me.

"—send out his short films in his scholarship applications. But, yeah, sure. Get one of those while you're at it?" He leaned in, whispering dramatically, "You're not very good at improvising."

"Wait, that's what you were so embarrassed about? You have to send out *short films*?"

Instead of answering me, he told Ryan, "We gotta keep going. But why don't you talk louder, it's not like people are trying to watch a movie or anything." Then he sped past him on his hoverboard.

Ryan nodded. "Yep. He's about to get moody."

"Why? What's the big deal about him sending out short films?"

"Ethan's not the most confident guy." He shrugged. "He holds himself to this, like, impossible standard and he's really passionate about movies. But he doesn't like to show his to people because he doesn't want to find out he's bad at it. Which he isn't, so that's why I bet he would have to send them out. They're pretty good."

Ethan was near the hedges around the exit for the screen, spinning around when he realized I wasn't beside him. Ever since I'd met Ethan Denvers, I'd given him the brutal and uncut truth about who I thought he was. He didn't want me to find out about what he'd bet, not because he was embarrassed, because it *mattered* to him.

We were quiet for about an hour. He didn't ask me where my sarcastic comments were or what I thought about him making short films, and I didn't say anything either. Then, after intermission, he asked, "Want to take a break?"

When we went back to the concession stand, Andi was behind the counter, leaning beside the popcorn machine and laughing at something Taylor-Elise said as she cleaned the crusty tops of the reusable ketchup bottles.

"No," Taylor-Elise scolded when she saw us coming in. I thought she meant me, until I noticed she was pointing at Ethan's hoverboard. "*No.* That thing gets scuff marks all over the floor. Walk, like a normal person."

Ethan spun circles around the tables. "I don't see anything."

"It gets marks everywhere and you never mop."

"I'm outside personnel. You don't mop the outside."

"Then get back outside," she countered.

I stood there awkwardly, waiting for Ethan to show me how to clock out, and glanced at Andi. She was smiling, which was unusual, and ignoring me, which was not.

The girl from the beach with the space buns emerged from the bathroom, holding a spray cleaner and a roll of paper towels. "I can hear you yelling from the men's room, which is *disgusting*, by the way. Like, why am *I* the one cleaning it?"

"Are there scuff marks on the floor?" Taylor-Elise asked pointedly.

"There are *worse* things on the floor," the girl answered, shuddering.

"Whatever it is, I didn't do it," Ethan said as he rolled his hover-board behind the counter and parked it. "You coming? Bronwyn? Hey, Bronwyn?"

I nodded, following him behind the counter then up to a flight of wooden stairs. At the top was an expansive room with small windows of thick glass in front of bulky projection equipment with lenses pointed in the directions of each of the five screens. There, sitting in a chair with a creased paperback, was the other girl from the beach, the one with the pixie cut. She looked up from her page and waved at Ethan. I followed behind him on creaking floorboards, wondering if there were any teenagers in Shelridge who *didn't* work here.

"Hey, Ginny," he said, bringing up what looked to be a timer on a computer near the door. "Okay, so just type in your name, first and last together, then the last four digits of your social security number."

"You're Bronwyn, right? The girl Ryan hit with the football?"

I hit the *Enter* key. "Yeah."

"You're also Andi's sister, right? The new one, not Natalie."

"Sure."

"That's so crazy," she commented, shaking her head. "I'm sorry about your mom, that sucks, it's just like, *huh*. I never knew that about Andi's dad. No politician is spared a scandal, I guess."

"Right," I mumbled.

Ethan cleared his throat. "Ginny, you need help with that?"

"Help with what?"

"Getting your foot out of your mouth?" he asked pointedly.

She shot him a look, then glanced somewhat apologetically to me. "Sorry, it's just new. But it's cool you're here. You get to see movies for free, like, every night. And take home leftover popcorn."

"All right, let's go get something to eat," Ethan said finally. "See you later."

The concession stand was still empty when we walked downstairs. Ethan walked to the counter, pulling out his wallet as the girl punched keys on the register wordlessly, like she already knew what he wanted. Probably because everyone here was friends, had known each other for years, for summers. Even hung out at the beach before work. That was the real reason Amy wanted me to get a job, *this* job. She wanted me to be a part of that. But she didn't get it. No one here wanted that, especially me.

I walked to the front doors, still propped open. Then Ethan called out, "You're leaving?"

"I have a half hour, right?"

There was a pause. "Yeah."

I nodded, then left the concession stand. There wasn't anywhere for me to sit, so I sat on the grass near the back for the fifth screen, eventually finding myself watching the second feature. I didn't recognize this one, either, but my intrigue grew as an older woman in a hospital gown followed a girl expressionlessly. For a moment, it was like everything else slipped away, too absorbed in what was happening on the screen to consider anything going on in real life, just waiting for what came next.

"There you are."

I looked away, the hoverboard appearing in front of my shoes, then realized it had been more than half an hour since I sat down. The girl in the movie—whose name I learned was Jay—was still being followed by *something*, although not the same woman from before. I had no idea what was happening, but I couldn't force myself to get up and leave.

"What are you doing out here?" Ethan asked. "I've been looking for you for, like, fifteen minutes."

I shrugged as Jay was told to sleep with someone, and the confusion I already felt intensified. "Do you remember the name of this movie?"

"*It Follows*," he informed me, taking in my bemused frown. "Do you have any idea what's happening in this movie?"

"Yes. It's . . . following Jay. It follows Jay."

He nodded drily as I stood up. "Okay, so Jay goes out on this date with a guy and they have sex in his car. Then he tells her *it* is going to follow her. Now, by *it*, I don't mean the Stephen King *It*, totally different *it*. A common term in horror films."

"Okay." Ethan quickly explained the ins and outs of the plot to me. "And that's what you call a cinematic masterpiece? A movie telling you not to have sex or you'll die. Like the coach from *Mean Girls*?"

"The movie isn't telling you not to have sex, but anyone who watches horror films knows it's a bad idea. They pretty much *scream* if you have sex, you're dead." He continued, "One of the brilliant things about *It Follows* is that it has several interpretations. There's *symbolism*. Is the entity a representation of the AIDS epidemic with no real cure, or does the violating experience represent sexual assault? The movie lets you figure things out yourself, it doesn't tell you everything."

"I don't like things being left to my imagination. I want everything crystal clear."

"You don't seem like the type to need everything spelled out for you," he remarked. It almost sounded like he was calling me smart, something I wasn't sure anyone else had before. "You just take what information you do have and fill in the blanks."

"What if you don't have all the information? What if you're missing very important pieces and *nothing* makes sense without it?"

"Then it would sound like you're watching a pretty bad movie."

"You're not the type to need things spelled out either. You know I'm not talking about a movie."

"Well, it's not like you're an open book. I mean, kind of. I think you are, anyway. But it's like you don't want anyone to read the pages," he said. "If it's about the tornado and your mom . . . I don't think there's much more information about it. Real life doesn't always have a deeper meaning to it. Some stuff just happens, like it's meaningless, you know?"

"It wasn't meaningless, though."

He shook his head, his eyes widening. "No, I'm not—that's not, no. I wasn't trying to say your mom was—"

"That's not what I meant."

"Okay, well, then what?"

On-screen, Jay scrambled across a beach while her friends ran after her, asking her what was happening, but she kept running. Almost like Ethan at that moment, except we weren't friends. We had nothing in common; everything we said seemed to create a bruise somewhere the other couldn't see. Around him, I felt uncomfortable and set apart. Around me, it was like he felt insecure and embarrassed.

But then, something occurred to me. Something we had in common, that brought us together before the Solidays. We had both been there, after the tornado.

I knew he couldn't have been there when she died. But he might've seen something after and thought nothing of it until now. And he didn't know my mom, so it wasn't like I would be exposing the investigation to her actual killer. More like a potential witness.

"What I meant was my mom wasn't killed during the tornado," I said. Crinkles formed around his eyes, but he didn't say anything. "When I was at her funeral, there were police officers there and one of them told me she was murdered before the tornado. Someone had . . . strangled her."

"Oh . . . Bronwyn, I'm really—"

I shook my head. "That's not why I told you. I told you because you were there too. When you were there volunteering, you might have seen something."

"What could I have seen after? Wouldn't she have already been . . .?"

"Dead, yeah. But after the tornado, whoever killed my mom might have gone back to make sure evidence had been destroyed or something. Took stuff, I don't know, but I've seen it on TV."

"A lot of people were taking stuff, though."

"What about dead bodies? Maybe whoever killed her moved her to make it look like she'd died in the tornado? Did you see anything like that?"

"What do you mean, dead bodies, or someone moving one? Because the answer to both is, well, yeah. There'd been a tornado. There were a lot of dead bodies, and people were putting them in trucks to get them to a hospital just in case. I guess someone could've taken your mom like that, but I wasn't playing detective."

"Will you just think about it?" I asked, more pleadingly than I wanted.

Maybe that was why he nodded. "Sure, yeah. Yeah."

Or maybe that wasn't why, I thought as we walked, thinking back to the smile he'd offered me earlier or how he waited for an explanation, searching for one like Jay's friends in the movie.

"It's pretty cool you make short films," I murmured, not sure how this went, like I was attempting a dance I didn't know the steps to. "Ryan said you were good at it. You should send them out."

"You're not going to tell me my parents are rich enough to pay for my education and I should leave scholarship money for the people who actually deserve it?"

"You don't deserve it any less just because you're *affluent*,"

I said. "Not if the scholarship rewards talent. And, technically, your parents are affluent. You have nothing. If you think about it, you're poor."

Ethan laughed. "Oh yeah. I'm poor. I had to buy my Gucci T-shirts on sale the other day."

"Okay, do you just sit around all day memorizing the things I say or something?" Then I remembered what Ryan had mentioned earlier, how Ethan wasn't the most confident. He remembered everything I said because it quickly attached to the insecurities he had. "So, do you do a lot of volunteering or something?"

He shrugged. "It's a requirement at my school to have so many hours of volunteering every year so that's how I got into it. Usually it's just stuff at a soup kitchen or nursing home, but I was already here in Shelridge when the tornado happened. A couple friends thought it would be a good idea to help clean up. We found a volunteer group and just went with them."

"That's cool," I said, nodding, when he glanced over at me with a raised eyebrow and I let out a sigh. "I'm trying to be . . . friendly. I'm not used to it."

"Okay, well, don't try too hard. Then you might smile, and I don't know if I can handle that."

"I know what you're doing and it's not going to work."

He spun around me for a moment on the hoverboard. "If you say so."

o

"Are you flipping kidding me, Bronwyn Chloe Larson?"

It took me a moment before I realized the voice admonishing me wasn't a part of my subconscious, sunlight bright against my closed eyelids. I opened them a second later, squinting blearily at Indie grasping onto the railing of my bunk bed, glaring.

"What are you doing here?"

"You text me on *Sunday* your mom was murdered. I text you a million times after and you don't respond *once*, and it's Wednesday. *Wednesday*!"

I glanced at Andi's bed across the room, seeing it was empty. "You came all the way here because I didn't text you?"

"It's like an hour, Bronwyn. It's not that far," she pointed out, dropping back down to the floor. "Why didn't you text me back, or call me? I was worried about you."

"How did you even know how to get here?"

She shot me a look. "I had my mom call Amy. Now would you stop deflecting and start talking to me?"

I climbed down the ladder. "I don't have much to talk about," I said, ignoring her frustrated glare as I went into the closet. "What's up with you? Are you back working at the pool?"

"What did you mean your mother was murdered?"

"I think that's what I meant," I said, pulling out a T-shirt with a band name on the front. "Have you ever listened to Pink Floyd before? I can't think of any of their songs."

"No, I've never listened to his stuff. Now can you—?"

"*Their* stuff. Pink Floyd is a band."

She scowled. "Fine, *their*. Whatever. Now cut it out and *talk to me*, Bronwyn. What is going on with your mom?"

"Nothing. She's dead. Kind of why I'm here instead of home."

"Bronwyn—"

"Look, someone strangled her, okay?" I interrupted, tearing off my pajamas and flinging them over Indie's head to my half of the bunk bed. I focused on not getting my foot caught in the distressed holes in my shorts instead of her face. "I don't know who. The police don't know who, and I don't know what else to tell you."

"Bronwyn . . . are you okay?"

I was zipping my shorts when I heard it in her voice, a tightness, a signal for how emotional she was about to become. And since her emotions tended to bring out mine, I did not want that to happen when either Andi or Natalie could walk in any second.

"Yeah. I mean, it sucks but it's not that different from my mom being dead, period, you know?"

She frowned, confusion squinting her tearful eyes. "But, like—?"

"Have you seen their backyard? They have a whole lake, in their *backyard*. With a dock and everything. You should see it. It's like the one decent thing about this place."

I spent the rest of the morning attempting to avoid or ignore any other questions Indie had about my mom's death—or, worse, my feelings about it—by pulling the kayaks out from the shed and fumbling with the paddles until Danny came outside and demonstrated how to use them. Then, after our shoulders felt decently sunburned, we went back inside, and I was about to tell her every single streaming channel known to North America was on their TV when Amy suggested we go shopping. I was going to tell her no, like I always did, when Andi and Taylor-Elise came into the kitchen to microwave chicken nuggets. I didn't want to hang out with Indie while the Solidays were around, trying to interject themselves in our conversations like Amy kept doing.

So, I agreed, reluctantly accepting the cash from Amy. She said, "If you see something you like, get it! And, Indie, honey, if you see something, there should be plenty for the both of you. Have fun, girls!"

The mall, about fifteen minutes away from the house, had more stores listed on the directory than I knew existed. I wasn't expecting to buy anything—I just wanted to look around—but in American Eagle, I realized if I came back empty-handed, Amy would wonder why I hadn't gotten anything. Plus, I hated wearing the clothes she'd picked out for me. Before I knew it, I was handing over twenties at the register for six T-shirts and two pairs of jeans.

"I'm spending too much money," I commented two stores later, the weight of the bag handles pressing into my arms. It was distracting, buying whatever I wanted instead of putting it back and wishing I could afford it. Which made me feel guilty, like I was conforming to their lifestyle and betraying the one I'd had with my mom.

"All your clothes *did* just get destroyed in a tornado and you have ridiculously rich new parents practically begging you to spend their money."

It wasn't long before I'd spent a few hundred dollars more on clothes that were not on sale, plus matching shoes. Then we found a cosmetics store, and I bought a couple of lipsticks I liked and mascaras Indie told me were good, wondering how many of these products were in Andi's PR packages piled in her filming room at the end of the hall. Eventually, Amy texted, asking if we were going to be home for dinner.

> We're grilling with veggie options! Indie said she was a vegetarian, right?

I sighed down at the screen.

"You can't just shop forever. Just like you can't avoid talking to me about your mom."

"I'm not avoiding it. There's just nothing left to say."

"You're not telling me how you're feeling, what you're thinking about it."

"Because I shouldn't have to," I moaned, the mango smoothie she got from the cafeteria stopping midway up her paper straw. "I'm angry. That should be obvious, but there's nothing I can do about it right now. I'm just going to have to live with it."

"You could talk to someone," she said, and I groaned. I was so sick of talking. "You could get angry at me. Yeah, get mad at me."

"I already am."

"No, but like *really* mad at me. Yell at me, tell me all the things you want to say to whoever killed your mom."

"No."

"I think it's a real thing they do in therapy. Or TV therapy, anyway."

"You're not a therapist. You're not even a high school senior yet."

"Fine, then just say something, *anything*! I'm your best friend, Bronwyn. I'm supposed to be the one you tell everything to, even the really hard stuff. *Especially* the really hard stuff. And for you, that's feelings. You can talk to me."

"Then listen to me when I'm telling you I don't want to talk about this anymore." I hesitated, realizing, as I strode forward, she hadn't moved from near the massage chairs. "Will you just . . . let me decide when to talk, okay? Is that a compromise you'll accept?"

"Are you just lying so I'll get off your back?"

"Maybe."

○

The Solidays were all in the backyard when Indie drove us back, the scent of warmed charcoal and grilled meats already drifting around to the front of the house. David was at the barbecue, wearing an apron with *Netflix and Grill* over the chest. Amy was in one of the Adirondack chairs, sipping a glass of wine as Danny raced off the dock into the water. Andi and Taylor-Elise were by the patio table, where an assortment of vegetables, chips, and buns were set out. Andi was showing Kimberly something on her phone. Jason was walking around Indie with an armful of sodas against his chest, saying, "Whoops, excuse me." And Natalie was at the table, trying to look over at what was on Andi's phone.

"Hey, girls," Amy said when she spotted us. "How was shopping?"

Indie reached for a celery stalk. "Good. I got a couple of new tank tops. Bronwyn bought, like, the whole mall, though."

Amy smiled, and it struck me just how *different* everyone was around here. Back in Shiloh, if your parents found out you'd spent even a hundred dollars of their money at the mall, you got in trouble for it. "You did?" she asked as I grabbed a carrot stick. "What all did you get?"

I chewed, stalling. "Just a couple of tops, some pants. Shoes."

Indie plopped in the chair beside Natalie. "Yeah, American Eagle was having a *huge* sale on their jeans."

Taylor-Elise's eyes widened, pointing to her. "I *love* their jeans. They're seriously the most comfortable. No one else gets my weird hips," she said, not noticing David glancing over his shoulder, his brow furrowing into a confused frown.

"Can I see?" Natalie asked.

"My hips?" Taylor-Elise asked, scrunching her nose.

She shot her a look, blushing. "No," she said, exasperated. "What Bronwyn bought at the mall."

"*Oh*."

I shrugged. "The stuff's in your room."

Something came over her expression as she looked down at her sandals and bit the inside of her lips.

"Did you get something to wear for the wedding? Because, if you didn't, I thought we might all go shopping together sometime. Maybe get our nails done while we're at it?" Amy suggested.

"No, I didn't see anything."

"You should get acrylics!" Indie exclaimed suddenly, holding out her hands. "Here, look, I got mine done last week."

I took another carrot stick from the vegetable tray, as Indie displayed her nails for Kimberly and then Andi, who complimented them. Indie was the friendliest person I knew. She struck up conversations all the time, and it never bothered me until then. There she was, talking about why she preferred acrylics to gel polish with Andi and Taylor-Elise, girls who barely acknowledged me. Indie was fitting right in. And I . . . wasn't.

But that was nothing new. My mom told me that after we'd left Andi's birthday party all those years ago. We didn't fit in then, or now. Ever.

I snapped my fingers to get Miles's attention and fed him the rest of my carrot.

It was getting dark outside when the Solidays finished with dinner, the dirtied dishes clinking together as they were brought back into the kitchen. Taylor-Elise left to get ready for another night shift at Starbright, and Andi was supposed to drive me even though she had the night off, probably to spend another couple hours at the concession stand with her friends. I carefully cradled the condiments in my arms to avoid staining my shirt as I walked into the kitchen. David was at the sink with his sleeves rolled up and splatters of dishwater against his shirt. He glanced over as I deposited the condiments in the fridge, realizing we were the only ones in the room.

"Did you like going out with Indie today?" he asked.

"Probably not as great as it would've been back home," I mumbled.

The sound of the dishes clinking against the sink paused. "Well, you could always hang out in Shiloh if you wanted," he said. "You would probably need a car for that."

"What?" I gawked.

He turned, grabbing a dishcloth to dry off his sudsy hands. "Amy and I have been talking, and we think it would be a good idea for you to have your own car. Jason had a car when he was your age, Andi has one. Plus, we know how much of your life is back in Shiloh and we want you to have the freedom to visit." He considered something for a moment. "Within reason, of course. And before curfew on school nights, but we can talk about that later."

"You want to give me . . . a car? After I literally spent hundreds of your dollars today at the mall? A *car*."

"Well, yes," he replied, sounding a little confused. "Didn't you need clothes? We want to give you the things you need, Bronwyn, and we feel like a car might be one of them."

"The things I need?" I asked, incredulous. "Where was that, like, sixteen years ago? I needed a lot of things then, like how about two parents? Or child support payments or—"

He held up the hand clutching the dishcloth. "Wait, your mother told you—"

"—that you never paid them? Even though you're superrich? Yeah. She was pretty mad about that."

He hesitated. "I can see how she *would* be."

"I just don't get it. I don't get why you wouldn't pay child support for years but now you want to give me a car and buy me an entire wardrobe? Where was all this when I needed it, when I actually wanted it?"

David sighed. "Politicians get their bank accounts hacked all the time. I didn't . . . I didn't want someone to track you down that way, involve you into some sort of political scandal."

"What a load of bull," I told him. "You're trying to make yourself look better, just like you did on that morning show. Keeping me out of your life was never about protecting me, it was about protecting you and your reputation. But no one made you cheat on your wife. I didn't choose to be born. That was a choice my mom made after you chose to stay with your wife."

"I know. But things weren't always that simple."

"The only reason you're doing these things is that people are watching. They know about me now, so I have to wear nicer clothes, drive my own car, end up at some prestigious private school. It's not because that's what's best for me, it's what looks best for *you*. You don't care about me any more than you did back then." I shook my head as Indie stepped into the kitchen, and I grabbed her hand. "Screw you and your new car."

I pulled her out of the kitchen, her feet stumbling as I stormed outside. "What's going on? Where are we going?" she asked.

I let go of her hand, walking around to the passenger side and yanking open the door. "Home."

I turned my phone off when the road signs started to look

familiar and I recognized the storefront signs, even though no one texted or called me. In one mile, I would be home.

It was dark when Indie pulled into the trailer park, and it was quieter than I remembered it. I found the muddied tangerine walls of my trailer under the beam of the flashlight app on my phone. Indie followed me cautiously, glancing around the woods.

"When you said home," she said after a moment, "I thought you just meant Shiloh. I didn't think you wanted to come *here*."

"This is my home," I told her. "I'm kind of used to seeing it as a dump, anyway."

"This place is creepy in the dark."

"Then you shouldn't think about how my mom could've been strangled here." I glanced over the dilapidating walls, metal rusted and bent, the glimpses of the living room and kitchen I could see from outside, and I wondered if that might have been true. Detective Marsh told me the trailer was searched, while I was in Shelridge, but days had passed since the murder—and tornado—and nothing conclusive was found. Rainwater and wind had washed everything away.

I wondered if she had been scared, or if it had all happened so suddenly she didn't have a chance to be. What had her thoughts been when she realized what was happening? Were any of them about me? Was she thinking about what would happen to me, or just relieved I was at school?

Or was she hoping I would come home early and stop it? I had always saved her before—flushed pills down the toilet, drove her to meetings whenever she was *trying*. That night she told me she needed my help and my ATM card. I *always* saved her. Except for the one time it mattered. And maybe she spent her last moments, waiting, pleading, hoping I would do it again.

Instead, I'd sat on the curb at school, cursing her out for being late again.

Stop, stop, stop.

I sniffled, rubbing the back of my hand against my nose and glancing over to the dead grass where Kingston's trailer used to be. "You can go home," I told Indie, pulling out my phone and turning it back on. "I'm going to see if Kingston wants to hang out."

"Yeah, I'm not leaving you in the sketchy, abandoned woods by yourself, Bronwyn. I've seen horror movies before."

For a moment, as I typed out a quick text message to Kingston, I thought about the shift at Starbright I had blown off, then forced it out of my head.

> Back in Shiloh, staying. You want to do
> something tonight?

Wow, really? Ok. I'm at a friend's, you need a
ride?

> Sounds fun.

○

"Bronwyn, this is a *party*. On a *Wednesday*."

Indie peered out from behind her steering wheel, approaching the address Kingston texted, about a dozen cars parked on the lawn and on the shoulder of the road. The front door was open, a couple of people hanging out on the porch, smoking and drinking from tinted bottles. Music wasn't pulsating, no shrieks of laughter or yelling. I had never been to a college party before, even though I wasn't sure if anyone here was actually in college or if they were like Kingston, part of the workforce straight out of high school. It was obvious there was beer here, and I could smell marijuana, but it was also calm. Casual, laid-back.

There was an archway leading into the living room from the hallway, the sight of the matted and stained beige carpet almost comforting to me. People were crammed together on a couch covered with quilted blankets, feet propped up on a coffee table with scratches across the finish, an ashtray near beer bottles without coasters. There was a television across the room with a multiplayer video game on the screen. Pizza and buffalo wings were in the adjoining kitchen. The scent of cigarettes reminded me of my mom, smoking on the futon as we watched whatever was on TV.

I took in a breath, buffalo sauce and smoke mingling together, and finally felt at home for the first time since the tornado had struck. Then I spotted Kingston near the back of the room.

"Hey," he smiled, then waved at Indie behind me, who crossed her arms and looked disapprovingly over her shoulder at the people on the couch, drinking and smoking. She wasn't his biggest fan. She thought he was too old for me, too *experienced*, as she phrased it, and didn't like that he smoked, did some weed. One time, she tried to tell me I was looking for a less problematic version of my mom.

"There's some more pizza if you guys want some," he said, leading us into the kitchen. The sink was filled with melting ice and beer bottles, a discarded bottle opener tucked behind the faucet with the scrub brush. "You want anything to drink?"

Indie looked skeptical. "It looks like it's all beer."

He stared at her blankly until it seemed to dawn on him that Indie and I were still teenagers. "I think there might be something in the fridge," he said, before pulling out a quart of milk.

I scrunched my nose, already deciding I wasn't going to be the youngest one here drinking *milk* at a party. "I don't think Jonny will care if you use his cups."

"I don't think it matters if we have one beer."

"It's against the law," Indie pointed out, her gaze turning into more of a glare each second it focused on me. Maybe this was part of the reason she didn't like Kingston. Around him, I was someone a little more daring, which to her meant a little more careless. But it was one of the reasons I liked him. I felt unrestrained, loose, and free.

I reached out and grabbed one of the bottles. "You met my mom," I told her. "She gave me beer before, it's fine."

"Yeah, addiction runs in your family. All the more reason not to do it, especially when it's *illegal*."

"Drink some milk if you don't want a beer."

Kingston pulled one out for himself, ice clattering against the sink filling the silence before she reluctantly took the milk. We followed him into the living room with our pizza and drinks, sitting on the carpet and watching his friends play *Mario Kart*. I checked my phone to see if anyone texted, only to find nothing but a low battery notification. I felt relieved, but also bitter and right and not exactly surprised. I finished my beer in several long gulps after turning my phone off again.

After that, everything went soft. I wasn't drunk, but my thoughts weren't as sharp, flowing and slipping through instead of getting clogged in this endless mantra of the same old things. *Strangled, dead, Shelridge.* My mouth went dry after finishing my pizza, so I grabbed another beer when it was Kingston's turn to play, ignoring the pensive look on Indie's face.

Then, when everyone was tired of *Mario Kart*, someone started a campfire in the backyard and we went outside to roast jumbo marshmallows. Kingston and I found sticks under a crabapple tree and speared them through our marshmallows while Indie sat on the corner of the back steps, shifting closer to the railing whenever someone went around her, looking more bored now than concerned.

"Your marshmallow is burning!" I laughed. When he lifted it to inspect it, it fell on the grass. "First *Mario Kart*, now this. You're full of failure tonight, Kingston."

"Okay, wow," he said, feigning offense. I reached out to shove his shoulder, but he stayed firm under my palm. "I didn't know Shelridge could've made you mean*er*."

"Shelridge *sucks*!" I groaned. "Everyone is so fake and they spend *so* much money. Before I left, David the Sperm Donor offered me a car. A *car*."

He shook his head. "That's so stupid."

"I know!"

"No, that you would leave without getting the car first. I would've been like, *yeah, sure, dad, let's go get my Prius*. Then I would've booked it out the dealership."

I grinned, wondering when I'd last laughed so much, then if it had anything to do with the beers or because I was home. I broke my s'more in half and gave one piece to Kingston, feeling the warmth of the melted marshmallow against my fingers. Or maybe that was his hand.

When we went back inside, I grabbed another beer, shrieking as I plunged my hand into the melting ice water. Kingston laughed, so close it felt like it was in my ear, smelling like cigarettes and soap.

"That's your third beer. Maybe you should wait a couple of hours."

I took a long, pointed sip. "You know. Just because my mom's dead doesn't mean everyone has to try to take her place. Amy, Indie, don't make me add you to the list."

"You know that's not what I'm trying to do. I worry about you, sometimes."

"What about the other times?"

I was alive and crackling like the fire outside, wisps of energy reaching out into the night, and I wanted something to cling to. And maybe he did, too, because something shifted in his expression, going from flushed to thoughtful.

"You know how much I think about you," he said. It wasn't whispered like a secret, and it wasn't hesitant, either, spoken like a fact known to the universe. "What do you think of me?"

I brought my lips to his, letting him know exactly what I thought of him, barely waiting a second before I felt him respond, hands on my arms, then my back, tangled in my hair. He tasted like cigarettes and marshmallows. Then, after a moment, he pulled away.

"You're kind of drunk. But you're not, like, *really* drunk, are you?"

"I'm the perfect amount of drunk. Brave drunk, not stupid drunk."

And maybe because I was in the brave category of drunk, I kissed him again before catching a glimpse of the staircase in the next room. I wanted this, him, enough to pull away and smile at his pouty expression. "Do you think there's somewhere up there we can go?"

"You want to—?"

"I do. I want to. And if you want to, then we should." I frowned, hearing how that sounded. "What?"

"Are you sure you're not stupid drunk?"

"I'm not stupid drunk, I'm brave drunk. Because stupid drunk would mean this just *suddenly* looks like a good idea when, in reality, I've thought about this *so* many times. I'm not stupid drunk for wanting this, I'm brave drunk for finally admitting it to you."

Kingston bridged the gap between us, lips impatiently finding mine again. I knew it would be only a few minutes before Indie realized we weren't outside and came looking for me, so I threaded my fingers through his and tugged him to the staircase.

The bedroom upstairs was locked. Farther down the hall, we found an open bathroom door and slipped inside, locking it behind us. I was against him, his hands still on my sides, exploring my rib cage. I brought mine down his shirt, feeling the hitch in his breath as my nails touched the skin near his waistband before pulling the shirt over his head and tossing it into the bathtub. Then he lifted my shirt, knuckles brushing against my skin. I felt so aware of everything his hands, fingers, and lips were doing. It was all I was focused on. All my body would let me think about.

The back of his head bumped against the door when he broke away. The room was so dark, I could barely see his face. "I don't have anything. Are you on the pill?"

"No."

"I could go ask my friends if they have a condom."

I thought about sitting on the edge of a stranger's bathtub, thoughts resurfacing and swirling in my head while I waited for him to come back. Whatever was happening right now would be severed, and anything could slither into that break. "Or we could keep going," I whispered, pressing my lips to his throat. "You don't have a killer STD, do you?"

"What?"

"It doesn't matter. You can pull out, right?"

"Yeah." He didn't sound convinced, so I kissed down his chest. He let out a breath I felt against my hair. "You sure?"

"Do I look like I'm not sure?"

Kingston didn't answer; instead, he pulled me closer, our bare skin bumping together as his hands went down to his belt, metal clinking together before his pants fell around his ankles. I did the same, stumbling as I tried to pull my feet, still in my shoes, through the pant legs. He brought me over to the sink, spinning me around so I was leaned over the porcelain and caught a glimpse of myself in the mirror. The bare moonlight streaming in through the window caught my hair, tangled into blond knots from his hands running through it. My eyes looked dilated and glassy. I was flushed, breathless, and in the reflection behind me, I saw him pull down his boxers. This was about to happen. And instead of feeling exhilarated, the campfire smoke coming in through the window started to choke me. I looked like my mother. Drunk, untamed, desperate. I saw in my eyes what I had seen in hers so many times before.

I was so caught up in not wanting to be like the Solidays, I'd forgotten I never wanted to be like my mother either.

"I'm sorry," I said suddenly, turning around and seeing him, *all* of him. I looked away, embarrassed and flustered. "I can't—we can't. I'm sorry. This isn't . . ."

"It's fine," he said, scrambling to grab his pants, sliding his legs through the holes and forgetting his underwear on the bath mat. "It's fine. Really. I get it."

"I'm sorry," I said again, finding my clothes scattered across the floor and hurriedly pulled them back on. "I'm sorry."

My face felt warm as I opened the door, like all the energy coursing through me before was concentrated into a pounding in my ears. Seconds ago, I was clinging to him, desperate to keep him close, and now I couldn't wait to get away.

I headed out and sat on the front porch steps, closing my eyes to keep everything still, but the party was vibrating, loud. I felt like I was spinning even though my limbs were sluggish and heavy.

"Bronwyn?" Indie crouched in front of me. "Are you okay? Were you roofied?"

"No. I had three beers," I said, leaning my forehead against the railing. "I want to go home, but I don't have one."

"That's not true."

"Shelridge isn't my home. I don't belong there. No one even wants me there. It's only because," I said, lowering my voice to a whisper, "my mom was *murdered*."

She sat beside me. "I don't think that's true. About them not wanting you, I mean." It was quiet for a moment, then tires crunched on the gravel. "Please don't get mad at me."

"What did you do?" I asked, my eyes still closed.

"You were drunk and when I couldn't find you, I got worried, so I called the Solidays."

I groaned. "Why would you do that? Why didn't you just text me?"

"I did! You didn't answer," she whispered. "You've been gone for, like, an *hour*, Bronwyn! I was worried."

"I don't want to deal with Amy and David."

"Lucky for you," a man who was definitely not David said, "you're not."

I pried my eyelids open to see there, on the lawn, were Jason and Kimberly. Kimberly was in her pajamas, her black hair pulled into a messy bun. Jason was dressed, frowning disapprovingly.

"What are you doing here?"

"Giving you a ride home," Jason replied, his voice flat. He held out a bottle of water to me. When I took it, it was heavy and slippery, taking me seconds to realize it was made of thick glass instead of plastic.

"No."

"Jason answered the phone when Indie called," Kimberly clarified. "We didn't tell your parents when we left."

"They're not my parents."

"How much did you have to drink?"

I held up three fingers around the glass. "Beers," Indie elaborated.

"What are you even doing here?" Jason asked as he took in the run-down house, the empty bottles on the porch railing, the scent of marijuana coming through the screen door. "We thought Indie drove you to work."

"I wanted to go home."

"And instead," Indie continued, "we ended up at some random guy's house so she could hang out with Kingston Castaneda."

Kimberly frowned. "Who's Kingston Castaneda?"

"My neighbor."

"Her crush. He gave Bronwyn all the beers."

"Why don't you tell them my social security number while you're at it?" I snapped.

"Were the beers opened or in cups?" Kimberly asked, sounding so concerned it was almost laughable that someone, even a stranger, could think *that* of Kingston.

"No. I opened them myself. He's not *that* kind of guy, okay?

I'm just drunk." *Stupid drunk*, I added in my head. "I'll be fine. You can go."

"Yeah. Right, okay," Jason said, grasping my elbows and bringing me to my feet. The concrete felt unsteady under my shoes, tree branches moving even though I didn't feel a breeze. "Come on."

"I don't want to go back there. This—here, Shiloh, is my home."

"Yeah, well, you can't live on this guy's porch."

"Well, it's better than *Shelridge*. I'm not a *Soliday*. I'm a Larson. I'm a Bronwyn."

We approached their car, a coupe with black gleaming paint, because he was rich too. Only twenty-three years old and he was already making six figures as an IT manager, thanks to his father's connections, spending most mornings and afternoons in his bedroom working from the lake house. Kimberly, on the other hand, was a Pilates-slash-yoga instructor who commuted only when she wasn't making smoothies or reading books with *inspire* or *empower* in the title.

"Okay," Jason said, leaning me against the car. "What does that have to do with anything? No one is asking you to change who you are. We just want you to accept who *we* are."

My eyes narrowed, incredulous and confused that this was coming from him. The Solidays weren't concerned with acceptance, at least not from me, anyway. Maybe from the public, the friends I kept seeing around, other politicians. Not me. But before I could say anything else, Jason nudged me inside the car before Kimberly handed me a paper bag, asking if Indie needed a ride home, and she shook her head, mouthing *text me*. I leaned back against the headrest, about to close my eyes, when someone exited the front door of the house. A part of me hoped it would be Kingston, another part relieved it wasn't.

But that quickly faded when I saw the person letting the door slam behind him was Jude Carney. My mother's boyfriend. He was leaving the party, but I hadn't seen him there. And he didn't see me when I waved to him as he passed Jason's car.

I was confused—everyone I saw inside had been older than me, but definitely decades younger than Jude—because he wasn't that partying kind of person, and he walked right past me in the backseat. I blamed it on the tinted windows, before blaming the unsettling feeling I had on the beer and questionable pizza as we drove back to Shelridge.

○

It wasn't like I'd actively thought about the kind of music Jason listened to, but soundtracks from Broadway musicals definitely wouldn't have occurred to me. And yet, that was what came through the speakers a few minutes into the drive. According to the screen on the console, his taste included numbers from *In The Heights*, *Into the Woods*, and *Hamilton*. I watched from the backseat as his fingers tapped against the steering wheel, nodding his head.

Besides the intermittent rapping of Lin-Manuel Miranda, the ride was quiet. Jason didn't lecture me for drinking underage, and I sipped the water they gave me, thinking about Jude. My thoughts weren't totally coherent, slipping and bumping into each other, Kingston also emerging randomly, but it still didn't make sense to me. I couldn't think of a reason why they'd been at the party together.

When Jason pulled into the driveway of the lake house, the curtains were drawn behind the windows. He shifted around in his seat after I opened my door, just as headlights beamed across his dashboard from another car. He paused, until it pulled into the Denvers' driveway. "Wait. You should stay here for a second, okay? Let me go see if Mom and Dad are awake."

"I don't care if they are."

"Trust me, that's not what you want," he warned. "Do you want to be grounded and have your phone taken away for the summer?"

Jason stared at me until I answered, reluctantly. "No."

"Then wait here," he instructed, glancing over at Kimberly. "Maybe you should wake up Andi."

My eyes widened. "*No.*"

"I don't think we should leave her alone," Kimberly said.

"I don't know how to get her up on the top bunk, and we can't tell Natalie."

"We can't tell *Andi.* She *hates* me." I tried to stand up, my head grazing against the interior roof of the car. "I can go up the bunk bed."

"I could—" The sound of a fourth voice broke through our whispered deliberation, and there was Ethan, wearing a gray hoodie over his Starbright uniform. "I could stay with her."

Jason eased me back into the backseat.

"I don't need a babysitter."

He ignored me, patting Ethan on the shoulder. "Thanks, man."

A sentimental ballad oozed from the speakers while Jason left his car running. Ethan hadn't moved, his head tilted like he was waiting for something from me, but I didn't have anything to say. I was embarrassed, vaguely nauseated, and scared I was becoming the worst parts of my mother. The song was from *Waitress,* and it reminded me of my mom. She, too, had been a waitress, in a little diner on the street corner, when she met the man who would change everything for her, but in all the wrong ways. The waitress sang of the girl she used to be, bringing herself to the honest moment of wishing the girl she used to be had had a different ending. Like everything she cherished was dimmed and burnt out, leaving nothing but a pregnant waitress who had given up everything to keep a baby she'd never asked for.

Something in my chest broke apart, and the muscles in my face involuntarily scrunched together, hot tears spilling over my cheeks before I realized what was happening or that Ethan was there to witness it. The more I tried to hold it back, the harder it pushed through.

"Bronwyn?" Ethan tentatively approached the car. "Hey, are you okay?"

"I miss my mom," I choked out, my voice so tight, it kept breaking the words I tried to speak. "And it's so st-stupidly obvious I don't belong here. I don't have anyone, and I just keep thinking that—that this would be easier if I could talk to my m-mom."

Ethan crouched in front of me. "I'm so sorry your mom died."

"Did you remember anything?"

He hesitated, which was enough to deflate my hopes. "No," he said, then added quickly, "but I could. It's possible."

"No, it's not," I whimpered. "If you were going to remember anything, you would already. This is just . . . how things are going to be. How is that fair? How is anything that ever happened in my mom's life fair? She had the suckiest life and the suckiest daughter and then she was murdered. The end."

"You're not the suckiest daughter."

"Yeah, I was! I *hated* her. I wanted a normal mom," I said. "I should've wanted her just the way she was because that's all I want now. I don't care if she's on something or flaky, I just—I want her back. And, maybe that's why they didn't want me. Maybe they knew already what a terrible daughter I am."

"Is that what you really think?"

"Their mansions are huge and there's still not enough room for me. No one here gets me, and I act like I'm okay with that but . . . I'm not."

"You're not alone right now," Ethan said quietly.

I shook my head, attempting a snort but somehow it turned into a sob. "You're saying that because I'm crying. I'm mean to you too. I called you spoiled. I objectify your body just because you're good-looking."

"I understand why you do it, though," he told me, shifting so he was sitting on the pavement, his back against a tire. "You do it because you feel vulnerable—"

I scrunched my nose. "Ew, don't say *vulnerable*."

"—and that freaks you out. So, you bring up stuff to level the playing field and distract me . . . and you." The gentle breeze brushed his hair against my bare legs, but I didn't pull them back. "You could have friends here, you know."

"We don't know each other. I just pretend to know you. I say things that make sense when I'm angry and fill in these blanks about you."

"You're not wrong about me," he told me, his voice murmured and low, almost lost in a number from *Dear Evan Hansen* about how we weren't alone. "My parents aren't here. They normally aren't. Right now, they're back home in Niagara Falls for work. And even when they are around, they're so distracted, they might as well be somewhere else. You know, I get straight As in school, I'm on the debate team, I do odd jobs for, yeah, my parents' *connections*."

I leaned over, my leg pressed against his arm now, but neither of us moved.

"You weren't wrong about me—I am nothing without my parents' money. If I was, I wouldn't have to try so hard just to . . . be noticed."

"Are you kidding me? If I were you, *they*," I said, gesturing to the lake house, "wouldn't have been so ashamed of me they practically disowned me."

"Well, my parents don't even care. It's great to have kids for as long as they can make small talk about us at parties. I'm not convinced that isn't the whole reason they had us, to have that reputation of a traditional American family. And it's not even just them. Before I started doing all this stuff—working out, wearing nice clothes, using *hair gel*—nobody cared about me. I was just this dork who talked too much about movies."

"I can't picture it. You're not a dork, you have *abs*."

He scoffed. "Like, half the week. Then I eat, like, a slice of pizza and they're gone."

"I don't have abs. Ever. Even if I don't eat pizza," I pointed out. "You aren't a dork."

"I was a buck twenty soaking wet, had braces until I was fifteen, and when I asked Summer Marston if she wanted to go to the winter formal, she told me she'd think about and let me know if anyone else asked her. Which, of course someone did but she didn't tell me, so I went to the dance anyway and then there she was with Michael Danner."

"Did you get your revenge when you came back all hot?"

"That's the problem. I don't want revenge. I still want their approval. I did it all to fit in, not rubs their noses in it." He took in a breath, glancing over his shoulder at me. "But like, I still have parents and I don't even care about Summer Marston anymore. I shouldn't be saying any of this—"

He stood up, and I said, "It sucks when your parents don't care. Or Summer Marston."

"I'm sorry," he blurted out. "I shouldn't have talked about me when you were upset about your mom. That's not the same as—"

I slid out of the backseat, and my movements felt like they were with Kingston, everything slippery and soft, easier. Maybe that was why it seemed so simple to wrap my arms around his broad shoulders, feeling his muscles tighten as he hesitated. It might have been because of the beers I'd had earlier that night, or maybe that piece of me still left over from whenever I saw my mom or my best friend cry, which was often. It was easier to do this, to reach out, like that steadied me as much as it did them, than to try to navigate through my own emotions.

"I think this is backward," he said, but his chest relaxed against my cheek, his arms finding their way around me.

"You're enough on your own, you know," I said, muffled against his hoodie. "You're enough to be proud of right now, without anything else."

"You sound like you're still drunk," he said.

"Why do you think I'm saying it out loud?" I pulled back, staring at him before ruffling his hair between my fingers. He tilted his head lower. I was about to say more, and I knew it would be frightening to me later, but now out in the open under the starlight, it felt smaller. Like, of course he got so easily under my nerves—he knew where each one of them was.

But then someone called out for me, saying Amy and David were asleep.

I walked away, letting Kimberly lead me into the bedroom where Natalie was softly snoring, Andi already in the top bunk. As I crawled into her bed, I looked out the window to the Denvers' but everything was dark, like Ethan walking into an empty house.

CHAPTER TWELVE

When I ambled into the kitchen the next morning, I was surprised to find Amy and David weren't there. Jason was, sitting at the island with his laptop in front of him on the counter. Kimberly was dropping frozen dragonfruit into a blender filled with ice cubes.

"Dad left for work and Mom went out for a run," he explained. "She does that sometimes, when she's frustrated."

"Are you feeling okay?" Kimberly asked. "I could make you some toast?"

"I'm fine."

Jason suddenly closed his laptop, startling me as he ran a hand over his jawline. "Did you seriously leave last night because Mom and Dad offered to get you a car?"

"Yeah," I said, confused. "You're acting like that's not a big deal. Just like they did."

"It's a big deal but not one that makes you run away from home. You went out and got drunk with strangers at a party because they wanted to give you a car."

"I don't think that's the whole reason. You've missed home a lot, haven't you, Bronwyn?" Kimberly interjected.

"Which was why they were offering to give her a car," Jason said, "so she could go visit."

"But I don't want to just *visit*. That's my home. I wasn't running *away* from home. I was running back *to* it because that's where I'm supposed to be. *Home*."

He wanted to say more, but then shook his head and opened his laptop again, quiet as he aggressively typed. "Getting drunk at a party with people you don't know, not responding to texts, not telling anyone where you are, that's a stupid idea, no matter where your home is."

"But you're not stupid," Kimberly added, shooting Jason a look over her shoulder.

"No, you're not. Which makes what you did even stupider."

"I don't remember asking what you thought was stupid," I snapped, because I was so *done* with everyone acting like they had some sort of say in what I did after all these years.

He resumed his typing. "Maybe you need someone to tell you. Anyone else would've been sensible enough to figure it out on their own."

"*Honey*," Kimberly murmured, drawing out the vowels on her tongue as she gave him another look. I realized as my frustration ebbed that he was *angry*. Maybe not the kind I was used to, loud and overemotional, but more reserved. I'd never seen any of the Solidays angry before. Polite, upset, placating, disappointed. Annoyance from Andi, mostly, but here was Jason, of all people, expressing a negative emotion.

"Why are *you* angry?" I asked, quieter and softer than before.

"I'm angry because no one knew where you were," he told me,

his voice *not* quieter or softer. "Your mom was murdered, the police don't know who did it, and you go back home without telling anyone. Then we get a call in the middle of the night, saying they can't find you. We tried to help you, but you're just so *focused* on hating everything we do, it's—" He stopped abruptly, looking back at the screen. "I have a work email to finish."

"Why do you care now? Why, after all these years, are you acting like you care?"

"I'm not acting, I do care," he snapped. "We all do, and we always have."

I snorted. "Yeah, okay."

"Look, we invited you to come up for the summers, birthday parties, my graduation. We even sent a wedding invitation. You're the one who never showed up."

"What?" I said. "You actually sent those to me?"

"Yeah, of course—"

"No, besides the wedding invitation. Were *you* the one sending invitations for parties and summers, sleepovers, and whatever?"

"No," he said, "I guess my parents would've probably done that."

That made sense. David told him, maybe the rest of them, too, that he'd invited me to things, like he was this brilliant and shining father he wanted them and the public to think he was, but it wasn't real. He'd pretended to send them, told his family I never answered, that I didn't want anything to do with them.

Like a typical politician, he lied to everyone.

○

"There are cuts all over my hands, but I have no idea where they came from. I think someone's been playing rock, paper, scissors with me in my sleep." Ethan paused, thoughtfully. "But with the real objects."

I glimpsed his hands out of the corner of my eye as he brought them up from his sides, approaching me on his hoverboard. I was standing farther away, tugging on my reflective vest. I felt all too aware of him at that moment. I cried in front of him, not just tearful but sputtering with snot. I'd told him things I hadn't even told Indie, then I'd *hugged* him.

I planned to avoid him for the rest of the summer, but when Andi was about to leave for her shift, Amy wondered why I wasn't also in my uniform. Because I didn't want to deal with a lingering hangover and the repercussions of telling her I was probably fired, I left with Andi. I was going to just hang out in one of the booths by myself when Sheila spotted me outside and told me she hoped I felt better, and to not forget the vest. So, apparently, I wasn't fired.

Which meant I still had to work with Ethan, and not only did I feel awkward and embarrassed but now I was confused too. Especially when, after I didn't respond, he abruptly turned to me.

"No, don't you do that," he warned, his voice startlingly firm and scolding. "You're retreating, like a turtle, back into your emotional shell. Knock it off."

I shrugged. "I'm not doing that."

"Yes, you are."

"No! I'm just not—"

"You're embarrassed because you admitted things last night that wouldn't have taken a genius to figure out, anyway. You were honest with someone out here for the first time in a way that *wasn't* out of anger, and it freaks you out. But it shouldn't."

"Good, it doesn't."

"Okay, well, it freaks *me* out," he said. "I was honest, too, you know. I admitted I use *hair gel*. I basically admitted to being vain."

"Not sure that's how hair gel works."

"Seriously?" He looked disappointed. "You're not going to crack some joke? You're just going to shut down on me."

"I'm not acting weird. *You* are. And don't think I can't tell why. You're pitying me. I said . . . things, and now you're trying to pity friend me because of it but I don't need a pity friend, okay? That's worse."

The Starbright was still closed, with at least another twenty minutes before we started letting in cars for the first showing. Before I could think of somewhere to wait out the next half hour, Ethan swerved in front of me on the hoverboard.

"Do you really think we're so different that we can't possibly be friends?" he asked. "I don't pity you. I *like* you. Believe it or not, I think you're funny, even when I'm the punchline of your jokes. You tell me things none of my other friends do. And when you're drunk, you're even kind of cute."

"Is this you getting back at me for calling you an Abercrombie model?"

"No, I'm serious. Kind of like one of those poisonous frogs in the Amazon. Bright and pretty, but if you get too close, it kills you." He tilted his head to the side, feigning an adoring look. "Like you."

"So, like gender-reversed *Princess and The Frog* then?"

"Yeah, exactly like that," he said. "But it doesn't break any spells. You just poison him."

I snorted, because that sounded like it might have gone over easier than what actually happened last night with Kingston.

Then, I glanced up and noticed Ethan raising an eyebrow. There wasn't much I hadn't already told him. "I kind of . . . have a thing for this guy who lives next to us."

His eyes went wide, dramatically. "*What*?"

Not understanding his reaction, I remembered he lived next door to the lake house, then shoved his arm as he laughed. "Yeah, right, I'll be sure to jump in that line," I said sarcastically. "I meant back home. His name is Kingston. He had a trailer across from ours and he's, just . . . I don't know. Fun? We've always flirted but last night at a party, we . . . *almost*."

"Okay," he said, sounding confused. "And you wished you had?"

"No, I mean, not when I was drunk, and we didn't have protection. I—I felt like I was becoming my mom. Under the influence of something, about to have sex with some guy and maybe get pregnant, like her."

"But you weren't, though. You didn't go through with it."

"But I was acting like her, all emotional and intoxicated. And the thing is, I like Kingston. But when I changed my mind, I just left. Like, I barely said anything to him, and I haven't heard from him since. I think I blew it."

"You can't blow it with a guy who sincerely likes you for not wanting to have sex," he said. "It's basic human respect. He'll get it."

"I know, but what if I hurt his feelings with how I told him I didn't want to have sex? Or, didn't tell him. I just ran out of the bathroom."

"Bathroom?" He raised his eyebrows. "You must have been really drunk to want to have sex in someone else's bathroom. Like if it's your bathroom, that's one thing, but someone else's? No. I mean, can you imagine all the horrible things that happen in a bathroom?"

"Like the men's room here?"

"Yes, but worse. Also, I'm still not responsible for any of *that*." He glanced over at me, his smile softening. "If I were your friend, I would tell you to call him. Explain what happened and if he's not cool with it, then forget about him. You're enough on your own."

You're enough on your own, I'd told him the night before. *You're enough to be proud of right now, without anything else.*

I smiled, just slightly.

"But what do I know? I'm not your friend."

"Maybe we'll be friends. Someone needs to keep your hair gel usage in check."

He ran a hand through his hair. "It's bad."

Nodding, I told him, "I know."

○

After a couple hours assigning parking spaces and wandering the Starbright property, Ethan and I decided to go for our break before intermission. We weren't always talking to each other, but the silence wasn't uncomfortable or awkward. It was easier than I thought to bridge that gap from whatever we'd been before to what was beginning to look like friendship.

"I don't know if I should bring up what happened or if I should say hi or something first," I said after pulling out my phone and realizing Kingston still hadn't texted. "Should I apologize?"

He shook his head, weaving his hoverboard around a crack in the pavement. "Don't apologize for not wanting to have sex. Be honest with him, and if you feel that badly about it, apologize for walking out when you realized it was a bad idea."

"I don't know."

"Come on, you're honest to a fault. This should be easy for you."

"Sure, but this is *too* honest. Like, about feelings, and I don't know how to do that."

"You like him, don't you?" Reluctantly, I nodded. "So, you should want to be honest about your feelings with him. That's how a relationship works."

I made a face. "We don't have a relationship."

"No, but you want one."

"No, I don't. Relationships are a lot of work, responsibility, commitment. And it's not like I have a good example of what one looks like. I want . . . fun, casual flirting, maybe hanging out sometimes."

Ethan nodded. "Okay, so tell him."

"What if that's not what he wants?"

"Bronwyn, he was ready to have sex with you in a *bathroom*."

"Maybe he changed his mind after I freaked out on him, or maybe he just wanted to have sex with no strings attached? I don't know," I groaned. "Why does everything have to get so complicated?"

"Because you're doing that annoying thing when you're not just honest and upfront with a person about what's going on. Instead, you're doing this dumb little dance, trying to figure out what he's thinking instead of *asking him*."

We were approaching the concession stand, the light from inside stretching out over the pavement. Through the windows, I caught a glimpse of Andi, restocking the candy display. I was still watching her when Taylor-Elise called out, "If you *dare*. . .!"

"It's right there, relax," he responded, pointing to the parked hoverboard over his shoulder as he followed me upstairs and clocked out. On the way back down, I pulled up my texts with Kingston and began typing.

Hey, King.

I paused, not sure what else to write until Ethan looked pointedly at my phone.

I'm sorry if I hurt your feelings when I left last night. Are we still okay?

"It looks too . . . perfect. Too polite," I said to him, holding out my phone for him to read it before I sent it. Then my eyes widened. "I'm becoming the Solidays."

Ethan laughed. "It's what you mean, though, right?"

My thumb lingered over the *Send* button, then I hesitated. "Did you ever send in your short films after losing that bet with Ryan?"

"Oh, no, you're not deflecting that easily here."

"Yeah, unlike you," I retorted, heading into the locker room. I stood in the doorway in case he wanted to change or something. "You're telling me to send my thing when you still haven't sent out your movies. You're just as afraid of rejection as I am."

He scoffed. "No one's going to reject you," he said, so matter-of-factly, I laughed.

"Hi, sorry, have we met? I'm Bronwyn, the estranged illegitimate daughter of a senator. I'm here now only because my mom's dead, but not from the OD I always worried would kill her. She always kind of rejected me a little every time she used."

He paused. "I know, I'm sorry. I shouldn't have said it like that. This guy clearly likes you back and if you talked to him then things will work out." I turned my head slightly, glancing over to where he was standing in front of his cubby. He had thrown a hoodie over his shoulders, his shirt bunched above his waistband for a moment.

"Have you ever shown your parents your movies?" I asked, stepping into the locker room and walking over to my cubby, grabbing my water bottle from inside.

"They know about them, I guess." Ethan shrugged. "It's not like they're disapproving, but they kind of think it's a hobby or something."

"Are you serious about it, though?" I asked. He paused, grabbing his reflective vest from where he had draped it over a chair. Then he nodded sheepishly. "Then send them!"

"Scholarship money shouldn't go to me anyway. It should go to someone who needs it. I don't."

"What did I tell you when we met? Your parents are filthy rich, not you. You could use it as an opportunity to put yourself through school, cut the financial cord, join the real world." He nodded distractedly as he pulled out his wallet. "Okay, wait, just . . . people might like you because you're good-looking. You have abs, nice hair, even a dimple when you're really smiling. And they might like you because you get good grades, do debate or whatever. Water senators' gardens."

A small smile tugged at his lips.

"But they'll *love* you for what you're passionate about. No one could be prouder of you than when you're doing something that makes you happy."

He glanced down at my phone. "Does Kingston make you happy?"

Happiness wasn't exactly the word I would've used, but it felt adjacent. "Do your movies make you happy?"

Like me, he paused, but it seemed more like self-consciousness than anything. "Yeah."

"Then send out your movies."

"Are you going to text him? I'm not trying to pressure you. If you don't want to, then don't. But if you're just scared, then you shouldn't let that hold you back either."

I pulled out my phone and tapped the *Send* button. "There, it's done," I told him, showing him. "I'm doomed."

The dimple appeared in his cheek. "I think if anyone is doomed here, it's me."

○

The soundtrack from the first screen was still coming through the speakers when we left the locker room, with Ethan already calling out his order for a large onion ring and root beer. I stopped short when I realized someone was standing on the counter. It was the other girl who worked here—not Ginny, but the one whose name I still didn't know. Her arm was extended, standing on the tiptoes of her high-top sneakers, with a lighter in her hand, waving the flame in front of the wall.

"She's trying to get the AC to go on," Taylor-Elise explained, clipping the note with Ethan's order inside a window frame in the kitchen. "It's controlled by how hot the room is, so she uses the lighter to trick it into thinking it's hotter."

"Cass, you're using the lighter again?" Ethan said. "Don't you remember when you singed the wallpaper last summer?"

Cass waved her other hand dismissively at him. "It works the best and the fastest. I'm dying," she said. "Coffee doesn't work as well as you think."

"You put coffee on the thermostat?" I asked him, confused.

"No, you just hold up a cup and wave it around like the lighter," he explained. "Except it doesn't start a fire when someone gets startled by a car horn."

"I mean, who hits the horn at a drive-in?" she hollered back, dropping down from the counter. "Besides, it wasn't *really* a fire. I think it's gotta last longer than five seconds to be considered a fire."

"I think fire is *fire*."

I pulled my phone out to see if Kingston had texted back yet, but my screen was still blank. He could've been at work, or asleep. I knew there were more reasonable explanations than him not wanting to talk to me anymore, but those weren't as loud in my head. So, I found the contact for the Shiloh Police Department as I stepped outside.

"You're leaving?" Ethan said. I looked over my shoulder, seeing Ethan with a cardboard container of onion rings, so fresh the oil was already seeping through the box.

"Yeah," I said. "I thought I would call the detective on my mom's case again. I don't know if he'll be there this late but maybe he won't be as busy if he is."

"Which makes more sense? That you want to call the detective on your mom's case at midnight, *or* you're avoiding Andi and everyone else?"

"How about *C*?"

"I didn't give a third option."

"Why do you think that's the one I'm picking?"

His familiar deadpan expression stared back at me, the faintest tug at his lips. "Look, I know that this sort of thing is hard for you. But this is how people get you. You have to give them the chance to get to know you, get to know them. It's what happened to us. This isn't so bad, right?"

"Not exactly how it feels right now."

"Cass is insanely easy to get along with. He's not working tonight, but Ryan thinks you're all right. Standoffish, but all right. And Taylor-Elise doesn't have anything against you; she's just siding with Andi until she comes around."

"Which will be never."

"You won't even talk to her," he replied.

"Because she won't talk to me," I pointed out.

"Yeah, she's freakishly stubborn like you. It's almost like you two are sisters."

I glared at him before letting my gaze drift over to where Andi was standing behind the counter, using a pair of scissors to slice through the tape on the bottom of the empty candy box. *Sisters* wouldn't have been the word I used to describe what we were, whatever that was.

"Come on," Ethan said, nudging me. "You don't have to keep going off on your own all the time."

I sighed. "For a minute."

"A minute's just fine."

○

One minute soon became several after Ethan sat on one of the bar stools in front of the counter where Cass had just been standing before patting the one beside him. He angled his onion rings down so they were in front of both of us, but I kept my hands on my water bottle. It seemed too quiet with me in there. Taylor-Elise, Andi, and Cass were all cleaning, more focused than I thought they would've been if I hadn't been sitting on one of the bar stools.

I looked at my phone—still no text from Kingston.

After another few minutes—during which I looked longingly at the doors, but it felt like leaving was even weirder than staying now—Cass and Taylor-Elise started debating about the length of Cass's shorts, since the dress code for Starbright stated shorts had to be at least fingertip length, and what exactly qualified as *fingertip length*.

"No one walks around with their fingers like this," Cass told her, her arms stretched rigidly at her sides as she straightened out her fingers. Then she relaxed them. "This is what hands normally look like, so this is what constitutes as fingertip length."

Taylor-Elise shook her head. "No, it's with your fingers fully extended so they go down as far as possible. That's what it means."

"No, okay, I'm texting Ginny."

Andi was in the corner with the Pepsi machine disassembled on the counter as she cleaned it, aggressively rubbing against the sticky, dried splatters of soda. She'd barely looked at me since I sat down. "I'm right here, you know," she called out.

Cass was still texting. "Yeah, but you're going to agree with Taylor-Elise. I need someone impartial."

"If that's what you want, ask Bronwyn," Ethan said, ignoring the look I gave him. "She's annoyingly honest about stuff."

"Okay," Cass said, coming around the counter and putting her hands back down at her sides. "Which do you think is more natural? This, or *this*?"

Taylor-Elise waved her wet wipe in the air. "No, no, no. That's not the question! The question was, *is this fingertip length*."

"That's what I said!"

"No, you're trying to plant subconscious signals in her brain or something. Doesn't matter what looks more natural, what matters is which one is true fingertip—"

"I know, that's what I'm asking—!"

"—length!"

I paused, glancing back and forth at them uncertainly. "When your fingers are relaxed," I answered slowly.

"Told you! Thank you, Bronwyn."

Taylor-Elise shook her head. "If you really wanted to know, you'd ask Sheila, but you know your fingers are supposed to be extended."

"You're such a sore loser. Just admit when you're wrong," Cass said.

Ethan snorted. "That's never going to happen. Remember my bloody nose?"

"That was an accident," Taylor-Elise retorted quickly, prepared like this was an argument they had been having for years.

"See? It's physically impossible for her."

I looked back over at Andi at the Pepsi machine, reassembling it, and thought about what Ethan had said earlier, how it wasn't just her not wanting to talk, it was me too. He was still in the middle of an argument with Taylor-Elise, but he nudged his elbow against mine, nodding to her.

All I had to do was ask her what she thought of the fingertip-length rule. Simple, casual, inclusive. But then she went into the kitchen without even looking over her shoulder.

Fine, I thought. *Whatever, who cares. It was stupid to listen to Ethan in the first place. He doesn't know anything about us, anyway.*

Whatever.

It wasn't until after two in the morning that the last cars left and our shifts finally ended. Ethan and I clocked out after locking the gates to the property. When we walked out of the concession stand, Taylor-Elise was already in his passenger seat. Her window was rolled down and facing Andi in her car, on her phone but she wasn't texting, just holding it in her hand. Her face looked flushed, eyes glittering as she held it out to Taylor-Elise.

She was still turned to Taylor-Elise when I got into the passenger seat of her car. "I can't believe how close you are," Taylor-Elise said, grinning, but Andi seemed more reserved, maybe even nervous. "It's going to happen tonight."

"It might not," Andi said, bringing her arm back inside the car. "I could lose, like, five hundred in twenty minutes or something. It happens."

Taylor-Elise shook her head then turned to Ethan, who was tugging on his locked seat belt in mild frustration while simultaneously fiddling with the radio. "She's about to get her Gold Play Button," she said. "*Tonight.*"

Although I was still confused over what was happening—and what a *Gold Play Button* was—Ethan seemed to understand. "Hey, that's awesome. Good for you, Andi."

A moment later, they waved and pulled out of the parking space beside us, but Andi still stared down at her phone. Then, she begrudgingly turned to me. "Okay, would you just . . . hold this. Let me know if it gets close to one million."

I tentatively took her phone from her, heavier and with a bigger screen than mine. Now that I was holding it, I realized it was a YouTube subscriber count with the channel name *AndiSoliday* above the fluctuating numbers.

"Wait," I said, as she pulled out onto the road, "are you about to hit a million subscribers?"

She didn't answer, instead smacking her palm against the radio, an advertisement for a used car dealership now loudly echoing throughout the car. I thought this was her response, but then she turned it back off. "I don't know. What number is it on now?"

"It's at 999,968."

Andi let out a breath. "Is the number going down at all? Because sometimes, it goes down."

"It went down by, like, two a second ago but then up like six. Do you seriously have that many people watching your makeup tutorials?"

"More, usually. Not everyone subscribes so there are more casual views than anything." She reached to flip on the turn signal, but her finger missed and tapped the console instead. "What number is it on now?"

"It's 999,983." Andi's shoulders seemed tense, her back lifted away from her seat and stretching out her seat belt. "You're about to hit a million."

"*What?!*" she blurted out. "Right now?"

"Yes, pull over! You're six subscribers away."

Her hands fumbled around the steering wheel and the gearshifts. "I don't know what I'm doing!" she cried out.

"Just pull over," I said, grateful the late hour meant no one else was on the road. She finally managed to pull over to the shoulder of the road near an embankment, the silver of a white moon reflected in the lake water. I held her phone out while she tried to put it in Park, and just as she took it, her fingers brushing against mine, one million lit up the screen.

It happened so suddenly, skipping several numbers, and Andi barely had a second to take it in, scrambling to get a screenshot but her fingers kept slipping off the buttons, then it was gone. Jumped to one million and four. She went still then, and it took me a second in the dim lighting from the dashboard controls to realize her chin was trembling. I was stunned, feeling even more alarmed when she suddenly burst into tears.

"Are . . . is this normal?" I asked tentatively. "Do you want me to call your mom?"

She was still crying, text notifications appearing at the top of her screen, but she gave a sputtering laugh. "Call my *mom*?" she said, and, for the first time, there was an openness in her eyes. It was more startling than the tears. "*Call my mom*? What am I, five?"

"I don't know!" Maybe it was because, lately, whenever I cried it was because I wanted my mom. "Aren't you upset about not getting a screenshot?"

She shook her head. "No, I just—I hit a million subscribers. I've been making videos for three years, and I never thought this would happen. A million people care about what I do."

"A million and sixteen," I corrected, gently.

"A million and sixteen," she echoed, then giving another watery laugh. "A million and twenty-one." She was still staring at it when she gasped. "I was supposed to film it! I told everyone I was going to film when we hit one million and I missed it."

"You could just tell them that—" I was interrupted when Andi practically thrust her phone in my hands again, flipping down her sun visor and patting her thumbs underneath her eyes. "What are you doing?"

She ran her fingers through her hair and teased her roots, before flipping on the interior light. "Will you film me? I need something to put in a video. Please?"

"Okay," I said slowly. "Just start whenever?"

She nodded, taking in another breath. "Hey, everyone, welcome back to my channel," she said, her voice more energetic but still somewhat hoarse. "I'm in my car, it's, like, two in the morning. I just got off work. And on the drive back home, we . . . we hit a million subscribers!" She got tearful again, glancing over her phone at me. "Thank you all so much. I really can't believe . . . Wow, I just keep crying. I'm totally freaking out, Bronwyn. She's filming me on my phone right now."

She laughed, patting her thumb under her cheeks again. I wasn't sure if she'd ever said my name before.

"There's going to be more to the video than this, but I just really wanted to thank you. This is more of an accomplishment for you than me. A million of you. I just—I love you. I'm not even thinking straight, and it's so late! It is *so* late right now. Okay, so much love to . . . all one million of you."

I stopped recording and handed her phone back, sitting quietly as she watched it. "I look like such a mess," she murmured, shaking her head.

I took her in under the bluish glow from the dashboard and how, even with the blotchy cheeks and swollen eyes, she was still admittedly beautiful. I remembered what I thought the first time I saw her, when she was in a bathing suit at her birthday party ten years ago, how she looked like me, but not quite me.

"Do you remember the year I came to your birthday party?" I asked.

She frowned, and I was sure she was about to tell me that, no, she didn't, which shouldn't have been that surprising. We'd never actually spoken to each other back then—my mom had kept her hand clamped around mine the whole time. It occurred to me that she might not have even realized that was *me*.

"Yeah," she replied. "I invited you."

"*You* invited me? On purpose?"

"Yes, on purpose. I invited you every year."

"You invited me every year? *You* did?" I asked.

"Yeah, why are you saying it like that? We always invited you to things. I sent letters sometimes, because I thought if you couldn't come to stuff then maybe we could be pen pals or something, but you never wrote back." Her befuddled scowl softened the longer she looked at me, clearly not understanding. "Didn't you know about those?"

"I only got that one birthday party invitation. You wrote letters to me?" There were a lot of things I would've considered unthinkable before—someone strangling my mom, a tornado ripping through my home minutes later, me living with a senator's family—but Andi *writing letters* to me seemed to be the most unbelievable right then.

"That's what I said, wasn't it?" she tossed her phone on the dashboard.

"What did you write in them?"

"Stuff, okay. Did you seriously never get them?"

"No. Did you mail them, or did you give them to David to mail?"

"I mailed them. It's not that hard to stick an envelope in a mailbox."

Her phone lit up with another text message and she paused to reach for it. I glanced away, unsure what any of this meant.

The isolated birthday invitation never really made sense to me before, but now it felt even more confusing than when I was younger, waiting for another the next year but it never came. Eventually, I started believing what my mother had told me: that seeing me made them question my paternity. She said it was because we were poor, and he was making a name for himself as a politician. It looked like we wanted money, and she was too indignant to comply with a DNA test. That was the truth I knew, the ending to the bedtime story that was her relationship with my father. But now there was another piece, something she'd never told me, something I'd never known. But I'd waited at the mailbox, watched out the windows when it rained. If she'd written to me, then why didn't I ever find her letters?

"Is that why you don't like me?" I asked. "Because I didn't answer your letters?"

"It was part of it, I guess," she admitted. "It seemed pretty obvious you didn't want anything to do with us, and then when you came here, it was just so in-your-face you didn't want to be here. It just made me mad, I don't know."

"I didn't know about the letters, I never got any of them," I said. "But, yeah, I don't want to be here. This isn't my home."

"I know. For the longest time, my parents fought about what was going on with you and your mom. You never wrote back, we never saw you, and it just sucked. For a long time. Then, when things were starting to get better, you finally showed up and, I don't know."

"What kind of fights did they have?"

She shrugged. "Normal fights you have when your husband gets another woman pregnant, I guess? I mean, they were separated when it happened, but it still hurt my mom. They fought about it a lot. She was worried he was in love with her, and eventually, my dad just wanted to move on. And she thought he should've been more involved with you."

"Amy thought that?"

"Yeah, and he was, but after you were born, your mom thought they were going to file for custody, so she pushed them away."

"No," I shook my head, "that's not how it happened. He stayed with your mom after mine told him she was pregnant. She didn't see him again until your party when he asked her for a DNA test."

She was quiet for a second before the blinding light from the flashlight on her phone shone in my face. I shielded my eyes as she told me, flatly, "You literally have his entire face. Not to mention you could practically be my twin if you learned to moisturize."

"Not everyone has companies sending them PR packages of free skincare products like you. Now turn that off, you're about to blind me."

She waved the light over my face then turned it off. "No one asked for a DNA test. He went to the doctor with your mom and the dates lined up. Then you were born the spitting image of his mom, so yeah, no. That didn't happen."

"His mom?" I said as it occurred to me I probably still hadn't met all the Solidays yet. There were aunts, uncles, cousins, *grandparents* I had no idea about. "Is she still alive?"

"Yeah. But Mom and Dad told everyone to hold off for a couple of months to not freak you out. They knew you probably weren't used to big families."

"Then they went and put me on TV," I remarked.

She laughed. It was soft and quiet, but it made me realize I'd never made any of the Solidays laugh before. "Yeah, I don't know what they were thinking with that one. It was probably Deshaun's idea. Throw the media a bone and they'll stop digging. For, like, a minute."

Silence stretched over the car before Andi pulled back onto the road. I was about to find something to add, like it was pretty impressive she had over a million subscribers or I would've written her back if I knew, but then another light shone in the car, another text.

But this time it was my phone, from Kingston.

> Yeah, we're okay. I was just worried I did something wrong.

                                        No, it wasn't you.

I paused, remembering how Ethan said I should want to be honest with him if I liked him.

                    I got freaked out, started thinking I was
                                        becoming my mom.

> Gotcha. But that wouldn't be a totally bad thing, though. Your mom was cool too.

                                        I know

I typed, although I had this unsettling feeling that maybe I didn't.

There would always be only one side of the story for me to hear, hers before and theirs now, and for the first time, I wasn't sure which one I believed.

CHAPTER THIRTEEN

Grasping a weed in one of the ceramic planters on the patio, I shook the dirt from the roots over the gerbera daisies, my favorite flower. Weeding was one of my least favorite things about gardening, but I always went back to it whenever I felt frustrated. Usually, when my garden looked the most immaculate, things were falling apart with my mom. No thistles meant my mom was on something. No dandelions masquerading as one of my flowers meant she was apologizing for something I'd pretended didn't disappoint me.

It was Saturday, a little over a week since I'd found out Andi used to write letters to me, and I still wasn't sure what it meant. It seemed clear, to Andi at least, that it meant my mother had hidden them from me because she was jealous or scared, but that didn't make sense. My mother insisted she was the one reaching out to them and we were ignored. David admitted to not paying child support, and if my mother was ignoring them, there were legal things he could've done. His name was on my birth certificate. As a politician, he had access to so many resources if he wanted and, obviously, he didn't.

I couldn't even ask anyone about it. My mother was dead. David was working again now that his vacation was over, commuting to the office before I woke up and coming back after I left for Starbright. According to Natalie, he normally went on a lot of business trips and during the summer, he tried to do most of those meetings remotely, but it wouldn't have surprised me if I found out one morning he left for Washington, D.C., again. And I didn't want to ask Amy about the letters, because then she'd want to talk about the emotions of it all instead of just the facts.

Another weed snapped, unsatisfying.

After Andi hit a million subscribers, things were *slightly* different between us. It wasn't like we were suddenly sisters, or even friends, but she wasn't so sullen around me anymore. She even acknowledged me a couple of times in front of her friends at Starbright. I didn't usually spend much time at the concession stand with them, but when Cass made an inside joke and I was the only one who didn't laugh, Andi explained it to me.

It wasn't like her friends were mine, though, except for Ethan. Taylor-Elise, Cass, Ginny, and Ryan all seemed okay with me, but it was obvious I was still the dandelion among beautiful gerbera daisies. Last weekend, after our shifts were over and they made plans to go somewhere called Dive Right In!, I pulled out my phone and started texting Kingston. Andi paused while they discussed if they wanted to go straight from Starbright, then Ethan outright asked me if I was going. I shook my head and finished my text.

I hadn't seen Kingston since the party, but we were back to texting and sending flirty emojis back and forth. I was thinking about asking him out, but that meant him coming up to Shelridge, probably the lake house, and meeting everyone here. That, I didn't want, but every time I tried to explain—either to myself or to Ethan whenever he asked why I kept Kingston at arm's length—I couldn't.

I stabbed the trowel through the soil, digging for the roots of the severed dandelion, frustrated this time by the phone call I'd had earlier with Detective Marsh. Maybe he was equally frustrated with me for calling every other day about my mom's case. Normally, he repeated whatever he'd said during the previous call, and the one before that. A slew of familiar catchphrases like *pursuing every lead*, *pouring everything we've got into this*, *we'll let you know if there are any new developments*. At first, I thought it was because they wanted to keep their leads quiet, like the investigation, but I was beginning to think it was because they had nothing to tell me.

The door opened and Natalie, with a rocket popsicle staining her lips a bright shade of red, walked out and plopped down in one of the Adirondack chairs. She was quieter lately, not asking me if I'd seen all the *Twilight* movies or talking about her friends back at school. I wasn't sure I minded, though, especially after my opinion on vampire romance seemed to mildly offend her.

"Did you see the video Andi posted on YouTube?" she asked, shifting her fingers on the popsicle stick to reveal one half of the joke written on the stained wood. "About her one million subscribers?"

"I saw part of it, I guess," I said. Andi had brought her laptop into the kitchen a couple of days ago and showed everyone the intro she was in the middle of editing. She glanced over to me during the clip from the car, when she'd mentioned me filming.

If I squinted, I could make out my reflection in the driver's side window.

"You're in it. You were there when she hit a million subscribers."

"Yeah, it happened right after we left work. She needed someone to film it."

"You guys were together without me," she said, biting into the white-lime third of the popsicle. "We're all sisters, you know."

I was a little thrown hearing her refer to us as *sisters*. "I mean, sure," I said, because I knew not to be as blunt with Natalie about this. She was more emotional, sensitive, only fourteen. "It just happened, though. We didn't plan it without you."

"You guys go to the drive-in all the time together without me."

"Because we work there, Natalie. We don't even see each other most of the time. She's in the concession stand and I'm outside. We're not hanging out or anything without you."

"But you get to drive there together, and you know all her friends' names."

"Most of the time, Andi and I don't talk."

She gave me a look, not quite as withering as the ones Andi gave but it was reminiscent. "I don't want you to, like, not get along. But I'm your sister, too, and we never do anything. You sit in our room all day until you have to go to the drive-in."

"We're talking right now," I pointed out.

"You could come to the beach with my friends sometime, meet them like you did Andi's friends."

I scrunched my nose. "Hang out with fourteen-year-olds?"

"You're not that much older," she snapped, or maybe whined. It was kind of hard to tell with her teeth biting into the popsicle. "It's like you don't even want to do anything."

"Natalie," I said, then hesitated, not sure how to explain that, even though we were technically sisters, we weren't *sisters*. Not her and Andi, with years of teasing and countless braid crowns and old arguments time made funny. "I'm still getting used to this, okay?"

"What do you call a man with no body and no nose?"

"Nobody knows—" I was interrupted when the doors opened again, just enough for Danny to lean outside, folding his flip-flops under his feet.

"Mom wants you to come inside," he told me.

"Tell her I'm busy."

"*She says she's busy!*" he hollered over his shoulder.

"No, go tell her."

Danny kept his head turned. "I don't want to," he replied, his flip-flop slipping out from under his foot and smacking against the hardwood floor inside. "She says right now."

"Why?"

"*Why?*"

"Will you just go talk to her?" Natalie snapped, and I didn't know if she meant me or Danny.

Danny looked back at me, his face startlingly casual for what he was about to repeat. "You're on the news."

o

I found everyone in the living room. David was standing in front of the television, his arms crossed and the remote clutched in his one hand, staring pensively at the screen, while Amy was distractedly petting Miles on one of the ottomans. Old footage of David walking into a brick building in the winter was playing, the collar of his coat fluttering around his stoic expression. I was confused because Danny had told me *I* was on the news, then I read the headline. Natalie came up behind me, asking, "Why is Bronwyn on the news?"

*'Police Conduct Murder Investigation
for Senator's Former Lover'*

Then footage from the interview with Kelly Bright a couple of weeks ago came on, me saddled between Amy and David. "Senator David Soliday announced earlier this month he had fathered a daughter with the victim, Donna Larson, during a separation between him and his wife in 2001. Donna Larson was said to have been killed during the EF4 tornado that devastated the Shiloh area three weeks ago, but now sources are saying that police are treating her death as a homicide."

David turned to me. "Do you have any idea how the press found out about this?"

I stared, dumbfounded, at the screen. "I told . . . a few people."

"Who did you tell, sweetie?" Amy asked.

"I told Indie," I admitted. "And this guy I know, my neighbor. Kingston."

David frowned. "This *guy you know*?"

"We—we hang out sometimes. He was at the funeral and after, he found me upset and I . . . told him. But he wouldn't leak it. I told him the police wanted to keep it quiet."

David stared at me for a long moment, and everyone else did too. Especially Jason and Kimberly, who apparently hadn't forgotten about Kingston after coming to Shiloh in the middle of the night to find me drunk at a party.

"Was there anyone else you told?"

"And Ethan Denvers," I begrudgingly confessed, stifling my groan.

"*Ethan Denvers?*" David repeated.

Andi, who had been watching the news coverage from the floor with her back propped against the couch, turned to me, confused. "What? You told *Ethan*?"

"We'd met before," I said. "He volunteered in Shiloh after the tornado, and I thought maybe he might have seen something? And look, you know the guy better than I do, but I don't think he would've told anyone."

David muted the television. "It was probably a reporter with a contact at the police station. I'm honestly surprised they made it this long into the investigation without it going public already."

"Could it hurt, though? Like, does the press knowing about this make it worse?" I asked.

"It could go either way. Now that it's gone public, the police will probably get more tips, maybe a couple of witnesses, but they'll have more to weed through. Not all of it will be relevant, or helpful. Plus, this," he said, gesturing to the screen with the remote, "isn't going to go away any time soon."

"But media coverage can be good, right? Get more exposure?"

"It can be. But it all depends on which direction they spin it. They could focus on the more . . . scandalous aspects of it instead of the case itself."

I sighed, the headline still in bold capitalized letters at the bottom of the screen. "Can we go to the police station? We should probably talk to them about this, right?"

David considered this for a moment before his phone rang. "It's Deshaun. He probably wants to talk damage control on this."

"Can't it wait?" I asked.

"I'm sorry, kiddo, it can't," he told me, pausing when he real-ized he called me *kiddo*, like it was casual and something he always did, which it might have been, just not with me. "I'm sorry. I promise we'll go down there as soon we can, okay?"

A commercial for a heartburn medication replaced the news coverage as he stepped out of the room and into the kitchen, his voice muffled when he answered his phone.

"Bronwyn," Amy said. "Do you want to—?"

"No, it's okay," I blurted out. "Like he said, this could be a good thing, so it's fine. I think I'm going to go talk to Ethan. Since he knows already, he probably wants to make sure things are okay."

Andi narrowed her eyes as Amy nodded, somewhat surprised. "Yeah, okay. But if you ever want to talk here about things—"

"I know, you're here," I finished. "Yup. Cool, I'll be back later."

I found Ethan outside a couple of minutes later, pulling open his mailbox and trying to yank out a package jammed inside. He waved when he noticed me crossing his driveway. "Hey. Did you see what the mailman did? I don't know how to get this out of here."

"Look, can I ask you something?"

"Shoot."

"Can you drive me somewhere?" When he finally managed to pull the cardboard box out of his mailbox with a triumphant grin, I continued. "Can you drive me back to Shiloh?"

"Are you running away again?" he asked drily.

"No, I want to talk to the detective on my mom's case. It was leaked and, like, that's something we should talk about, right? But David's busy and I don't want to ask Amy so—"

"Or me, apparently."

I blinked, turning around to find Andi behind me with her

arms crossed. "I . . . didn't think you'd want to," I stammered. "You don't even like driving me to work."

"My dad said he would take you later."

"And I kind of get the feeling *later* usually turns into *never* with him."

She glared at me for a moment, then her gaze softened almost begrudgingly. "Fine, whatever. Go get Taylor-Elise."

Ethan made a face. "Why?"

"Because I'm coming too."

○

An hour later, the receptionist behind the main desk at the police station told me to wait across the room where Andi, Ethan, and Taylor-Elise were already sitting. She tapped her long fingernails against the keyboard and told me Detective Marsh would be out in a minute. I sat down in one of the chairs beside Andi. She was quiet for most of the ride here and I didn't say much either; we listened to Ethan and Taylor-Elise argue about directions, which became her pointing to roads and saying, "Turn here," and Ethan repeating over her, "I've *driven* here before!"

I pulled out my phone and texted Kingston.

Guess where I am?

You're in Shiloh?

It's not fun if you don't guess.

I did guess. I'm just right. Where are you?

The police station. Did you see my mom's murder was leaked to the news?

That sucks, I'm sorry.

I came to talk to the police about it.
Solidays wanted to wait.

You're here by yourself?

> Not exactly . . . I asked this guy I work
> with at the drive-in to take me
> here since I don't have a car.

What guy?

> His name's Ethan. His little sister is best friends
> with Andi, so I see him around sometimes.

Why would you ask him to take you? I could've
come up to get you.

> I don't know. I think we're friends?

I waited for his response after seeing he'd read the text. After my apology, we were texting each other almost every other day, but we never mentioned how close we'd come to doing it. I wondered if me drunkenly freaking out on him after he got naked dampened, if not totally extinguished, whatever spark we had. But now he was acting *jealous*. I wasn't sure if that meant he had feelings for me, or if he thought someone else was about to play with the toy he'd set down.

"Bronwyn?" Detective Marsh rounded the corner into the waiting room. "How are you doing today?"

"I've been better," I told him, and he nodded sympathetically. "Are your parents here?"

"No, my mom's dead, but you know that already. I came by myself." Pausing, I glanced over my shoulder at the others. "Sort of."

"How about we go talk in my office?"

"Okay."

I followed him back down the hallway and through his open office door. If I thought the bland white walls and furniture in the Denvers' home appeared bleak, then the inside of Detective Marsh's office looked stripped and half finished, with similarly white walls and a desk near the center of the room. The carpet was navy and matted under our feet as we walked in, certificates and diplomas framed on the wall.

"I've seen the leak on the news, we all have," Detective Marsh said. "It's not going to change how we handle the investigation. It just means it's going to be more high profile, more pressure from the public. But it's nothing my department hasn't handled before."

"*Okay.* But you were concerned the media would sensational-ize this if they found out about her involvement with David. Are you not worried about that anymore?"

"It's true, this wasn't how I wanted to handle this investigation but what's done is done. We can't take back a leak. We can only handle things as best we can. We're going to hold a press confer-ence tomorrow afternoon to try to get ahead of things."

"Sure," I said, uncertainly.

"Don't worry. We've got all the best people on this, Bronwyn. We're going to get this guy."

○

I stepped out of his office a few minutes later, when it became apparent he wasn't going to tell me any more. I was halfway down the hall when I caught a glimpse of Officer Porterfield in a break room in front of the water cooler, refilling her tumbler. I hesitated, glancing to make sure no one else was inside, then cautiously walked in.

"Bronwyn, hi, do you need help with something?"

"No." I shook my head. "I mean, kind of. It's just—you're the only one around here who's ever been honest with me. Like, about my mom and everything. So, I thought maybe you could be real with me again?"

She screwed the lid back on her tumbler. "Okay."

"Will the media knowing about the investigation hurt it? I

know Detective Marsh is trying to sound all confident, but no one wanted this to happen, right? So, I'm thinking it's a bad thing."

"It makes things harder," she admitted. "And it's going to make things harder for you too. People are going to want to know things about you, what your life was like, what's happening now. The media's going to badger you and your family, and it's going to turn this case into something it's not. Which is why we're doing a press conference and why David and his team are releasing statements already. To redirect the attention back to your mom."

"You must have a lot of high-profile cases around here for you to know all that much."

She snorted softly, shaking her head. "You're even younger than I thought."

I watched as she stepped around me, scrunching my nose. "Huh?"

o

My waffle cone curved under my fingers, the chocolate and strawberry twist turning the inside soggy as I leaned against the hood of Ethan's crossover. He was beside me, with a vanilla twist, cherry syrup sliding down the cone. Andi and Taylor-Elise were still inside Scoops, and through the storefront windows painted with cartoon ice cream cones, I could see they were still at the counter, debating ice cream flavors.

It was a little after nine, the lights from downtown obscuring the starlight in the parking lot. It was still humid, and whenever I breathed in, I kept expecting it to smell like pine and lake water.

"I think this is a bad idea."

I looked over at Ethan, the first half of his ice cream gone, my phone in his other hand. "I want to know what they're saying, but, if it's bad stuff about my mom I don't want to know. Maybe. That's why it's better you look and not me. Just read the headlines."

"'*Senator's Former Lover's Cause of Death Revealed as Homicide*,'" he read. "Then there's '*Foul Play Suspected in the Death of Senator Soliday's Former Lover.*' Lots of *former lovers*. And '*Murder Investigation Launched for Mother of Senator's Illegitimate Child.*'"

"That's me. Illegitimate child. Woo-hoo, I'm in the papers," I muttered sarcastically.

"*Earlier this month, Senator David Soliday came clean about an affair he had in 2001 with a waitress named Donna Larson, who gave birth to the pair's daughter the following year. Larson was thought to have been killed in the devastating EF4 tornado that struck the town of Shiloh last month, but it has since been reported she was actually murdered hours prior. So far, Senator Soliday has not responded to TMZ's request for comment, but a public statement was announced via his Twitter that he was cooperating with the investigation and asking for privacy for his family during this difficult time.*"

I sighed. "Last month, I had to grab spare change out of my mom's ashtray to buy dollar store conditioner and now *TMZ* is writing articles about me."

"In a couple of weeks, someone will go to rehab or get pregnant, and you'll be old news."

I pulled out my phone when I noticed Kingston had texted me again.

Are you still in Shiloh?

I stared down at the notification, considering my response, if I even had to give one. I could've left it until morning, then text him that I hadn't seen it, sorry, another time. It wasn't like I didn't want to see him—I did—but I wasn't alone, or just with Indie. I was with Ethan, Taylor-Elise, and Andi. Shelridge kids. *Rich kids.* Plus, Kingston was already acting weird about Ethan, and I wasn't sure what that would be like in person.

"What are you looking at?"

"Kingston wants to know if I'm still in Shiloh."

"Why aren't you answering?"

"He's going to want to meet up and it'll be weird with everyone here."

Ethan bit into the ice cream cone. "Who cares? He can't be your boyfriend if he never meets your sister."

"Don't call her that. Or him that," I groaned.

"I want to meet him too. I want to know what kind of guy managed to crack your cold exterior. One layered in a thick coating of brutal honesty, sprinkled with loathing sarcasm, and topped with class prejudice. I would like to give the man a trophy."

I shot him a look.

"Or maybe a hug," he conceded, and despite myself, I snorted. "I'll decide when I meet him. Text him. Tell him to come get ice cream."

"How long does it take to get ice cream?" I asked, in an attempt to change the subject but, of course, he never fell for it. Instead, he grabbed my phone. "Hey," I scolded, but I didn't take it from him.

"Hopefully," he said, finishing the text and handing the phone back to me, "it takes until he shows up."

> This is Ethan. Bronwyn would LOVE to meet up with you. We're over at Scoops if you're in the mood . . . for ice cream.

"Don't give me that look! Remember, I'm your ride home," he said as I smacked him with the stack of napkins on the hood.

○

We waited for almost twenty minutes, during which time Ethan thought it was pretty amusing that Kingston was jealous in the texts he'd sent earlier. Andi was less than thrilled when she found out Ethan had invited him to have ice cream with us. She mentioned to Ethan and Taylor-Elise that he looked *older*, too old in her opinion, when she'd caught a brief glimpse of him after the funeral at the trailer park.

Taylor-Elise eyed me skeptically. "Okay, how old is this guy?"

"Not old," I responded.

"He's got to be in his twenties," Andi pointed out.

"So, he's in his twenties. Not midtwenties or anything. He's, like, twenty-two at the most."

"You don't *know*?" Andi asked, her eyes widening when I sheepishly shrugged in response.

A few minutes later, still slumped against the hood of Ethan's crossover, I heard the familiar thunderous roar of Kingston's engine and felt a pang of self-consciousness. Before, I'd never really cared about our age difference. It never mattered. No one had acted like it was a *problem* before. He pulled into the parking space beside ours, opening his driver's side door carefully to keep from scratching Ethan's car.

"Hey," I said, then hesitated because I didn't know what else to say. I would've been flirtatious before, asked if ice cream was all he wanted, but I felt too aware of Andi and Ethan watching me. "What's up?"

"Nothing much," he replied, glancing around to Andi and Taylor-Elise, then Ethan. His eyes didn't stay on him long, turning to the napkins bunched on the hood. "Did you guys already get ice cream?"

"Yeah," Andi told him flatly.

"Oh," Kingston said, nodding. "Okay."

"Yeah, but you can still get some, man," Ethan said before holding out a hand. "How are you? I'm Ethan."

Kingston hesitantly shook his hand, glancing at me instead of holding Ethan's gaze. "Hey," he replied, just as uncertainly. "So, how long are you here in Shiloh?"

I thought for a moment that he was making conversation with Ethan, until I glanced up from my shoes to see him staring at me expectantly. "Just today. We have to leave in a little while."

"We have a *curfew*," Andi said, giving him a knowing look. "Because she's sixteen."

I turned over my shoulder. "For, like, two more months."

She ignored this. "Kingston, how old are you, exactly?"

"Twenty?" he answered, confused.

"Please go get some ice cream," Taylor-Elise sighed, and I didn't know if she meant Andi or Kingston.

Kingston seemed to take this to mean him. "Do you want more ice cream?"

I hesitated, and maybe it was because I'd seen him naked before or that we weren't alone, but it just felt *different*. It didn't feel casual anymore, and the look in his eyes only seemed to confirm this. That I'd invited him for ice cream with . . . whatever Ethan, Taylor-Elise, and Andi were to me. That seemed to be the opposite of casual, like I wanted him to meet them. Meanwhile, he was waiting for me to answer. So were Ethan, Taylor-Elise, and Andi.

"Sure," I said. "Let's get some ice cream."

We headed for the ice cream parlor. It was quiet except for the traffic in the distance, semis passing through town. I didn't know where to go from here, and somehow, being alone made it feel worse.

"I have a new trailer now. Insurance payout finally came through," Kingston said after a moment. "Are those your new friends?"

"Oh yeah, I'm one of the Shelridge rich kids now. This evening I had to make the most difficult decision between bringing my Balenciaga or my Louis Vuitton handbag."

There was a slight pause before he cracked a quick smile that made me feel like my joke had missed the mark. "I noticed you were wearing new clothes. They look nice."

"You said *nice* the way some people say *root canal*."

"It's just—I'm not used to it. It's barely been a month and you already look different."

"That could just be because the last time you saw me I was topless," I blurted out. Kingston came to an abrupt stop as we reached the storefront. "Sorry, I was going to ignore it but then it turns out, ignoring it bugged me more than not ignoring it."

"No, I just—I'm a little confused. I thought you wanted to hang out or something, but then back at the car, you were all quiet and weird."

"I wasn't weird," I objected, even though I knew that wasn't exactly true. I'd let Ethan invite him here, then never met his eyes. But still, it stirred something in me when I heard it. Like maybe I really was different now and to him, that was weird. "It's just a little awkward, I guess. Because of them."

Kingston stuffed his hands into his pockets. "Like, Ethan?"

"Are you seriously mad because he drove me here?"

"I don't get why you're suddenly so comfortable with this guy. I mean, obviously you let him use your phone, and you spend like every night with him, right?" I scoffed, shaking my head because I couldn't believe he was getting like this over Ethan Denvers. "Okay, I'm not an idiot. I'm not even into guys and I know he's good-looking."

"Yeah, because you don't have to be attracted to him to admit it. His sexiness is practically objective."

"And now you just called him sexy," Kingston pointed out. "Like, if you want to go out with him, why even text me or ask me to come here? What, did you want me to check him out for you?"

"*He* was the one who asked *you* to come here!" I said, watching as the lights from the neon storefront sign reflected off his clenching jaw. "And you couldn't even say anything to him. You just said your name, that was it. You couldn't even try to have a conversation with them."

"Maybe that's because that girl kept making all these little snide comments about me."

"Yeah, her name's Andi," I told him, glaring.

Kingston stared at me, incredulous for a moment, and I turned away, staring at the cartoon ice creams on the window. "Did I do something?" he asked. "Did we take it too far the other night at the party? Because that's the only thing I can think—"

"It's not about that."

"So, what? Was it moving there?"

I shrugged, sighing as I leaned against the window, cold against my neck. "I don't know. Literally everything that could be different about me is different now. I went from a poor kid in a trailer home with only her mom to . . . someone who lives in

Shelridge for the summer. I'm probably never even going to find out why my mom was murdered."

His expression softened and he leaned against the window, too, beside me. "You don't think they're going to find who did it?"

I shrugged. "Who cares? No one else does."

"I do," he said. "That's one of the reasons I wanted to talk to you, actually. After the news leaked, some people have been talking."

"About her murder?"

"I heard her dealer was talking about it. Saying she owed him money."

"Did you talk to him?"

"No, I don't know who the guy is. It's just what I heard in town today."

I chewed the inside of my mouth because I wasn't sure who her dealer was either. But still, I shook my head. "No, she didn't owe him money."

"I'm just telling you what I heard." The clerk locked the front door of Scoops, flipping the *Open* sign to *Closed* against the glass. "Guess we're not getting ice cream."

"Nope. Guess not."

○

It was Horror Movie Tuesday on the fifth screen, and the first film was Jordan Peele's *Get Out*, followed by *Us*. Ethan was so excited for this, doling out random facts about the production or the brilliance of Jordan Peele's foreshadowing, that Ryan threatened to quit before Starbright even opened. Twice.

While we wandered around after the first films started, Ethan kept craning his neck to look through the shrubs separating the screens, remarking on where *Get Out* should've been. Then he told me he would be right back and minutes later, he came back with a handful of box candies and sodas. He brought me to the back corner of the fifth screen, already pouring Milk Duds into his mouth. When I reminded him that we weren't on break, he told me to hush.

"Okay, so that's Chris. He's the protagonist."

"There's only one girl in this movie. How is there supposed to be a Final Girl if she already starts as the Final Girl? And if Chris is the protagonist, what do we call him if he lives? Is Final Girl the term for any sole survivors at the end?"

"There're more girls. You're just impatient."

"You didn't answer my other questions."

"Are you one of *those* people at the movies? Do you just annoy whoever you're with by asking all the questions the movie will answer if you just *paid attention*?"

"Are you saying the movie is going to tell me if we call Chris a Final Girl or not?"

"No, Final Girl is just for girls. Like Laurie Strode or Nancy Thomson. It's a trope. The protagonists of most horror films are younger women who spend most of the movie abstaining from things like sex or drinking, a symbolism for purity while her more immoral friends get killed off. Usually shirtless."

"Ah, and your obsession finally makes sense."

I was chewing my Sour Patch Kids, and noticed Ethan wasn't watching the screen; instead he was looking at me like he was waiting to see what I thought. Then something flashed behind his shoulder. A quick dot of light, gone almost as soon as I saw it. Then there was another and a third closer to me.

"Are these fireflies?" I asked, surprised I hadn't noticed sooner.

"They like the plants here. This corner has fireflies all over it every summer. It's kind of cool until one flies in your ear."

"You know, bringing me to watch a movie in your firefly corner is probably why Kingston is so jealous of you," I remarked, handing him one of the orange Sour Patch Kids, which was one of his favorites and the only flavor I never liked.

"Was that why he was acting weird the other night?"

I widened my eyes. "You thought he was weird?"

"He wasn't exactly friendly," he pointed out.

"You're starting to sound like Andi. She's still going on about him, asking every time my phone goes off if that's him texting."

While attempting to prove Kingston was weird, Andi herself started acting strange. Even when she was finished berating him, she would say other stuff to me too. The other day, she gave me a foundation she said matched my skin type better than hers.

"It was weird. He was meeting you all at once and it was so obvious Andi didn't like him. But he doesn't normally act like that. I told you about the Bill Paxton thing he did at the funeral, right?"

"Yeah. But he should make an effort with your friends, don't you think? And don't do that thing when you wrinkle your eyebrows and you're like, *we're friends? I'm poor, you're rich, go away, I'm going back to my emotionally repellent shell.* Stop it. But my point still stands. Cass, last summer, had this boyfriend who never liked her hanging out with us. Always wanted her to himself, and it was so controlling. Don't put up with someone like that."

"He's not. He's just in his own emotionally repellent shell and is incredibly intimidated by your abs. Could practically see them through your shirt."

"You're a little objectifying, you know. I don't talk about you like that."

"I know, I know," I murmured, feeling a twinge of guilt because I knew he didn't think of himself like that. Whenever I teased Kingston about his attractiveness, he liked it, wanted more. Ethan seemed to retreat or ask about whatever I was trying to ignore. "But if you did, what would you say? I'm curious."

"Oh no. I'm not falling for that."

"What? I can take it. You could tell me my hair's a weird shade of blond or my bottom teeth are crooked too. And I clearly don't work out, unlike yourself."

"You're missing the movie."

"Wow, am I that ugly you have to deflect the conversation?"

"You know you're not ugly. Your hair's fine and I didn't even notice your teeth were crooked until you pointed it out."

"This is what Kingston is jealous over? I'm a little underwhelmed right now."

"Yeah, which is why I'm not saying anything. You got that thing going on with him, and I'm not adding to his preexisting jealousy by counting all the ways you're beautiful."

"But you do think I'm beautiful, though?"

"Bronwyn."

"Ethan," I said, mimicking his stern tone.

He sighed. "You're like a firefly. Pretty, bright, often found in a corner. But ultimately a constant buzzing in my ear."

I feigned a stunned expression, although the smile sneaking through felt real. "Wow, I just asked if you thought I was beautiful, and I got bright and in a corner too. I get the jealousy now."

He was in the middle of rolling his eyes when a firefly flew close to my hair and I flinched, jerking back and accidentally spilling half my Sour Patch Kids on the ground, and he paused his exasperation to laugh. A second later, swatting the bug away from me, I was laughing too.

○

"So, now do you see how the movie is fantastic?" Ethan gushed, and I nodded. The corners of his bright eyes were crinkled when he spoke. "And you have to watch the house party scene again. Actually, you have to watch the entire movie again. Like, when Mr. Armitage is showing Chris the kitchen, he says—"

"Oh my *gosh*. I can't take another Tuesday with you talking about the symbolism in *horror* movies," Taylor-Elise groaned as we walked into the concession stand. Ethan made the sweeping gesture of leaving the hoverboard at the front door, waving until Taylor-Elise noticed. "Stop, I see you. You're so annoying."

"I'm going to stop spending my money here if I'm going to be continually harassed by the employees."

"Ooh, what are we going to do without your eight bucks?" Taylor-Elise retorted. "And no tip."

"Your tip is the passenger seat of my car that I let you sit in every night," he replied swiftly, handing Cass a twenty for his usual order of a large root beer and onion rings. "Where you sit for free, because you've given me gas money, wait, let me think, *zero* times."

"I'm going home with Andi."

"Only if you give me gas money," Andi said.

"I don't give you gas money," I pointed out.

"Then don't get in my car either."

"I'll take you home," Ethan told me.

"Why her but not me?" Taylor-Elise called out.

"Because she likes *Get Out*, which is what I'll be saying to you when you try to get in my car later tonight."

Cass looked up from the register, holding the ten-dollar bill for Ethan's change. "Wait, so you guys aren't coming then?"

Ethan shook his head. "Nah, we're coming. If I don't give her a ride, our parents would find a way to ground us from Niagara Falls."

Andi was focused on wiping down one of the booths, her hair a curtain over her profile. "Ginny's dad owns a pool business in town. Sometimes, we sneak in and swim in the display models at night," she explained.

"Oh, okay. That's cool," I said.

The soundtrack from the film on the first screen echoed through the speakers in the room. I reached out to take the onion ring Ethan extended to me when Andi sighed.

"Did you buy a bathing suit at the mall before or do you not have one?"

"Yeah, but I didn't bring it," I said, then took a bite of the onion ring when she, Taylor-Elise, and Ethan turned to me. "It's fine, though. I don't need one."

Cass raised her eyebrows. "You want to skinny dip?"

"No, I—I don't need one because I'll just head back."

"Why?" Taylor-Elise asked. "You don't want to go swimming? Or do you not know how? I mean, it's a shallow pool. I think you'd be fine standing."

"No, I know how to swim. But—"

"You should come," Ethan interrupted after gulping his soda. Then he placatingly handed me another onion ring. "You can't keep up your reputation forever. We'll wear you down. Just look at Andi."

I glared but took the onion ring. "It's going to be late when we get off."

"That's the point. Otherwise, we can't sneak in because *people* are there."

"Like, I said, I don't have my bathing suit."

"We can figure out when we get there," Cass pointed out. "Or you could just sit on the edge and put your feet in or something. But you should come! It'll be fun."

I thought about trying to distract them with a joke, but then Ethan made a pointed glance over to Andi, her complexion a little blotchier under her foundation than before.

For the first time since we were little, she was inviting me to something.

"I mean, I guess as long as you don't mind me swimming in my clothes," I said, not quite looking at her face, more like the microfiber cloth with which she was cleaning the tables.

"You can swim in whatever you want," she replied.

I was wandering throughout Starbright around an hour later, alone after Ethan ran into a couple of parents smoking at the third screen. I was shaking out a piece of gravel from my shoe when shadows stretched over mine.

"Hey, do you know when the concession stand closes?"

I turned, still holding my shoe in my hand. A girl, maybe a little older than me, was standing there with a guy beside her, their hands grasped together. "Yeah, it closes at one. They shut the fryer and popcorn machine down at twelve-thirty, though."

"What can we get now if everything's already shut down?"

"Anything that's prepared already, like candy. Even though they stop making popcorn at twelve-thirty, there's usually some from the last batch available."

The girl narrowed her eyes, and I thought it was because she was unsatisfied with the concession options, when she asked, "You look familiar. Do I know you from somewhere?"

"You've probably seen me around here."

"I've never been here before," she said, sounding confused. "*Oh*! You were that girl on the TV, that senator's new daughter."

"Not exactly new," I deadpanned. "Been around Earth for several years now."

"Yeah, but you're, like, *new* to us, though," she explained. "That sucks what happened to your mom."

"Yeah, murder usually does," I replied, and the guy blinked, his eyes focusing after staring at his phone, uninterested. "Anyway, the concession stand's about to close soon, if you still want something."

She hesitated—in the dark, it was harder to tell if she thought I was rude or debating if she wanted anything that wasn't fried—before nodding, tugging at the guy's hand until he followed her away. I was about to go find Ethan when I overheard the guy say, "Who was murdered?"

"Her mom. She had an affair with a senator while he was still married and had that girl, and she was just murdered last month," she whispered not very quietly, "I watch her sister's YouTube videos sometimes, and she was in one. Now, like, all the comments are conspiracy theories on who killed her mom."

I paused, realizing she meant the video Andi had posted when she'd reached one million subscribers. But I hadn't read any of the comments on it. It never even occurred to me that they might have been about me and not her.

"Who does everyone think did it?"

"Her dad."

HOMEWRECKER

○

It was a fifteen-minute drive from Starbright to Ginny's father's pool business, Dive Right In!, but I still spent most of it on my phone, scrolling through the comments section of Andi's video. Some were congratulating her on reaching one million subscribers, but the girl at the drive-in was right when she said most were about me. Some had links to the time stamp where people could best make out my face in the window behind Andi, others bet it wasn't even me and it was just something Andi had said to get views. But the majority were about the leaked murder investigation.

> WAIT did you see her mom was actually murdered?

> Guys her mom didn't die in the tornado like they said, it was leaked the police are treating it as a homicide case.

> Anyone have links for this?

> You guys all know her dad probably did it to keep her from talking about the affair, right?

> He probably didn't do it himself, he probably paid someone to kill her because she wanted money or something, like maybe take him to one of those court shows and do a DNA test.

> OMG, could you imagine him on Lauren Lake?

> YOU ARE THE FATHER AND THE KILLER!!!!

I glanced over at Andi, watching as she adjusted her bikini straps at the red light. She must have seen the comments, but she never said anything. She seemed normal, about to go late-night swimming with her friends, like thousands of people on the internet weren't accusing her father of murder. But she grew up surrounded by public opinions. She was probably used to outrageous rumors and, to her, this was just another one.

But I wasn't used to it. It startled me every time I answered my phone and a reporter was on the other line. Jason was there one of the times it happened and explained I should answer calls only from my contacts and block the texts coming from gossip magazines or cable networks. I barely checked my email anymore after my email address was leaked too. Sometimes I caught a couple of people staring at me at Starbright, like tonight. It wasn't like everyone stared and pointed, not like it felt, but once in a while, I would look over and see someone quickly glance away after meeting my eyes. The same thing must have been happening to Andi in the concession stand, but she could just brush it off.

I couldn't. I might have been able to stop answering unknown numbers, but I couldn't stop scrolling through the comments on her video. Most of the theories didn't even make sense, like having her killed because she threatened to expose their affair. I came to live with them because she'd been killed, and they'd come clean about the affair themselves. Killing my mother didn't erase what happened. It brought me to their doorstep, something they would've known.

And maybe that was the part that bugged me.

"Are you texting *him*?" Andi asked as she turned into one of the stores along the quiet street, bricks painted pale blue. Even though I shook my head, she continued anyway. "You know, I don't like him. He's too old. I mean, could you imagine being with someone four years younger than you? Could you imagine wanting to be with a twelve-year-old?"

"But I'm not twelve. I'm sixteen. And I told you, I'm not texting him. We haven't talked since we met up."

"I'm not trying to insult your friends," she continued, ignoring this, as she parked and dropped her keys in the cupholder. "But could it work even if he wasn't too old? You don't live across the road anymore. You have a new life now."

"It doesn't feel like mine."

Andi paused after unbuckling her seat belt, staring through the windshield as Ethan and Taylor-Elise parked and stepped out of the car. There was a towel draped over Taylor-Elise's arm as she motioned for Andi to hurry up. Then she pointed two fingers at the passenger and driver's sides. "It could be."

Andi left the car, and like when she first drove me to Starbright, she didn't look back. But somehow, unlike then, I knew she was waiting.

So, I got out of the car too.

○

The scent of chlorine hung in the air, glimpses of teal from the pool lights rippling across Andi's features as she discarded her towel on the chain-link fence encasing the inground pool. Cass and Taylor-Elise were already sitting on the edge with their feet in the water, with Ginny using the remote to set the pool's lights to multicolor. Ryan stretched in front of the pool, and I noticed Andi glance over her shoulder at him, the teal reflecting in her eyes as she watched him before the color shifted to lavender.

It wasn't long before everyone else was in the pool, shrieking when Ryan decided to cannonball and splashed everyone. Everyone except me, since I was still in my uniform, but I took off my sneakers and slipped my feet into the deep end. Ethan swam around aimlessly, going under and emerging a few seconds later near me. We were farther away from everyone, lounging in the shallow end, leaning against the side.

"You could come in, you know," he said.

"Don't pull me in."

"I won't. Just making sure you're aware of your options."

"I don't have a swimsuit. Or a towel."

"I have a towel," he replied. "You can swim in your clothes."

"Are you just trying to see me in a wet T-shirt?"

"Excuse me, ma'am, you have an undefined thing with Kingston What's-His-Name. I would never violate such a covenant."

I smiled. "I'm fine with just watching."

He hesitated, water dripping from the wet tendrils of his hair, his expression softening. The teasing, playful glint left his eyes as the water turned a green hue to match them, pinking slightly from the chlorine. "I'm not," he said, his voice low but not whispered. "I don't want you to be alone."

I blinked, softly realizing that no one had ever told me they didn't want me to be alone before. I knew it was because of what I'd told him before, when I was drunk and crying and alone, except I wasn't, because I was with him. And he was alone, too, outside in the middle of the night with me because there was no one waiting for him when he walked back home. Except, he wasn't, because he was with me.

"I'm not alone right now," I said quietly. Then, when the silence turned expecting and awkward, I splashed him with my foot.

"Fine, whatever. I'll get in. I hate sliding in on the side, though. It scrapes your thighs."

He watched me as I went to stand up, then tilted his head. "You want a way in without scraping your thighs?"

"Cannonballing?" I asked drily. "The ladder?"

He shifted around so his back was to me and then dipped underwater. I felt his hands reaching for my legs, maneuvering them over his shoulders. I shook my head but scooted closer to the edge, waiting. When he emerged and his shoulders were level with the concrete, I slid onto his back and wobbled as he immediately went back underwater. I slipped from his shoulders and crashed into the water, the blurry color of pink all around me. When I came back to the surface, Ethan was laughing.

"I think I should've tried that in the shallow end," he said as I sputtered, water having gone up my nose. "Oh man, I'm sorry. I didn't think I was going to drown you."

"I need to stop hanging out with you all. You keep finding ways to hurt my nose," I said, coughing as he patted me on the back.

"Yeah, but it's a tough old schnoz."

"Were you guys trying to play chicken by yourselves?" Ginny called out. "In the deep end?"

At the mention of this, Ryan started nodding enthusiastically. "Yes! Yes, chicken, yes! Come on, guys, just sitting around feels like a waste of breaking and entering."

"You know it makes me nervous when you call it that. Can't we call it anything else?" Cass asked, concerned.

Ethan looked over to me. "Well?"

I smoothed the wet hair plastered against my forehead behind my ears. "If someone has to be your partner . . ."

"Okay, who wants to be my partner?" Ryan called out.

Glancing over to where she was adjusting her bikini strap again, I said, "Andi will!"

It seemed having her own inground pool back home gave Andi an advantage when it came to playing chicken, easily toppling me from Ethan's shoulders. Her grin brightened her whole face each time and it didn't look so unfamiliar to me anymore. The one time I managed to knock her off, after at least four losses, she came up from the water laughing and shouting, "*Finally*!"

Eventually, Ethan's shoulders started to hurt and the girls got tired of being thrown in the water so Ryan suggested a game of Marco Polo, with accusations of cheating quickly declared. While Cass had her eyes closed, calling out *Marco,* I swam over to the shallow end, the water changing colors under my chin. Quiet except with Cass's increasingly frustrated *Marco*s and water gently shifting against shoulders as they passed her outstretched hands.

Then something caught my eye, blue flashing against the fence while the water was still orange. Everyone else in the pool noticed it, too, as tires crunched on the asphalt. A patrol car, pulling into the parking lot, just as Cass's fingers brushed my neck.

"Ha! Got you!"

○

The officer made us all call our parents, especially when Ginny tried to convince him her dad owned the store. We had to wait until he arrived around ten minutes later, looking less than pleased when he got there, still in his pajamas. He confirmed with the officer he owned the store and didn't want to press charges, adding a few exasperated remarks about some *definite* grounding. Meanwhile, Andi was on the phone with Amy explaining what was going on, and Ethan was trying unsuccessfully to get a hold of his dad as Taylor-Elise comforted Cass, on the verge of tears.

After the patrol officer left, Ginny's father had deep frown lines set in his skin when he turned to us. "I think it's time you all go home," he announced. "And this isn't to happen again. If one of you kids had gotten hurt, that could've been the end of my business. You understand?"

We nodded, which seemed to satisfy him.

"All right. Now get on home to your parents."

Andi kept the air conditioning on a lower setting as she drove back to the lake house, my clothes still completely soaked and dripping down my legs. The lights were on when she pulled into the driveway. My shorts made awkward suctioning noises as we walked in to find Amy and David in the kitchen, both in their robes, waiting.

Amy stared tiredly at us, leaning her cheek against her knuckles. "Did you girls have a good swim?"

Andi had her arms crossed with the towel draped over them. Droplets from her wet hair were still slipping down her shoulders.

"I wasn't having a fun time when I got this phone call," Amy continued. "Your father and I are very disappointed in both of you. You know better."

"It was Ginny's idea. She said it was okay," Andi said.

"So, if it was Ginny's idea to jump off a bridge, you would do that too?" David asked.

"No one does that. That's not even a thing."

"You could've gotten into serious trouble tonight," he scolded. It struck me that this was the first time a parent had *ever* reprimanded me for something. "What if Mr. Warren wanted to press charges? Or someone got hurt? What were you even doing, swimming at three in the morning?"

"Ginny asked us to go, okay? She never told me her dad didn't know."

I tried not to look at Andi, feeling fairly certain that wasn't the truth.

"Girls," David sighed, running a hand over his face, "right now is not the time we can afford to make decisions like this."

"Or ever," Amy added.

"Yes, or ever, but especially now. The media has become . . . *focused* on our family and we have to be careful we don't add to their fire right now. I don't want this to be still going on when school starts."

"And by *this*, you mean my mother's murder investigation?" I said.

David was standing in the corner of the kitchen with his back against the marble countertops near the sink. I wondered if he knew about the comments on Andi's video, what he would say if he thought I knew about them too.

"I was referring to the media scrutiny, but yes. I want them to solve your mother's case, and the sooner the better."

"Better for who?" I murmured, arching an eyebrow at him.

"Bronwyn, we'll talk about the investigation in a moment. Right now, you girls are still in trouble for swimming at Mr. Warren's business without his permission—" Amy was interrupted when a bedroom door creaked open. Natalie padded down the hall midyawn a second later, acne treatments dotting her forehead and her pupils small like ink marks. "Hey, sweetheart. Did we wake you?"

Natalie nodded as she took us in, particularly me in my soaking wet Starbright Drive-In uniform. "Why are you all wet?"

"Natalie, go back to bed, please," David told her.

"Are they in trouble?" she asked, slowly inching back to the hall. "What did you guys do?"

Andi glared at her. "Dad already told you to buzz off."

"Andrea," Amy warned.

"Well, he did!"

"Stop," she said, lifting her hand. "Natalie, sweetie, you need to go back to bed."

Natalie, her face pinched in frustration, reluctantly left the kitchen and slammed the bedroom door behind her. It was still echoing in my ears when Amy spoke again, "You girls know what you did was wrong, right?"

She hesitated, but eventually Andi nodded. Amy looked at me expectedly until I did the same.

"Okay. You will apologize for abusing Mr. Warren's trust," she said. "I also think you need to come straight home after your shifts instead of hanging out with your friends."

David nodded. "That's too late to be out."

"Fine," Andi said, her voice strained. "We won't. Can we go to bed now?"

"Yes. Go get some sleep. We'll talk more tomorrow."

Andi's face fell. "Talk *more?*"

"Did you think you weren't going to be punished for breaking and entering?" she asked, although from her tone it didn't sound as if she wanted an answer. "But for now, we should all go to bed. Oh, and Bronwyn, you can just leave those clothes in the tub. I'll take care of them later."

I followed Andi down the hall to the bedroom. Inside, Natalie was still awake, lying across her unmade bed with her feet propped up on the wall. "So, what did you guys do?"

Andi pulled open a drawer. "Nothing."

"Yes, you did! What happened?"

"Stop being so nosy all the time."

"I wouldn't have to be if you ever took me with you. You guys are always doing stuff without me!"

"Bronwyn has been here for, like, a month. Good use of the word *always*."

"Always in the past month!" Natalie whined. "You guys are *always* doing stuff on your own, like going to the drive-in or Shiloh, and you just leave me with the boys all the time! It sucks."

"What do you want me to say, Natalie? We'll just quit our jobs to hang out with you all the time?" Andi asked sarcastically, abandoning her towel on the floor near her bed.

Natalie groaned and brought one of her pillows to her chest. "You're not *getting* it."

"I don't know what else you want because that's pretty much the only time we've hung out without you."

"No, it's not—!" I grabbed my pajamas and headed for the door when Natalie abruptly lifted her head and paused. "Where are you going?"

"I'm just going to change."

She was quiet so I tiptoed out of the room, but before I could make it down the hall, I heard her voice again, muffled against the pillowcase. "You guys don't even want to argue together."

CHAPTER FOURTEEN

Even though it took me until around five in the morning to fall asleep, chlorine still clinging to my hair and now thoroughly embedded in my pillowcase, I was awake again a few hours later. Andi and Natalie were still asleep as I gingerly walked out into the hallway, breathing in the pungent smell of brewing coffee.

Amy was in the kitchen, dressed in a floral blouse, her hair pulled back into a tight ponytail. Pie plates were on the counter with scrambled egg yolks and cinnamon sticking to the glass, an opened package of whole wheat bread beside it, and a griddle with three slices of sizzling French toast already cooking. The window above the sink was open, the early morning breeze coming in from off the lake rustling the curtain.

"The first batch will be ready in a few minutes if you want some," she said, without looking over her shoulder. "There's also some raspberries from the farmers' market in the fridge."

I hesitated, then shuffled over to the refrigerator and grabbed the raspberries inside.

"David left already for work, but I thought we should talk about a few things." She slid the spatula under one of the French toast slices, flipping it and revealing a golden brown marbled top.

I ran the raspberries under the faucet. "Like my punishment?"

"We decided to leave that at you girls coming straight home after your shifts," she said. "There's a lot going on right now, and I was the one who encouraged you to hang out with Andi and her friends. I don't want to ground you and take that away just when you were getting along with everyone."

"What about Andi?"

"I'm more disappointed in her. Don't think I didn't notice she was in a bathing suit and you weren't," she pointed out. "But I can't ground only one of you." She turned around. "But that's not what I wanted to talk to you about. You seemed upset last night about what's going on with your mother's investigation."

"It's fine."

"Bronwyn, if something's bothering you, we want to know about it. We haven't even talked about the investigation being leaked. Maybe we can help."

I turned back to the refrigerator, pulling out a pitcher of orange juice so she wouldn't notice the look on my face. "Well, I think David's a little too busy trying to salvage his reputation for that."

"Is that what you're upset about it? You think David's more interested in his career than you?"

"He does have, like, sixteen years' worth of practice."

"Bronwyn," she warned, like she did earlier when Andi and Natalie were arguing. It was strange, hearing her say my name like that. "Do you really feel like you've been unwanted this whole time?"

I thought about the invitations Jason told me were mailed and never answered, the letters Andi wrote. It contradicted what I knew, the neglected child support payments, their absence, everything my mom told me. The longer I stayed here with them, the less sense everything made.

"If you wanted me, why didn't you do anything about it?"

She reached into the package of bread, grabbed three slices, and then dropped them into the pie plate. "That's not entirely true," she admitted reluctantly. "You remember when you and your mom came to Andi's birthday party a few years ago?"

"Yeah."

"Did your mother ever explain why you left so soon?"

"She said David had asked for a DNA test after accusing her of being a gold digger."

Amy let out a soft laugh before quickly pressing her lips together. "No, sweetheart. He never asked for a DNA test, he didn't have to. When you were born, you looked *exactly* like Andi. We couldn't believe how much you looked like her. You both were such frowny babies!"

"You were there when I was born?" My mom always told me she was at the hospital alone, that nurses had to take the pictures of her holding me.

"Not for your birth. Your mother wanted her privacy, but we were in the waiting room. Then we went in and saw you. So tiny and sweet. You were bald like Jason and Andi too. Actually, we brought them to see you and took a couple of pictures of you together. They're back at the house, otherwise I'd pull them out to show you."

I glanced down at the French toast slices sizzling on the grid-dle as she slid a spatula under one, having mentioned something so casually that went against everything I ever knew. The few times I asked Mom about what the Solidays had done after I was born, she spoke bitterly. *They did nothing, sweetheart. Nothing.*

"What does that have to do with Andi's birthday party?"

"We wanted to reach a custody agreement with Donna, out of court. And she was not very happy with that idea. She got upset and left. We didn't hear much from her after that."

"You wanted . . . custody?" I asked skeptically.

"We did," Amy said. "We were supposed to see you more than we actually did, maybe get a couple of weekends with you. But there was always an excuse—you weren't weaned, you had a fever. When we finally saw your mother for the first time in years, we talked about creating some sort of agreement. It went about as badly we'd expected."

"If that were really true, you could've gone to court."

"We didn't want to put you through that. Ethan's father is a divorce attorney. He has stories of these bitter custody cases. People tear each other apart, trying to prove they can be the happiest home for their children. Besides, David knew there was a good chance your mother wasn't going to honor a custody agreement anyway. Then what? Your mother has to pay a fine we knew she couldn't afford, or worse, jail time? No. We wanted to work something out with your mother, but as time went on, it only got harder and harder. Eventually, we just . . . had to hope when you turned eighteen, we could have more of a relationship with you."

I paused, remembering the comments on Andi's video. "You wanted me the whole time? Both of you?"

She handed me a plate of French toast, still steaming. "Yes, sweetheart. We always wanted you to be a part of our family.

Maple syrup's in the fridge, and there's powdered sugar if you want some."

I was about to ask her about the child support payments David admitted to never sending, and why he would've done that if apparently they wanted me all this time, when Kimberly wandered into the kitchen in her yoga clothes with her mat tucked under her arm. "That smells good."

"I'll save you a plate in the microwave," Amy told her, then noticed me staring down at my plate. "Bronwyn? Everything okay with your toast?"

"Yeah. It's fine," I said quietly.

o

The next afternoon, I leaned against the passenger side of Andi's car after she'd forgotten her keys and dashed back inside. The scent from the grill was lingering after David had cooked chicken and zucchini for dinner. He and Amy were still outside on the patio, watching Danny and his friends do cannonballs off the dock into the lake. As I waited, my phone lit up with a text from Kingston. We hadn't really texted since meeting in Shiloh—I told myself it was just because I was busy, not because things felt weird. And if I was being honest, things did feel weird. We'd only kissed once, but he'd acted so jealous that night at Scoops, not even listening to me. I thought we were casual and laid-back, mature. That was what I liked about him. He was more mature than the guys at high school; or at least that's what it seemed like before he'd acted so jealous and insecure.

Do you think you'll come down sometime?

I mean, I'd like to, but I work a lot of nights and
I'd have to ask someone to drive me.

I could drive you.

I made a face down at my phone, before confusion settled in. I'd had a crush on him for months, flirting back and forth over the gravel between our trailers. I used to sit outside on the cinderblock steps around the time he got home from work to strike up another conversation with him. I didn't understand it, or me anymore—I used to want it, him. But now I didn't know what I wanted.

"Okay, found them. Let's go," Andi announced as she jogged back over to the car, pausing when she noticed my phone. "*Ugh*. You're not texting him, are you?"

I looked down, receiving a new text from a different number.

Hi, Bronwyn! This is Deborah Zhao from Read Between the Lines. I was wondering if we could set up an interview with you for an article we're writing about your family.

"Nope, now I'm talking to Deborah Zhao."

"Block," she replied. "But seriously. You're texting him, aren't you?"

"I know, you don't like him."

"Do *you* even like him? Because you kept making this face at Scoops, like you couldn't wait for him to leave."

"He wants to see me again," I admitted, reluctantly, as she unlocked the door. "And I—"

"Who wants to see you again?" Amy asked, approaching the driveway with an intrigued smile barely contained on her face. "Do you have a boyfriend?"

"No—" I started to say.

"Pretty much," Andi answered.

Amy grinned. "I didn't know that! Wow, so what's his name? When do we get to meet him? Or do we already know him?" she asked, turning to look over her shoulder.

"Shouldn't we get to work?" I pleaded with Andi.

Instead of getting in the car, Andi smiled mischievously. "Actually, I think we should *all* meet him. Wouldn't it be so nice if the whole family got to meet your boyfriend? I'm sure we're all going to love him, as do you."

"You love him?" Amy asked.

"*No.*"

"Okay, well, we should get to know him," Amy said, nodding as she considered this. "How about you invite him down this weekend for a barbeque? And invite Indie, too, she's just so sweet. David?! Do you have anything planned for this Sunday?"

I glared at Andi as Amy walked back toward the patio. "Why did you do that?"

"What?" she asked, innocently. "You're not ashamed of him, are you? Or perhaps, embarrassed by the fact he's in his twenties? But it'll be fun. We'll get out the cornhole."

"I'm going to kill you." I opened the passenger side door, slamming it when I was inside.

"Fine. We'll do ladder golf."

CHAPTER FIFTEEN

"You knew they were going to have to meet him eventually."

Ethan was setting up the cornhole while I watered the flowerbeds. He was wearing a Jason Voorhees T-shirt from the *Friday the 13th* sequel—I knew that only because he'd gone off on a tangent about how Jason wasn't actually the slasher from the first movie, just the ensuing sequels.

"I had hope."

Amy had spent the last week going to and from the grocery store, asking Jason to get the lawn games out of the shed and dust them off, all while trying to get information out of me about Kingston. She kept getting this look in her eyes every time, like this was romantic and dreamy. That was normally when I left to go outside and weed.

Ethan stepped back from the cornhole boards. "All right, so here's what I don't get."

"You're supposed to get the beanbag through the hole."

He shot me a look over his shoulder. "You said you like him, but whenever we try to get to know him or hang out, your face gets all scrunched. Whenever I like a girl, I want all my friends to meet her, and like her too. That's not what you're doing."

"Is that what happened with Summer Marston?"

"What?" he said, frowning, then blinked. "Oh."

"You're such a hypocrite. You didn't want her to meet your friends."

"That's not—I haven't thought about Summer Marston in ages."

"You brought her up, like, two weeks ago."

"Yeah, ages ago," he replied, and when I tilted my head and raised my eyebrow, he sighed reluctantly. "Okay, fine. Dorky, scrawny fifteen-year-old me didn't want her to meet my other dorky, scrawny friends. All two of them. I wanted her to like me, but she still didn't. And I'm not like that anymore. I don't keep the girl I like away from my friends because I'm worried she'll realize what a loser I am."

"You're not a loser. And what girl are you talking about? If you want her to meet all your friends, why haven't I met her? I *knew* it! We're not really friends. Can't say I'm surprised, since you're rich and I'm poor." Then I grinned. "See, I can make jokes about myself too."

He shook his head. "I'm just being hypothetical. My point was, I grew up."

"It's not like anyone has ever liked me and Kingston together. Indie doesn't like him. Andi doesn't. As soon as Amy and David see how old he is, I bet they won't either." I eyed him, rearranging the cornhole boards. "Do you like him?"

"I don't know him. I met him once."

"Do you think he's too old?"

He threw a beanbag and, as it landed in the grass a few inches away from the board, he turned to me with a sheepish expression.

"You do! You think he's too old for me."

"He's *twenty*," he pointed out. "You're sixteen."

"I'll be seventeen in two months."

"Okay, *almost seventeen*. But still, doesn't it seem kind of weird he wants to be with a teenager instead of someone his age?"

"I'm mature for my age, don't you think? After all, I spent my whole life taking care of my drug-addled mother."

"You also sprayed me with the hose twenty minutes ago," he replied.

"You looked hot."

"Thank you, but we're not talking about that right now, Bronwyn—" he paused as I lifted the hose and sprayed his chest, grinning as he looked down at the water beating against Jason Voorhees on his shirt with a deadpan expression. It lasted only a second before he cracked a smile. "You know, water is actually Jason Voorhees's greatest weakness."

I stopped spraying. "Why do you think I did it?"

"Did you really know that?"

"Yeah, because he drowned at Camp Crystal Lake when he was a kid. I've been paying attention."

There was a softness in his eyes for a moment, his grin slighter but more endearing than before. "I'm not sure I'm used to this. Usually people just tune me out."

"Oh, I definitely do that too," I said, and he laughed. "But people don't tune you out. The endless barrage of horror movie fun facts, maybe, but not you. You're pretty magnetic that way."

His eyes crinkled a little in confusion at the corners when one of the doors opened and Miles sprinted onto the lawn.

Jason followed behind him, the corner of a doggie bag in his one pocket.

Ethan tossed him one of the beanbags and said, "Hey, man, what's up?"

"Nothing much," Jason replied, tossing the beanbag and missing. "Just wedding planning. Your parents home?"

He shook his head. "Back home in Niagara Falls, but they said they'll make it back down for the wedding so . . ." he said, shrugging.

"You haven't met Bronwyn's friends yet, right?"

I released my grip around the nozzle for a second, looking over at Ethan throwing his beanbag underhand at the board. He'd met Kingston before, but not Indie. I already knew he would like her, people usually did, but a part of me was worried she wouldn't like him. She never liked any of the boys I hung out with, and even though Ethan was different, like we weren't *hanging* out, I wanted him to be the exception. Which was confusing because she was carpooling with Kingston, and he should've been the one I wanted her to like.

"I met Kingston before, not Indie," he said, scratching Miles behind the ears.

"You met him?" Jason asked. "I didn't get the chance last time, since he'd just left Bronwyn drunk by herself at a party. And he's practically my age."

"I left him," I pointed out. "It wasn't that big of a deal. And no, he's not. He's only twenty."

"Oh, *only* twenty." I glared at him, and he shrugged. "Look, I get I don't know the guy. And I don't really know you that well, either, but that's not what I think people should do. You might have left, but he had legs. He could've made sure you got home safe, but he didn't."

"Maybe he has the confidence in me to know I can take care of myself."

"Not the kind of drunk you are," Ethan mumbled.

"You might be able to take care of yourself, but you shouldn't have to all the time. It's not so much to ask that your partner gives you a hand when you need one."

"Maybe we just have different ideas of what a relationship is. Maybe I think it's better to know when to step back and give your partner some space."

Ethan snorted. "Your idea of *space* is Mercury to Neptune."

"Hey."

"Sorry. It's just if you want this to work, you have to both be on the same page. Or planet, at least. Because right now, he's stony and you're icy." He paused. "Are you going to spray me again—"

I did.

When I finished, Jason piped up, "Hey, wait, are you wearing a Jason shirt?"

o

It wasn't until David started grilling that Kingston finally pulled in. The kayaks were already out of the shed, paddles tossed down onto the grass with life jackets crammed into the seats. Ethan finished assembling the ladder golf about a half an hour earlier and was in the midst of a game with Danny, Jason, and Natalie. Amy set out the salads and chip bowls. Drinks were submerged in ice water in one of the coolers on the patio. Everyone was already there, lounging in lawn chairs scattered around the backyard, waiting.

Indie came around the corner of the house a couple minutes after the rumbling of Kingston's truck quieted, smiling but her jaw looked clenched, like whenever she was frustrated. She was holding a Crock-Pot of baked beans and didn't look to see if Kingston was following.

"Hi, Indie. It's so good to see you again," Amy said. "Oh, those smell great!"

"My mom's recipe," Indie said. "Do you have somewhere we could plug it in? It took longer getting here than I thought and they're probably cold by now."

"I'll take care of that for you," Amy said, nodding. "Help yourself to drinks in the cooler, dinner should be ready in about ten minutes. I found this recipe for mushroom burgers, I hope you like them." She was about to step away when she paused. "Kingston is with you, right?"

Amy might not have noticed the way Indie's eyelids drooped a little at the mention of his name, but I did. "Yeah, he's here. He's just getting stuff out of his truck."

"Really? Wow, you kids are so considerate. Thank you."

Amy turned to go up onto the patio with the Crock-Pot. I was watching as she passed David at the grill, informing him they were here, when Indie groaned. "That was so awkward."

I shrugged. "That's Amy."

She smacked my arm. "No, spending an hour and a half alone in a car with Kingston. We had nothing to talk about, and he got lost because when I told him to take the turn on Monroe, he didn't listen and kept going down Belknap. When I said I've driven here before and it's *Monroe,* he got all quiet and mad in that way guys do whenever they're wrong. It took twice as long as it should have to get here."

"Hey, I wasn't the one who invited him here. Go whisper-yell at Andi if you're mad."

"I hated it," she whined. "Then I have to do it all over again tonight."

She was still pouting when Kingston came around to the back, a foil pan balanced on his open palm, the arm of his sunglasses in between his teeth. He smiled when he noticed me near the patio, and when he didn't look away, I offered a small wave but it felt awkward to me. My wave, his smile, everything.

He came over and handed me the pan. "They're vegan. I figured rich people are always on those weird kinds of diets, right?"

Indie sighed. "Veganism isn't a *weird kind of diet.*"

"He just means it's something usually only rich people can afford," I replied with a halfhearted shrug, feeling like I needed to soften his opinions when I wasn't even sure if that's what he meant. Back home, people ate what they could afford, and vegan or gluten-free diets were almost always out of the question. But here, I had been living with Kimberly, who ate things like chickpea pasta and seaweed chips. On the nights she cooked dinner, it tasted better than I expected it to. It wasn't *weird,* just privileged.

Cheering erupted from behind me as I gave Indie a pleading glance she deliberately ignored. I was still giving her that look when Ethan strode over. "Natalie and I won," he said instead of a greeting, before glancing over to Kingston and Indie. "Hey, Kingston. How are you doing?"

"Good, how about you?" Kingston asked stiffly, the muscles in his jaw twitching.

"Oh, I'm great. I just won at ladder golf." Then Ethan held out his hand past me to Indie. "Hey, Indie. Nice to finally meet you."

Indie shook his hand, looking confused.

"That's just how he talks," I explained. "Like a very old man. Trapped in a young Herculean body."

"Herculean?" Kingston and Ethan repeated over each other, their inflections different. Ethan laughed, one eyebrow arched and Kingston sounded confused, *offended*. I never thought it was weird how I talked to Ethan before, but with Kingston standing right there and analyzing every word, I started to feel uncomfortable.

"Where did you learn a big word like that?" Ethan asked.

I shrugged. "I don't know. Probably just preparing for that big fancy private school."

"You're going to a private school?" Kingston asked with a small snort, like he couldn't believe it. It bothered me, even if most of the time, I couldn't believe it either.

"Yeah. You don't think I could make it at a private school?"

Beside me, Indie smiled and covered it by pretending to cough into her hand.

"No, that's not what I said—" He paused, looking quickly over to Ethan. "You've just never cared about any of this stuff, like private schools. They're just expensive ways to prove you're better than everyone else without even trying."

Ethan tensed. "On that note, I think I have a Ferrari to go polish."

"Ethan, wait, hang on—" I turned to Kingston, glaring as Ethan just smiled with a small shrug and headed toward the patio. "Why would you say something like that?"

"That's the sort of stuff you said," he replied defensively, and I felt a part of me flinching away from him as I heard it because he was right, remembering all of the things I'd said to Ethan right here in the same backyard. "All the time when you talked about this place, how it's just insane privilege everywhere they don't even have to earn."

"Yeah, it's not fair," I said, my mouth still open because I wanted to say so much more than that, but I felt too confused to string together the words. I remembered the words I'd spoken about this place and the people who lived here and next door, the exact sentiments he was echoing now, but before it felt self-righteous. It felt like the truth. And now things felt different, like the way I saw things was distorted and bitter. Maybe not totally wrong, but not . . . right, either.

"Look, he's one of my friends, okay? And, you know, if you get to know—"

"Sorry, maybe I should've stroked his ego by calling him *Herculean* like you."

I paused, taken aback again but this time by his tone, sarcastic and annoyed, and the confusion I felt before started to slip away, becoming replaced with my own sense of anger. "Right. I didn't realize you were so insecure you couldn't handle me having other guys for friends."

"What's going on?" Andi asked, approaching us.

Indie smiled. "Everything I ever wanted."

Kingston gestured to her. "See, why can she say that stuff about me, but I can't point out what's true about Hercules? Whenever we're around your friends, they're what's most important to you. You don't care about me at all."

"No, the problem is she doesn't care *only* about you," Andi retorted, bringing her drink close to her lips without taking a sip from it. Instead, she just watched him over the rim. "Not everyone's stuck in their trailer."

I frowned, turning to her. "What's *that* supposed to mean?"

Something shifted in her eyes for a second. "I didn't mean you—"

"Except, you did," Kingston pointed out. "Because she came from a trailer, just like me. But I guess after one month of living with you, she's already forgotten that."

"This must be Kingston!"

David came down the patio with Amy beside him, holding spoons for the cold salads, neither of them apparently realizing we were in the middle of an argument. I noticed the slight flinch in their smiles as Kingston turned around and they took him in.

"Hi, yes," Kingston replied, distracted. He paused then held out his hand, and I tried not to roll my eyes. "I'm Kingston Castaneda."

"Kingston. Good to meet you. I understand you had a bit of a drive up here."

Indie nodded before he could answer. "Yeah, we got lost. He took Belknap."

"Belknap?" David repeated with a bemused laugh, before quieting himself. "As long as you both got here safely, that's all that matters. We've got some games set up over there, kayaks if you want to take a ride, and burgers are coming up in a minute. Speaking of which—" He turned, flashed a smile, and jogged back up to the grill.

Amy extended her hand, and Kingston's eyes widened as he realized he'd overlooked shaking hers. "It's good to have you. And, oh, did you make brownies? How thoughtful."

I handed them to her. "Vegan brownies."

"I'll go set these up with the other desserts. Bronwyn, how about you go introduce Kingston to all your friends," she said, glancing pointedly to the others in the backyard.

I waited quietly until she walked back up to the patio, something in me still simmering with Andi and Kingston on either side of me before I mumbled, "I'm going to go play horseshoes."

○

I was roasting marshmallows a couple of hours after dinner, with Kingston across the flames in a lawn chair, a sweating can of Pepsi in his hand. I'd barely spoken to him after my heated battle of horseshoes with Danny. It bothered me because he was right. Lakeshore summer homes, private educations, it was all extravagant to me. Gawdy and suffocating. I used to live in the trailer across from his. My phone screen was cracked, the clothes I'd worn had been someone else's before they'd been mine. Every time someone did something—like go out on the lake in the kayaks, argue over croquet arrangements—I wondered what he thought. How *much* everything was, and it made me feel like I was becoming numb to it. I felt different around him, like I was becoming someone else, and to him, that was worse.

But I didn't know how to be that girl anymore, sitting sun-burned on cinderblocks and listening to the classic rock blaring from his trailer like it was a soundtrack I always wanted to replay. Now, I wore the name brand clothes I used to think were too much and lived with minor celebrities in a lake house. It was something I hadn't felt a part of until Kingston looked at me the same way he looked at the rest of the Solidays, at Ethan.

Or maybe he judged me for trying to blend in somewhere he knew firsthand I didn't belong. But I was starting to feel tethered, and how Kingston felt about them changed how I felt about him. He was supposed to like my friends, get to know them, get along with them, but he didn't. He was sitting next to Taylor-Elise, and instead of talking to her about how she'd dominated cornhole, he watched me. I was his whole focal point, and I didn't want to be.

Laughter floated from across the campfire. Ethan was between Natalie and Indie, her fallen s'more melting onto the grass. Unlike Kingston, Indie was getting along with Ethan. She commented on his Jason Voorhees T-shirt, he complimented her mom's baked beans recipe, and they even teamed up for a game of ladder golf. She looked like she liked him, like she really *liked* him. As my marshmallow dropped, so did my smile.

Because she looked like she liked him, like she really *liked* him.

"Bronwyn, your marshmallow's burning—and it's gone," Ethan remarked.

"Right," I said, feeling suddenly very aware of myself and him looking at me, before promptly standing up. "I'm going to get another drink."

"Didn't you just get one—?" Andi asked.

I walked away before I caught any more of her confused question, or heard Ethan explain to Indie how terrific a Final Girl Alice Hardy was—like that was something he told everyone, and maybe it was, it wasn't like I knew—and headed for the patio. I told myself with each step this was what I wanted. I wanted them to like each other and if they liked each other like that, then great. *Great.*

I plunged my hand deep into the ice water in the cooler, focusing on the flinching cold instead of the thought of them together, around me all the time, maybe even at Starbright discussing whether *Alien* counted as horror or sci-fi, and the confusion of why that *bothered* me. It made me feel like my muscles were seizing up when it shouldn't have because they were my friends. I wanted this. I wanted them to get along.

I just didn't think it would be like *that*.

"Bronwyn?" Kingston approached me on the patio. "Can we talk?"

Sighing, I tapped on my can of lemonade then nodded.

"Earlier, what I said—I didn't mean you couldn't make it in a private school. You're, like, ten thousand times smarter than anyone I know," he said. "You would also look cute in one of those little uniforms."

"Do you ever think sometimes I'm too young for you?"

"What? No, I'm not *that* much older than you."

"But I'm in high school. I have a curfew. I mean, I'm . . . sixteen. That's like me dating a twelve-year-old."

"I never thought that bothered you. And it didn't until you started letting what other people thought change how you feel about me."

"They're my friends. Do you not want me to have friends? Because that's how it's beginning to sound."

He groaned. "You know that's not what I meant. But things are so different now—"

"Well, what do you want me to say? I'll go back to that little trailer . . . on my own, with no one except for you? Because that was when this felt okay."

"Then let's go back to that!" he implored.

"I don't want to," I blurted out, taking both him and me aback. Then it was quiet, a deafening silence barely touched by the muffled conversation near the lake. "Look, I know it's weird because I didn't want to come here, but what am I going back to? My mom's gone, my trailer, my stuff, everything."

"I'm still there. I never left, Bronwyn!"

"That's not enough for me. And it shouldn't be for you either. I mean, I want you to have friends! I want you to talk to *my* friends, not just me. I want you to have hobbies and care about things, but you don't."

"I'm sorry I'm not like the other people here who have all the time and the money in the world to pursue their *hobbies*, okay? I actually have to work. I'm in a factory, not just sitting around at a desk, ordering other people around."

I narrowed my gaze. "You don't sound proud. You just sound jealous. Maybe if you actually talked to any of the people here, you would see what I mean."

"Okay, okay. So, are we talking about what you mean *this* month or what you meant *last* month?" He clenched his jaw, then shook his head. "What happened to you not being a Soliday?"

I swallowed, feeling his grumbled words sting against my skin because I thought I might have been losing pieces of myself since I came here, becoming a version of myself I never wanted to be—numbed to privilege, soaked in wealth, deadened to the real world—and he'd just confirmed it. I didn't want to be that person, but I was starting to realize I didn't want to be his version either: resentful, jealous, alone.

I remembered what Ethan had asked me a few weeks ago—did Kingston made me happy? In that moment on the patio, the shadows from the moths fluttering around the porch lights shifting across his face, I couldn't remember the last time Kingston and I had talked instead of argued. The last time I'd felt excited to see him. The last time I'd wanted to kiss him. The last time he'd made me happy.

"If you don't want to be here, then maybe you should just go," I mumbled.

"You want me to leave?" he asked, incredulous, and when I

nodded, he let out a sardonic laugh. "Fine, I'll go tell Indie you're sending us poor, lower-class scum back to Shiloh where we belong. Never mind that you used to be one of us."

"If you don't want to be sent home like lower-class scum, then don't act like it," I snapped. "Don't worry about Indie. She doesn't want to go back with you anyway."

"If I'm the lower-class scum, then why is your mother's drug dealer still going on about how she owed him money, huh? What'd that make *her*? Or *you*? You would've ended up just like her if you hadn't won the lottery—!" I was still staring at him, feeling like he'd just reached out and slapped me across my face, too stunned to speak when he suddenly stopped. His face was still red, veins flared in his neck, but the anger in his eyes melted away as footsteps creaked behind me.

"Kingston," David warned. "I think you've outstayed your welcome."

Kingston glanced back at me like he thought I would defend him, but I didn't, clenching my teeth together and counting the seconds until he walked away and went around the house.

David sighed. "He left his brownies."

I nodded, not meeting his eyes.

"They weren't good. You know what he did to them?"

"They're vegan."

"Your mom used to make really good brownies. From a box, but she would add things to make it taste better. Weird things, like maple syrup or condensed milk, but they always tasted good." He took the fork out of the foil pan Kingston left, the brownies missing only a couple squares, and tossed the rest into the garbage can. "Amy's going to be mad I did that. She hates wasting food."

"Amy told me you wanted custody," I said quietly. "That you

wanted me this whole time, but if that's true, then I don't get why you wouldn't pay child support. It doesn't make sense, not after everything you've bought me in, like, the month I've been here."

He paused. "Bronwyn, this might not be the time to talk about that."

"Right, we have company. Got it."

"It's not that. I think we should talk about this when you're not upset. We can talk in the morning if you'd like."

I wondered if that was to give him time to think of another excuse, but I mumbled *sure*, anyway, smoothing my hands under my eyes before leaving the patio. Instead of going back to the campfire, I picked up the scattered horseshoes and tethered golf balls in the grass.

A moment later, I looked over my shoulder and noticed David cleaning up, too, grabbing the cornhole boards and bringing them to the shed.

o

I slipped my feet in the lake after gathering all the pieces of the lawn games and shoving them back into the shed, watching in the moonlight as the ripples spread out from my ankles with peepers chirping around me. Then exaggerated grunting noises silenced them as Ethan plopped down beside me. The dock swayed and then settled under his weight as he kicked off his shoes.

"Kingston's truck is gone," he stated, dropping his feet into the water.

"I told him to leave."

"How come?"

I gave him a look. "Don't pretend like you liked him. No one did."

"You did," he pointed out, his voice soft.

"Not anymore," I replied. "I'm sorry about what he said before. You're not better than everyone else. Except, you are. But not because you're rich. You're passionate, you talk to everyone in the room, you take Monroe . . ."

"Okay, you didn't send him home because of what he said back there, did you? Because I don't care about—"

"Yes, you do, and so do I. But no, I told him to leave because we got into a fight. He was . . . suffocating me. And you were right. He's too old. Like, we started talking about private school again and he said I would look cute in high school uniform. I thought, that doesn't sound right. Something like that shouldn't turn him on. Am I crazy for thinking that?"

"Not if you don't want him to."

"I don't. So, whatever we were is over now and he said my mom was lower-class scum who died owing her drug dealer money and I would've ended up like her if I hadn't *won the lottery*, so I told him to leave."

It was quiet again as I stared down at my ankles in the water, swirling around in the water beside his, still. The only piece of him I could see with my head tilted down. "You know what he said about your mom wasn't true, though, right?

"Oh, I know. And I also know she didn't owe her dealer money. She was sober when she died, and I know this because I used my college savings to pay off her debt."

"You paid her dealer with your college savings?"

"Back in April before she died, she woke me up in the middle of the night and told me she needed money. I was angry, but I did it."

I focused on the chirping of the peepers resuming in the grass near the shore instead of wondering what he thought about that as I brought my knees up to my chest, his profile staring out over the water for a moment. "Where were you going to go? Like, what schools were you thinking of?"

"That's your response? Where I wanted to go to school?"

"She's your mom," he replied. "It sucks, and you shouldn't have had to do it, but I get it. She's your mom."

"I don't know where I wanted to go. All I wanted was to get out of Shiloh. Didn't think about where I would go or even what I would do."

He leaned back against the warped wooden boards. "Well, you could—"

"So, it looked like you and Indie got along tonight," I blurted out.

"Yeah, she's nice. Said she liked my shirt."

"Well, now she's going to need a new ride home." I paused, watching to see if he smiled or if his eyes brightened when he realized what I was implying. Instead, he stared expectantly at me. "How about you give her one?"

"Like, tonight?"

"Or tomorrow. But it would be a good way to spend some more time with her . . ." I let my sentence trail off, not sure if that was because it sounded more suggestive or because then all the blanks were left unfilled.

Ethan frowned. "You want me to spend more time with her?"

I shrugged, feigning indifference. "It doesn't matter to me. It just looked like the two of you were getting along, and—I mean, if you liked her then I wondered if you wanted to take her home."

"You think I like Indie?"

"I don't know! Who wouldn't like her? She's cute, adorable,

smells like cinnamon. It's everything you could ever want in a girl."

His befuddled frown turned into a slight smile as he shook his head. "You know, for someone who says big words like *Herculean*, you can be a little clueless sometimes."

"About what?" When he didn't answer, I shoved his shoulder with my hand. "About what?"

"I don't like Indie like that," he answered after a moment.

"So, what am I clueless about?"

"You're clueless in many ways. Like how you don't like root beer floats."

I pointed a finger at him. "You're deflecting! Are you lying about Indie? Are you saying that because you think I'll get weird about it?"

He raised his eyebrows, hoisting himself on his elbows. "Why would you get weird about it?"

"I wouldn't," I retorted after hesitating when everything in me felt twisted tight and exposed. "*You're* the one who'd probably get weird about it."

"*I* wouldn't."

"Well, if neither of us is weird about it then go offer to take her home."

"Maybe I will."

"Go do it then. She's on the patio."

He considered this for a moment before leaning his head against the dock, grimacing at the soft *thud*. "Nah, she'd probably get weird about it."

A disconcerting surge of relief come over me before I pushed it away. I didn't have a reason to feel relieved he'd backed out. Still, I leaned back against my hands and stared out at the pine trees so distant in the darkness across the lake, they almost blended in with the sky.

"Wait, if you paid off her drug dealer, why would Kingston say she owes him money?"

"I think he wants more. I'm betting he heard about who my biological father is and how much money *he* has." I shifted toward him. "You know what I thought the other day?"

He groaned. "All your bad ideas start this way."

I gestured for him to sit up. "No, come on. Just hear me out. Okay, so I thought maybe . . . maybe David and Amy hired someone to kill my mom."

He was expressionless until it occurred to him I was being serious. "I was right."

"It's the only thing that makes sense! I've been thinking ever since I got here how weird it is that, all of a sudden, they're super involved. Like, how does that make sense after basically ignoring me all those years? It doesn't unless they wanted me this whole time like they said."

"How does any of that mean they wanted to kill your mom?"

"Because she'd kept them from me. With her out of the way, I had to come live with them."

He rested his elbows on his knees, still frowning. "There are easier, more legal ways to do that than to hire a hitman."

"Yeah, Amy told me they wanted custody, but they didn't think she would listen. She said my mom was the one who shoved them away, not the other way around. Andi and Jason said the same thing."

"Except I didn't say they killed your mom."

I turned, startled by the cold sound of her voice and as soon as I heard it, everything inside me froze. Her hands were down at her sides, clutching a bag of marshmallows, her hair getting caught in her lip gloss as she glared at me but there was something else underneath that made me blurt out her name. "Andi—"

But she stormed back toward the house before I could get anything else out, slamming one of the patio doors behind her so hard it popped back open.

o

I slept on the sectional couch in the entertainment room that night. Indie slept on the other sectional and now, hours later, was softly snoring into one of the couch cushions. I must have fallen asleep at some point, this restlessness now becoming a habit. But once the birds started chirping outside, I quietly hoisted myself up from the couch.

I shuffled out of the entertainment room and through the hallway, hesitating when I saw David in the dining room. He was sitting at the head of the table, his phone in one hand and half a rainbow bagel with cream cheese in the other. He was dressed, but more casually than he should've been before work, adorned in a weathered T-shirt from Old Navy for the Fourth of July, still a couple of days away. Papers were on the table as he glanced up.

"There you are." He gestured to a chair, and I wondered if Andi mentioned what she overheard me telling Ethan last night. "I was wondering when you'd wake up. Bagel? I think Andi bought them yesterday for an Instagram picture or something."

I paused, still in the door frame. "You're not at work."

He nodded. "I called the office early this morning and told them I wouldn't be coming in today. I wanted to talk to you, like I said last night."

"Wait, you were going to do that? I thought you were trying to brush me off."

"No, I meant what I said about not wanting to upset you further. And I wanted time to find documents to prove what I'm about to tell you."

I cautiously walked over and pulled out a chair. "Tell me what?"

Instead of responding, he handed me one of the papers. It was a bank statement, a transfer from one account I didn't recognize to one that I did. My mom's. The amount was for five thousand dollars, then he handed me another bank statement for the following month with another five thousand dollars transferred.

"This is a file of every transfer I made to your mother's bank account every month on the first. It wasn't court ordered, so I can't technically prove it was for child support, but that was its intended purpose."

Some of the pages inside the file were older, tinged a different color the further back I went. Even the style of the bank statements changed sometime in 2015, but the account numbers remained the same. "Is this real? Because she said you never paid. *You* said it."

"When you mentioned what your mother had told you, it, well ... I didn't want to hurt your opinion of your mom. And considering the struggles she had, it didn't take long for me to figure out where she was probably spending the money."

I set down the file. "You think she used it on drugs."

"Not all of it. But a good portion. Cigarettes if she still smoked."

I nodded. "She did."

"I'm sorry. When I realized that's what you thought, Amy and I decided to keep the truth from you. We hoped that eventually, in time, we'd be able to make amends and you'd forgive us. We wanted to protect your memory of your mom."

Every word my mother had said about my biological father, told to me like he was the dragon in the middle of the sunlit path to happily ever after, was a word I believed. I clung to them. They were all I had. But now there were other pieces, other paths, other dragons. And my mother was one of them.

"Were you really separated when you guys went out, or was it an affair like she said?"

"Amy and I were separated at the time. Between my career and two young children, our relationship was strained. Amy felt like she'd sacrificed more for our family than I did."

"Was she right?"

"If that was how she felt, but at the time, I didn't agree. I was putting in fewer hours, leaving work earlier than my supervisors liked. At the time, I was a lawyer. And Amy and I had always talked about how I needed to invest this time into my career. It was our plan, but after Andi was born . . . well, family and work got harder to manage." David sighed, taking another bite of his bagel, gesturing to the folded paper bag across from me. "There's more in there if you want some. Anyway, we separated, and I rented an apartment near Shiloh. I met your mom while she was waitressing at this diner in town. I'm not even sure if it's still there, but they had a great Dutch apple pie."

"And you came in late, and she wanted you to leave."

He laughed under his breath. "It was open twenty-four hours, but I guess I was her last table and she had to wait until I left. And she told me as much when I'd asked if she wanted me to go; she didn't even think about it. *Yeah, I do.*"

For the first time, I was hearing how they'd met from his side.

The weathered details sounded just the same, except softer and more nostalgic rather than bitter and resentful, like my mom had spun it. It also made me realize there was truth in her side too.

"Your mom was fun. She made me feel fun. I was in my thirties, but I felt like my life was over already. I'm not proud of it, but being with your mom for those few months was so freeing to me. I still look back on them fondly."

"But you didn't stay with her."

"No, I didn't. I had a family. I was still involved, and eventually Amy and I talked about ending our separation. We still loved each other, and I started to miss our life together. Which was when things started to unravel between your mom and me. Fun is fun for about three months, then you feel like you lost control of your life."

"Getting another girl pregnant tends to do that."

"Actually, your mother told me she was pregnant about three weeks after I moved back home," David said. "Told me the pill wasn't effective, and she was going to have you. She was very . . . *upset* when we broke up, so I think if she knew then, she would've brought it up."

I looked at him, taking in the face he made when mentioning her birth control. "You don't think she was actually on the pill."

He hesitated. "Your mother was lonely. And she knew I was married with kids, so even if we did get divorced like she wanted, they would still be in my life. I can't prove it, but I don't think you were that much of an accident."

"Did you ever ask her to get an abortion?"

"No, but I was scared. I didn't know what it would mean for my marriage or what my family would think. Truthfully . . . it was hard, although that's not something I blame you for. It was our decisions that brought you here and every decision we made after was in your best interest."

I raised an eyebrow. "You sure?"

"I don't think your mother expected Amy and me to stay together after she got pregnant," he said sheepishly. "When she realized we weren't going to divorce, she felt threatened. We were a prominent family with old money and a lot to offer you. She was afraid of losing you, which we never wanted. But, after you were born, we never heard from her. And we didn't want to lose you, either, so when you both came to Andi's birthday party, we *talked*."

"Amy said you wanted shared custody."

"Yes. We just wanted to see you. But Donna got angry and left. We considered pursuing it legally, but you were six. You didn't know us and we didn't want to drag you into what we believed would be a bitter custody battle. Your mom probably wouldn't have listened anyway."

"Did you know she was on drugs?"

He shook his head. "No. Not until you got here a few weeks ago. To be honest, I thought things were better for you than they actually were. I didn't know she wasn't working anymore, or that you were living in a trailer. The address she gave me was a PO Box number."

I thought back to the bright pink envelope near her purse that summer afternoon as she dyed her hair over the sink, the letters Andi said she'd mailed but that I never saw. I waited at the mailbox every morning before school, but all I ever found were bills and advertisements.

Because the letters and invitations had all gone to a PO Box she'd never told me about.

"Why didn't you fight harder to see me? I mean, you're a senator. If you'd wanted to, you could've."

David sighed, staring down at the half-eaten bagel on his plate before he answered. "A lot of it had to do with the pressure from my career choice, truthfully. The scandal it would've caused, and how that would've affected everyone, including you. But I shouldn't have let those things, or anything else, keep me from seeing you. I should've fought harder, and I'm sorry I didn't."

I looked down at the papers on the table, still confused. "Okay."

"Have a look over these papers. There are more bank statements, some papers from the insurance company since we put you under our policy. And, enjoy some bagels. Did you notice they're blue?"

"They're supposed to be rainbow."

"Where?" he asked, frowning as he tilted it over then smiled. "*Oh*, I see now. Hey, that's pretty neat. Okay, I'll leave you to it, and if there's anything in here you want to talk about, I'm going to be outside."

I grabbed one of the folders as he went outside. I was still looking through it when he dragged a rototiller out from the shed and started churning up the lawn.

o

Since the previous night, I had barely seen Andi, catching a glimpse of her hair while she successfully dodged me and snuck into her filming room after Danny brought in a couple of PR packages from Benefit off the porch. She seemed so focused on ignoring me I slept in the entertainment room again, and when Amy found me and asked why I wasn't sleeping in my room, I lied and said I'd fallen asleep watching a movie.

Her ignoring me also meant that on Tuesday night, when it was time for my shift, I walked outside to find she'd already left without me. I knew I couldn't ask Amy for a ride without her questioning why Andi would leave me behind, so I walked over to the Denvers', hoping Ethan wouldn't be as upset with me as she was. Not that he had a reason to be, but I still found myself worried anyway, when he answered the door and said, "*Hush.*"

Which turned out to be the name of the first horror feature tonight.

"I think Andi must have told him," I explained later, while we watched *Hush* in the corner, after telling him David was starting a vegetable garden for me. "Not only is it a bribe, but he's trying to coax me into thinking, *how could he kill my mom if he's making a vegetable garden for me*?"

"Well, you did want one."

"That's why it's suspicious. Before I accuse him of murder, he's at work all the time. After? Suddenly he's at home, making me a garden. Does that make sense to you? Summer's half over; I'll be gone before anything's ready to harvest."

"So, grow radishes. Stuff that only takes a month." He held out his bag of popcorn. "Do you believe him about the child support?"

"Yes. He has paperwork with my mom's account number on it. And it makes my theory work even better. Maybe David found out she was spending the money on drugs and killed her for it?"

"Yeah, but—and hear me out on this—if he knew your mom was on drugs, it would've made more sense to take her to court and get full custody with *no* legal repercussions than hire some-one, who could implicate them later, to kill her."

"Maybe you're biased," I suggested.

He gave me a look. "And maybe *you* are trying to find new ways to hate Amy and David now that the old ones don't make sense anymore."

"I'm doing it because it makes sense, not because I'm bitter."

"But you *are* bitter, that's the thing. And you're not wrong for feeling that way, but if you want to do something about this, then I think you should make sure you're doing it for the right reasons."

"So, you don't think I'm right."

Ethan sighed. "I think you need more than a hunch to convict someone of murder."

I turned away from him and looked back over at the screen. "Why is *Hush* so great?" I asked after a moment. "Unleash the can of worms."

"Okay, so the Final Girl is Maddie, deaf as you can tell, and the film is a take on the classic home invasion trope. Maddie's a writer so she goes through all these scenarios in her mind to defeat the assailant credited as The Man. And did you know *Hush* was written by a husband and wife—the wife's Maddie, by the way—who tested out ways to break into a house by trying to break into theirs?"

I took another handful of his popcorn. "You sound jealous."

He swatted a firefly from his ear. "Yeah, for whatever reason, whenever I try to break into a house on a first date, the police are always called."

o

When I walked into the concession stand after the intermission, Taylor-Elise was hoisting herself onto the counter again with a lighter in her hand for the thermostat. There were a couple of customers still in the restaurant, probably waiting for their orders to come out of the fryer, a few preteen girls trying to cram themselves into the photo booth in the corner. I hesitated near the doors as Ethan reached for his wallet and Cass held up her hand. "I already know your order, Ethan."

Andi was near the popcorn machine, using the collar of her shirt to fan herself as she stared at the shifting curtain of the photo booth before realizing I was there.

She didn't look at me for more than a second before turning around and heading for the kitchen, but before I realized what I was doing, I was following her. "Andi, will you just wait a second? Please?"

"Don't think so."

"Wait, what's going on?" Cass asked, handing Ethan his change.

"They're fighting," Taylor-Elise filled in, waving the lighter in front of the thermostat.

"No, we're not *fighting*," Andi corrected. "She didn't just steal my clothes or something. She accused my parents of murder."

Cass blinked, her mouth falling agape. Taylor-Elise, on the other hand, didn't look as surprised as she continued manipulating the air conditioning unit.

"Look, can we just talk for a minute?" I asked her. "It's not like this is easy—"

She shook her head, interrupting me. "No, no, okay, don't say this isn't easy for you, because truthfully, it came a little *too* easy to you. Ever since you got here, you acted like just because you grew up poor it gave you some sort of character. Made you better than all these rich snobs who have only ever tried to give you *everything*!"

"Okay, well, maybe I'm not materialistic like you," I retorted. "All you've ever cared about was stuff. You have a million subscribers watching you review makeup no one else can afford!"

Ethan leaned over. "Is this how you're trying to get her to forgive you?"

"You're so . . . *narrow-minded*! My parents didn't just buy you stuff, they gave you somewhere to live when all you had was a broken-down, rusted old trailer, and that was before the tornado hit it! My mom got you a therapist for when we go home, she enrolled you in private school, and Dad has been making you a freaking vegetable garden because you wanted one!"

"That's just more stuff, more money thrown at everything like that makes it all better—"

She laughed sardonically. "Seriously? *You're* the one who's so hung up on money."

"Because I never had any! You're, like, numb to it. You don't even care."

"*We* don't care? We do all of those things for *you*! To make you happy, but you're the one who never cares. When your mom died, I gave you my bed so you didn't have to sleep on the floor. When you blew off work to get drunk with Kingston, I covered for you with Sheila and Hank. Jason and Kimberly have been scrambling to find something for you at their wedding so you don't feel left out. And all of this, literally everything we've done since you got here, was such a waste because it didn't matter to you at all."

I was quiet for a moment, a tightness building in my chest.

"And the fact you think my parents would kill someone to have an ungrateful brat like you, that's honestly one of the most laughable things I've ever heard—"

She quickly clamped her mouth shut when the cook, a middle-aged man named Wayne I usually never saw, stepped out from the kitchen with his sweating brow furrowed. "What's with all the shouting?" he asked, pointing his spatula out at the few customers in booths waiting for their orders, trying not to stare. "We've got customers in here."

"Sorry," Andi and I murmured, though not to each other.

○

The next afternoon, I was alone in the kitchen with Miles while I picked off pieces of my turkey club sandwich to toss onto the floor when the door to the garage opened and David stepped inside. His briefcase was in one hand, his suit jacket draped over the same arm. He was also home about three hours earlier than usual.

"Hey," he said, glancing down at Miles licking the tiles. "Do you have a second? There was something I wanted to talk to you about."

I paused, another piece of turkey between my fingers. "Did the detective call you?"

"No, it's not about that. Also, don't feed him too much turkey or he'll throw it up," he warned, placing his briefcase down on a bar stool. "How are you holding up, with everything going on in the media?"

"It's fine," I told him. I wasn't answering phone calls from unknown numbers anymore, like Jason told me, and I usually just deleted the text messages without reading them. I was still getting tagged in posts and getting emails, but since it had been a couple of weeks and there was no new information—for them or us—it was starting to let up.

"We could get your number changed."

I shook my head. "I don't want to change it."

"Okay. Just remember, don't respond to anything, even the condolences. Did Deshaun talk to you about social media?"

"Yes, and I barely even use it anyway. I haven't posted anything since the tornado. And *no*, I don't read my DMs and turned all the comments off the old posts."

He smoothed a hand over the dark stubble over his cheeks. "Perhaps you could rub off some of that cooperation on Andi. She's still refusing to turn the comments off on her videos," he said, and I pulled off another piece of my turkey just to have something to do with my fingers. He had to know what those comments said about him.

"Speaking of Andi, she told us about this theory you have . . . about us hiring someone to kill your mother?"

I felt myself paling. "Look—"

"I'm not angry about it. Unlike Andi," he said. "I know how it looks, and you don't have much reason to trust me. I don't hold it against you for considering all the possibilities. It would be hard not to."

"So, what? That's what you think I'm worried about? That you'll be mad if you find out I *considered* you killing my mom?"

"No. I just wanted you to know that. I didn't kill your mom or ask anyone else to. Your mother and I had a complicated relationship, but we would never hurt you like that just to get custody."

"Okay."

"You can be honest with me, Bronwyn," he sighed. "You can tell me what you're thinking or feeling about all this. You don't have to keep it from me. I am your dad. You might not feel like it because you've only had your mom until now, but I am your father and I love you."

I held back the snort I felt bubbling in my throat, born out of the disbelief I was hearing this from *him*. One second, he empathetically informed me he understood why I couldn't trust him, then wanted me to be the kind of honest with him I couldn't even be with my mom.

"You don't get it, do you? You're not my dad. Okay, you might be one half of the biological reason for my existence but you're not my dad. You're not someone I can come to about *stuff*. You're just this guy who got my mom pregnant and left. And it doesn't matter if that was my mom's fault. You never even *tried* to be my dad, ever."

David was quiet for a moment, only the sound of Miles licking the tiles filling the room. "I know," he finally murmured.

I shook my head. "Will you stop saying you know? You *don't*. You don't know anything, and you don't know me! Ugh," I groaned, turning away from him. My nerves felt tight like my chest, but something was slipping out of my grasp. "You know what I know? Not you. You just . . . the only way I could ever see you was on TV. I would read magazines at the checkout in grocery stores when you were on the cover. Those were the only ways I knew you because . . . you weren't there. You were off with your perfect family in your perfect house living this perfect life. And it was perfect because I wasn't anywhere near it."

If he was offended or hurt, angered or saddened, I didn't know, I couldn't look up. This was why I kept everything buried, kept all those things close, because those feelings were something he could never see.

I took in a soft breath. "It is *so* disappointing to find out your dad can just live without you."

"Bronwyn," he said, his voice soft but . . . different. There was a fragility to it that almost made me glance up. "I am so sorry. I shouldn't have let it get to that point—"

"Stop putting all the blame on my mom," I mumbled.

"Okay," he murmured. "I am apologizing for the pain you've had in your life because of me and what I did or didn't do. And you should know I would never add to that by taking your mom away from you."

I didn't look up or answer; instead, I waited until he walked out of the room a moment later, then tightly squeezed my eyes closed.

CHAPTER SIXTEEN

I was stretched out over a beach towel, grains of sand scratching against my neck as I stared up at the sky, cloudless except for the tinge of smoke from the fireworks curling in the air. Starbright was closed on the Fourth of July because, according to Ethan, sales weren't that great when there were fireworks and drinking elsewhere. It was his idea to come to the beach that night with everyone, and I came with him early to help set up. Also, because he was my ride everywhere since Andi still wasn't speaking to me. Or driving me.

After summarizing my conversation with David, I said, "I don't know what to think."

"I think you do, but you don't like it, so you don't think it," Ethan replied.

"Well, Andi did say no one would kill to have an ungrateful brat like me," I mumbled.

"I wouldn't kill, but maybe I'd do a little jaywalking," Ethan teased, opening a package of red licorice and holding one out to me. "You know she said that because she was upset, right? Not because she thinks it."

"I think people tend to say a lot of things they mean when they're upset."

"*When* they're upset," he repeated. "If I believed everything you meant when you were upset, we wouldn't be friends."

I lifted my head. "Are you still mad about that?"

"No, because I considered how you were feeling when you said those things. Let a little forgiveness go a long way." I plopped my head back down on the towel. "Plus, you gave me a proper apology, which you didn't give Andi."

"I tried!"

"Calling her materialistic isn't trying."

"Well, was I wrong?"

"At that moment, yeah, you were."

I hated that he was right, but it wasn't like Andi was just hanging around the lake house, waiting for the moment I admitted that to her. She was spending more time at Taylor-Elise's, completely ignoring me. And Amy made me stop sleeping in the entertainment room. Most nights, Andi didn't even come into the room until I fell asleep. And I was fine with that. I was pretty used to Andi Soliday ignoring me.

I rolled onto my stomach, wanting to change the subject. "So, if your parents keep going back to Niagara Falls all the time, why even bother with a summer home in Shelridge for, like, the two weekends they're here?"

Ethan shrugged. "They own both houses so it doesn't cost them anything except gas. Plus, then we're out of their hair for most of the summer and Taylor-Elise gets to see Andi. That's probably one of the biggest reasons we still come up."

"So, they only see each other in the summer?" I asked, my voice sounding more hesitant than I wanted it to so I took a bite of my licorice, like that somehow made me look more nonchalant.

"I wouldn't say that, but it's not as often. They usually plan something for birthdays, sometimes holidays or spring break, but three hours is a long way to just hang out."

"One way?"

He nodded, then tilted his head, as another isolated firework shot into the sky. "You're going to miss me," he grinned, reaching out to touch me with his licorice. I jerked my arm back.

"I won't. I'm relishing how I'm going to be three hours away from another Jordan Peele fun-fact explosion."

Ethan was quiet, the dimple carved into one cheek as I reached for the bag of Sour Patch Kids he brought. I was chewing when my phone vibrated in my back pocket.

Adelaide's white shirt gets progressively bloodier throughout the film, foreshadowing the plot twist at the end.

"Just because you can't see me in person doesn't mean you'll be free of Jordan Peele fun facts," he said.

I responded to his texts with an onslaught of rabbit emojis, noticing as his face broke out into a grin. Then, to keep it there, I typed:

run run run.

"I think this is just proof *you're* going to miss *me*."

"Absolutely not," he said distractedly, texting me the teacup emoji now. "I am going to be . . ."

If he had a conclusion for his trailed-off sentence, it was forgotten when headlights beamed across the sand beside our towels.

He waved a hand at Cass's car, saying to me, "In a moment, I'm going to need you to remember how much you're going to miss me when the summer's over."

"What?"

Car doors slammed behind me, metal scraping against the asphalt while I eyed him skeptically before turning around. Andi was in the parking lot, grasping a folded lawn chair in one hand, the skirt of her sundress fluttering around her knees as she stared at me.

Ethan leaned over, whispering, "I might have told her you weren't going to be here."

I shrugged as she turned to Taylor-Elise getting out of the car. "I don't care. She's the one with a problem."

He grabbed another licorice piece, prodding my nose with it until I tried to take a bite, but he pulled it back too quickly. "Now look, this took some planning, and if you ruin it with your big mouth, *this* is going up your nose."

"What planning?" I asked. "What are you talking about?"

He hit me on the head with the licorice. "Did you think I just randomly decided to host a Fourth of July party for no reason? Taylor-Elise and I planned this because you're both hopeless."

I glanced at Andi, who had since abandoned the lawn chair against one of the tires, her arms crossed with a crease between her brows as she spoke to Taylor-Elise. "Why do you care so much if Andi and I are talking?" I asked him, annoyed.

"You remember how much of a weepy drunk you are?"

"No, I remember nothing."

"Liar, you do. You told me you weren't okay with being on your own. And I told you at the pool I wasn't okay with you being on your own either. But . . . you're going to be when summer's over if you leave things like this."

"So, you've been thinking about summer ending."

Ethan was quiet for a moment, then admitted, "Yeah." His voice sounded different. "I don't think you believe Amy and David had your mom killed. You're trying to push them and everyone else away because then you can't get hurt again."

"I don't like how you're making it sound like I'm emotional about this when I'm not. They have an actual motive, which is more than I can say for anyone else," I said.

"I'm sorry. But do you really think they could've done something like that? Even if it was to get you back in their lives? You have to know there are so many other *better* options."

I didn't say anything.

"And if you want to be logical about it, then be logical. Your mom was strangled, and that's a personal way of killing someone. If they hired someone, they would've shot her, not strangled. Did Amy and David have alibis?"

"Yes," I mumbled reluctantly. "They cleared them with Detective Marsh at the beginning of the investigation when they did mine."

"So, maybe you need to consider alternative suspects."

I sighed. "But I can't think of anyone else who would want my mom dead. When the police asked me, I was like, *I don't know. My mom never* did *anything. Except drugs, I guess.*"

"What if that's it? I'm not saying she wasn't still sober, but I don't know. Maybe when her dealer got the college savings from your mom, he thought he could get more money from her? He could've tried to rob you guys and she surprised him."

I hoisted myself up. "Kingston said he saw Jude at home before the tornado hit." It hadn't struck me as odd when he mentioned it after her funeral, since he usually came over after I left for school since he was unemployed and on disability after injuring his back working construction. But what if that was just another lie? She'd never said how they'd met but told me the story of how she'd met David regularly like some sort of cautionary tale. Jude had been acting distant since she died. He didn't want to help plan her funeral and was practically forced to sit up front for the service.

And he was at that party last month.

Jude wasn't someone who went to parties. He smoked, lounged on the couch, drank a couple of beers without getting drunk, and guessed the answers to game show questions and called it a good time. I knew he couldn't have been there long, either, otherwise I would've seen him before I went upstairs with Kingston.

"Ethan," I said. "Do you think he could've—"

I was interrupted when lawn chairs clattering together were dropped into the sand beside me. Andi's expression was still perturbed, and she was farther away from the beach towels than the others, but at least she'd left the parking lot.

"All right," Ryan declared, grabbing a lighter with a grin. "I'm ready to play with fire."

"Ryan, no—"

o

Even though she might have been talked into staying, Andi kept to herself, as if she were just waiting for the moment she could stand up and trudge through the sand back to Cass's car. She ignored most of the conversation, stared at her phone, and hadn't looked at me once since sitting down. I pretended I hadn't noticed, eating cinnamon gummy bears and wondering if texting Ethan about Jude would be weird in front of everyone.

While we were still waiting for the fireworks across the lake, Ginny suggested we go swimming, which was met with immediate approval from Ryan, who tossed off his shirt at the mention. Andi lingered behind as I shrugged off my shorts, grateful I was wearing a swimsuit this time, telling myself if she didn't want to come, she didn't have to.

But there was a part of me that felt I was taking over. A month ago, it was me on the beach behind everyone else, not a part of this, the friendships constructed over a handful of summers. But now that was Andi, and these were *her* friends. It felt unfair, like I was shoving her out of her own life and forcing her to take my old place. And that wasn't what I wanted.

I stepped out of the water as Ethan and Ryan waded up to their waists, complaining about the sharp rocks under their feet, and I decided I would text him later. Orchestrating this was nice—but it wasn't going to work if Andi edged herself out. But I made it only a couple of steps up the beach before someone called out from the water.

"You're not leaving, are you?"

I looked over, surprised to see it was Taylor-Elise, ankle-deep in the lake. "Ethan told me Andi came only because he said I wasn't going to be here," I said.

"Yeah, but she didn't leave."

"You mean that little beach chair she's been sitting in all night?" I asked, noting her frown when she saw Andi was still there by the coolers. "I can walk back. I know the way."

She trudged out of the water. "You can't leave. The fireworks haven't even started yet. And Andi is still going to mope around whether you're here or not."

"Look, you guys are her friends," I said. "She came here to

hang out with you, not sit on the sidelines the whole night. And I don't mind being by myself. She does."

"Okay, but how about instead of leaving, you just go talk to her?"

"She doesn't want to talk to me."

"Ugh, you're both being freakishly stubborn right now," Taylor-Elise groaned, clenching her hands. "When you were younger, both of you wanted to be sisters but it was your parents who got in the way. Now it's your own pride doing that. And that you're both a little emotionally stunted."

"When we were kids—"

"When you were kids, she wrote you letters all the time. When we met, she told me she had this secret sister and we made up all these lives for you to explain where you were. A boarding school in Sweden, undercover in California. Even though she knew you lived just a couple hours away."

"Just because she did that when she was a kid doesn't mean anything now. When I got here, she—"

"Still had the birthday present you gave her."

"What?"

"The mystery bag? She opened it after you left. It had one of those eyeshadow palettes for kids. She hit pan on most of the shades, but she still has it at home. It's how she started getting into makeup."

A firework screeched as it exploded down the beach, popping and crackling, something sinking in my chest like the embers into the water. *We do all of those things for you*, she'd shouted at me a couple of days ago.

"Whatever's happening with your parents, it doesn't have anything to do with her," Taylor-Elise went on. "I'm Andi's best friend, I want her to be happy, and right now neither of you are happy."

"Which was why I was trying to leave," I pointed out.

"Maybe you should stop trying to leave and learn how to stay."

"At a Fourth of July beach party?"

Taylor-Elise gave me a look. "You mean the one my brother basically planned for you?"

There was a knowing glint in her familiar green eyes that made me turn away, grateful it was dark enough she couldn't see the warmth I felt in my cheeks at the thought of it being put like *that*. "She's been happy before without me, you know that."

"Oh my gosh. Do you need to be smacked over the head that people *care* about you?" she groaned. "I know we're not close *friends*, but you matter to Ethan and you matter to Andi whether either of you admits it, so you matter to me too!" She paused, letting out a breath. "Sorry, I'm yelling but I'm just frustrated. You're frustrating me."

"I don't mean to."

"I don't think that's entirely true, but whatever. Point is, even if I'm frustrated with you or Andi's angry with you, we're still here, you know? We're not going anywhere, and it would be nice if we could stop running after you all the time."

We were interrupted a second later by the chiming of electronic bells as an actual ice cream truck pulled into the parking lot, pastel pink paint gleaming under the streetlights and multicolored sprinkles decorating the rubber wheels. It took me a moment to realize it was decorated like an oversized strawberry ice cream cone.

"Is that a real ice cream truck, or an abduction waiting to happen?" I asked.

"It's a real ice cream truck," she answered, walking over to where our clothes were scattered in the sand around the coolers. "Having a real one makes the abductions go smoother."

I smiled, just for a second, then spotted Andi looking behind her at the ice cream truck, a window opening. I followed Taylor-Elise over to the towels, rifling through my pockets on the ground for my wallet.

"Come on," I said, somewhat hesitantly even though I was trying to sound normal. "We should get some ice cream." Andi turned her phone back on, ignoring me. "It's an actual ice cream truck," I added, and when she continued scrolling through Instagram instead of acknowledging me, I stifled a sigh. "I've never seen one before. We don't have any in Shiloh. They're practically an urban legend."

"Are you going to blame growing up in some podunk town on my parents too?"

Taylor-Elise grabbed one of the shirts from off the ground and whipped it at the back of Andi's head. "Get up, Andrea."

"Ow, what the—you could've got sand in my eye!"

"We're getting ice cream," she snapped. "End of discussion."

The others came in from the water and went searching through their clothes for their wallets. Then Andi stood up and followed Taylor-Elise to the ice cream truck, looking over her shoulder once to see if I was following.

"I'm not sure this is what I ordered," Ryan announced a few minutes later, after purchasing a Teenage Mutant Ninja Turtles ice cream popsicle. The turtle looked to be slanted on the stick, the blue smile unevenly centered on a frostbitten face. Andi was beside him with a rocket pop. She was trying to look casual, but I knew she was trying to get a picture of herself with the themed popsicle for her Instagram. Normally, Taylor-Elise took the photos for her, but she was at the window, taking longer than I anticipated to choose between an ice cream sandwich and a rocket pop.

I already knew I wanted a chocolate taco, so I stepped out of line. Andi was frowning at her phone when I held my hand out, eyeing me skeptically. "I'm not giving you my popsicle."

"I don't want your rocket pop," I said. "I want a Choco Taco, but I know how you feel about the selfie camera quality."

Andi hesitated, then reluctantly handed her phone to me. "I want to get the lake in the picture," she instructed me, posing with her back to the beach before she stopped. "Actually, I want both the beach and the ice cream truck in the picture."

"Turn that way then."

She did. "Okay, let me see," she said after I took a couple of shots.

I gave her phone back to her, watching quietly as she scrolled through the pictures. In the background of one, I noticed Taylor-Elise glancing over her shoulder, finally receiving an ice cream sandwich.

"I'm sorry I called you materialistic," I murmured while she scrolled, pausing midswipe without looking up. "I shouldn't have done that when I was trying to apologize, or . . . at least, talk."

"About you accusing my parents of killing your mom?" she asked. Her biting tone was back, and I realized it wasn't there a moment earlier.

"Well, yeah. I didn't want you to find out that way. And I get it, they're your parents. You—"

"But that's the thing, Bronwyn. They're not just *my* parents. They're yours too," she said, adjusting her grip around the popsicle stick as melting blue raspberry started to drip. "And that doesn't mean anything to you. You'd rather be alone, so fine, you get your wish."

"But what I said about Amy and David has nothing to do with that. For weeks, they talked about how my mom kept me away from them. Can't you see how that would look to me?"

She sighed. "Do you still think they did it?"

I thought of Jude for a moment, his car at our trailer before the tornado struck. Then shrugged as the ice cream truck's jingle sounded again. "I'm not sure," I admitted. "It's just—I want . . . I want to know what happened to my mom."

Not knowing who killed my mom was killing me. And I couldn't say that out loud because I didn't know what would happen after. But I still wanted her to know it.

"Yeah," she mumbled softly.

I wasn't sure what that meant—yeah, as in she understood what I meant, or yeah, she was trying to end this conversation—but then the engine for the ice cream truck rumbled again. I glanced over my shoulder as it pulled out of the parking lot, and when I turned back Andi was halfway down the beach.

Sighing, I started to walk away when I felt something strikingly cold against the back of my neck. I gasped, turning to see Ethan behind me, holding out a chocolate taco.

"Eavesdropper," I scolded, taking it from him.

"*Proud* eavesdropper," he corrected, his gaze warm and his dimple exposed. It felt good and awkward at the same time, so I was grateful when a red-and-blue firework exploded over the lake, the cascading sparks dripping down and mirrored in the undulating waves. As the fireworks show finally started, I noticed Ryan was sitting with Andi on her beach chair, his legs stretched out over hers.

Pointing to them, I whispered, "I think they like each other."

Ethan was closer than I thought, my arm brushing against his as I dropped it back down to my side. "He definitely likes her. A couple of summers ago, he pulled a bunch of pranks at Starbright and canceled a date she had with this guy, Dennis, over the phone, pretending to be him."

"Does she know?"

"Oh yeah. Dennis still showed up for their date and she figured out what Ryan had tried to do, so she had Dennis call Sheila at Starbright, pretending to be Ryan's dad, asking he have *special consideration* at work after surgery on his *abnormally sized* hemorrhoids. It's why we have the hoverboard."

I grinned. "Did she *really*?"

"She did. Sheila gave him baby wipes and put up signs in the bathroom for *rectal health*, gave him a tube of *Preparation H*, saying it worked wonders. And whenever Ryan tried to deny he had hemorrhoids, Sheila would tell him stories about hers and that he had nothing to be embarrassed about," he laughed. "It started a bit of a prank war between them, which Hank put a stop to in August after a tampered batch of popcorn was accidentally handed out at intermission."

Fireworks split into the air and rained down multicolored sparks over the stars. "So, since Andi still isn't really speaking to me, do you think you could drive me back to Shiloh?"

He looked hesitant. "Why?"

"I want to talk to Jude, you know, my mom's boyfriend with the stairs? I think he might have been her drug dealer."

o

The next morning, while I waited for Ethan, I grabbed the radish seed packets Amy brought from the store and was going to plant them. I'd decided not to call or text Jude, knowing he'd tell me not to come, and I had some time to kill before we were leaving. Putting the seeds into the soil would calm my nerves. Not as satisfying as weeding, but at least it was something.

The patio doors opened and flip-flops frantically smacked against the grass before Danny barreled down the dock and cannonballed into the lake, with David leisurely following behind him and squinting without his sunglasses.

"Danny," David called out. "Take your sandals off. If you lose those in the lake again, it's coming out of your allowance."

I buried a couple of the seeds as Danny grabbed his soaked flip-flops and tossed them onto the dock.

"How's your garden coming?" David asked.

I nodded. "It's good. Big. Hope you like radishes."

"Well, I wanted it to be big enough for next summer when you have time to grow more vegetables. But yes, I do like radishes." He looked over to Danny running back up to the shore, wobbling barefoot on the pebbles where the water lapped against the ground. "Think you could use a hand?"

Even though Ethan had made a couple of valid points last night, I still felt reserved around him. Like, after almost seventeen years of living without him, I didn't know how to live *with* him. Especially now that I knew our situation wasn't his fault.

I didn't look at him as I held out a packet of icicle radish seeds. I focused on depositing my seeds as he read the back, then wandered over to the shed, grabbing a pair of dirtied gardening gloves from inside. We were quiet, only the sound of water splashing whenever Danny cannonballed. Then, after a few minutes, Ethan called my name across the yard.

"Is that you, Ethan?" David asked, holding his hand out over his eyes. "Hey, there. What can we do you for?"

Ethan was staring down at his phone in his other hand when David responded instead of me. His back straightened almost immediately, his head jerking, and he quickly stuck his phone in his pocket. "Hey, Mr. Soliday," he said, approaching us. "How are you, sir?"

Sir? I mouthed, then *straighten up, soldier*! Ethan glanced at me, then promptly ignored me.

"Good, good. How are you?"

"Good," he said, nodding.

David waited a moment, then asked, "Was there something you needed?"

"He's picking me up," I said when Ethan stalled. "We were going to go out."

"Go out?"

"Yeah," I said slowly.

"Where are you going?" he asked, speaking just as slowly.

"We were going to go visit Shiloh," I responded, which wasn't a total lie.

David nodded, his gaze lingering on Ethan. "So, how long has this been going on?"

"Has *what* been going on—*oh*, no. No, no, no," I said to him, shaking my head after Ethan cleared his throat when I was half-way through my first sentence. I had to focus hard on what I was saying to keep myself from stammering in front of them. "We're not *going out*. We're friends."

I wasn't sure if David looked convinced, but I knew hammering home the point too hard would look even worse. "Oh," he said skeptically. "Okay, then. Be home before ten, alrighty?"

I nodded and then realized he wasn't looking at me. He was still staring at Ethan.

"Okay, bye," I said, grabbing Ethan by the arm and pulling him away. When we were halfway across the backyard, I whispered to him. "What was that? Why were you acting so weird?"

"I wasn't weird."

I exaggeratedly stiffened my back. "Yes, sir. Good, sir. How are you, sir?"

"I only said sir once. It's respectful. Let me guess, where you come from, you greet your elders with a spit handshake."

"Don't forget the duet of duck-call imitations," I replied, reaching the pine trees separating the properties when I noticed through the windows of the Denvers' home that Andi was in their kitchen, peeling back the skin from a tangerine. She spotted us too and came around to the back door.

"Where are you going?"

"Shiloh."

"Are you running away again?"

"Worse. I'm going to confront my mom's drug dealer about his possible involvement in her murder."

Andi sighed. "Let me get my shoes."

"You're coming?" Ethan and I asked at the same time.

"Jinx!" I yelled before he could. "You owe me a soda."

She groaned. "I'm regretting it already."

"Actually," I said, pausing to look behind me. "Speaking of things we might regret . . ."

o

I was crammed in the middle seats of Ethan's car after Andi came back from the lake house with not just Natalie but Jason trailing behind her too. I wondered how much Andi had told him, since I'd suggested only bringing Natalie. She suppressed a grin when she climbed in between me and Andi, barely even arguing when Andi said she was sitting on her seat belt buckle.

I wasn't sure how good an idea this was, confronting my mother's potential drug dealer with a fourteen-year-old in the car, but after Andi and I had spent the Fourth of July at the beach, and she'd spent it with her parents and brothers, I started to feel guilty. She didn't even complain anymore or ask what we did, just looked disappointed whenever we left for our shifts. It reminded me too much of a version of myself waiting on the front porch for letters I was realizing weren't ever coming, and so, here we were.

We were about halfway there when Jason, in the passenger seat, turned around. "Natalie, put in your headphones, okay?"

Her eyes widened. "I'm not even doing anything!"

"Just put them in."

"I don't have any."

Jason looked at Andi. "Give her your AirPods."

She scrunched her nose. "No. What's your problem?"

"We have to talk. Will you just give them to her?"

"What's wrong with the air?" Taylor-Elise, who had also tagged along, called out from the back. "I can't hear anything back here."

"What do you have to talk about?" Natalie asked, glancing suspiciously at Andi. "What did you do?"

"Nothing," she snapped.

"I think she can hear this," I interjected, shrugging, which caused Jason to give me a look. "She's fourteen, not four."

Andi made an unconvinced noise in her throat.

"Shut up," Natalie grumbled. "Just tell me."

"She's going to find out when we get there," I said.

"Wait, what's going on?" Taylor-Elise asked, leaning forward.

Ethan looked in the rearview mirror. "Don't worry about it."

"Why did he say worry?"

"I said *don't worry about it*!" he shouted.

"Why are we worried?" Natalie cried out.

"Because we're going to meet my mom's drug dealer," I blurted out. "Except we're not worried because he's a pretty chill guy who used to be her boyfriend. I know him so it's fine. He practically lived with us."

It was quiet for a moment—probably still enough Taylor-Elise could've heard the turn signal chiming in the back—and Natalie grew pale, staring at the back of Ethan's headrest with widened eyes.

"Well, now she knows so you should just talk," I mumbled.

Jason sighed. "You shouldn't talk to him."

"I've known him since I was Natalie's age. He's not going to do anything. We're just going to have a normal conversation."

"Why can't you just tell the police about this?"

"I might, but I want to be sure first."

"Okay, say he's truthful with you—which I doubt—and then you're *sure*. Then what are you going to do?"

"I'll ask about what Kingston said about him being at the trailer the day my mom died."

Natalie turned to me. "He's a *murdering* drug dealer?"

I scrunched my nose. "I meant to leave that part out."

"Wait, do you really think he killed your mom?" she asked.

"I don't know," I moaned. "No? Like, Jude was always so laid-back. He never got stressed out over anything, but if he was her dealer, maybe she wanted to break up with him when she got clean? I don't know."

"You should tell the police what you think. Not play Nancy Drew," Jason said.

"Look, if he admits he was her dealer, or I think he's lying about it, then I'll tell the police and let them handle it but I don't want to turn him in without at least talking to him first. As long as he didn't kill my mom, I liked Jude. They were together for three years, he was over all the time, took us out for breakfast on our birthdays."

Something in Jason's gaze shifted, as he seemed to consider something, and I realized it was that Jude had been like a father to me. He might not have been especially paternal, but he did things like remember birthdays when my mom didn't always or make pancakes on random school mornings, without blueberries. I had more memories and years with him than I did my actual father.

"You shouldn't talk to him by yourself," he finally said.

"He's not going to tell me anything if you're all with me. He doesn't know you guys."

"Then why am I even here?" Natalie asked.

Andi shot her a look. "Okay, you can't complain you never get to come, and then complain when you come. That's why you never get invited."

"Andi," Jason scolded.

"I can talk to Jude. I've done it, like, a thousand times before. It'll be fine."

"Uh oh," Ethan said. "That's exactly the kind of thing you say before you get slashed in a horror movie."

"*What*?" Taylor-Elise yelled.

A few minutes later, Ethan turned onto Jude's street and

caught a glimpse of his home through the windshield. A part of me had thought it would look different from the last time I saw it, that he would have repaired the storm damage by now. The sun-bleached yellow siding was still peeling, exposing the decaying wood underneath, and the white porch steps were sagging but the caution tape had been taken down. There were still holes in the screen door, black garbage bags puckering behind the broken windows. I did notice, however, there was a cat dish on the first step as a makeshift ashtray. It looked almost the same as it did when I came here looking for my mom. Except, his truck was in the driveway.

"I didn't know you well enough to say it before," Ethan said, "but I think *It* lives here."

"What lives here?" Natalie asked, frowning.

"*It.*"

"Yeah, what's it?"

"He's the titular character from a Stephen King novel—"

"It's from a movie," Jason interrupted as I unbuckled my seat belt. "Do you really think it's safe to go in by yourself?"

"You're right outside. If you see him carrying out my body in a rug, I'm sure you'll do the right thing."

Ethan nodded. "Absolutely. Help him load you into the car."

"Exactly," I replied. "Be back in a minute."

I slammed the car door before I heard any further protests, or horror film references, and started what I hoped looked like a confident stride to everyone in the car. Then, when I approached the sagging steps, I got a text from Ethan.

Ma'am? Hey, sorry, ma'am?

I bit back a smile.

I'm not used to being called ma'am.
Thought you meant someone else.
Those stairs aren't safe to walk on.
I was going to walk on the side.
Okay, you should go in now. Jason's starting to
freak out because he thinks you're freaking out.

There was a pause, then,

But really, watch the stairs.

I slipped my phone into my pocket, deciding if Jude could somehow make it inside without fixing them—with about a hundred extra pounds on him—then so could I. They creaked and groaned under my shoes, plummeting a little more than I would've liked, but I managed to get onto the porch. Then I knocked over the cat dish. I looked down, picking it up and realizing it was filled with . . . cat food.

I was scooping it up in my hand, wondering when Jude had gotten a cat, when the hinges to the front door behind the screen squeaked. Jude stepped in front of the torn mesh, shirtless, his thinning but long brown hair frizzing from the humidity against his back. He held the remote in one hand as he spotted me, frowning.

"Bronwyn? What are you doing here?" he asked, opening the screen door and holding it out for me.

I dumped the dry cat food into the bowl. "When did you get a cat?"

"I didn't," he explained. "I'm feeding the strays. They're probably someone's stinking pets but the tornado got everyone's stuff all over. Found a salad spinner in my backyard, still don't know who it belongs to."

I took a cautious step inside, his house not exactly unfamiliar to me but I didn't come here often. The wallpaper was outdated, cracks in the baseboards and near the ceiling, and I knew whenever it rained, it leaked. I followed him into the living room, sat down on his lumpy couch while he excused himself to go find a shirt.

When he came back a moment later, he sat down on the armchair across from me, moving aside newspapers and jackets. "So, you never did tell me. What are you doing all the way down here?"

"Well, I just . . . hadn't heard from you in a while."

"Yeah, I imagine you're pretty busy up in Shelridge. They treating you good up there?"

"Yeah. I have a job now," I said. "I work at this drive-in movie theater a couple of miles from their house, telling people to turn off their headlights."

"You know, it's a shame drive-ins aren't as popular anymore. I loved going as a kid. In fact, I took your mom and you to one once, right? I don't think it was up in Shelridge, though. Maybe Burlington."

"Yeah, that was fun," I said. It was one of the times my mom had tried to stay clean for a couple of months when I was fifteen. "Mom was sober then."

"She was," Jude remarked. "Hey, did you want something to drink—"

"I saw you at a party last month," I interrupted, blurting it out before I realized he was even speaking to me. "With a bunch of kids, and you left by yourself. Did you see me there?"

He thought for a moment. "No, I don't remember seeing you somewhere. What were you doing at a party here in Shiloh? Don't they got those up in Shelridge?" he laughed.

"Why were you at a party, with, like, a bunch of younger people?"

I asked. Then, before he responded, I continued. "Where did you meet my mom? You guys were together for three years and no one ever told me how you met."

"At a party, maybe about ten years ago? Maybe not that long, but we knew each other for a few years before we dated. Your mom was a nice woman, and I liked her."

"She never talked about you, before you were dating."

"Maybe she didn't like me as much," he said, smiling.

I looked down at my hands. "Were you her drug dealer, Jude?"

A sense of incredulousness came into his eyes and in the seconds he took to reply, I couldn't tell if it was because I knew, or because he wasn't and I'd ruined his entire opinion of me. But then he just leaned back in his chair, the newspapers crinkling under him. "I'm not proud of it."

"Wait, so you were really her drug dealer?"

"It was how we met, although that was at a party. She was one of my nicer ones, real friendly and sometimes she brought me Burger King. We got to liking each other, and then we started dating a few years later. She was nervous bringing guys around the house with her daughter being there."

"Yeah," I mumbled, even though that wasn't something I knew about her. She never really talked about dating to me until she was with Jude, so I never realized she'd considered that. I thought she just couldn't get over David. "Did you ever get upset when she tried to get clean?"

"Nah. I mean, I know what horrible stuff that is, and truthfully, I shouldn't be selling it but after I hurt my back, there didn't seem to be that much of an option. Unemployment pays next to nothing and my mom was still living then. She needed care, medicine, stuff like that. Besides, could you imagine me working behind some desk? No, it was either sell drugs or go homeless. I chose to sell drugs."

"Weren't you worried about her overdosing?" I asked him, frowning.

"I was, and I told her to be careful, but Donna knew what she wanted. If she didn't get it from me, she would've gotten it from some other guy who could've been a total weirdo, preying on her addiction."

"Unlike you?"

He looked taken aback for a second. "Well, I told you I'm not proud of it."

"Kingston—one of our neighbors—told me he saw your truck at our house when I was at school, around the time she would've been murdered."

If he looked taken aback before, he looked completely affronted now. "I stopped by the house, but there's no way I killed your mom. I had some errands to run, and while I was out, I went by your place to give Donna your money back."

"Wait, what?" I said, shaking my head. "You mean my college savings? You didn't give that back."

"I most certainly did, young lady," he informed me. "Your mom told me later the money came from your college savings, so I said, *well, then I don't want it. That girl needs an education, so she doesn't end up like us, messed up in drugs and all that.* So, I gave it back, we had lunch, and then I left. And she was very much alive when I last saw her."

"Did you tell the police any of this?"

"Part. I said that I was there, but I'm not going to cop to being a dealer if I don't have to. It's not relevant."

"We never found any money."

"Probably blew away in that tornado. Maybe the person who owned this salad spinner."

"Wait, if that's true, then why did Kingston say you've been telling people she owed you money?"

"She didn't owe me money. Well, okay, she did, but I told her to forget about it if it meant using your college money."

"And that's what you've been telling people?"

"I haven't been telling any*one* any*thing*. You think I'm some blabbermouth drug dealer, telling anyone who'll listen that a murdered woman owed me money? I'm not the sharpest tool in the shed, but I'm not that stupid."

"That's not what Kingston said," I told him.

He threw up a hand. "Who's Kingston? Why's this guy talking about me?"

"Our neighbor. He lived across the yard from us. Buzzed hair, glasses, kind of short."

"Oh. Yeah, yeah, yeah. That guy. Your mom mentioned him a couple of times. I don't think she was too fond of him."

"No, she liked him. They talked sometimes, both liked rock music."

Jude shook his head. "She thought he had a crush on you and was too old for something like that. I mean, I don't think she personally disliked him or anything, just thought he should be flirting with girls his age."

"Yeah, so I've heard," I mumbled.

"Truthfully, I think he reminded her a little bit of your father. He was a bit older than her when they met, right? Yeah, so I think it just made her a little uneasy. Made her think you were following in her footsteps." Jude hoisted himself up from his armchair, grunting. "So, how about that drink? I got water, milk. Just let me check the date on it."

"Water, please." Then, while Jude was in the kitchen, something occurred to me. "Wait, so if you never said she owed you money, who was Kingston talking about?"

"I don't know," he called back. "Someone else, I suppose."

I stood up. "Do you think she could've had another dealer?"

"Your mom? No way. She was supportive of my business," he said, coming back into the door frame, holding a plastic cup with fading cartoon animals. "Well, as supportive as you can be with a drug business, anyway. Besides, I usually let your mom off the hook a little bit. She wouldn't have got a better price anywhere else. Would've given them to her for free, but I gotta pay my suppliers. That's why she got clean that last time—she was tired of disappointing you. I took care of it."

"It's a little weird hearing you talk about drug dealing like it's an actual business."

He shrugged. "It's not too different. Just more illegal. Now, not to be intimidating here, but I just want to make sure you're not going to turn me in to anyone."

"Well, selling drugs is bad, Jude."

"Economy's worse," he pointed out.

"But not as bad as the opioid epidemic."

"Arguable, but I see your point," he replied, gesturing to me with his cup.

"I don't want to see you go to prison," I said, glancing around the house that in some small way was even more familiar to me than the one in which I currently lived. Then I wondered if I'd ever have another reason to see him. "You haven't been caught. If you stopped dealing, found a way to work things out, then it's like this never happened."

"Have you seen what they've got going on prisons nowadays?

Free meals and iPads, gym equipment, TV. Heck, prisoners live better than I do. I'm not afraid of it."

I made a face. "People out there are waiting for me, so I should probably get going."

"Right, right," he said, walking over to give me a quick hug, which he'd never done before. Maybe he also thought with Mom gone, so was our connection to one another. "You stay out of trouble now, and find some boys your own age, but make sure they treat you well. You keep going to school too."

"I'm enrolled in a private school for this fall."

"No kidding," he said, starting to smile. "See, we always knew you were smarter. Too smart for us, anyway. Thought for sure you knew I was her dealer years ago, but didn't say nothing just in case I was wrong. I'm not that stupid."

"I never thought you were stupid. But was that why I never heard from you after Mom died?" I asked him, watching as he looked away. "You barely answered my texts."

"I know, and I feel bad about that. It's just hard, you know," he said, his voice a little deeper than a moment ago.

I nodded. "I know. But it was nice seeing you again."

"Pleasure was all mine," he told me, then a crease formed between his eyebrows as he watched me walk toward the front door. "What are you doing?"

"Leaving? I—"

"What, do you have a death wish? Have you seen those stairs, girl?" Then, before I could answer, he waved a hand for me to follow him through the dining room. "Come on. I've been going out through the back. Those stairs are going to kill somebody if I don't get that money from the insurance company."

"Well, look who made it out of the haunted house alive."

I hoisted myself into the car, motioning for Natalie to scooch out of my seat and back into the middle. "I told you everything would be fine. Natalie, you're on my seat belt buckle."

Jason leaned over as Ethan started the engine. "Is he a drug dealer?"

I hesitated, then reluctantly admitted, "Yes."

"Wait, you were right?" Andi blurted out.

"Yeah, I wasn't expecting that, either, but yes, he's a drug dealer and *please* don't say anything. I mean, he's not a bad person, he's just in a bad place."

Ethan looked at Jason. "Was half an hour long enough for Stockholm Syndrome?"

I flicked a finger at his neck.

"Ow, driving."

"Bronwyn, he's driving," Jason scolded at the same time, and a part of me wanted to roll my eyes even though I wasn't annoyed with him, instead he was just *bugging* me. It was weird, finding someone annoying without actually being annoyed with them. "Him being a drug dealer is a serious offense, Bronwyn. The opioid epidemic is a very real problem in the United—"

"Dude, she knows. Her mom was an addict," Andi interrupted.

"Which is why she should understand how serious this is. He didn't just run a red light—he's been enabling the progression of a serious disease for his profit, and one of the people he did that to was her mother."

"I said all of that. But I can't turn him in. He's okay with getting caught and going to prison, but I can't put him there. He's not sleazy, just . . . poor."

"Wait," Taylor-Elise piped up from the back. "So, you're not going to turn him in for killing your mom either?"

"No, because I don't think he did. Like, he admitted to selling her drugs, but he never got upset whenever she tried to get clean; in fact, he wanted that for her. And he said the reason he was there that morning was to return my college savings."

Ethan glanced at me through the rearview mirror. "He did?"

"Why did he have your college savings?" Jason asked.

I made a sheepish face. "Because I gave it to my mom to pay off her drug debt."

"*What?*"

Even Andi peered over Natalie, whose eyes had widened. "You did *what*?"

"Wait, what's going on?" Taylor-Elise called.

"She needed money," I moaned. "But when he found out it had come from my college savings, he returned it. A tornado came by a moment later and sucked it all up, but I don't think that's his fault."

Jason looked at Ethan. "Did you know?"

"Yeah."

"You told him?" Andi asked, looking almost . . . *hurt*. Again.

Which caused me to shake my head, although technically, it was the truth. "I mean, I did but I tell him a lot of weird stuff walking around the drive-in all night."

"It's true, and sometimes a little frightening," Ethan remarked.

"Are you sure you can trust Jude about any of this? It's not like people readily confess to murder," Jason said.

"I know, but I don't think he did it. They never fought. She didn't owe him money, he wanted her to get clean, so why would he want her dead?"

"Well, then who was Kingston talking about?" Andi asked. "Didn't he say it was her dealer?"

I slumped against my seat, offering a halfhearted shrug. If Jude was her drug dealer, and he said he'd forgiven her debt and had never told anyone otherwise, then what Kingston said didn't make sense. Unless it was something floating around town to throw off suspicion, make it look like her death was related to drugs, but I couldn't understand who would do that. Then I wondered if maybe the Solidays had paid someone, but I couldn't see how someone would be okay with implicating themselves, even in the poor economy around here.

As I considered if anyone would be *that* desperate for money, I remembered what Jude had said about the front porch steps, how he was waiting on the insurance payout so he could finally get them fixed.

Kingston had received his weeks ago, using it to buy himself a new camper.

Maybe they used different insurance companies. But, in the mess of our waterlogged trailer, I'd never found a single bill from the cash Jude said he'd given back to my mom that morning.

But Kingston had been there, across the gravel path, that morning.

He was the one who said her dealer was talking about her owing money.

Before the tornado touched down, after I walked home from school, he kept talking to me, like he didn't want me to go inside the trailer.

Her van had been parked there. She hadn't gone anywhere.

At the funeral, Detective Marsh told the Solidays whoever killed my mom might be there, paying extra attention to them or me, soaking it all in. He was in the back, holding up Bill Paxton movie posters on his phone. Then he came back to the trailer park after.

But his trailer had been destroyed.

He didn't have any reason to be there that afternoon.

"Bronwyn?" Natalie waved a hand over my face. "Did you hear Andi? Do you want to get milk shakes?"

"Why would Kingston lie?" I asked instead of answering, my voice quiet and deeper, like it was all caught in my throat. "Why would Kingston lie to me about her owing money?"

No one said anything for a moment, nothing but the muffled humming of the engine as I waited for some sort of answer, even though I should've known better than for any of them to come to Kingston's defense. But thinking, even for a second, that he might've . . . that it could've been him all this time . . .

It could've been him when I met him at that party in Shiloh, when I kissed him and let him kiss me back, when we'd walked upstairs alone together.

We'd almost had sex.

"Bronwyn?"

Everything sounded mangled and distorted, like my name was being melted as it was spoken, and every other thought in my mind was pushed out by this looming, indescribable feeling. I was light-headed and vaguely nauseated, my palms sticking to the leather seats. Someone was talking to me, but I wasn't listening. It all kept coming back to him.

Across the gravel, talking to my mom so casually, smiling at me after her funeral in the trailer park on the cinderblocks. His hands in my hair when he'd kissed me, his hands on her throat when he'd killed her.

"Bronwyn?" A voice broke through the melting and the memories, finding my eyes through the rearview mirror.

"I think maybe we should talk to the police," I finally croaked.

CHAPTER SEVENTEEN

When Ethan pulled into the police station about ten minutes later, I sat there for a moment, still strapped under my seat belt, suddenly feeling unsure now that we were here and the station was right behind me. "Do I wait for Amy and David?"

Jason leaned forward in his seat. "They were on their way when we hung up, but it's probably still going to be another half hour."

"Do you want them there?" Andi asked.

My movements were slow as I shook my head, glancing through the rearview back at the police station, although I wasn't so sure, realizing I was about to suggest my neighbor, the boy I'd crushed on for months, might have killed my mom. Truthfully, she was the one I wanted. I wanted my mom, and I wanted her to tell me what to do, even if I'd never listened to her advice before. Her advice normally meant something like confronting Erin Hall when she'd spread a rumor around school that I'd stolen tampons from the nurse because I was so poor, which I didn't. Then she wanted me to stuff her locker with tampons to prove a point, which I also didn't. I just ignored Erin Hall. But my mom had listened; she'd been there.

I took a moment to breathe out the feeling that came over me whenever I thought about her too much, and looked at Andi before thinking better of it. "Can you get your mom on the phone?"

She wasn't *my* mom. But she was still *a* mom. A mom who was there.

"Bronwyn?" Amy's voice coming through Andi's phone was comforting. I climbed out of the car, shutting the door behind me, stepping away from everyone. "Bronwyn, sweetheart. What's going on? Jason told David you think Kingston had something to do with your mom's death?"

"He told me her drug dealer was saying she owed him money, but I found out that wasn't true. And then I thought, during the tornado he wouldn't let me go inside and warn her. He was at the trailer park after her funeral. I think he followed me there. You know, paying special attention like the detective said."

"Okay, honey—"

"I think he stole from my mom too. We were supposed to have a couple thousand dollars at the house, and I don't think it got destroyed in the tornado. He stole it and used it to buy a new camper."

"Honey, where are you?"

"We're at the police station, still in the car. Should I wait for you? Do I need a lawyer to talk to the police? I don't know what I'm supposed to do."

"Just go inside. Tell them you have some new information about your mother's case. Once you do that, you can decide if you want to wait for us. I don't think you'll need a lawyer, but if you want one, I can call for one."

"No, that's—if you don't think I need one, then I don't."

There was a pause on the other end. "Okay. Well, then, go in and tell them your name and who you want to talk to. Jason can help if you need anything until we get there. We'll be there soon, all right?"

"All right, but should I even tell them? What if I'm wrong again?"

"Bronwyn, you're not giving this boy a life sentence by telling the police your suspicions. They will take that information and use it to find more. And that information will let them know if he needs to be arrested." I was quiet, looking over at the police station. "Remember, your loyalty is to your mother. Not him, or anyone else."

"Is that what you would've said if I'd told the police when I thought you and David did it?" I asked her, somewhat tentatively, because I'd never talked to her about it or even asked David if she knew. She never brought it up or acted any differently around me, didn't try to force me to *talk* about it, but I was starting to get the feeling she knew, nonetheless.

She chuckled. "Yes, because I know I'd have nothing to hide."

"I should probably go in," I told her.

"Then go. We'll see you soon, sweetheart."

○

I decided after walking into the police station a few minutes later I would do what Amy instructed. I told the officer I had new information about my mother's death, then said I wanted to wait for—the words sounding awkward and garbled when I heard them—my parents, before going to the plastic chairs across the room. Jason was asking the receptionist if I needed to fill any-thing out while I waited, like I was at the doctor's office, and Andi eventually told Natalie to stop bugging her with dumb questions. Taylor-Elise took up answering her after that, and Ethan sat beside me.

"Don't say reassuring things," I murmured. "I almost had sex in a bathroom with the guy who might've killed my mom. What horror movie is that from?"

"You don't have to be funny all the time, you know," he said. "I know you think saying what you feel makes you look weak, but as someone who's heard a lot of what you thought, you've never looked that way to me."

"I told you not to say reassuring things."

"Are you okay?"

"That's worse," I mumbled, sighing as I stared down at the scuffed tiles under my shoes. "I don't know. I'm such an idiot either way. I'm an idiot for thinking he could've done this if he didn't and I'm an idiot if he did it because I never noticed. Ugh, like, I'm so stupid. Everyone saw it but me."

"You're not an idiot. You liked him."

I shot him a look. "Yeah, *I* liked him. No one else did, you didn't, and it turns out, even my mom didn't like him. And I just ignored all of you and thought things like *you just have to get to know him*. That's stupid. I'm stupid, and I kissed the guy who killed my mom."

"Bronwyn—" When I glared at him and the softened tone he started to use, he leaned back into his chair. "Do you want me to leave you alone? No hard feelings."

"No. I'm sorry—I'm just really angry right now."

"I get it. I'm pretty angry right now too," he admitted. "Look, I never liked Kingston. But you did and if you're right, then . . ." He trailed off, shaking his head.

"If I'm right, then what?"

"Then he hurt you. That's what makes me angry."

I knew we were friends, and it was normal whenever someone hurt your friend that you felt upset on their behalf—like when Indie found out her second boyfriend, Malcolm, had kissed another girl at the Valentine's Day Dance—but, for a moment, I thought there might have been something else underneath it, maybe in the way he was looking at me. It was enough to give me pause until he nudged me with his elbow when Amy and David walked in. "Speaking of angry."

"I thought she was at a friend's house," Amy was whispering to David when I approached them near the front doors, turning to me with a disapproving frown. "Why is Natalie here?"

"We brought her."

"You brought her to meet your mother's *drug dealer*?" she hissed.

"I didn't say that exactly."

"No, but your brother did," David replied. "Bronwyn, do you have any idea how—"

"She stayed in the car," I said defensively.

"Why would *you* do that? Why would you be so careless to confront her drug dealer, Bronwyn?" Amy demanded. "This should've been your first step. This, here, the police. What if something happened to you?"

"Well, they were all outside."

"Really? What good do you think a van full of teenagers is going to do in an emergency?"

"Okay, yes, it was stupid but if I didn't do it, then I wouldn't have found out what I know about Kingston. And look, I'm fine. See?"

She pointed a finger at me. "Don't get smart. You're still in so much trouble right now. You're looking at a grounding from now until graduation. *College* graduation."

I looked over at David, preparing my response when he made a pointed glance at Amy then shook his head slowly. Reluctantly, I stifled the rest of my defense as Detective Marsh came around the corner.

"How we all doing?" he called out, waving.

Amy let out a breath. "We'll discuss punishments later." Then she smiled, holding out a hand to Detective Marsh. "Fine, how are you today, Detective?"

○

It seemed like we spent hours in the interrogation room with Detective Marsh and Officer Porterfield. Amy and David were on either side of me as I explained over and over again about what I'd learned. Whenever it came back to the question about her dealer, how I could've known Kingston was lying without telling them *how* exactly I knew, I kept insisting I just did and focused more on what I *could* talk about. Him at the trailer park after the funeral, the money missing from our house, that I thought he lied about getting an insurance payout when he bought a new camper.

"Bronwyn, you've never mentioned money was missing from your house before," Detective Marsh commented.

"I just found out about it," I said uncertainly. "Someone told me they gave my mom money that morning, and I never found any of it. I think Kingston might have stolen it when he killed my mom."

He sighed. "Bronwyn. I'm not an idiot. I know you're leaving out a lot of details involving your mother's drug dealer. I'm betting you know who he is and you're trying to protect him."

"Look, can't you just start investigating Kingston? Even if I can't prove what I'm saying, if you investigate, maybe you'll find new evidence."

"We'll talk to him. But it would be helpful if we could also talk to her dealer and get him to come forward about this."

"I'm sure it would, but I don't know who he is, and I don't want to answer any more questions about that."

Detective Marsh sighed, glancing swiftly at David. "All right then. Well, we'll be back in a moment to fill out a written statement and then you can be on your way. We'll contact Kingston and see what comes of that."

"Okay."

"Please make sure to keep us informed," David added, and I heard the shift in his voice. He went from sounding like his normal self to sounding like a politician as he stood up, buttoned the inside of his blazer, and shook Detective Marsh's hand without once looking away.

I wasn't sure how I felt about it, but it felt different to me.

Not foreign or forced, awkward or misleading. Not exactly normal, either, but I remembered what Andi told me at Starbright before—*we do those things for you.* So, I let that thought be there and didn't push it away as we left.

○

One of the several punishments doled out from Amy and David to Andi and me for confronting my mom's dealer—and bringing

Natalie with us, who readily confessed to not knowing what we were doing before we left—was running errands for Kimberly for the upcoming wedding. Over the next week we drove around town picking up bridesmaid dresses, met with the florist, went to the catering business, and dropped off the check. And now we were making wedding favors. Neither of us said much, except when we accidentally burned ourselves trying to glue labels onto glass jars, which was how it normally went whenever we had to do something together. I was torn between saying something and, well, not. I could've asked her about the silent disco party Jason and Kimberly were having for their reception, whatever that was, or I could've kept gluing things to candle jars.

"Are you still mad at me? Because I can't tell anymore," I blurted, when I decided after my fifteenth candle I was tired of this. Her not talking to me, me continually wondering if I should say something. Even her anger was better than this weird silence, like I couldn't tell if we were in a truce or the middle of a pause.

She shrugged. "I don't know. I can't tell either. Sometimes, maybe."

"I don't think Amy and David did it anymore," I told her, which I realized was the truth when I said it out loud. "People might have been right when they said I was just using it as an excuse to stay angry at them."

"Do you only think that because of everything going on with Kingston?"

"No. But it helps a little bit. Okay, and I know that sucks, but I don't know them like you do. My whole life, I only heard bad things about them. Not saying I still believe those things, but it's all I knew for a long time."

"I know. It just . . . it sucked, okay? It sucked waiting *my* whole life to meet you only for you to hate it here and accuse my parents of murder. And I know," she said, holding up her hand, "I didn't want you here at first, but after so many years of never hearing from you and listening to my parents argue about what to do, I freaked out."

"It's okay."

"It was so obvious when you arrived that you didn't want to be here. And accusing my parents of murder just felt like another way to get out of it. And if you don't want to be . . ." she trailed off, gesturing with the glue gun through the air.

"Careful, that's still on."

". . . then I don't know what I'm supposed to do."

"Do you remember when Kingston left the barbeque?" I asked, and she shrugged. "He wanted me to come back home, but I told him I didn't want to. And I don't. I don't want it to be just me anymore, but I'm not used to it. I want to be, though."

She hesitated, then grabbed another candle.

I sighed. "I'm also sorry for hurting your feelings and I don't want you to be mad at me anymore, okay?"

"Fine."

"Wait, *fine*? Just like that? I thought I was going to have to do something sappy like finally write you back a letter or something."

She shuddered. "No. If you want to get used to this, then you need to get used to fighting and we don't do some dramatic gesture every time we're sorry. We just say it, okay? Regular apologies, no weirdness. Or feelings. Keep those back."

I bit back a smile then let it show, just a little. "Cool."

o

Later that night, I lay out over the top bunk, my legs dangling over the sides. Natalie was brushing her teeth and Andi was in the middle of her shift at Starbright. I stared up at the ceiling as I waited for Indie to pick up my call. "Bronwyn? What time is it?"

"It's not that late," I said. "It's not even ten yet. But, hey, do you want to be my date?"

"Huh?" There was some shifting around on the other end for a moment. "You mean to Jason's wedding?"

"Nope, the other major event I was invited to this summer. Yes, Jason's wedding. Will you come?"

"Wait, seriously?" she asked, sounding more alert as I heard bedsprings creaking in the background. "I mean, this is all so sudden. We haven't even gone out on a regular date first and now you want to take me to your brother's wedding. This is all moving so fast."

I wrinkled my nose, smiling somewhat at her wistfully spoken sarcasm. "How about we just say Jason's wedding? Besides, the last guy I invited to anything probably killed my mom so . . ." I trailed off, then remembered I was talking to Indie, who would definitely want to talk about *that* more. So far, she seemed torn between wanting to discuss what this meant for me and wanting to say *I told you so.*

"You're not internalizing all your feelings about that, right?"

"I just don't have much to say about it right now. I haven't even heard back from the police yet about what's going on. They could've ignored me for all I know."

"Look, I know I said a lot of stuff about him. And I knew I was right about him, but I didn't want to be *this* right, you know? I didn't want you to get hurt, Bronwyn."

"I know," I mumbled. "You're coming, though? To the wedding?"

"I mean, if you're going to twist my arm and *force* me to go to an extravagant, upper-class social event where anybody who's anybody is going to be there."

I shook my head. "You're insane."

"I'm also in. Okay, now what do you want to hear about? What's happening with the robotics club in the fall or the latest gossip at the pool after Cayden Bruni came back from visiting family in Long Island and found out Lola Belle was with the new lifeguard?" she asked as I brought my pillow to my chest and said yes to all of it, to every bit of home she could share with me.

○

The next day, a garment bag arrived at the house. After dinner, we were all settling in to watch a movie when Amy announced she wanted Andi and Natalie to try on their bridesmaid dresses again. I was somewhat confused—the garment bag couldn't have held Andi and Natalie's dresses, because those had been hanging in our bedroom for a couple of weeks. And then Kimberly informed me it was my dress. I just stood there, speechless.

"When we started planning our wedding," Kimberly said, "I knew I wanted all of Jason's sisters as bridesmaids. It's why the styles are different for each bridesmaid. We were hoping you'd be there, even last minute."

I swallowed. "You don't even know me, though. Shouldn't your bridesmaids be, like, your best friends?"

"You know, I'm more excited about our future, and isn't that the whole point of a wedding? Embracing your future?" Her eyes drifted over me again, warmly. "But if that's too much, that's fine too. You don't have to be a bridesmaid if you don't want to be."

"I mean, if you want me to be a bridesmaid . . . I could be."

Kimberly nodded. "You'll make a beautiful one, I just know it."

A few minutes later, Andi changed into her dress in the bathroom. Amy was by the door, knocking every couple seconds to see if Andi needed help getting dressed, which she didn't. Kimberly was beside me, her legs near Natalie, already in her dress, on the floor, eating a popcorn ball.

"I love this movie," Kimberly said, pointing to *When Harry Met Sally . . .*, paused on the screen. "And Harry, but I can't get over how he dresses like my grandpa."

"That was the style in the '80s!" Amy said.

After the bathroom door unlocked, Andi stepped out sheepishly, a flush coming over her cheeks as Amy fawned over her, ignoring the leggings and fluffy socks she had on underneath her skirt. The fabric was powder blue, a chiffon skirt flowing around her legs with a halter bodice.

Amy was still gasping when Andi carefully sat down on the sectional. "You look so beautiful, honey. You're growing up so fast; before I know it, it'll be your wedding day."

"Mom," Andi groaned.

"To Ryan," Natalie teased.

Andi's nostrils flared as she grabbed one of the throw pillows on the couch. "Shut up."

"Andrea," Amy warned as the pillow soared over the ottoman and collided against Natalie's chest with a hollow *thwack*, causing Miles—lying beside her, patiently waiting for a bite of her popcorn ball—to perk up. "Girls, stop. You're going to ruin the dresses."

"Can she even eat popcorn balls? Won't they get all stuck in her braces?"

Amy paused. "Yes."

"Mom! Can't I just have one? It's no fair everyone else gets to have them."

"Not everyone else has such horrendously crooked teeth," Andi retorted.

"*Andrea.*"

I pulled back my bottom lip. "My teeth are crooked."

"*Okay,*" Kimberly interrupted, heading over to the recliner where the other dresses were in their garment bags. "Let's see how Bronwyn looks in her dress."

I took the bag from her and went into the bathroom. When I opened it, I noticed the material was a similar shade of blue as Andi's, with a haltered bodice too. When I put it on, also refusing Amy's offers to help through the door, the skirt was light, close to my hips and legs.

I walked out a moment later and Amy made the gasping sound again, which I ignored like Andi had, and Kimberly smiled from the couch. "That dress looks so beautiful on you, Bronwyn," Kimberly remarked. "The color complements your hair."

"You look like Cinderella," Amy murmured.

I glanced down at the skirt, grasping the material between my fingers. "It's blue."

Andi was still on the sectional with her legs crossed, chewing on a popcorn ball as she took me in, tilting her head. "Some gold glitter eyeshadows on the lid would complement it."

"Glitter?" I asked skeptically.

She nodded, starting to smile. "Definitely glitter."

○

The Monday before Jason and Kimberly's wedding, David received a phone call from Detective Marsh asking us to meet him at the station. Barely an hour later I was ushered into the detective's office with Amy and David following behind me.

"Please, sit. thanks for coming in," Detective Marsh said, more to Amy and David than me. "I know this must be a frustrating time for you all, and I want to assure you everything we have is going into this case."

"Thank you, Detective," David replied.

"That being said, unfortunately, we're at a standstill here with the investigation. We've interviewed Kingston Castaneda. It's suspicious, certainly, but right now, we don't have any evidence and he isn't confessing to any involvement at the moment."

"What does that mean?" I asked.

"It means that right now what we need is an admission of guilt, something we can take to trial, which we just don't have," he explained with a sigh. "You mentioned you had been in a romantic relationship with him, correct? You two were friends, a little more?"

Reluctantly, I admitted, "Yeah."

"What we would like to do is use that to our advantage, Bronwyn. You have a rapport with him, a connection. And, we understand how much we're asking for here," he said, briefly breaking eye contact with me to look at David, "but we would like you to set up a meeting with him while wearing a wire. We would be outside the whole time, listening in, and if anything went south, we would be right there."

"Okay," I readily agreed. "When—?"

"I'm sorry, you can't be serious," Amy interrupted, shaking her head as she held up a hand, incredulous. "You want Bronwyn—a sixteen-year-old child—to wear a wire to trap what could be a very dangerous man into confessing to murder?"

"Like I said, I know how much we're asking for here, but it could be our best shot. We would need your consent for this—"

"Well, you don't have it," Amy told him, laughing sardonically. "If you can't coax a confession out of him, what makes you think an untrained teenager can do it?"

"We would educate her beforehand on this matter. But she has a relationship with him. She's expressed he's interested in continuing that relationship. If we play to that angle, then he could come clean about any involvement he had."

"I have to agree with my wife here, Detective," David said, glancing over at me apologetically. "For all we know, Donna could've been killed because of that relationship he wants with her, and none of us know what he might do if he gets her alone. He could know that she was the one who turned him in."

"Okay, could everyone just hold on for a second?" I asked. "I'm right here and I said I would do it. It's fine, I know him. I want to find out what happened to my mom and I'm okay with whatever could happen. I'll sign a waiver or something."

"Bronwyn, we all want that, too, but we can't risk your safety. I'm sure the police can find another way of getting justice for your mom," Amy said, her voice hardening. "Right, Detective?"

"Right. It was just a suggestion, and we're going to continue to pursue this for as long as it takes. Rest assured."

Amy and David nodded, standing up on either side of me, but I hesitated because I wasn't sure if I could just rest assured anymore. Not when the lead detective was saying things like *for as long as it takes*, and there was something I could do about it.

Then, as we were on the way out of the station, I saw Officer

Porterfield pulling out of the parking lot in her patrol car and realized maybe there was still something I could do.

○

I asked Ethan if I could borrow his car the next evening, mostly trying to convince him that, yes, I did know how to drive, and no, I wouldn't wreck his car in a fiery collision. He mentioned coming with me—and driving instead—but I insisted on going alone because I knew if he came, he would talk me out of what I was planning to do. I parked under a streetlight in the corner of a Chinese restaurant parking lot across from the police station and leaned against the bumper with a carton of sweet-and-sour chicken I was lazily picking over with my chopsticks while I waited. It probably looked stalkerish, but it wasn't like I had Officer Porterfield's number or anything. Besides, I did grab her some eggrolls.

Most of my sweet-and-sour chicken was gone when her patrol car finally pulled into the police station. I was relieved this hadn't turned out to be her night off and waved when she stepped out of the car. It took her a second to figure out who I was.

"Sorry!" I called out. "Can I talk to you? I have eggrolls."

Officer Porterfield hesitated, too far away for me to make out her expression but there was something about her that almost looked . . . skittish. But a moment later, she approached Ethan's crossover, eyeing my extended eggrolls wearily. "Is everything okay?"

"Yeah, they're kind of cold, but I think they'll still be good," I said. "The other day, Detective Marsh mentioned he wanted me to wear a wire and confront Kingston about my mom. But Amy and David shot him down."

"Right."

I held out the eggrolls again, and with a small sigh, she accepted them. "So, I was wondering if there was some way we could just . . . forget about that. Like, maybe forge their signatures or just forget that part."

"Bronwyn, that's illegal. We can't just do something like that without your parents' consent."

"But it could work! I know it's risky, and I'm okay with that. Kingston and I were, like, flirting for most of the summer, we hung out a couple of times. He'll think that's exactly what we're doing again," I tried to be convincing. "And, like Detective Marsh said, you'll be right outside, listening in so if anything happens, *bam*! You take him down."

"It's not me you have to convince. Your parents are the ones withholding consent. And they're right, it's incredibly dangerous. There are all kinds of things that can happen when you're alone with someone like that."

"But I wouldn't be. You'd be right there. Okay, I mean . . ." I sighed, leaning back until I was lying against the hood of Ethan's crossover. After a moment, she leaned against the bumper beside me. "I hated my mom. I spent most of my life wishing I could get away and we got into this fight a few months ago. I never really forgave her for it and then she just—she just died. And I think it was because of him. I trusted him. I liked him. I've kissed him before. If I did this, it would be . . . like finally making it up to my mom and getting revenge on him all at the same time."

In the darkness with nothing but the gold streetlight cast over her features, she looked younger. "The police's hands are tied. They can't legally do anything without your parents' consent."

Maybe I should've tried to bribe her with more than luke-warm eggrolls.

"You know, this is the first murder investigation I've ever worked as an officer," she admitted. "And I might have taken it too personally, which is why I keep telling you things I probably shouldn't. Because I know what it's like to be . . . *blindsided* by someone you trusted."

I sat up, confused. "What do you mean?"

"It happened about seven years ago. I was sixteen, like you. And I trusted a boy like you did, except it wasn't my mom he hurt." She looked away, something clouding her eyes for a moment as a delayed sense of understanding came over me. "There was other stuff too. You were probably too young to remember any of it but the whole reason I became a cop was to stop something like that from happening again. No one stopped him from hurting me, but I thought maybe . . . maybe I could do that for someone else."

"Okay."

She set down the empty eggroll container between us. "We can't do it officially. Like I said, the police's hands are tied. But I've done something kind of like this before, with some help. I could probably do it again."

I broke out into a smile. "Seriously? You'll do it? You'll help me?"

"Against my better judgment."

CHAPTER EIGHTEEN

The venue for the wedding was on the lake, glimpses of shimmery blue water through the open windows in the lodge where members of the wedding party were getting ready, everything constructed of wood with expansive panes of glass peeking out over the property, including the floral arch with dainty white flowers contrasting the greenery. Wooden chairs had been arranged over the grass, petals sprinkled down the aisle with additional ones to be thrown by Kimberly's nieces during the ceremony. The breeze off the lake was cool, and the wedding planner kept promising it was going to warm up before the ceremony as bridesmaids came in, dressed in hoodies with hot coffees.

I told Andi she could do my makeup and after a debate over a warm-toned nude eyeshadow palette and one with gold shimmer shades, I learned Andi wasn't actually asking for my opinion when she listed her options out loud. She also did my hair, pinning it up with teased braids and baby's breath attached with bobby pins, after finishing her makeup.

I waited as she held up two compacts of blush against my complexion before deciding on peachy beige. "So, I've been confused about something for weeks now," I said.

"It's called blush," Andi quipped.

"Oh, ha, ha. Andi *does* know how to make a joke," I replied drily, watching as she tapped her brush against the side of the compact. "I meant the silent disco party. What is that?"

"You just wear headphones. And it's only for half the reception. They compromised."

"It sounds weird, though. You're just listening to music and dancing like you're alone except you're in front of three hundred people. And you're all listening to different songs."

"It's fun. It allows people who don't want to dance to still carry on conversations without having to yell over loud music. You can dance around people, or with people . . ." she said, suggestively.

"Andi, do you want to dance with me?"

She made a face. "No. But I might be able to think of someone who does." When I frowned at her, confused, she let out an exasperated sigh and grabbed a tube of liquid lipstick. "Ethan. Ethan wants to dance with you. How can you figure out who killed your mom but not that?"

I pulled back. "Are you out of your mind?"

"What? This is a nice, tanned rose shade. It'll look good with your skin tone."

"You know what I mean," I snapped, which she ignored, motioning for me to hold still. When she was done applying it, I continued, "We don't dance. We're not a dancing thing.

We're not a thing at all, actually, unless that thing is friends."

She twisted the lid back on the liquid lipstick, shrugging. "Well, as someone who's known Ethan for a long time, that's not how he treats his friends."

I wasn't sure what to make of this or how I felt hearing it. I wanted to know why she'd said that, but it felt like giving in to something I didn't want to admit was there. Ethan and I were friends, good friends. Summer friends, probably. He never said anything about wanting to be anything *but* friends, except there were moments when . . .

Ugh, knock it off, I thought to myself, shaking my head. *This is Ethan. Your good friend, Ethan. Who is definitely* not *thinking like this right now, no matter what Andi says.*

But, as I distractedly watched her gather her makeup brushes from the vanity we were sitting next to and cram them back into an overflowing travel case of makeup, tubes smeared with traces of foundation and black mascara, curiosity eroded through my thoughts. "He's never said anything about . . . dancing."

"Yeah, because he's *Ethan*. It's hard for him to ask anyone out, let alone you," she told me, and when I made a face, she elaborated. "He's never been good at putting himself out there, especially when it comes to girls he likes. He doesn't want to find out they don't like him back. And how could he think it would be any different with you? You came here, hating everything he's ever known and liking someone else. But despite that, somehow, you kind of became his best friend, which just makes it even harder."

I frowned. "Has he told you any of this?"

She shrugged. "Not exactly, but I know him. And *I'm* best friends with his little sister, who knows him even better." I glanced away, not wanting to admit I felt almost . . . disappointed. "Okay, I can't tell you when he started liking you or that he ever admitted it, but he does. Trust me."

I sighed, then told her, "You could dance with Ryan."

"We're just friends."

"Well, as someone who's known Ryan for basically no time at all—"

She grabbed a black cylinder from the table. "Shut up, it's time for your setting spray."

○

A little over an hour later, after the guests had arrived and found their seats and the bouquets were handed out, I stood near the entrance of the lodge as the DJ transitioned to the instrumental music. Through the door frame, I saw Jason at the end of the aisle. Flower petals thrown by Kimberly's nieces were at his feet, and as the music swelled, Andi strode down the aisle with her arm around Danny's. Mine was linked with a groomsman named Michael, one of Jason's old college roommates, as we waited for our turn.

A moment later, Michael and I came out of the lodge together, my shoulders stiffening as guests turned to look over their chairs. But then I caught a glimpse of Indie toward the back, and a few rows in front of her were the Denvers, realizing with some surprise their parents were with them. Ethan turned in his seat like everyone else, but his eyes weren't bored or casually going over me while waiting for the bride. He was smiling and looking right at *me*.

I gave him a small smile, wiggling my fingers around Michael's arm.

Then, as we reached the front, I noticed in the first row of seats that Amy and David had turned in their chairs too, smiling. So was Jason at the front beside the minister. Even Andi had a soft smile on her lips as I released Michael's arm and turned to stand behind her, glancing at Danny to the left of Jason, tugging at his tie until Amy made the quick motion for him to stop. Then I watched as Natalie came down the aisle after me, linked arms with another one of the groomsmen, seeing how hard she was struggling to stifle her grin, the slightest peek of her metal braces showing through. For a moment, it didn't feel like them, the Solidays, and me, a Larson. Instead, it felt different, like a piece finally falling into place.

Then I waited, with everyone else as they stood, for the bride to join us.

○

It was almost dark when the DJ announced the silent disco half of the evening would be starting soon, after we'd spent hours with the photographer. I was still seeing camera flashes every time I blinked when Andi pulled me toward the dance floor instead of the buffet table where chocolate strawberries were still being served.

She handed me a bulky set of headphones, lit bright green over the ears in her hands. "Okay, so there are three channels you can choose from. This is how you change the song. Kimberly said they've got classics on one channel, new hits on another, and the last one is like their playlist or something."

"I don't like this," I mumbled, holding it carefully and frowning over at Ethan, who had already slipped his on. "It's going to look stupid to everyone else not wearing headphones."

Andi paused putting her headphones on. "You mean all the people more focused on the macaroons than you?"

"I think it's cool," Indie said, her voice a little too loud as Queen blared through her headphones. "Hey, what channel do you think the song from *Shrek* would be on?"

"Put it on," Andi ordered.

I reluctantly slipped them on, standing still as Andi and Taylor-Elise started dancing, with Ryan close beside them, making wild, somewhat dangerous arm gestures. Indie danced, too, doing some sort of bouncing thing that also proved to be dangerous when she accidentally bumped into another wedding guest. Cass and Ginny were waltzing together, and when Cass gestured for me to dance, I nodded. But didn't dance.

Then a hand reached for mine when the song coming through my headphones changed to "Dancing Queen" by ABBA. Indie's headphones were the same color, meaning she was listening to the same channel, and she grinned.

"That's so original!" I shouted, then flinched, realizing the only people who could've heard me were the guests, *not* dancing.

Indie pulled me closer to the center, where most of the people were, mouthing along to the lyrics. Her movements weren't entirely fluid, but her eyes looked radiant. I was limp for a moment, but when she let go of my hand to start mimicking playing the piano notes, I laughed. Then, feeling more stilted and aware of myself than she looked, I bounced on my heels and shifted my hips, laughing embarrassedly at myself but Indie started copying me. And before I knew what I was doing, I lifted my hands over my head and danced like I did whenever I was home alone. I felt stupid and free and open, and then I caught eyes with Ethan.

I pointed to him, awkwardly swaying, as I mouthed the part about looking for a king. Ethan laughed as I danced over to him, forcing the pieces of me down that wondered if I looked like an idiot—because right then, I was just dancing.

And I knew him. The boy always a little bit worried about how he looked, how he sounded, or what he said, wanting to be liked a little too much by those around him. I grabbed onto his arms and pulled him closer, still mouthing the chorus to him, how he could dance, wondering if he understood I was saying it to him, not just repeating lyrics. A second later, he switched his channel to mine, mouthing the lyrics with me. His dancing wasn't entirely unabashed, but it was in sync with mine, his face broken out in a grin that brought out his dimple.

Somehow, without any conscious thought, we got closer, the warmth from his chest against my arms, our hands sometimes brushing together. It wasn't until we mouthed one of the drawn-out *oohs* that I realized how close we were.

He seemed to notice it, too, because he paused, something shifting in his eyes, not as bright but now almost timid. Endearing. For a moment, as everything slowed, I let myself hear the echo of Andi's words.

That's not how he treats his friends.

Then he reached out and grasped one side of my head-phones, before carefully slipping them down around my neck. My breath caught in my throat, like everything in me was awake and completely aware of every possible thing that could happen, and I wasn't sure if I was more afraid of them happening or not happening. I lifted a hand, not sure if I was going to touch his headphones or his tentative dimple.

Then someone bumped against my back, sending me stumbling forward against his chest as the song finished, the silence that stretched between the songs somehow sounded louder than ABBA singing in my ears. I laughed and took a step back, only realizing after I did it that it wasn't what I'd wanted to do. He smiled, his headphones still on, but his gaze looked distracted.

"You dance well," I said after a moment, then scrunched my nose.

He pulled one side of his headphones down. "What?"

I shook my head. "Nothing. I'm going to . . ." I pointed toward the refreshment table, watching as he'd glanced over his shoulder and nodded. I realized with some disappointment that whatever look he had in his eyes a moment ago was fading, returning to normal Ethan and his normal shade of green. I didn't want that. I didn't want normal. But then the song changed, and Indie pulled me away again, Ethan and I turned away from each other.

○

I handed back my headphones an hour later when the silent disco half was over and walked to the buffet table, when Danny nearly bumped into me. "Geez, kid," I muttered. "Slow down."

"You're not the boss of me," he retorted, grabbing a plate.

We barely spoke to each other, Danny and I, both off doing our own things, an age difference of nearly seven years between us. Which was fine, except I didn't know what would happen after tonight, when the wedding was over, and I drove back to Shiloh. And if something happened, then fine really wasn't fine at all.

I turned to him, putting down my plate. "Danny—"

"I'm still deciding," he said, almost defensively, before turning back to the macaroons.

"I don't want a dessert. I want to dance with you."

Danny was already frowning when he turned to me. "I don't want to dance. This song sucks. It sounds like something Mom listens to."

"Danny, come on."

He groaned and stepped away from the buffet table, reluctantly following me to the dance floor and glaring down at my arms as I reached out for him. "This looks weird."

"You know, I really haven't seen you all summer," I told him, ignoring this. "You're always off with your friends, which is cool. You've got so many friends here, always playing outside. You're probably even more outdoorsy than me."

"We play basketball too. And I always win."

I raised an eyebrow. "Always?"

"Always. Really."

"I just . . . I wanted to make sure the reason we haven't talked was because you're off having so much fun, not because you're upset I'm living with you now."

Danny shrugged. "Well, you're not that fun. You just look mad all the time."

"I normally am," I conceded, nodding. "But you know, you're the only one here I've never actually been mad at before. You just mind your own business. I like it."

"Who are you mad at the most?"

"Usually David or your mom. Or Andi."

Danny groaned. "She's so annoying."

I smiled as the song ended and I let my hand fall away from his shoulder. "Okay, go, get your dessert. Thanks for dancing with me, kid."

He narrowed his eyes. "You're acting weird, even for you."

"You'll get it soon."

I watched as he sprinted toward the dessert table, his shoes squeaking against the hardwood when Jason approached me. There was a hint of a smile on his face as he made a pointed glance at Danny, grabbing a peach macaroon, before he held out his arms. I grasped his hand, setting my other hand on his shoulder.

"You danced with Danny," he commented, like he was amused.

"And now I'm dancing with you."

"Two weeks ago, you didn't even want to be in a car with me."

"And I still don't, but this is dancing. And your wedding. I've never danced at a wedding before," I confided. "The last wedding I went to had coolers. And the hors d'oeuvres were chips, served in the bag."

"I bet you loved every moment of it."

I pretended to look appalled. "I do *not* enjoy myself at establishments that offer only *two* silver, handcrafted salad forks for my meal. It was disgraceful."

Jason smiled, giving a slight nod while his gaze drifted away for a moment. "Do you really feel that out of place here? Not just here at the wedding, but with us?"

"Sometimes," I admitted, staring at my hand on his shoulder instead of his face. "We never knew each other until we were supposed to be family, and by then . . . we grew up differently. I was thinking when we were all in the car together, listening to you three bicker, that's never going to be something I can do. I'm still that only child who doesn't get it."

"You know, there were a lot of things I never thought I'd have with you. I always knew you were out there, but I never thought I'd know you. I never thought I'd talk to you, or dance with you," he said, pausing to spin me slowly. "I never thought I'd see where you went to school. Get on your nerves, or you get on mine. But all those things happened already, and summer isn't even over yet."

I thought back to where I was going when this was over, wondering if this summer would be enough for him when he remembered it if something went wrong.

"I've waited for you to be my sister for a long time," he confessed softly. "And whatever that looks like, I'm okay with it. It's more than I ever thought I'd get."

When the song ended, he pulled back and looked over my shoulder. "Now, there's one guy you still haven't danced with yet. And he's probably the one who wants to dance with you the most."

David stood near the edge of the dance floor. Then, I straightened my shoulders and focused on the sound of my heels against the floor as I approached him, brisk at first but then tentative when I got close.

"Jason says I should dance with you," I blurted out.

He took a second to process this. "Would . . . would you like to?"

"We could just . . . dance around each other or something," I offered.

David nodded eagerly. "Sure, I'd like that. That would be nice."

"Yeah," I mumbled, swaying my hips somewhat awkwardly as he mirrored my actions. Then, in an attempt to be dorky or funny, he started doing a bad impression of the dance from *Saturday Night Fever*. He was smiling, until he saw my expression, then he dropped his hands down to his sides.

"I'm not trying to be mean to you," I told him.

"You're not being mean. No one likes my dance moves."

"You're pretty dorky, but I think you do it on purpose to make your kids laugh."

David chuckled. "That's why all dads make those jokes. That, and we just really appreciate a good pun."

"Like the one about haircuts?"

"If I ask Andi which hair she got cut one more time, I think she's going to put herself up for adoption," he laughed. "When you went to visit your mother's drug dealer, I remembered a good one, but Amy didn't think it would be appropriate, considering the situation. She was right, of course. What you did was incredibly dangerous and even with my joke, I still don't approve."

"What was it?"

"I got these new shoes from a drug dealer. I don't know what they've laced them with, but I've been tripping all day!"

"That's dumb."

"Want to hear a joke about construction? I'd tell you, but I'm still working on it."

"I tell dad jokes, but I don't have any kids. I'm a faux pa."

David grinned, pointing at me as warmth grew over my cheeks and chest. "You know, I'd like to be your dorky dad. I want to be someone you trust with things. But I want to go at your pace because I've made mistakes that need to heal first. But no matter what, no matter who you think of me as, I am always going to love you because you've always been my daughter."

I looked away, not exactly skeptical but . . . timid, which wasn't something I was used to feeling. "That's hard for me to believe."

"I know. But I'm going to work hard to prove it to you. And a part of that is apologizing for the mistakes I made when you were younger. I should've been there for you. I'm sorry for letting you down."

I swallowed. "Okay."

"Do you think Ethan wants his old job back? Because that's the only reason I can think of as to why he's looking over here so much," David pointed out teasingly.

I didn't look. "I don't know."

He laughed. "I'd be more than happy if you had no interest in anyone, especially teenage boys. In fact, celibacy until marriage is a great thing, even a couple years after marriage, just to make sure things work out." When I shot him a look, he smiled knowingly. "But Ethan's a good kid. And that's all I can really hope for."

"We're friends."

"Maybe you should tell him that," he replied. "But you don't look like you believe it so much yourself either. Remember, a good twelve inches between dance partners is how the professionals do it. And no leaning in either. That's bad for your spine."

"Okay, David."

"I know that tone. Just don't forget there are hundreds of people watching."

As David retreated from the dance floor, my eyes met Ethan's through the wedding guests crowding the dance floor, the song crooning through the speakers changed to one from *Waitress*, the musical playing in Jason's car the night he found me drunk at a party. It wasn't the one that made me burst into tears in front of Ethan, but it was soft, with a gentle guitar strumming to an echoing voice about sad eyes. Coming out of hiding. Mattering.

Which he did, I knew with a softened recognition, like it wasn't a surprise to me at all. Like it was clear and obvious underneath the lights strewn around outside, in the feeling coming over my chest when he smiled as the song became a duet. The waitress singing she always ran away, but for the first time, she wanted to stay.

"Do you want to dance?" I asked.

Ethan smiled and held out a hand. "Yeah." I smiled at this, like he was thinking too much to speak too. "You look beautiful. You usually do, but I like the flowers in your hair."

If my hand hadn't been clasped in his, I would've reached up to touch them. "Thank you," I said. "And you usually look smoldering, but I almost think I prefer you in a suit and tie than shirtless."

"I'm sure everyone else does too. Last time I went shirtless to a wedding, it didn't end well."

"Let me guess, the bride wanted to run off with you instead."

"No, the groom," Ethan joked, and his smile broadened when I laughed. "Look, so, you've been making a lot of jokes about me liking Indie and I just, I wanted you to know—"

I tried not to stumble over his feet as we danced, a cold panic coming over where the warmth had been starting to feel comfortable.

"—I don't. But we get along, and I wanted us to. I want to get along with your friends," he admitted, his gaze earnest and open, maybe even vulnerable. "And you mentioned she didn't like Kingston, so I tried harder for her to like me and I think that's why—"

"You don't ever have to worry about being compared to Kingston," I told him. "You don't have to worry about being liked so much either. You're absurdly close to perfect."

"Bronwyn."

"I mean it. And it's not because of your eye color or how fit you are. It's because of your passion. You're funny, quick-witted. You care, and it's not because you want others to notice. You're going to start your own production company someday, giving equal opportunity to everyone and *listening*. Because you're you. Wonderful, already, right now. And just not a rich boy. You have privilege, yes, but I know you're going to use it to do good things for people who don't."

He smiled bashfully. "You remember that one movie, *Hush*? Cowritten by the director and his wife?" When I nodded, he hesitated. "Sometimes, I think maybe . . . maybe that could be us someday. I mean—I'm not, like, I'm not saying that—"

I bit down on a laugh at how red his face was turning.

"Shut up, I'm dying right now. I'm . . . I'm not saying *that*. But I think we could work well together if that was something you wanted. Someday. Cowriting and directing movies together, which is so far-fetched, I know, but it's just something I was thinking about."

"It sounds nice to think about."

"I think so."

"It would be even nicer to do," I said, glancing away and my eyes widening. "Look, look. Ryan and Andi are dancing together. And her head's actually resting on his chest."

"I guess she likes him after all."

"I think they might be inevitable."

"Like, right now?"

"Probably not. They'll probably wait until they're alone, and not at someone else's wedding, which is essentially an homage to another romance."

He nodded. "That is kind of tasteless."

"They'll wait until they're somewhere that matters to both of them, and then it'll happen. Inevitability will take over."

He smiled back at me knowingly. "For now, they'll just dance."

"Yeah," I whispered. "For now, they'll just dance."

CHAPTER NINETEEN

It was the Monday after the wedding—everything still felt serene, pieces of it still lingering around the house like the heels I wore shoved against the wall or the makeup Andi brought with her still in its Kaboodle—when I pretended to take on an extra shift at Starbright. No one took much interest, just wished me a good shift before continuing dinner preparations, and I could tell they didn't have that warning, that *feeling*, I wished I had had the last night with my mom. I thought about saying something they could remember if everything went wrong, but the problem with a warning is it's a warning. So, I just took Andi's car—with her begrudging permission—and left.

I pulled into the parking lot of a closed pharmacy about an hour later, where a gold van was idling, doors pulled open and Officer Porterfield standing outside, dressed in plainclothes. The friend she'd texted me she'd be bringing along—beware, she's a little pink—was behind the steering wheel. The interior lights were on, revealing the long black hair down to her lower back, and also the pink. She wore a pink camisole with a pink lace choker on, and her nails were hot pink as she typed on her phone.

"What happened to pink being too loud for spy missions?" Officer Porterfield was saying as I approached the car, her back turned to me.

"Well, I'm not on the spy mission. I'm just the technical crew. Besides, if we have to intervene, the pink might be distracting."

"Hey," I interrupted, watching as Officer Porterfield turned and the woman behind the wheel quickly typed out something on her phone before tossing it, almost aggressively, onto the cluttered dashboard. "Nice pink."

"Finally. Someone compliments me on it. *Thank you*, Bronwyn."

"Yeah, sure. So, um, you are . . . ?"

"Aniston Hale. Yes, Aniston like the actress. I'm also, like, Clara's best friend, although you probably call her Officer Porterfield. Like, I'm proud but it sounds weird, like, you're a grown-up or something," the woman replied, in a single breath. "You actually might already know me. I'm a journalist, got my own true-crime podcast. I've been writing a couple articles about what's been going on with your family, sent you a couple DMs on Instagram?"

I shook my head. "Sorry. I haven't checked my DMs in weeks. David's manager said not to."

She paused, her nose wrinkling for a second. "That's fine. Yeah. That's totally fine."

Officer Porterfield waved her hand dismissively. "Okay, so we bought this wire on the internet. It's not going to be as good as the ones we have at the station, but cops tend to notice stealing so this is what we've got. It's going to go under your shirt, so try not to let him touch your back. We'll be able to hear everything you say, record it, but we can't communicate with you."

"I wanted you to just use your phone to tape the whole thing but apparently, what worked when we were teenagers is considered *low-tech* nowadays," Aniston muttered.

"Aniston," Officer Porterfield said.

She sighed. "I'm starting to think my name's code for *be quiet*."

"She's here to call 911 in case anything happens while I rush in," she explained.

"Speaking of codes, we should come up with one in case something does go south. You know, like kangaroo or pastel. Ooh, or maybe a shade of pink! How does everyone feel about bubblegum? It's subtle too. Like, you can just say, *hey, do you have some bubblegum*? Then Clara goes right in!"

I frowned. "Why can't *help* be our code word?"

Aniston shook her head, disappointed. "Fine, if you want to take all the fun out of it."

"*Anyway*, let's hook this up. If he starts to talk, act like you understand. Hold back your judgments, lie to him. Act casual about the entire conversation, maybe even talk to him about other stuff first."

I nodded as she untangled the wire. "Sure, okay."

"If he confesses, find a way to end the conversation and come back to the van. We'll be just out of sight from the park, and then we'll take the recording to the police. After that, we should be able to arrest him."

I lifted up my shirt so she could attach the wire. "Will you get in trouble for this?"

"Don't worry about that."

"She probably will!" Aniston called out, checking her phone

again. "But she's cool with it. Plus, this is going to make an amazing article for my blog."

I shot Officer Porterfield a look. "Seriously?"

"Sorry. My boyfriend was busy."

Aniston looked up from her phone, offended. "Ouch, Clara. *Ouch.*"

○

Fifteen minutes later, I was wired and sitting on the cinderblocks where my trailer used to be, the broken pieces of it recovered and the ground without grass. Pieces of flowerpots and glass were scattered around the gravel still, glinting under the light. My heart was beating now that this was happening—wondering if Officer Porterfield and Aniston could hear it through the wire—but this had to happen. And before I could think of a reason it shouldn't, his headlights beamed over me.

Kingston got out of his truck. It was darker, so I couldn't make out his expression seeing me there on the cinderblocks, offering him a slight wave. "Hey. What are you doing here?"

"I wanted to see the new camper for myself. Looks even smaller than I thought."

"Even smaller inside too."

I tried not to let it throw me how casually he could talk to me, knowing what he'd probably done to my mom, what he must have seen or what she could've said or pleaded. "I was hoping you'd show me," I said, swallowing the bile in my throat until nothing but careful and determined words came through.

Kingston hesitated, a soup thermos tucked under one arm and a large soft drink from McDonald's grasped in the same hand, ice rattling inside. "I didn't think you'd want to talk to me again."

"Why, because you pretty much called my mom lower-class scum or because you're being investigated for her murder?"

Something came over his face, his other hand fumbling with his keys. "You don't think I actually did that, right? You know I could never do that."

"I talked to her drug dealer, Kingston. He never said anything about her owing him money because she didn't," I said, standing up when he approached the door of the camper, accidentally putting the wrong key in the lock. "When the tornado was coming, you didn't let me go inside to get my mom."

"Because it was coming right for us, Bronwyn. Did you want to get killed by it?"

"Funny hearing that from you," I remarked, but when he shot me a look, I eased back. "Look, can we at least talk? Please?"

He sighed, then threw open his door and gestured for me to go inside.

I sat down on the cracked vinyl of his couch, which was attached to the wall and nestled behind a table bolted to the floor. He walked in front of the fridge, pulling out a plastic bag of tomatoes and an opened package of precooked bacon, a mayonnaise jar tucked in the crook of his arm. "You want anything?"

"No, thanks." It was quiet in his camper as he unscrewed the lid to the half-empty jar of store-brand mayonnaise, it spinning on the counter after he tossed it aside. I stared at his hands, remembering all of the things they'd touched.

"I didn't kill your mom," he told me. "You should know I could never do anything like that. I don't even know why I've gotten caught up in all this."

I leaned over the table, frowning as it wobbled under my arms. "Look, I know who my mom was, all right? You don't have to lie about it. I just want you to be honest with me. That's all I've ever wanted from anyone."

"I *am* being honest with you. I didn't kill your mom. I don't know why I gotta keep saying that. If I'd killed your mom, then there would be evidence to arrest me, right? Well, there's not and they haven't."

Yet, I wanted to tell him.

"Kingston, you're frustrating me, you know that?"

"Yeah, well, try being accused of murder every time you go outside. *That's* frustrating."

"I'm not even saying you did it on purpose," I said. "My mom was probably on something when you went to talk to her, and maybe she fell. You could've just hit her because you were angry, and she died."

"Except I didn't. I didn't kill your mom. I liked her."

"Yeah, I know. But killing her and hating her are two different things."

He swore under his breath, shaking his head as he pulled open one of the drawers, silverware clattering inside as he got out a paring knife. I went still, watching him carefully while he tore the plastic bag of tomatoes and set one out on the counter, wishing I could explain how fidgety he was to Officer Porterfield. His hand smoothing over his stubble or wiping a smudge off his glasses with his shirt.

He was lying to me.

"Kingston, we've never been anything but honest with each other. It's been me and you from the start, but if you're going to lie to me then . . . I don't know what I'm supposed to do. Because that's not what I came here for."

"What did you come here for?"

"I've only asked you to admit it, like, ten times."

"What? You want to admit I saw her that day? Fine, yeah, I saw her."

"After Jude left?"

The knife hitting against the counter as it sliced through the tomato. "Yeah."

I tried to keep myself composed, because he'd said after her funeral he never saw her after Jude left. It was one piece closer to the whole truth. "Did you go over to the trailer?"

"No, I was outside, having a smoke and she came out a few minutes later. We talked and then she went inside. That was the last time I saw her, really."

"What did you talk about?"

"The tornado watch and how dumb it was since we never get tornadoes around here," he explained, laughing under his breath at this. "She mentioned she was going to pick you up from school and you were going to go out shopping for plants or something."

"With her first check from Good Greens."

"Yeah, all one hundred and forty bucks of it. You know, I don't want to talk badly about her, but maybe if she'd been better with money, life wouldn't have been so rough for you guys."

I blinked. "How did you know it was one hundred and forty dollars?"

He paused with the knife halfway through another slice of tomato. "I don't know. She must have told me."

"No, she didn't. She was leaving it in the envelope until we left for the store. She didn't know how much it was," I told him, remembering how it was still on the kitchen counter when I left for school that morning, labeled *Bronwyn's Flower Money*, sealed.

He must have seen it, too, knew it was exactly what he'd come for. Money.

"I don't know. She probably opened it after you left for school to cash it or something."

"You know, I've had enough," I snapped, sliding out from the vinyl seats. "You've done nothing but lie to me since I got here, and you think I can't tell? I know there was money at the house, and I know you stole it after you killed her. But what's making me mad is that you won't tell me the truth."

"Yes, I am. I don't know what happened to your mom."

"If you killed my mom, then I deserve to know. Okay, Kingston, we . . . were friends, we were *more* than friends. You were the first guy," I said to him, the breathless words catching in my mouth, "I thought cared about me. Or was that a lie too?"

"You know it wasn't."

"Stop telling me what I know! If you cared about me, you would tell me the truth. If you cared about me at all, you would be honest with me."

His expression contorted with anger, reddened, and he turned around and punched his clenched fist into one of the cupboards beside his microwave, swearing as his knuckles made contact with a hollow *thunk*. I stood there, quiet as he breathed, even the movements with his back and shoulders exaggerated, like he wanted to look aggressive. But it was a show. He pretended to act volatile and threatening, but he was just a pathetic coward, low-life scum, wanting to be something he wasn't.

"Don't," I said, but not to him, to Officer Porterfield listening. "You're going to wreck your cupboards."

He held his hand for a moment, then quietly mumbled, "I didn't mean for it to happen."

I stepped closer. "What?"

"She told me about what happened to your college savings. I saw her car leave so I broke into your house to take it, but she came back while I was still inside. We started fighting. She said she was going to tell you I was stealing from you guys and then she fell trying to shove me and hit her head. I panicked. I hoped it would look like an accident when you got home."

I tried to consider my words carefully, since I knew she had been strangled. "So, she was still in the trailer when I got home from school. That was why you didn't want me to go inside."

"Yeah," he admitted sheepishly, grabbing the paring knife again. "I was kind of waiting for you to get home, planned it all out in my head, but when you started to go in, I felt bad. I didn't want you to be the one to find her. Then a tornado started coming right for us."

"Why did you help me? Why would you save me from the tornado?"

He shrugged, taking the sliced tomatoes and setting them on a slice of white bread. "I just kind of reacted, you know? And like I told you, what happened with your mom was an accident. I didn't mean to hurt her."

"What a load of bull," I muttered, my voice shaking but irate. "She didn't die because she hit her head. She was strangled. Something I *told* you after her funeral, and you still can't get the lie right. No wonder she caught you stealing. You're as stupid as you are a coward."

"I didn't strangle her. Someone else must have come in and did that. Or maybe the police are wrong, but I didn't do anything like that." He paused, taking the bacon out of the package and tossing it back in the fridge. Then he took the paring knife to scrape mayonnaise from the jar. "Look, I didn't mean to hurt your mom. It all happened so fast."

"That's what you say when you cheat, not kill someone's mom."

"I'm sorry, Bronwyn. I really am, okay? I liked your mom. But when she found me in your place, I panicked. My job pays nothing, my truck's engine light has been on for weeks, I'm eating *this* crap," he told me, gesturing to his sandwich. "I don't even have the *L* for a stupid BLT. When your mom said she had some extra cash at home, I thought it would be easy."

I crossed my arms around myself, not even relieved to finally know what had happened to my mom. Instead, I felt bruised and saddened because this came from someone she trusted—someone *I* trusted, had brought into our lives—and it was for a couple thousand dollars. My mom died for two thousand dollars. "It all comes back to money, doesn't it?" I mumbled.

"It makes the world go 'round. Not that you need to worry about it anymore."

"What, do you want me to thank you? Thank you, Kingston, for killing my mom because now I can afford BLTs with all the ingredients?" I turned away and shook my head.

"You said you just wanted me to be honest with you." He was quiet for a moment, the knife scratching against the counter as he cut the sandwich into triangles. "What are you doing here, Bronwyn?"

"You know why I'm here."

"Why did you come here to ask me about your mom?"

"The police told me you were a suspect. I had to know for myself."

He turned toward me, the knife still in his hand. "But you didn't ask me. You just wanted me to say it." I glanced down at the knife, the fluorescent lights glinting against the somewhat bent blade, tomato seeds clinging to it. Then he used the tip to point to me, my heart tensing. "Are you pulling something?"

"No."

Something shifted in his eyes. "Were you the one who turned me in?"

"No one turned you in, Kingston. The cops figured it out."

"The cops said I lied about her owing money and you were the only one I'd told about that," he said as something came over his voice, desperation and frustration, the veins in his neck bulging. "Are you serious, Bronwyn? You sent them after me!"

I stepped back but I bumped into the table behind me, feeling it wobble against my back. "Hey, do you have any bubblegum?" I asked.

"I can't believe you!" he yelled, taking a step closer until I was wedged between him and the table, the knife ominously close to my hip. "I don't even know why I bother with you. You're just like her."

My anger flared, drowning out everything else because there it was. Underneath it all, a current rushing beneath the surface that never slowed. A pulse that never stopped.

He'd killed my mom.

"You know, my mother might have been a lot of things. A drug addict, a liar, a homewrecker. A bastard, just like the one she raised, but she knew a deadbeat when she saw one. And that was what she saw in you, wasn't it? You didn't kill her because she found you. You killed her because she told you exactly what she thought of you. That you were, and always will be, a pathetic piece of trailer park trash who gets off on teenage girls like the loser freak you are—"

I caught a glimpse of his hand before it loudly cracked against my face, tears springing to my eyes as I crumpled onto the tiles, my ears ringing. I fell over his feet as he tried to pull me up by the collar of my shirt. It might have exposed the wire taped to my back, but if he saw it, he never said anything as he hoisted me against the kitchen cabinets. He was still holding the knife as I kicked my legs to push him away, stabbing at the air around me when I remembered one of Ethan's favorite moments from *Get Out*.

I screamed when I pierced my palm through the knife as it came toward me instead of trying to block it or kicking against his legs. Blood spilled over my legs and made the floor wet as he grunted, trying to pull the knife out of my hand. Then the screen door burst open and I pulled away from him as his eyes darted to the doorway.

Officer Porterfield rushed him, an electric zapping sound echoing throughout the scuffle as I fell against the floor, blood smearing into my hair. She pulled her taser away from his neck while he slumped down to the ground, banging against his wobbling table.

"You stopped him from hurting me," I murmured to her against the floor as she handcuffed his wrists behind his back, glancing at me when the metal clicked.

CHAPTER TWENTY

An ambulance pulled into the trailer park about ten minutes after Officer Porterfield stopped Kingston, the red and blue lights beaming back and forth against the pine trees. Paramedics bandaged my hand, took my blood pressure, and checked my pupils before driving with sirens blaring to the hospital. There, the receptionist had to call Amy and David while I waited with a blood-soaked gauze loosely wrapped around my hand in an exam room, expecting some fury, probably mostly from Amy. It wasn't until they were brought back to my exam room, still dressed in their pajamas, that I realized they weren't angry at all.

The muscles in Amy's neck were bulging and rigid, her eyes bloodshot and her skin blotchy, with her flannel pajamas shifting against her shoulders as she let out a shuddering breath. But she still stood back, clutching the strap of her purse, with David behind her. His hair was tousled with cowlicks in the back, pale.

"Hey," I said slowly as they shuffled into the room. Then I sighed. "Look, I know you're mad, but I had to do it! And I'm not really hurt. Like, this is fine." Neither of them spoke. "So . . . am I grounded?"

Amy squeezed her eyes shut and shook her head, letting out something between a breath and a sob as she turned away, wiping her hand under her eyes. David leaned against the wall, arms crossed, and eyes pointed to the ground.

"Amy? I'm okay, you know," I said. "I didn't do it to hurt you."

"Bronwyn," she breathed against her hands. "How could we not be hurt? You could've been. . . Ugh, Bronwyn." She pulled her hands from her face and opened her tearful eyes. "I don't know how . . . how I'm supposed to do this."

"What are you talking about?"

"I haven't done anything but fail since you came to us," she confessed, her words tight and choked. "I don't know how to keep you safe, how to make you feel loved, how to give you what you need. If I was a good mother, then I could do this, but I can't, and I'm not your mother. I—I don't know what to do."

Her composure was gone. The graciousness had ebbed. And all that was left was her, and the honest truth she had been clinging to all this time.

"Amy," I said. "You're enough on your own."

"You're just saying that because I'm a mess. You don't even like me," she sniffled with a breathy laugh, sitting on the foot of the bed. "And I understand why, I really do, Bronwyn. You just lost your mother and I would never want to replace her. But I tried so hard to be more than just your stepmother and I've . . . pushed you even further away."

I brought my knees down from my chest and crossed them, leaning forward as I looked over at David, realizing how red his eyes looked too. I felt a knot in my chest that had been tightening all summer begin to unravel, spilling and coming apart. "What teen likes her parents?" I whispered.

She looked up, her expression almost completely blank before it crumpled again, reaching over and enveloping me into a tight embrace. Then, after a second, when I was too surprised to react, she started to pull away. "I'm sorry, I know—"

I pulled her back. "It's okay," I said into her hair, glancing at David across the room, tentatively watching us. Then I held out a hand to him, waiting the three seconds it took for him to walk over and take it in his.

"I'm sorry," I whispered as his fingers intertwined with mine and Amy untangled herself from me, taking my face in her hands and brushing her thumbs under my eyes. "I'm sorry."

"Oh, Bronwyn." She was still crying, but her lips held a wobbling smile. "Thank you for forgiving us."

She hugged me again, David tenderly smoothing back the strands of my hair and mouthing *our girl*.

And we stayed like that until the nurse came in to check on us.

○

I had to have surgery on my hand and the day after, Officer Porterfield visited me while Amy and David ventured down to the cafeteria, noting my request for any Sour Patch Kids they might stumble upon there, and I smiled when she walked in. She was dressed in a pair of shorts with a camo T-shirt that hung loose around her shoulders, her glasses sliding down her nose.

"How's your hand?"

"It's not bad. Plus, what's one more scar? At least there's a pretty cool story behind it," I said as she sat in one of the chairs. "What's going on? They didn't release him, right?"

"No, he's still in custody and in the process of being charged with the murder of your mother," she informed me. "After he found out you were wearing a wire, he confessed at the station."

"Did you get in trouble for that?"

"Oh yeah, I was fired."

"Wait, what? Like, seriously, you were *fired*?"

"That's normally what happens when you go behind a senator's back and endanger his daughter's life after he explicitly said not to," she replied. "Not that he was responsible for anything, but I knew it would probably happen."

"I'm sorry. I guess I should've . . . thought about that."

She shrugged. "You know, I'm not that upset about it. I was beginning to think I didn't share the same ideals as the police, anyway."

"So, what will you do now?"

Her smile was somewhat bashful as she stared at her hands for a second. "When I was in high school, I loved doing musicals. I think I was kind of good at it too. So, maybe I'll go back to that, enroll in a theater program. And self-defense techniques aren't that much different from choreography, so I'd like to do that, too, maybe teach a class on it someday."

"I'd sign up," I said. "I don't know what all happened when you were in high school. But the police weren't really the ones who helped me. That was you. So whatever choices you made, they got you here. And without you here, I would've had more than just a hole in my hand."

"I guess it all worked out then," she remarked.

I held out my unbandaged hand as she went to stand up, glancing at it warily for a second as a small part of me wanted to smile, tell her about an inside joke she wouldn't understand. "Thanks, Officer Porterfield."

She shook my hand. "It's just Clara now."

○

When I was released from the hospital, I arrived back home to see a hand-drawn banner draped along the siding, uneven letters written with a mixture of capitals and lowercases welcoming me home. Balloons were attached to the mailbox, fluttering in the wind. When I was getting out of the car, I heard Miles barking inside, his nose shifting the curtains at the windows.

Everyone was standing in the kitchen, where even *more* balloons were tied around the room, onto the handles of the refrigerator and the oven, pizza boxes stacked on the island. And a cake on the kitchen counter. I realized then that half the balloons said *Happy Birthday* on them.

Natalie bolted over and hugged me. It caught me off guard, but I wrapped one arm over her shoulders after a slight hesitation. "Why do these say happy birthday on them?"

Natalie pulled back, frowning. "Isn't your birthday tomorrow?"

"It's not September."

The color drained from her face as she whirled around to look at Andi. "You told me her birthday was in July and we should do something!"

"Whoops," she offered drily. "Doesn't matter, my birthday's sooner anyway."

"You were close, girls. September 1," David said, opening the cupboard where the plates were kept. "But now we have cake. Who calls a corner piece?"

"Me!" Danny shouted.

"Not before dinner," Amy interjected firmly, looking over the Styrofoam containers beside the pizza boxes. "I'm guessing it's too much to assume one of these is a salad?"

"No, but the wings come with celery," Jason pointed out.

Andi stood in the door frame, just staring at me, or, more specifically, at the bulky white bandage wrapped around my hand. I knew she was holding back, like me, but holding myself back so much was starting to feel more exhausting than just letting it go. I walked over and wrapped my arms around her.

She was quiet for a moment, then muttered into my hair, "What are you doing?"

"Hugging you," I explained. "It's only weird if you make it weird."

"It's a little weird already," she mumbled, but then hugged me back. "You're so stupid, you know that?"

"Yeah. I know."

"And I'm mad at you too."

"You usually are," I remarked.

"Yeah, except I'm really mad this time." She tried to hide a sniffle from me, pretending to cough as she pulled back, wiping at her nose. "Because Mom made me give you my bed, so I have to sleep on the top bunk now."

"It's too hard for her to climb with her hand right now, Andrea," Amy said.

Natalie snickered, picking off a mushroom from her pizza. "She's just mad because she's afraid of heights."

"Shut up, I am not."

"Don't tell each other to shut up," David scolded.

"I didn't, she did!"

"Enough," Amy warned, holding up her hand. "Finish up your pizza, everyone. David, where are our candles?"

He pulled open a drawer. "Right here."

She grabbed a lighter from the top of the refrigerator after pressing a handful of partially melted candles through the white frosting with multicolored floral designs piped around the edges. "Okay, so we could celebrate one of the sixteen birthdays we missed with Bronwyn? Or the fact she's alive and well?"

"Or that she recorded her mother's killer confessing?" Andi added.

"Which was dangerous," David said then, while Amy, preoccupied with lighting the candles, offered me a wink.

"Okay, so what are we celebrating?"

When no one else responded, I shrugged as she lit the last candle. "Who knows? Let's just blow out some candles."

"Wait, can't we choose something meaningful—?" she started to ask, but it was too late, everyone was already drawing in a deep breath and blowing out the candles, wisps of smoke unfurling in front of her before she laughed. "You *kids*! You never let me have cute family moments!"

A couple hours later after dinner, I walked into the bedroom and noticed three gerbera daisies tied together with a ribbon, knotted with uneven loops on Andi's bed, now mine apparently. Beside it was a plastic baggie of Sour Patch Kids, just the blues. My favorites.

And a Blu-ray copy of *Get Out*, with a Post-it note stuck to the cover.

Heard how you stabbed your hand. That's my (Final) Girl.

I smiled, smoothing my thumb over the letters before looking at the lights shining through the windows of his house.

o

Getting yourself stabbed in the hand toward the end of July effectively terminates your position at your summer job with well-wishes and a promise for next summer. But the following Tuesday night, I stole a jean skirt from Andi's side of the closet—hoping she wouldn't notice, then arguing with her for fifteen minutes when she did—and a black T-shirt with an embroidered daisy. Not exactly a gerbera daisy, but it was close enough. I asked Natalie to do my hair into a braid, like the one Ethan had earlier in the summer.

When she was finished, I asked, "You want to come?"

She spent most of the drive to Starbright asking what movies were playing, following up with what movies were going to be on the first screen visible through the restaurant's windows. Andi gave me a look at one of the red lights, but she was smiling a little bit too.

When we got there, I was somewhat disappointed Ethan wasn't in the concession stand with everyone else but also relieved because the conversations I wanted to have weren't ones I wanted to have in front of everyone else, particularly two teasing sisters. Taylor-Elise was there, though, rotating the theater boxes of candy and tossing the box of Dots on the counter when I walked in.

"Hey!" she yelled, maneuvering around the tables as she jogged over, enveloping me in a hug. "Wow, hey, oh. What the crap were you thinking?"

I scrunched my nose. "The police were the ones who came up with the idea."

"I'd smack you if you didn't already look so rough," she mumbled, pulling away and squinting her eyes in a glare she maintained for about two seconds. "I would've come! And I have pepper spray, too, like on a little keychain."

A squeal came from the stairwell as Cass clumsily came down in chunky heels. "Bronwyn!" she called out, awkwardly holding her arms out, like she wasn't sure if we should hug, and I walked in. "Your hand! Look at your hand. But are you okay? Is this hurting you? Am I hurting you?"

"Only her ears," Ginny remarked from one of the booths, chewing on licorice and using it to wave at me. "Hi, glad to see that you haven't died."

Cass detached herself from me abruptly. "Ginny, your mouth needs an *Off* switch."

I slid into the half of the booth opposite from her, accepting one of the licorices she held out to me as Andi left to go clock in, scooting to make room for Natalie. Ryan came in from outside a few minutes later, grinning when he noticed me. "Hey, it's you!"

I nodded. "Looks like it."

"Aw, I thought you had a cast. Someone told me you had a cast on. I was all pumped to sign it."

"Sign the bandage," I said, shrugging. "I have to change it tomorrow, though."

"Ooh, get me a marker," Ginny said.

Ryan ran over to the cash register to grab one of the Sharpies from a plastic medium-sized cup on the counter. I watched as he handed it over to Ginny to scribble down her name. Then when it was his turn, he started drawing a cartoon depiction of me uppercutting someone I assumed was Kingston. "I didn't punch him in the face you, you know."

"Shh," he whispered, "you can't say that when I've already started."

Despite the historical inaccuracy, the cartoon didn't look that bad. "You know," I said, "it looked like you and Andi were pretty close together at the wedding. When you were dancing."

"Yeah. Dad was stressed out, because she was dancing too," Natalie said, pointing to me. "You were all dancing pretty close, actually."

"Yeah, but we're not talking about me right now. We're talking about Andi."

"Who will kill us *all* if she hears this conversation," Ryan dramatically muttered.

"I'm not scared. You should ask her out."

He shot me a look. "Are you kidding me?"

My face fell. "What, you don't like her?"

Ryan paused, writing *boom!* and *pow!* around a cartoon Kingston stumbling backward. "She's great," he admitted, "but I'm . . ." Instead of finishing, he shrugged.

"Kinda obnoxious?" Ginny interjected.

"*Ginny!*" Cass hollered. "For the love of—!"

"No, yeah, that. She's, like, so serious all the time and I never take anything seriously. She graduated high school at the top of her class and I was nearly suspended right before graduation for gluing pennies all over the principal's office. With, like, the good superglue. Even the computer. Can you imagine Andi wanting someone like that?"

"No," I admitted, and he nodded. "But she does, anyway. She probably likes you because of it. Maybe being so uptight all the time, she finds it kind of nice to hang out with the class clown."

"She just gets annoyed with everything I say."

"That's how she expresses affection!"

"It really is," Natalie agreed. "If that's a love language, it's hers."

"Just think about it," I said. "Is Ethan here tonight? I haven't seen him."

He nodded, focused on drawing my hair. "Yeah, he's picking up trash outside. He's going to be pumped when he sees you. Dude's getting lonely out there. He tried talking to me about *A Quiet Place* last week and I was like, huh?"

"It's actually really good. It's an allegory for parenthood—"

Ryan glanced up, unamused. "Yeah, I *know*."

o

I spotted his reflective orange vest through the shrubs a few minutes into the first feature near the fifth screen where *Happy Death Day* had just started, steering between bumpers on his hoverboard to ride over to the grass near the corner where fireflies blinked behind him.

His eyes were focused on the film when I approached him, a smile tugging on my lips when it took him a moment to realize it was me, without the Starbright uniform and vest he was used to seeing me in. Then there was a shift in the shadow over his face.

"Hey." He was grinning, dimple carved, as he met me halfway. "How's the other guy look?"

"Oh, I wouldn't know. He's currently in jail right now where, rumor has it, he's considering a plea deal to avoid a trial."

Ethan looked down at my hand, the bandage scribbled with signatures and the cartoon drawing Ryan had spent almost twenty minutes perfecting. "I would've come, you know."

"I know," I said. Something started to flutter around in my chest like the fireflies around us. "Okay, so, there's been this thing I've wanted to do *all* summer."

He paused, his expression slowly turning serious and uncertain and searching.

"I want to ride the hoverboard," I declared.

For a moment, he was completely still, like he wasn't sure he heard me right, before he laughed and shook his head. "No way."

"Come on. You haven't given me a turn all summer. You're hogging it."

"Because it's mine."

"Except it's not. It's Ryan's. For his monstrous hemorrhoids, remember?"

"I'm the only one who rides it."

"Because you *hog* it," I retorted. "Please, I just want to ride it for two seconds."

He stared at me, deadpanned. "How many stitches do you have in your hand?"

I took a step closer, tilting my head down. "*Ethan—*"

"Don't say my name like that."

"—I just want to take it out for a spin. One spin. A metaphorical spin, which would be more like a straight, supervised line. Like when a cop pulls you over for a DUI."

He let out a reluctant sigh. "Just . . . don't go fast, okay? Or move, for that matter." He stepped down from the hoverboard, glancing wearily at me when I stepped on it, holding out my arms and grinning at Ethan, who did not look as enthused, his hand not *exactly* touching my back, but whenever I shifted, I felt his fingertips against my shirt.

"How do I make it go?"

"Can't you just practice standing for right now?"

"You worry too much."

"You don't worry enough."

"That's why we make such a good team," I said. "Will you at least tell me how to turn?"

"You just kind of lean which way you want to turn but—" I leaned my weight onto my right foot and Ethan slowly came into view behind me, still holding out his hands. "Okay, you turned, it's been two seconds. Get off."

"Wait, just one moment," I said, much to his apparent chagrin, "there's one more thing I wanted to do."

"Bronwyn—" he groaned.

"You see," I blurted, "there's this height difference between us and with this, I'm almost as tall as you."

"If you tell me to shut my eyes, you'll give me a surprise, I'm not falling for it."

"Actually, I don't want this to be a surprise. Because what if you don't want to be surprised? It wouldn't be okay to surprise you when you don't want to be *surprised*." I paused, taking in his furrowed brow. "Could you just get what I'm hinting at here?"

"What are you saying?"

I sighed. "I want—ugh, I want to kiss you, okay? With fireflies and baby-face killers in the background. Because I like you, and that's our thing. I think. I want it to be, anyway, and I want what you talked about at the wedding. I want to cowrite and codirect with you, even if you say right now you don't want to kiss me. Because we're friends too. Or, only, depending on what you say next."

Ethan was quiet for a moment, and it wasn't until I squinted in the darkness that I noticed his dimple was soft beside his smile. "Wow," he remarked. "I just wanted you to admit you wanted to kiss me."

My eyes widened. "You made me say all that when you knew what I was talking about?"

"Don't slap me, you're going to fall," he laughed. "I'm almost kind of insulted. You didn't think I would get it when you mentioned height differences?"

"Oh, this is mine now. This hoverboard is—" I paused, something occurring to me. "Wait, you didn't find some weird sort of way of phrasing that. You talked about yourself kind of positively. You were direct about me wanting to kiss you."

"Yeah, and maybe even one day I won't say *affluent*."

He bridged the gap between us, his hands no longer lingering nervously in midair around me, but letting them reach out and brush against my sides. I nudged myself forward, bringing my hands up to his shoulders and leaning in. He met me halfway for the second time that night, his lips finding mine in a way that clenched the muscles in my chest, then turned them soft and melted.

The fireflies were blinking over his shoulders when I opened my eyes a few seconds later, resting my forehead against his as he glanced at the screen, his voice in my hair as he murmured, "You're missing the best part."

My laugh was breathy and quiet before I turned my head too. Because the best part was never really the tropes or the conventions, the Final Girls or the slashers, or even the symbolism. It was him, the enthusiasm in his voice as he relayed them all back to me through his eyes.

So, I watched and waited for the moment that would inevitably come when he whispered why, exactly, *this* was the best part.

EPILOGUE

"Natalie, if you don't hurry up, I'm leaving without you!"

"You can't. Mom will get mad," Danny informed me from the backseat, a toaster pastry between his teeth as he buckled his seat belt.

I pressed my hand against the horn again. "If she doesn't hurry up, I'm about to not care if she gets mad," I grumbled, grabbing my phone out of the cupholder and noticing I had a text from Andi.

It included a picture of the succulent I'd brought her in its terracotta pot, perched on the windowsill in her dorm about five hours away in Connecticut—*not* Yale, she always had to clarify. But it was just four miles from the college Ryan attended, and if her Instastories were any indication, they were spending quite a bit of time together, although she still wouldn't admit if they were dating whenever I asked. Beneath the picture, she sent a single text, without emojis like usual.

Still not dead yet.

Another text dinged, this time from Ethan, responding to the picture I'd sent him of me in my new school uniform. I was in front of the wall-length mirror in my bedroom with a disgruntled glare at my reflection, adorned in a black plaid skirt and tie David had to do for me under my white collar, my matching cardigan wrapped around my waist.

> I love this. This is becoming my lock screen.

It's so hot. Doesn't this school realize it's still hot in September?

> You're right. That is very hot.

I sent him a side-eyeing emoji, then continued typing.

Are we on for tomorrow? Wait, do private schools have a lot of homework the first week?

> You can't hear it from three hours away, but I'm laughing right now.

Noooooo.

> But, yeah, we're on. In fact, while we're at it, I could tutor you in calculus.

I responded with a crying emoji, several.

> It's going to be FINE. I gotta go before I miss first period. Remember, don't text me during lunch. Go make new friends. Text old friends (and boyfriend) after school.

After summer ended, Ethan and I texted every evening, sent pictures to each other of random things we saw, trailers to upcoming horror films and our reactions. But what I looked forward to most was watching a horror movie with him every Tuesday night while video chatting. Sometimes we were interrupted by our siblings, but it never really bothered us. Eventually, we started bothering *them* with all of the facts we had been storing up.

A moment later, the front door opened, and I glanced up, seeing David on the porch. "Your sister's waiting," he called out, holding the door open, soap suds clinging to his arms from washing the dishes left over from breakfast.

I still couldn't call him Dad yet, at least not in front of him, but I was finding it easier to introduce myself as his daughter or say things like *my parents* about him and Amy. It still felt awkward to me, to call someone I'd known for only three months something that meant so much, but he was giving me the time I needed, never flinching when I called him by his given name. He also decided to work from home more or waited until we left for school before heading into the office, although he would still travel often now that summer was over. But he promised to take me to the Washington D.C. sometime in the fall.

"Finally," I groaned when Natalie approached the car. "What took you so long? We said eight o'clock, remember? Eight *a.m.*"

She ignored me, flipping down the visor to glance at her reflection in the mirror, smoothing her tongue over her teeth, after recently getting her braces off. "Did you see the pictures Jason sent Mom from Hawaii?"

"Yeah." Between showing me pictures from Jason and Kimberly's honeymoon, Amy asked me repeatedly how I felt about starting senior year—if I was nervous, about making new friends or the classes, what the other students might already know about me.

It wasn't like it never occurred to me. After all, I was the illegitimate daughter of a married senator and a murdered drug addict, with her mom's killer currently in prison after pleading guilty. Part of the plea deal the lawyers arranged meant I had to drop the assault charges against him, and I agreed to avoid a trial.

I was ready to leave those pieces behind in Shiloh, or wherever he was now. It didn't matter. I'd kept what was important close to me.

Indie was planning to visit almost every weekend, excited to come to the football games at the private school on Friday nights, texting me frequently and moaning about how boring Shiloh was now. I also texted Jude sometimes. He still chose to keep himself out of my mom's case, but after he found out Kingston had broken into our trailer to steal the money he'd given back to Mom, he stopped dealing. Last I heard, he was applying to be a manager at a gas station down the road from his house.

And I kept my mom with me, too, as best as I could, but it was still hard. David had arranged earlier that summer to have her buried in a cemetery nearby and on my dresser I had a framed picture of her that he had given me. Grinning, with her hair wrapped in a towel, her skin bare and bright, just like her eyes, squinted in the flash. It looked imperfect and spontaneous, like her. Claiming it was an early birthday present, David also gave me a necklace of shining gold, a bar with her birthstone next to mine.

A few minutes later, I pulled into the parking lot, then followed behind Natalie and Danny until we stepped inside the school. As usual, Danny offered a quick and disinterested wave before barreling down one of the halls, yelling at one of his friends, who had his head in his locker.

"Do you know where you need to go?" Natalie asked me, lingering uncertainly.

"I've been to school before. Plus, I have this paper map thingy."

"You can text me if you get lost, though. Like, wasn't your last school as big as our house?"

I turned around, calling out to her, "See you later, Natalie!"

She wasn't entirely wrong, I soon learned after stumbling around a couple of hallways before finally locating my first class of the morning. I slid behind a desk near the middle as the teacher stood up, a thick stack of papers gripped in one hand. She surveyed the classroom before taking attendance. Then, after a few names had been called, I heard mine.

"Bronwyn Larson-Soliday?"

Holding up my hand, I answered, "Here."

ACKNOWLEDGMENTS

Here we go again. Didn't we just do this? I feel like we just did this. And that's probably something to acknowledge right there because having another one of your books published? That's like having your dream multiplied.

First, thanks to God for giving me another idea to write after literally four years. Honestly thought for a minute that writing was over for me already when I'd just published my debut. And then to Deanna McFadden, for scaring the crap out of me when she wanted to talk about another book after I'd abandoned another unfinished manuscript, my seventh or eighth in a row. At the time, I had a half-baked idea about a girl and a tornado and a summer, sure it would flop, too, but she encouraged me to write it even when I wanted to play it safe. It soon became the best experience I had writing, and I finished it—which alone felt like a huge accomplishment after four years of *not* doing that—in less than a year. I haven't done that in maybe ten years. I also want to thank Deanna for editing the second one of my books in a row.

I have my talent manager, Monica Pacheco, to thank for so much of this too. There have been a lot of wonderful opportunities she has talked me through, and this was another one of them. Thank you to Holley Corfield for all of the promotion that's gone into *Homewrecker* and to Jen Hale, not just for the helpful copyediting notes but her shared enthusiasm for *Get Out*. And, of course, to everyone working behind the scenes at Wattpad, who have made this and so many other things possible for me.

The biggest thanks go to the readers who loved *Homewrecker* before I even announced its publication. Reading your comments, the excitement, the *swooning*, made my day every Tuesday and Friday. There was a love for this book that was unlike anything I'd experienced before on the website, and for that, for your love and devotion, I thank you.

Thanks also to the friends I've made online through this community, especially Tay Marley after her book *The QB Bad Boy and Me* was published through Wattpad Books as well. It's been really nice to have a friend who's gone through this same process. Plus, she helped me proofread, so she's just awesome all around. The support that comes from the online writing community is *insane*. I could list you all by name, but even books have character limits.

I can hear the music from award shows when they're trying to hurry you up, so lastly, I have the people in my everyday life to thank. My parents, siblings, IRL friends. Thanks for only telling me sometimes I should be writing.

Wait, does this mean I have to write another book now?

And that, my friends, are what true horror movies should really be about.

(I mean, I'm still going to write. But, like, for real.)

ABOUT THE AUTHOR

Deanna Cameron began posting her stories on Wattpad under the pseudonym, LyssFrom1996, when she was just sixteen years old. Since then her debut novel, *What Happened That Night,* has been published in North America and France, after gaining over a million reads on Wattpad. Originally born in Canada, Deanna now attends university in Western New York and writes in the early hours of the morning.